OUR HAWAII

JACK LONDON AT WAIKIKI, 1915.

OUR HAWAII

BY

CHARMIAN KITTREDGE LONDON

(MRS. JACK LONDON)

AUTHOR OF "THE LOG OF THE SNARK"

1917

ILLUSTRATED WORKS OF JACK AND CHARMIAN LONDON
PUBLISHED BY

SEAWOLF PRESS

OUR HAWAII
Copyright ©2018 by SeaWolf Press

FIRST EDITION INFORMATION
The first edition was published by The Macmillan Company in 1917. There was an updated version published five years later that included some of Jack's articles as well as some other revisions. This cover is from the first edition.

SeaWolf Press
P.O. Box 961
Orinda, CA 94563
Email: support@seawolfpress.com
Web: http://www.SeaWolfPress.com

About *Our Hawaii*

Charmian London kept a journal during her trip to the South Pacific with Jack on their sailboat Snark. Jack went on to publish his version, *The Cruise of the Snark,* while Charmian later released her version, *The Log of the Snark.* She removed the section about Hawaii and made it into this separate book. It is both an interesting travel book about the islands as well as an insightful look into island life and the effects of encroaching civilization that accompanied becoming a U.S. Territory. She and Jack loved Hawaii.

About Charmian Kittredge London

Charmian Kittredge London was raised and educated by her Aunt in Oakland, California. Charmian became a symbol of the New Woman at the turn of the century. She met Jack in 1900, and finally married him in 1905 after his divorce from his first wife, Bess. Charmian and Jack built a sailboat, the Snark, and set out for an around-the-world trip in 1907 which ended prematurely the next year. She became Jack's "mate woman" and loved to accompany him on his adventures. Charmian published four books and died in 1955 at the age of 83.

Books by Jack London

Son of the Wolf (1900)

The God of His Fathers (1901)

Children of the Frost (1902)

The Cruise of the Dazzler (1902)

A Daughter of the Snows (1902)

Kempton-Wace Letters (1903)

The Call of the Wild (1903)

The People of the Abyss (1903)

The Faith of Men (1904)

The Sea-Wolf (1904)

War of the Classes (1905)

The Game (1905)

Tales of the Fish Patrol (1905)

Moon-Face (1906)

White Fang (1906)

Scorn of Women (1906)

Before Adam (1907)

Love of Life (1907)

The Road (1907)

The Iron Heel (1908)

Martin Eden (1909)

Lost Face (1910)

Revolution (1910)

Burning Daylight (1910)

Theft (1910)

When God Laughs (1911)

Adventure (1911)

The Cruise of the Snark (1911)

South Sea Tales (1911)

The House of Pride (1912)

A Son of the Sun (1912)

Smoke Bellew (1912)

The Night Born (1913)

The Abysmal Brute (1913)

John Barleycorn (1913)

The Valley of the Moon (1913)

The Strength of the Strong (1914)

The Mutiny of the Elsinore (1914)

The Scarlet Plague (1915)

The Star Rover (1915)

Little Lady of the Big House (1916)

The Acorn Planter (1916)

The Turtles of Tasman (1916)

The Human Drift (1917)

Jerry of the Islands (1917)

Michael, Brother of Jerry (1917)

The Red One (1918)

On the Makaloa Mat (1919)

Hearts of Three (1920)

Dutch Courage (1922)

Books by Charmian London

The Log of the Snark (1915)

Our Hawaii (1917)

The Book of Jack London (1921)

(2 volumes)

To
HAWAII

.

"A sense of marvel drifts to me—
Of morning on a purple sea,
And fragrant islands far away."
                —George Sterling.

FOREWORD

Jack London and Hawaii! From the years of his youth the two names have been entwined in the minds of those who knew him best— since that day when, bound for the Japan sealing grounds and Bering Sea on the *Sophie Sutherland* (his model for the schooner Ghost of "The Sea Wolf"), he first glimpsed to northward the smoke and fire of Kilauea. Through successive visits, including eighteen months spent in the Islands during the last two years of his life, through early misunderstanding and final loving comprehension of him, Jack London and Hawaii have drawn together, with increasing devotion in his heart for "Aloha-land"—"Love-land" in his fashion of speech—until at the end he could answer to the long-desired appellation, *kamaaina*, one-who-belongs, and more.

"They don't know what they've got!" he said of the American public, when, a decade ago, headed for the South Seas in his own small-boat voyage around the world, he sailed far out of his course that Hawaii might be the first port of call, and threw himself into learning the manifold beauty and wonder of this territory of Uncle Sam. And "They don't know what they've got," he repeated to each new unscrolling of its wonder and beauty during five months of enjoyment and study of land and people. Again in Hawaii after the breaking out of the Great War, he amended : "Because they have no other place to go, they are just beginning to realize what they've got."

And, really, the knowledge of the citizen of the States is woefully scant concerning this possession but a few days distant by steamer, and woefully he distorts its very name in conversation and song into something like Haw-way'ah. To the adept in the lovely language there are fine nuances in the vowelly word ; but simple Hah-wy'ee serves well.

What does the average middle-aged American know of the amazing history of this amazing "native" people now voting as American citizens? The name Hawaii calls to memory vague dots on a soiled map of the Pacific Ocean, bearing a vaguely gastronomic caption that in no wise reminds him of the Earl of Sandwich, Lord of the British Admiralty, and patron of the intrepid discoverer, Captain Cook, whose valiant bones even now rest on the Kona Coast. Savage, remote, alluring, adventurous, are the impressions ; but few have grasped the fact that that pure Polynesian, Kamehameha the Great, deserves to rank as one of the most remarkable figures in history for his revolutionary genius, unaided by outland ideas. Dying in 1819, little more than a year before the first missionaries sailed from Boston, he had fought his way to the consolidation under one government of the group of eight islands, ended feudal monarchy, abolished idolatry, and all unknowing made the land ripe for Christian civilization.

Of those whom I have questioned, only one even heard that, before this generation, indeed previous to the discovery of gold in California and the starting of our forbears over the Plains by oxteam or across the Isthmus of Panama, early settlers in California were sending their children to be educated in the excellent missionary schools of these isles of inconsequential name, and importing their wheat from the same "savage" port.

In this journal covering a few months spent a decade ago in Hawaii, concluding with a résumé of experiences there in 1915-1916, I have tried to limn a picture of the charm of the Hawaiian Islander as he was, and of his becoming, together with the enchantment of his lofty isles and their abundant hospitality.

During the original writing, many elisions were advised by Jack London, as being too personal of himself for me, being me, to publish. However, in the circumstances of his untimely passing, and in view of a desire made evident to me, in countless letters as well as in the press, for biographical work, I have been led to reinstate and elaborate much of the mass of data. Even in the face of his objections at the time, I had stoutly disagreed, maintaining that the lovers of his soul and his work would value revelation of his personality and manner of living life.

And so, missing incalculably the grace of his final censorship, I am chancing the test. If the personal pronoun *I* too lavishly peppers the story, take the rôle of "the gentle reader" toward me, I pray, and consider the inevitable handicap of one who writes intimately of a dear and gracious subject.

CHARMIAN KITTREDGE LONDON.

GLEN ELLEN, CALIFORNIA,
IN THE VALLEY OF THE MOON,
    September 1, 1917.

ILLUSTRATIONS

Jack London at Waikiki, 1915 . . . . *Frontispiece*

The Pennisula—The Hobron Bungalow—The Snark,
  and the owner ashore. 19

Damon Gardens, Honolulu—"And then Martin must snap us." 40

Working Garb in Elysium—Duke Kahanamoku, 1915. 59

Seen from Nuuanu Pali: Jack London, Lorrin A.
  Thurston, J.P. Cooke—The Sudden Vision—The
  Mirrored Mountains (Painting by Hitchcock) 77

L. G. Kellogg and Jack London at Wahiawa, 1907—
  The Brown Tent Cottage at Waikiki—Jack at corner—
  A Pair of Jacks—Atkinson and London—Ahuimanu 93

Princess Likelike (Mrs. Cleghorn)—Princess Victoria
  Kaiulani—Kaiulani at Ainahau—"Kaiulani's Banyan." 111

Landing at Kalaupapa, 1907—The Forbidden Pali Trail,
  1907—Coast of Molokai—Federal Leprosarium on shore—
  Jack in the Leper Settlement, 1907—Father Damien's
  Grave, 1907 129

Hana—The Red Ruin of Haleakala—Von and Kakina. 147

Prince Cupid—Original "Monument."—The Prince's
  Canoe—At Keauhou, Preparing the Feast—Jack at
  Cook Monument—Jack at Keauhou—Kealakekua
  Bay—Captain Cook Monument 163

By-ways of Hilo—and—Waiakea, Hilo—Riding the
  Flume: Londons (Center), Baldings (Right)—The Flume
  across a Gulch. 179

Waikiki, 1915: Mr. and Mrs. London (Center);
  Mr. A. H. Ford (Right)—A Fragment of Paradise—
  Coconut Island, Hilo—Jack—Rainbow Falls, Hawaii 197

Halemaumau, Kilauea, 1907—Jack in Kilauea—
  Bedecked with Leis—Halemaumau, 1917. 219

ILLUSTRATIONS

Kahilis at Funeral of Prince David Kawananakoa—
Kamehameha the Great—and—Sport of Kings. 235

Jack and Charmian London, Waikiki—A Race around
Oahu—Sailor Jack Aboard the Hawaii—Jack on
Beach Walk. 255

Queen Lydia Kamakaeha Liliuokalani—Governor
John Owen Dominis, the Queen's Consort—A Honolulu
Garden—Residence of Queen Emma. 271

OUR HAWAII

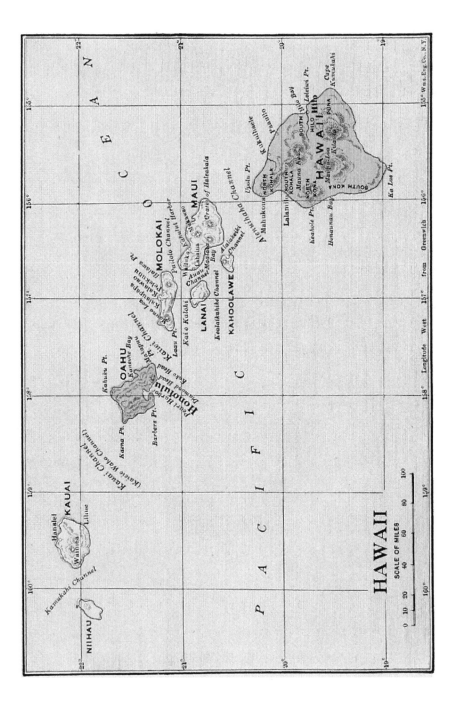

OUR HAWAII

Pearl Harbor, Oahu,
Territory of Hawaii,
Tuesday, May 21, 1907.

COME tread with me a little space of Paradise. Many pleasant acres have I trod hitherto, but never an acre like this. It is so beautiful and restful and green. Green upon green. With blue-depthed shadows imposed from green-depthed foliage of great trees upon thick deep lawn that cushions underfoot. Bare foot. For one somehow dissociates the idea of footwear with an acre of Elysium. It is one of the paradisal blessings of this new Sweet Home of ours that we may blissfully pace it unshod, and for the most part unobserved.

The street is a mere white, meandering, coral-powdered by-way; no thing less inquisitive than the birds abides in the adjoining garden, where a rustic dwelling shows but vaguely amidst a riot of foliage; and on our southern boundary is a tropic tangle of uninhabited wildwood, fronting upon a native fishpond—an elongated bit of bay inclosed by a low wall of masonry of such antiquity that no tradition of Hawaii can place its origin.

Bayward the outlook is a rosy coral reef, swept by tepid pea-green tides; and to its outer rim extends a slender wooden jetty, at the end of which our ship's boat can lie even at low tide.

An eighth of a mile beyond in the rippling chrysoprase flood of Pearl Harbor, "Dream Harbor" Jack loves to call it, swings our Boat of Dreams, our little *Snark*, anchored in the first port of call on her mission of pure golden adventure—a gallant foolishness, perhaps, but if we be fools, let us be gallant ones. Whenever my happy eyes come to rest on her shining shape, I feel them growing big with visions of the coming years on her deck; and then, remembering vivid incidents of the voyage, I drift back to the lovely earth with a filling sense of several laps of adventure already run. Not the least of these is mere living in a shady nook of Paradise where one's eyes must quest twice in the green gloom among enormous trees to discover, near the waterside, the habitation—a very small, very rustic, very simple brown bungalow of three rooms—only one, our big breezy bedroom, quite deserving of the name of room. The others are: one, a long and narrow seaward strip like an inclosed veranda; the other, a cozy cubby of a kitchen. A tiny pantry, an ample bathroom, and windows, windows everywhere, make perfect the indoor aspect of this arcadian acre.

Already, in swimming suits, we have ventured the reef at high tide, with unbounded delight in the sun-washed liquid silk. Our goal for to-morrow is the yacht, as there is scant danger from man-eating sharks in this sheltered harbor.

Beyond the *Snark*, across this arm of the sea, over low green vol-canic hills lying southeast between Pearl Lochs and Honolulu, one is just able to glimpse the rosy bulk of Diamond Head, trembling in the fervent sunlight. To the north, over vast rice fields and upland planta-tions, shrug the rugged, riven Kolau Loa Mountains, their heads lost in heavy cloud masses that seem everlastingly to roll and shift above these tropic ranges.

Pearl Harbor embraces some twelve square miles, divided naturally into three lochs, or arms of the sea, by two peninsulas, on the eastern of which lies the village dignified by the suggestive name of Pearl City. Trust me for having already gleaned the information that the locality has been these many years filched of its jewels.

On the southeastern extremity of our particular "neck of the woods," stray a few suburban homes of Honolulans, of which ours is one. Tochigi, Nipponese and poet-browed cabin boy of the *Snark*, is to live ashore with us and resume his erstwhile household service, while the rest of the yacht's complement—Roscoe, sailing-master, Bert, en-gineer of our ruined machinery, and Martin, cook because there was no other berth vacant—will retain their accommodations aboard. In these protected waters, the boat lies at least as steady as a house on wheels, as she swings to ebb and flow.

Strangely content are we in the unwonted tranquillity of motion and sound, lacking wish to venture afield, even to Honolulu, about twelve miles distant by the railroad. Enough just to rest and rest, and gaze around upon the beautiful, long-desired world of island. Scarcely can we glance athwart the apple-green water but there curves a span of rainbow between our eyes and the far hills, and like as not a double-span, with promise of a triple-bow; while frequent warm showers delicately veil the land's vivid emerald with all melting tints of opal.

Very florid, all this, you will smile—a bit overdone, perhaps? Gird at my word-storms if you will. Then consider . . . and take ship for this "fleet of islands" in the western ocean. It isn't real; it can't be—too sweet it is, day and night, the round twenty-four hours. Here but the one night and day, already we grope for new forms of expression, as will you an you follow the sinking sun.

The heat is not oppressive, even though the season is close to summer. But one must realize that Hawaii is only subtropical. To be precise, the group of eight inhabited islands occupies a central position in the North Pacific, and lies just within the northern tropic. For the benefit of any sailor who may run and read, Jack says I might as well be still more explicit, and record that the *Snark*, anchored about 2000 sea miles southwest of her native shore, lies between 18° 54' and 22° 15' north latitude, and between 154° 50' and 160° 30' of longitude west of Greenwich. Figures never did stick with me—there seems to be a positive lack in my brain that is the despair of my thoroughly mathematical and practical commander, who can reduce anything in the world to his eternal "arithmetic." (Almost anything, I hear him disavow, for none so humble as he to offer that there are holy things of the human heart and mind far from amenable to rule of thumb.) What does penetrate my senses in this particular case is the immutable truth that this ocean paradise is blessed with a lower temperature than any other country in the same latitude. The reasons are simple enough—the prevailing "orderly trades" that blow over a large extent of the ocean, and the ocean itself that is cooled by the return current from the region of Bering Straits. Pleasantly warm though we found the waters of Pearl Harbor this bright morning, yet are they less warm by ten degrees than the waters of other regions in similar latitudes.

And now, to go back a little and recount how we came to rest in this fair haven—Fair Haven, in passing, was the name bestowed upon Honolulu Harbor by one of her discoverers, Captain Brown, when, in 1794, in his schooner *Jackal*, accompanied by Captain Gordon in the sloop *Prince Lee Boo*, he entered the bay, and mixed in local affairs by selling arms and ammunition to King Kalanikupule of Oahu, who was resisting an invasion from the sovereign of the island of Maui, Kaeo. Right near us here, at Kalauao on the way to Honolulu, a red battle was waged, in which Kalanikupule, assisted by Captain Brown and his men, overthrew the powerful enemy. Poor Captain Brown was born unlucky, it would seem. Firing a salute the next day from the *Jackal*, in honor of the victory, a wad from his guns went wild and killed Captain Kendrick, who was quietly dining aboard his own vessel, the *Lady Washington*. The blameless skipper's funeral, being of a different sort from the native ceremony, was looked upon by the Hawaiians as an act of sorcery to induce the death of Captain Brown. Kalanikupule paid the latter four hundred hogs for his valorous part in the struggle with the vanquished Kaeo, and Brown, after the sailing of the *Lady Washington* for China, put his men to salting down the valuable pork at Kaihikapu, an ancient salt pond between Pearl Harbor and Honolulu.

One day while the *Jackal*'s mate, Mr. Lamport, and the sailors were gathering salt, Kamohomoho, uncle of Oahu's king, boarded the *Prince Lee Boo* and the *Jackal*, and more than made good the "act of sorcery" by dispatching poor Brown as well as Gordon, imprisoning those of the crews not employed ashore. Lamport and his men were captured, but their lives spared. The gratitude of the royal family for favors rendered had been outbalanced by ambition for a modern navy with which to attack Kamehameha the Great on the "Big Island," Hawaii. On the voyage, however, the white seamen regained possession of the vessels, sent the natives ashore in their own canoes which were being towed, and lost no time following the *Lady Washington* to the Orient.

But I become lost in the fascinating history of the men who blazed our trail to these romantic isles, and forget that this is the chronicle of a more modern adventure.

On the mainland, before sailing out through the Golden Gate, we made the fortunate acquaintance of one, Mr. Thomas W. Hobron, artist, merchant, good fellow, and citizen of Honolulu, who spoke in this wise: "I wonder if you two would care to put up in my little shack on the peninsula. It isn't much to look at, and there's only room enough for the two of you; but it's brimful of Aloha, if you care to use it."

So here are we, blessing good Tom Hobron, as we shall bless him all our years, for the gift of so idyllic a resting spot after the tumult of our first traverse on the bit of boat yonder.

And yet, casting back over those twenty-six days of ceaseless tossing, we are aware only of pleasure in the memory of every least happening, disagreeable and agreeable alike. In fact the last week aboard was so cozy and homelike that more than often we caught ourselves regretting the imminent termination of the cruise. Even at this moment of writing, despite blissful surroundings, did I not know that the *Snark*'s dear adventure were but just begun, I should be robbed indeed, so in love am I with sea and *Snark*:

"For the wind and waterways have stamped me with their seal."

We picked up a good slant of wind to make Honolulu yesterday morning—an immeasurable relief after the worrisome calm of the night before, during which we had taken our turns at the idle wheel and scanned the contrary compass with all emotions of anxiety, while the helpless yacht swung on every arc of the circle, with no slightest fan of air to fill her limp sails that flapped ponderously in the glassy offshore heave. Never shall I forget my own tense double-watch of four hours, straining eye and ear toward the all-too-nigh coral reefs off Koko Head, with Mokopuu Point light blinking to the northeast. But when a dart of sun through a decklight woke me from brief sleep, we were spanking along smartly in a cobalt sea threshed white on every rushing wave, with the green and gold island of Oahu shifting its scenery like a sliding screen as we swept past lovely rose-tawny Diamond Head and palm-dotted Waikiki toward Honolulu Harbor. After an oddly fish-less voyage of four weeks, we were joyously excited over a school of big porpoises, "puffing-pigs," intent as any flock of barnyard fowl to cross our fleeing forefoot. Undignified haste was their only resemblance to domestic poultry, for in general movement they were more like sportive colts hurdling in pasture with snort and puff—sleek sides glistening blue black in the brilliant sunlight.

To our land-eager eyes, the beautiful old city was the surpassing picture of her pictures, when, still outside, we came abreast of her wharves—the water front with ships and steamers moored beside the long sheds, and, behind, the Pompeian-red Punch Bowl, so often de-scribed by early voyagers; the suburban heights of Tantalus; the pur-ple-deep rifts of valleys and gorges; and the green-and-violet needled peaks upthrusting through dense dark cloud rack.

Barely had we finished Martin's eggless breakfast, when a govern-ment launch frothed alongside, and the engineer's cheery "Want a line, Jack—eh?" sounded classic assurance of Hawaii's far-famed grace of hospitality. Despite my sanguine temperament, I had been conscious of a premonition that something unfortunate would happen upon our ar-rival, probably due to the impression left by the hasty ship chandler of San Francisco, who unjustly libeled the *Snark* in Oakland and delayed our sailing; so this gracious "Want a line, Jack?" was music to my ears. You see, Jack London is not infrequently arrested, or nearly arrested, for one reason or another, whenever he sets his merry foot upon foreign soil (I have disquieting memories of Cuba, Japan, and Korea); and Hawaii seems like foreign soil, albeit annexed by the Stars and Stripes.

The morning paper, the *Pacific Commercial Advertiser*, preceded Immigration Inspector Brown and Customs Inspector Farmer over the rail, and they laughingly pointed to a conspicuously leaded item that the *Snark* was supposed to be lost with all on board—bright tidings already cabled to California and read by our horrified families and friends! We cannot help wishing we were early enough here to be handed the very first English newspaper published at Honolulu, in 1836—the *Sandwich Islands Gazette*. And two years before that, the Hawaiian sheets, *Kumu Hawaii* and *Lama Hawaii*, were the first newspapers issued in the Pacific Ocean.

Speed is not the object of our junketing in the Seven Seas; but if we of the *Snark* had known any hurt vanity about the length of our passage, it would have been amply offset by a report the inspectors made of the big bark *Edward May*, arriving six days before, which beat our tardy record but forty-eight hours, after an equally uneventful voyage.

Meanwhile the pilot had come aboard, a line was passed for'ard to the launch, and we now ripped and zipped over a billowy swell to meet the port physician, Dr. Sinclair, whose white launch could be seen putting out from a wharf. That dignitary, once on deck, scanned our clean bill of health, asked a few routine questions—one of which was whether we carried any rats or snakes; and all three officials pronounced us free to enter the port of Honolulu. Whereupon Jack stated that we were bound for Pearl Lochs, expecting there to find Mr. Tom Hobron, and was in return informed by the pilot that Mr. Hobron had been called to San Francisco for an indefinite period, but that he knew the cottage was at our disposal in accordance with the understanding. Furthermore, we were told that the wharves of Honolulu were lined with her citizens, waiting to garland us in welcome; but too impelling behind our eyes was the fancied picture of the promised retreat by the still waters of Pearl Lochs, so we thanked our kind visitors, secured a launch, and towed resolutely past the hospitable city.

"It does seem a darned shame," Jack mused regretfully. "But what can we do with all our plans made for Pearl Harbor?" "And anyway," he added, "I don't want the general public to see boat of mine sail in looking as if she's been half-built and then half-wrecked, the way this one does .... I've got *some* pride."

Then all attention was claimed by the beauty of our westward way to the harbor entrance, as we closely skirted a broad shoreward reef where greenest breakers combed and burst into fountains of tourmaline and turquoise, shot through with javelins of sun gold, and the air was filled with rainbow mist. Our boat slipped along in a world compounded of the very ravishment of melting colors—land and sea, it was all of a piece; while off to the southeastern horizon ocean and sky merged in palest silvery azure, softly gloomed by shadowy shapes of other Promised Islands.

Turning almost due north into the narrow reef entrance to the Lochs, we could easily have sailed unassisted, even with the light breeze then remaining, so well marked is the channel which has been dredged, full thirty feet deep, to admit passage of the largest vessels into this land-locked harbor, invaluable acquisition to the American government—the finest naval station in the Pacific, if not in the world. Its low banks show both lava and coral formation, and vast cane plantations and gently terraced rice fields slope their green leagues back to the foothills of the Waianae Mountains. Scattered over the rice areas are picturesquely tattered Mongolians, who utter long resonant calls to frighten the marauding ricebirds, which, swarming up in black, disturbed clouds, are brought down with shotguns.

We two, with oneness in love of our watery roaming, were happy and vociferous as a pair of children, entering this our first port. Had we given it a thought, we could have wished for a less civilized landfall, with conscious missing of a native face or two. But I am sure this never entered our busy heads—not mine, at any rate; and my memory of Jack's alert and beaming face precludes doubt of his contentment with things as they were.

Presently, as we wound along between the western peninsula and a little green islet, he called attention to the snowy bore of a tiny craft racing toward us. In short order a smart white launch was rounding up with dash and style befitting the commodore of the famed Hawaiian Yacht Club, Mr. Clarence Macfarlane, who, with Mr. Albert Waterhouse, a neighbor on this little eastern peninsula of ours, had learned by telephone from Honolulu of our arrival, and hurried out to make us welcome. Both of these "dandy fellows," as Jack promptly rated them, sent a warm glow through us by the unassuming good will of their greeting eyes and hand-grasp, while the first word on their lips was the beautiful Hawaiian "*Aloha!*" (ah-lo-hah) that is epitome of hearty welcome, broad hospitality, and unquestioning friendship. No noise nor flurry was theirs, as they set foot on the deck of the much-bruited *Snark*; only the kindest, quietest, make-yourself-at-home manner, as if we had all been acquainted for years, or else that it was the most usual thing in the world to receive a wild man and woman who had essayed to circumnavigate the globe in an absurd small shallop of outlandish rig. But those keen sailor eyes missed jot nor tittle of the vessel's lines and visible equipment, for to the mind of the world at large this boat, "the strongest of her size ever built," to quote her owner, with convenient English dogger bank sail plan, is a somewhat questionable experiment. I intercepted Albert Waterhouse's roving glance on its return from examining the stepping of the stout mizzenmast, which stepping constitutes the main difference between our imported ketch-rig and the more familiar yawl; and the comprehending laugh in my own eyes called out a roguish, half-embarrassed twinkle in his. But "Zing! She's some boat!" he appreciated, taking in the sturdy sticks and teak deck fittings, and the general compactness of our forty-five by fifteen foot ocean dwelling.

And then he related how he had been commissioned by Tom Hobron to turn over the bungalow and do what he could to make us at home. His first neighborly service was to see the *Snark* properly anchored off the Hobron jetty, the while I strained my eyes across the eighth mile of gray green water to glimpse the "not-much-to-look-at 'shack'" amongst the plumy depths of foliage.

Leaving the crew aboard to make everything snug, Jack and I were carried by launch farther up the Loch to a long wooden foot pier that leads over the shallow shore reef to a spacious suburban place where live Albert Waterhouse and his little family.

And here occurreth a teapotful of mischance. Let none question that negotiating several hundred feet of narrow, stationary, unrailed bridge above shifting water, by legs that for over three weeks have known only a pitching surface of forty-five by fifteen, is little short of tragedy for one who would make seeming entry into a hospitable strange land. I know how Jack looked; I can only tell how I felt. And he was distinctly unkind. He made no secret of his amusement at my astonishing gyrations, although to my jaundiced eye his own progress was open to criticism.

It still puzzles—how we ever traversed the distance without a ducking. Repeatedly I had to apologize to Mr. Waterhouse or Commodore Macfarlane for the frantic dabs made at them to prevent myself from going headlong into the water. It was outrageous, the way that interminable board walk would rise straight up until I felt obliged to lean acutely forward to the ascent, in terror of bumping a sunburnt nose—only to find that it had abruptly slanted downward, whereupon I must angle as giddily backward to preserve a becoming balance. From the rear, Jack, in difficulties of his own, tittered something about his wife's "sad walk," and I remember retorting with asperity that it was a pity he had never noticed it before. Then we all fell to laughing and, very much better acquainted for the fun, somehow gained the coral-graveled pathway that led into a garden of green lawns, hedged by scarlet-blooming shrubbery, and shaded by great gnarled trees that would have delighted *Doré*'s tortured imagination.

In response to her husband's shout of "Here they are, Gretchen! I've got 'm! Zing!" Mrs. Waterhouse, a cool and unruffled vision of woman, moved toward us on bare sandaled feet across the broad, shaded veranda of the big cool house, a stately figure in long unbroken lines of sheer muslin and lace.

"You poor child," was her greeting to me, with arm-around hovering me into a white bathroom all sweet-scented and piled with fluffy towels. "You must be nearly tired to death. I can just imagine how I'd feel after such a trip! Just come right in here and rest your bones in a good hot bath before lunch."

Rightly she guessed our tired bones; and rightly she prescribed the beneficence of steaming water. But the ache was from violent stresses of accommodating our precious skeletons to a stable environment, rather than from any hardships of sea-buffeting. Fifteen minutes' relaxation in that shining tub made me all new; and, once more in my blue silk bloomer-suit, I joined the happy captain of my boat and heart. Likewise bathed and refreshed, his wet hair wickedly though futilely brushed to snub the curling ends, sprawling in cool white ducks upon a broad flat couch spread deep with fine-woven native mats, he was immersed in a magazine of later date than our sailing from California. No one was about for the moment, and we lay and looked around with wordless content in this, our first household of Hawaii. Everything was restfully shaded, yet nothing dark, what of the light polished floors, light walls, and handsome rattan furniture from Orient and Philippines. Roomy window seats, banked with cushions, lovely pictures, and a "baby-grand" piano, furnished an air of city elegance to the equally refined summer rusticity. I did not even want to touch the alluring piano; to lie deep in that reclining chair of cool rattan and to know that it was there, golden-complete within its glossy casing, was all-satisfying.

Jack, watching under his long lashes, smiled indulgently. "Funny way to make a living, Mate-Woman!" Often he thinks aloud about his selection of a means of livelihood, and ever grows more convinced that he chose the best of all ways for him—and me. "I carry my office in my head, and see the world while I earn the money to see it with." And verily have my lines fallen in pleasant places, the garner from a congenial artistry making accessible those pleasant places.

Entered Gretchen Waterhouse, with her lovely babe in her arms, breathing beauty and comfort and cleanliness—such a sumptuous Germanic Madonna, with heavy hair parted smoothly over placid deep-blue eyes and wide, low brow, and piled high in a glossy tower. She was followed by that mischievous-eyed husband of hers, who announced luncheon with a jolly: "Come on, you famished seafarers, and see what there is to eat!" But first we must be crowned, I with a wreath of small pink rosebuds, dainty as a string of coral, while around Jack's neck was laid a wide circlet of limp green vine, glossy and fragrant. Commodore Macfarlane was also decorated in the same charming way that the white dwellers of the Islands have adopted from the sweet native custom.

The meal was furnished forth on a side veranda, or *lanai* (lah-nah-e quickly lahn-I) as they say here, screened with flowering vines, and our host and hostess were on tiptoe to see whether or not we would be "good sports" in trying the native dishes which form part of their daily menu. As Jack said afterward, they "let us down easy," because, instead of experimenting on our *malihini* (newcomer) palates with straight *poi*, Albert Waterhouse diluted some of the smooth pinkish gray paste with cold water and milk, and added a pinch of salt. Served in a long thin glass, he called this a poi cocktail. I scarcely see how any one could dislike it. The plain thick poi, unseasoned, would be debatable to those unfortunates who dread sampling anything "odd"; but we took to it instanter. It must have excellent food value, being as it is the staple of all Pacific native peoples who are lucky enough to have right conditions for its raising. They showed us how to combine the plain poi with accessories—a spoonful of the cool gray mush with a bite of meat or salt dried fish. Eaten by itself, poi is somewhat flat in taste, like slightly fermented starch. I do not know whether they were joking, but our friends told us that it is used successfully for wallpaper paste! In these days poi is manufactured by machinery in nice sanitary factories. Originally it was made by first roasting the tuber of the taro plant, wrapped in leaves, among heated rocks in the ground, then pounding the malleable mass with stone poi pounders and manipulating it with the hands. It would be noteworthy if foot work had not also been utilized, as by the Italians in macaroni making.

Also we were regaled with the tuber itself, fresh boiled—a very good vegetable, prepared like a potato, with butter, salt, and pepper. It would be hard to give an idea of the flavor, and so many writers have failed to describe foreign tastes that as yet I am not going to try, save to state that I feel sure taro would prove a palatable substitute for both bread and potatoes, if one were deprived of the old standbys.

Jack was interviewed by several perspiring newspaper men who had taken the first train to Pearl City after the elusive *Snark* had passed out of sight; and in the mid-afternoon Mr. Waterhouse guided us to our new dwelling, distant about ten minutes' walk. We met the entire crew bound for the village to see what they could see. Even the gentle Tochigi was bitten by the popular sightseeing bug. And Tochigi, alas, failed to return until evening, so that I was obliged to do the unpacking. For Jack had developed a vicious headache, and I hastened to reduce all confusion and establish a serene home atmosphere; but I must confess that the really happy task was an uphill one, when it wasn't downhill, due to the sad walk that led me devious ways and many extra steps, with frequent halts to orient a revolving brain.

By seven, with still no Tochigi, and not a scrap to eat, came a tap on the door. As if in answer to a wish, there stood a smiling woman bearing a tray of enormous tomatoes and cucumbers, a neatly napkined loaf of freshly baked bread, and a generous pat of homemade butter. She is our nearest neighbor, Miss Frances Johnson, with whom, upon a suggestion from Mrs. Waterhouse, we have this day made arrangements to board.

No sooner had she gone, than a cousin of Mr. Waterhouse brought an offering of papaias (pah-py'-ahs)—wonderful green-and-yellow melon things that grow on trees—and asked what further he could do for us. The combination of old-world and new-world neighborliness was quite overwhelming, and I was more than grateful, for by now poor

Jack had taken to the big white bed, although he weakly admitted that he might eat a tomato if urged.

Alas, for wifely solicitude. Old Ocean played a wicked trick. As I was nearing the pallid sufferer's bedside with a plateful of big red slices, which I had dressed with lemon and oil as he likes them, something distracted my attention, and I made to set the dish on a table. The house lurched and the floor gave a sickening jerk, and I actually missed the table. Of course the salad splashed on the floor, in a havoc of shattered porcelain. I do not know exactly what this particular confession is "good" for, but I might as well confess wholly while I am about it. A second salad was made, and ... went the way of the first. My sea-legs refused to stiffen into land-legs in one day, and little help they received from my eyes accustomed to shifting surroundings. When the second plate broke on the floor, the giggle that smothered Jack's "Poor little kid!" robbed me of pity for the painful shaking the giggle caused him.

Now that I am into the subject of Jack's illness, this day of his first landfall, with his permission I am going to divulge the cause. In fact, he mentioned it himself to one of the harbor officials this morning. And anyway, he is the frankest human being concerning his frailties that ever I knew. The majority of civilized humanity, being trained from without and within to repress their faults or peccadilloes, fail to comprehend this ingenuously open attitude. He is so candid that they think, without thinking, that he must be concealing something. Pardon the double paradox, but it seems to express what I am after. For example: if, in an autobiographical sketch or article, he mentions having been arrested, whether as boy tramp or as war correspondent, his charitable compeers of the press proceed to brand him as indisputably a jailbird and criminal "who should be behind the bars"; or, if he tells the thrilling tale of how, as a mere youth in the Klondike, he shot the notoriously difficult White Horse Rapids with a bracing glass of whisky in him, up goes a hue and cry about the pity of Jack London being a hopeless drunkard! Please believe, I am not exaggerating.

But to the case in point. Jack was thirty-one last January, and had smoked cigarettes ever since he was somewhere around fourteen. And when I say smoked, I mean smoked. He smoked all his waking hours—in the daytime, at work or at play, at night when reading and studying, stocking his remarkable brain with knowledge of every kind. His mind is like a library of infinite shelves, where he is endlessly cataloguing contributions from every source. Once, only, had I ever broached the subject of smoking—two years ago, shortly before we were wedded. From the conversation we held, swinging in a hammock under the laurels at Wake Robin Lodge, I seemed to gather that his smoking habit was a rather negligible detail in comparison with the thousand and one larger issues that occupied his mind. How shall I say?—that this habit, a mere habit, which requires none of his conscious attention in its pursuance, should not be too seriously considered by him or others. This, roughly, is the most I could conclude at the time, as to his outlook upon smoking in so far as concerned himself; and, having firmly philosophized these many years that my "not impossible he" should never be nagged, I had permitted myself no further reference to the ubiquitous cigarette. However, I did notice, during our months in the country, that occasionally he would restrict himself to only several a day, say on our long horseback jaunts through Northern California; and, once, with a certain rare little half-bashful smile that sits quaintly beneath the calm sweet of his gray eyes, he said: "I'm really trying to cut down a little, you see."

That was all; and never a word to me passed his lips until we cleared the Golden Gate, that he intended to forego his nerve-soothing custom on the passage to Hawaii. Naturally I was delighted at the well-executed surprise, meanwhile hiding misgivings as to the contentment of his nervous system under the unescapable shock of cutting off so abruptly the narcotic of seventeen years. Keenly as he felt the need at times, nevertheless it never once made him visibly irritable. Once or twice, he told me a couple of weeks out, he suffered from an illusion that there were cigarettes aboard if only he could find them, and that the rest of us were concealing them from him. His continual joy in the voyage went far to offset the deprivation, and after a little he ceased to miss his "Imperiales." But when the customs officer yesterday boarded the *Snark*, my young skipper immediately asked for a cigarette, with an "I'm going to see how it tastes." It did not taste "just right" and he tried another—and several. . . . In short, as the day wore, poor Jack found himself suffering with as absurd intensity as any surreptitious small limb of Satan during his first smoke. He was just merely "laid out," to quote his own words; and be it accredited to my good page that I did not giggle at his plight as did he when the second salad lapsed redly upon the floor.

At length, he fell sound asleep under the well-tucked cloud of fine bobinet that graces all Hawaiian beds (the mosquito seems to be the serpent of this Eden), and I breathed a sigh of relief, having this long time learned that sleep is the only medicine for any brand of a J. L. headache. Also, I was desperately weary, one might say land-sick, and more than ready to turn in upon my chosen canopied cot in a breezy corner of the big room.

My troubles had only begun.

When the crew passed through on their return to the yacht, I softly called Martin to look at the kitchen-sink faucet, which was not working properly. No sooner had he turned on the water, than up wriggled a truly appalling centipede all of five inches in length. The leathery toughness of the monstrous insect, which was as thick as my finger, made the slaying of it an eminently lively and disgusting tussle. Martin finally vanquished the leggy foe, but we kept a wary eye for its possible mate. Fate left it to me, alone in the bathroom—for I would not disturb Jack's healing slumbers,—to deal with the bereft one. After scissoring off its ugly fanged head, I fled to bed, fervently trusting to dream of things with wings—birds, butterflies, angels. No remembered assurances of the very mild venomousness of this transplanted little dragon can ever lessen its hideous offensiveness. In my mind there is filed away a word of protest for its every leg, of which, despite its name, I counted but seventy-four. The people here pay little attention to this insect's bite.

In the morning I summoned Tochigi to remove the mutilated remains. Oh, of course, before cremation they must be displayed to an admiring audience of husband; I had no call to forego the praise of his "Plucky kid!" For even more fussy is he than I, about crawly things, and he could see, by involuntary reminiscent tremors, that my overworn nerves had been somewhat shaken by the encounter. Not having laughed at me, we could laugh in company later in the morning, when, hair-brush in hand, he went right into the air with a "Great Scott!" before an ill-looking hairy gray spider, some four or five inches across, that dropped from the ceiling and clattered upon the bureau top. Was it Mark Twain who, disturbed at his writing by one of these, put the cuspidor upon it, claiming that a gray fringe of legs showed all around the vessel? Somewhere I have read that these spiders are descendants of the tarantula; but they have descended a long way, for the tarantulas that taught caution to my Southern California childhood were meaty monsters compared with these paper-and-fuzz household gods of Hawaii, which harm nothing more serious than mosquitoes and other dispensable vermin.

Jack had slept off the headache, and was able to enjoy his first luncheon at Miss Johnson's. (Tochigi is to cook our light breakfast at home.) Miss Johnson and her sisters, Miss Ellen and Mrs. Fyfe, served a most appetizing table for us seaworn pilgrims—a capital steak, done rare to a nicety, accompanied by taro which had been boiled and then sliced and fried lightly in fresh butter; cool platefuls of raw tomatoes and cucumbers, in oil and lemon; poi, with dried salt *aku* (ah-koo—bonita), papaias, and avocados—the almost prohibitively expensive alligator pears that we know in California, where they are sent by steamer and in shipping deteriorate; and bananas so luscious that we declared we had never before tasted bananas. These and sweet seedling oranges, as well as papaias, thrive in the fragrant garden of roses and hibiscus and palms, seen through Venetian blinds from where we sat at table, eating hothouse viands in the hothouse air.

We came away congratulating ourselves and each other upon such a feasting place within two minutes' walk of our own little red gate; and the trio of ladies granted indulgence to drop over in any garmenture that pleases our mood, and also offered the piano for my use. Although even on this warm leeward side of Oahu the temperature is said to range only from 6o° to 85°, with a mean of 74°, the humid quality of the atmosphere invites loose lines of apparel. Yesterday it was ducks and bloomers for Jack and me. This morning it was ducks and a summer lawn. But this afternoon, in the dreamy green privacy of our lovely acre, it is kimono and kimono, thank you, with not much else to mention. And I am already planning certain flowing gowns of muslin and lace, on the pattern of Gretchen Waterhouse's home attire, which flouncy robe is called a *holoku* (ho-lo-koo). It is a worthy development from the first clothing introduced by the missionaries, the simplest known design—like that cut by our childhood scissors for paper dolls, and called *muumuu* (moo-oo-moo-oo smoothly) by the Hawaiians. In time this evolved into the full-gathered Mother Hubbard atrocity; but in this year of grace (thanks be for that grace!) it is a sumptuous, swinging, trailing model of its own, just escaping the curse of the Mother Hubbard and somehow eliding the significance of wrapper. Not all women would look as well in the holoku as does Mrs. Albert, who is straight and tall and walks as if with pride in her fine height and proportion, as large women should walk. I believe a great measure of the holoku's good looks depends upon its being carried well. The muumuu, in its pristine simplicity, is still used by native women for an under-garment, and, in all colors of calico, for swimming, although I have yet to learn how it could permit any freedom of movement in the water.

"It hasn't taken you long to size up the styles in Hawaii," Jack smiled to me just now, after I had read him the above. But he added, appreciatively: "I hope you will get some of those loose white things. I like them."

Paucity of coast mail would indicate that relatives and friends have been chary of wasting energy on letters that might never be received by such reckless rovers. O ye of scant faith in the *Snark*'s oaken ribs and her owner's canny judgment! Not so with me, who am most concerned, after him, in the safety of the venture. Laying aside personal bias, there is not another man in the round world with whom I should care to risk my precious neck in a deep-sea vessel of the *Snark*'s measurements, because of Jack's life-long experience in *small*-boat sailing, a branch of sailor knowledge that stands by itself. Many's the gold-braided, grand old captain of great liners, who knows little or nothing of the handling of small sailing craft. Many's the deep-water seaman on big ships, who is quite ignorant of the ways of small boats. But the sailorman who has experience of both kinds pronounces: "Give me the small boat, every time, for safety at sea! She stays on top! And she rides one wave at a time!"

In addition to first-hand education in sailboats on San Francisco Bay, which unreliable expanse he knows from end to end, and seven months at sea in the *Sophie Sutherland* (the schooner *Ghost* of "The Sea Wolf"), Jack is possessed of swift right judgment in emergency. For many years I have yachted on the waterways of California, so little explored except by river dwellers and fishermen, and several times with Jack at the helm of his old sloop *Spray*, and never have I seen his equal for correlation of brain and body. All this for the doubting ones who curtail their unenthusiastic epistles to us of the *Snark*.

The mail was brought by a tiny "jerk-water," bobtail dummy and coach run by one, Tony, from Pearl City, a mile away, to a station near the end of the peninsula. Tony is a handsome little swarthy fellow, regarded by me with much interest, as my first Hawaiian on his native heath. Certain misgivings at sight of him rendered my surprise less to learn that he is full-blooded Portuguese.

Alack, my first Hawaiian is a Portuguese—and of course Jack is hilarious.

One other caller crossed the springy turf of our garden—Bert's uncle, Mr. Rowell of Honolulu, who, having been told we were looking for saddle animals, came to suggest that we bring up our saddles the first of next week, and ride two of his horses back to the peninsula, where we are welcome to them as long as we please. Truly, the face of Hawaii hospitality is fair to see. What a place to live, with the gift of a roof from the rain, tree tops from the noon-day sun, a peaceful space in which to work, strange pleasant foods irreproachably set forth, a warm vast bowl of jade for swimming, and fleet steeds for less than the asking! As this latest gift bringer departed, Jack, touched to huskiness, looking after him said:

"A sweet land, Mate, a sweet land."

And now our green gloom purples into twilight where we have lain upon the sward the long afternoon; and twice my companion has hinted at a dip before dinner. To him I have read from my chronicle, and he comments something as follows:

"You'll have to blue-pencil a lot of the stuff about me. You *do* 'get' me, somehow, and I love what you have written. But they'll make fun of you, my dear, and hurt your feelings. Listen to your father, now. I'm telling you! "

This is considered as it deserves. But I shake my head to him, and say:

"No. I don't believe they will."

Wednesday, May 22, 1907.

Too bright and warm the morning to stay asleep, even in this arboreal spot, we rose at six. Another and earlier riser played his part in the disturbance of rest—the saucy mynah bird, whose matin racket is full as soothing as that of our cheerfully impudent blue jay in the Valley of the Moon. "False" mynah though he is said to be, there is nothing false about either his voice or his manners, both of which are blatantly real and sincere in their abandon. Imported from India, to feed on the cutworm of a certain moth, he has made himself more familiarly at home than any other introduced bird, and has been known to pronounce words. He is a sagacious-looking and interesting rowdy; but could one have choice in feathered alarm clocks, the silver-throated skylark, another importation to Hawaii, would come first.

But who should complain? We had not stirred for nine solid, dreamless hours—speaking for myself, for Jack always dreams, and vividly. Nine hours, for either of us, is phenomenal, for I am more or less of what he calls an "insomniast," and he is one of those rare individuals

who seem to thrive on short sleep. Indeed, before our lives came together, he had for years resolutely held to as brief hours as four and
five; but even he was ripe to confess that this might prove destructive
to the nerves, and since then he allows himself a sliding scale which, in
the long run, averages well—some nights three hours, some seven, some
five or six, and, but very seldom a night like this last. He warns that
he will put on a large waist measure; but I am not to be frightened. At
the worst I would rather see his splendid body fat and long-lived than
his eyes hollow, and his fine nerves on edge. Oh, he is not a "nervous"
person, despite high-strung sensibilities. Rarely does he show his keen
tension in any fussiness of thought or speech or action. Nevertheless,
he has come to value a measure of relaxation, as have I; for it is a tense,
vivid life we lead in our happy hunt for adventure; meanwhile we work
for the feeding and housing of more than a few—to say nothing of the
upkeep of Jack's beauty-ranch in the Valley of the Moon.

Our rising young author, in search for an ideal work-room, pounced
upon a shaded, wafty space out of doors, mountainward of the bungalow. Tochigi found a small table and box-stool for that left foot which
always seeks for a rest when said author settles to writing. A larger
box serves to hold extra "tools of trade," such as books and notes. Each
morning, at home or abroad, Tochigi sharpens a half dozen or more
long yellow pencils with rubber tips, and dusts the table, but never
must he disturb the orderly litter of note-pads, scribbled and otherwise.

Within a couple of brisk hours, under my direction, the boy finished the work of settling, not the least item being the installing of
our big Victor and some three hundred disks; then nothing would do
but Jack would have me whirring off Wagnerian overtures and other
orchestral "numbers" while I pattered about in Japanese sandals.

The typewriter shares with the "music-box" a long table in the
narrow front room. Never anywhere are we quite at home until this indispensable factor of our business, with its accessories, is placed where
I may conveniently copy Jack's manuscript or notes, or take his letter
dictations. Since his office is under his hat, mine must be on a table
large enough to support the old Remington.

By nine, with a big palm fan I was joining Jack in the hammock
where he hung between two huge algarobas, surrounded by a batch
of periodicals forwarded from the Coast, and we felicitated ourselves
upon having risen in the comparative cool of the morning and done the
more active part of the day's work. Owing to a stoppage of the blessed

(1) The Pennisula. (2) The Hobron Bungalow. (3) The *Snark*, and the owner ashore.

Trades, the air was enervatingly heavy. For the past month Hawaii has known the same unusual atmospheric conditions that marked our passage. Only a mild south wind blows—the Kona, "the sick wind," and it does seem to draw the life out of one. We are warned that when a Kona really takes charge, all things that float must look lively. Because this is not the regular season for Konas, old sea-dogs are wagging their heads.

"Do you know what you are?" I quizzed Jack, having outrun him by a word or two in the race for knowledge.

"No, I don't. And I don't care. But do *you* know *where* you are?" he countered.

"No, *I* don't. *You* are a *malihini*—did you know that?"

"No, and I don't know it now. What is it?"

"It's a newcomer, a tenderfoot, a wayfarer on the shores of chance, a—"

"I like it—it's a beautiful word," Jack curbed my literary output. "And I can't help being it, anyway. But what shall I be if I stay here long enough?"

Recourse to a scratch-pad in my pocket divulged the fascinating sobriquet that even an outlander, be he the right kind of outlander, might come in time—a long time—to deserve. It is *kamaaina*, and its significance is that of old-timer, and more, much more. It means one who *belongs*, who has come to belong in the heart and life and soil of Hawaii; as one might say, a subtropical "sourdough."

"How should it be pronounced, since you know so much?"

"Kah-mah-ah-ee-nah," I struggled with careful notes and tongue. "But when Miss Frances says it quickly, it seems to run into 'Kah-mah-I'-nah.'—And you mustn't say 'Kammy-hammy-hah' for 'Kam-may-hah-may'-hah,'" I got back at him, for Kamehameha the Great's name had tripped us both in the books read aloud at sea.

"I'd rather be called '*Kamaaina*' than any name in the world, I think," Jack deliberately ignored my efforts at his education. "I love the land and I love the people."

For be it known this is not his first sight of these islands. Eleven or twelve years ago, on the way to the sealing grounds off the Japan coast in the *Sophie Sutherland*, he first saw the loom of the southernmost of the group, Hawaii, on its side Kilauea's pillar of smoke by day and fiery glow by night. In January of 1904, bound for Korea as correspondent to the Japanese-Russian War, he was in Honolulu for the short stopover of the *Manchuria*, and spent as brief a time there on his return aboard the *Korea* six months later. And ever since, despite the scantiness of acquaintance, he has been drawn to return—so irresistibly as now to make a very roundabout voyage to the Marquesas in the South Pacific, in order that Hawaii might be first port of call. Often have his friends in California heard him tell of the wonderful times in Honolulu on those two flying visits, and of how good to him was "Jack" Atkinson, then Acting Governor of the Territory.

"Here's something I didn't show you in the mail," Jack said presently, picking up a thick envelope addressed in his California agent's hand. It contained a sheaf of rejections of his novel "The Iron Heel" which has proved too radical for the editors, or at least for their owners' policies. "It's been turned down now by every big magazine in the United States," he went on, a trifle wistfully. "I had hoped it was *timely*, and would prove a ten-strike; but it seems I was wrong. Do you realize this means the clean loss of five or six thousand dollars?—some pinch just now, with all this *Snark* expense of repairs, and salaries both here and at home." He lay awhile, looking up into the green lace of the algarobas. "Darn them all—they think the stuff is an attempt on my part to prophesy. It isn't. *I* don't think the worst of these things are going to happen. I wrote, as you know, merely as a warning—a warning of what might happen if the proletariat weaken in their fight and allow the enemy to make terms with them." Before dismissing the entire matter until the day when he should answer the mail, he concluded:

"They're all afraid of it, Mate-Woman. They see their subscriptions dropping off if they run it; but they give hell to us poor devils of writers if they catch us writing for the mere sake of money instead of pure literature. What's a fellow to do? We've got to eat, and our families have got to eat. And we've got to buy *holo*—what do you call those flowy white things? for small wives;—and sail boats, and gather fresh material for more stories that will and won't sell . . ." he trailed off lugubriously.

Thus Jack on his unsuccessful and very expensive novel. Whereupon he shrugs his wide shoulders under the blue kimono, girds the fringed white obi a little more snugly, picks up a note-pad and long sharp pencil, and makes swift, sprawling notes for a Klondike yarn on which he has been working, "To Build a Fire." This, staged in the Frozen North, is bound to captivate editors and public alike, both of whom, mole-minded as ever, think every other subject but the Klondike out of his "sphere." *He* is the timely one; the masses are ever lagging behind these shining old-young thinkers. And I catch myself holding back tears of disappointment in his disappointment, and hoping he knows the half of how sorry I am. When I turn to look at him again, he is shaking uncontrollably in a fit of giggles over a cartoon in *Life*. Was there ever such a boy-man!

Although wellnigh demoralized on the voyage, due to hopeless sea-sickness and an equally hopeless disciplinary laxness aboard, Tochigi is rapidly regaining his old cheerful executiveness. We have had a good talk, for I have learned the value of once in a while holding friendly meetings with the servants when readjustments are to be made. Dissatisfied helpers are the doom of domestic happiness. Not all of the visitors at the Ranch have agreed with our refusal to allow any tipping. It has always seemed to us an offense to the sacred spirit of hospitality. "I pay my servants high wages to make my house a home, not a hotel," Jack states. "My guests are my guests in every sense. I do not want my servants to be paid for the hospitality of my house." The result has been a pleasant relation between our friends and our Japanese, who have entered wholly into the idea that they are truly sharers in the entertainment. Indeed, some sweetly amusing tales have come back from those whom we neglected to warn, of certain proud explanations that accompanied the declining of monetary favors. Of course, we do not carry this ethic beyond our own gates, wherever these may be; it would not be fair.

Tochigi, once this simple household system is under way, will find ample time for recreation and study. Being as he is a personal servant, he will go with us on many trips and see the land aspect of our wanderings. My work with Jack is of a nature that makes it necessary that I must be freed of a woman's usual tasks of mending, darning, brushing, packing, to say nothing of routine house duties.

"I don't want 'My Woman' to work like a horse," I remember Jack once saying, long before our marriage. "But I want her to be capable of working like a horse if it's necessary."

I like that. Every normal human being must surely pleasure in the ability to be "right there" in emergency—which is what Jack meant, of course. For instance, my "emergency" was quite unavoidable the first day ashore, when Tochigi forgot his. Also, that same night when the centipede had to be dealt with.

Perspiring this afternoon even in the thick shade of the great gnarled algarobas, we watched the "dear old tub" swirl on her chain cable in stiff little squalls, and noted with satisfaction that her anchors seem to have taken good hold despite the reputed "skaty" bottom of this part of the harbor. Although in bad weather we should be obliged to move her to better shelter on the other side of the peninsula, just now we want her near; otherwise it would mean a trudge of a mile to keep track of the repair work. And we both dislike walking.

After the exertion of a vociferous rubber of cribbage, which I lost, the crisp sage-green wavelets on the pink reef invited us to come out and play. So fine was the water that, once at the outer edge of the coral, I decided to venture a swim the like of which I had never known, either in length or roughness, for all my aquatic experience has been either in still creek pools or urban tanks. Not that it was actually rough; but the snappy little staccato seas slapping my face robbed me of breath and confidence of ever reaching the yacht, at a point when she was nearer than was the jetty. The various strokes I had learned availed nothing, and I was timid of floating lest I be smothered by water washing over my upturned face. In brief, I was "in a bad way." Quietly, reassuringly, Jack spoke to me every moment, meanwhile hailing the *Snark* for a boat. He told me not to struggle, and to rest a hand on his shoulder, while he swam slowly. Gasping and sputtering, but reassured by his calm as well as his support, by the time the lifeboat came up I was so far recovered that I merely used it for a tow to the yacht, where we rested for the return swim, on which Jack insisted that the boat escort us.

Martin, who vanished Honolulu-ward yesterday, returned this morning laden with an assortment of produce—all he could carry. His ambition was to be photographed rampant in the midst of tropical plenty, for the wonder and envy of his Kansan acquaintance. The fruity properties for the tender scene cost him all of five dollars. A mainlander might naturally conjecture Hawaii to be a land of almost automatic abundance; but the price Martin paid is illustration of the not economical cost of living. Meat is very high, and even fish, as this morning when Tochigi had to pay twenty-five cents for three small mullet, Hawaii's best "meat that swims" (that is Jack's), peddled by a Chinese fisherman. And everything else is in proportion.

Unfortunately for our purse, the papaia on our trees is not yet ripe. Jack is wild about this fruit, and has it for every breakfast. I like it, too, but the larger part of my pleasure is in looking at it, especially

on its tree, which is too artificially beautiful to seem a live and growing plant. Never have we read nor heard any adequate description of
a papaia tree; but for sheer beauty, in an artificial sense, it is the most
remarkable tree we have ever seen. The trunks of our papaias are six or
seven inches in diameter, rise perfectly straight without a branch nearly to the top, where the fruit clusters thick and close around the carven
bole, for so the ash-colored wood appears with its indented markings.
Among the "melons" and above them are very soft, large, palmated
leaves, some close to the trunk and some on slender stems. And then
there are the blossoms, on the axils of the leaves, twisting and twining
where the fruit comes later, little flowerlets not unlike orange blossoms
in appearance and odor. The trunk is said to be hollow, and there are
male and female trees, which should be planted in company to insure
a good yield—for both share in bearing. The young trees are not so
tall but one can easily reach the fruit; but the trees at Miss Johnson's
call for a stepladder, or stout hands and knees for climbing. Papaia
faintly resembles cantaloupe and muskmelon, although more evenly
surfaced; and it tastes—how does it taste? We have about decided upon
"sublimated pumpkin, very sublimated, but sweeter." For the table, it
is cut in half, lengthwise, its large canary-yellow interior scraped of a
fibrous lining and a handful of slippery black seeds coated with a sort
of mucus, that look for all the world like caviar, and is then set in the
ice box before serving with lemon. In conjunction with beauty and pal-
atableness, the papaia has strong peptonic virtues, and some one told us
it would disintegrate a raw beefsteak overnight.

So Martin had us "snap" him, properly alert amidst his Pacific
plentitude, banked under an algaroba at the waterside—cocoanuts,
watermelons, pineapples, oranges, lemons, mangoes (real mangoes but
tastelessly unripe), guavas, and bananas; not to mention papaias and
taro, and a homely cabbage or two for charm against nostalgia.

After which nothing would do for him but he must pose Jack and
myself, and I can only hope I did not look as silly as I felt. It was all
good fun, however, and Martin can now be heard developing films in
our bathroom, his principal noise a protest at the warmth of the "cold"
water.

Thursday, May 23, 1907.

Beginning to wonder why Tochigi was so late laying breakfast on
the end of the long table that holds the two machines, our surprise was

sweet when with a flush on his olive cheeks he led us out to where he had set a little table under the still trees, strewn with single red hibiscus and glossy coral peppers from a low hedge that trims the base of the cottage, and served a faultless meal of papaia, shirred eggs, a curled shaving of bacon, and fresh-buttered toast, with perfect coffee brewed in the *Snark*'s percolator.

Breakfast over, for an hour we lingered at table reading aloud snatches of books on Hawaii, and laughing over some of the freaks of her mythology, which are not in the main so dissimilar from those of other races, including the Caucasian, as entirely to justify our superior mirth.

All the time I am conscious of a wish that is almost a passion to share, with any who may read this diary, the loveliness of this smiling garden so green and so sweet-scented when little winds wake the acacia laces of the umbrageous algarobas; where nothing really exists beyond our red wicket, but dreams may be dreamed of mirage-like mountains shimmering in the tropic airs across the fairy lagoon.

Strolling to the bank, we sit in long grass with our feet over the seaweed-bearded coral, and lazily watch three native women—the first we have seen—in water to their ample waists, with holokus tucked high, wading slowly in the reef-shallows. One carries a small box with glass bottom, and now and again she bobs under with the box, and then comes up laughing and flinging back her dark hair that waves and ringlets in the sun. They are hunting crabs and other toothsome sea food, which they snare in small hooped nets with handles; and their mellow contralto voices strike the heavy air like full-throated bells, as they gossip and gurgle or break into barbaric measures of melody. Whether it be hymn or native song, the voices are musically barbaric just the same. Upon discovery of us, a truly feminine flurry of bashfulness overcomes them, but they smile like children when we call "Aloha!" and repeat the sweet greeting softly. The mirage effect of the scene is furthered by a motionless reflection of the yacht in the glassy water, as well as of the far shore and billowy reaches of snow-white cloud. The very thought of work is shocking in such drowsy unreality of air and water and earth. Poor Jack groans over self-discipline and there is a lag in his light and merry foot when he finally makes for the little work table, brushes off a brown pod and freshly dropped lace pattern from the algaroba, and dives into the completion of "To Build a Fire."

Before we were through the forenoon's business, he creating, I transcribing, there came stepping across the soundless lawn two dapper

Japanese gentlemen, one, the secretary of the Japanese Y. M. C. A. of Honolulu, the other a reporter on the *Hawaii Shinpo*. After a ceremonial short interview, the secretary, with many little bows and apologies, wanted to know if Mr. Jack London would obligingly consent to make him the proud possessor of "a sheet of document." Bless our souls, what was that? Tochigi avoided further embarrassment by explaining that his countryman desired a page of original manuscript.

"I can't—I'm sorry; they all belong to Mrs. London," Jack passed him on to me.

Since all of his manuscripts have been my most treasured property these three years, I compromised with a "sentiment and signature," which Mr. Secretary had the pleasure of seeing Jack write on the spot, and then departed with seeming elation.

We have rounded the day with a triumphal if slow swim to the yacht, and Jack struts with pride because I made it out and back, and even dived under the copper keel, without assistance other than his occasional advice, relaxing body and mind to float and rest whenever I grew tired.

Saturday, May 25, 1907.

Observing those native women (*wahines*—wah-he-nays) harvest crabs gave me an idea. Stirring betimes, virtuously I gathered a novel breakfast for my good man. In other words, I set baited lines along the jetty, and was soon easily netting the diminutive shellfish that hurried to the raw meat. Albert Waterhouse had furnished the method and the net, when he and Mrs. Albert dropped in last evening. No hooks are used; the crab furnishes his own hooks, and, being a creature of one idea, forgets to let go his juicy prize when the string begins to pull, so that by the time he does relinquish hold, the net is ready for his squirming fall. Although small, these yellowish gray red-spotted crabs are spicily worth the trouble of picking to pieces. Jack, however, does not think any food is worth "wasting that much time" on, when he might be using one hand to hold a book. But he was quite enthusiastic over the plateful of picked tidbits set before him.

Here is a peculiar thing: the fish of Pearl Lochs seldom bite, and must be either netted or speared native fashion. To be sure, there are the ancient fishponds, where it would be easy to use a seine; but these ponds are closely protected by their owners, and no uncertain penalties are exacted for poaching. There are no privileges connected with the long pond that flanks our boundary to the north, so we must depend upon the unromantic peddler for our sea fruit.

No lingering could we allow ourselves at table this morning, for we were bound Honolulu-ward on the forenoon train, to bring back the horses. "Wish I had a million dollars, so I could really enjoy life here," yawned Jack, arms above head and bare feet in the warm, wet grass (it had rained heavily overnight), as he moved toward his work, with a longing eye hammockward to unread magazines and files of newspapers.

Always have I remembered, in school days at Mills College, where I met and loved my first Hawaiian girls, the enthusiasm of Mrs. Susan L. Mills over the cross-saddle horse craft of women in Honolulu, where she and her husband founded a school in early days. So I do not hesitate to ride my Australian saddle here.

And so, trousered, divided-skirted, booted and spurred, both of us coatless, as the day promised to be sultry, we walked to Tony's little dummy-train, on which, with fellow passengers of every yellow and brown nationality except the Hawaiian, we traveled to the very Japanesque-Americanesque village of Pearl City, where the ten o'clock through-train picked us up. During the half-hour ride, we enjoyed the shining landscape of cane and terraced rice, long rolling hills, and the alluring purple gorges and blue valleys of the mountains to our left. The volcanic red of the turned fields is like ours in Sonoma County, with here and there splashes of more violent madder than any at home.

I had expected Oahu to be more tropical than this, palmy and jungly. But I woefully lacked information, and the disappointment is nobody's fault but my own. Even the coconut palms of Hawaii are not indigenous, nor yet the bananas, breadfruit, taro, oranges, sugar cane, mangoes—indeed, the fertile group does not lie in the path of seed-carrying birds, and it remained for early native geniuses navigating their great canoes by the stars, and white discoverers like Cook and Vancouver, to introduce a large proportion of the trees and plants that took like weeds to the sympathetic soil.

Of all imported trees, the algaroba (keawe—kay-ah'vay) has been the best "vegetable missionary" to the waiting territory, and flourishes better here than in its own countries, which seem to include the West Indies, the southern United States, and portions of South America. One writer fares farther, and claims that it is the Al-Korab, the husks of which the Prodigal Son fed to the swine he tended. The first seed of the algaroba was brought to Hawaii from France by Father Bachelot, founder of the Catholic Mission, and was planted by him in Honolulu, on Fort Street, near Beretania, the inscription giving the date as 1837. But an old journal of Brother Melchoir places the date as early as 1828. This tree is still alive and responsible for above 60,000 acres of algaroba growth in Hawaii. A busy tree these seventy-odd years! Left to itself, the algaroba seems to prefer an arid and stony bed, judging from the manner in which it has reclaimed and forested the reefy coast about Honolulu, which was formerly a bare waste. On this island as well as on Molokai and Hawaii, it has changed large tracts of rocky desert into abundantly wooded lands. The algaroba shades the ground with a dense brush, and attains all heights up to fifty and sixty feet—as these in our garden, where the boles have been kept trimmed and show their massive twisted trunks and limbs in contrast to their light and feathery foliage. The wood is of splendid quality, and the pods a most useful stock feed, while bees love the sweet of the blossoms and distill excellent honey. One of the two kinds of gum exuded is used like gum arabic. Containing no tannin, it has been used, dissolved in water, in laundries in other countries than Hawaii, where for some reason it is not appreciated.

Speeding along, we noticed a number of the exotic monkey-pod trees. The tropical-American name is *samang*, though sometimes it is called the rain-tree, from its custom of blossoming at the beginning of the rainy season. Broad-spreading, flat-topped, with enormous trunk, like the algaroba it is a member of the acacia family, folding its feathery leaves at night. It is wonderfully ornamental for large spaces, but cannot be used to shade streets, as its quick growth plays ludicrous havoc with sidewalks and gutters. I have read that a common sight in the Islands is a noonday monkey-pod shade of a hundred and fifty feet diameter.

"The Japanese city of Honolulu!" burst from my astonished lips, once we were out of the station and walking toward the far-famed fish market. For the Japanese are in full possession of block after block of tenements, stores, and eating places that fairly overlap one another, while both men and women go about their business in the national garb of kimono and sandals.

The market was more or less depleted of the beautiful colored fish Jack had been so desirous for me to see, and we plan to come back some time in the early morning, at which time both the fish and the quaint crowd are at their best.

Not until in the business center of the city proper were our eyes gladdened by the sight of our own kind and the native Hawaiians themselves, although the latter have become so intermixed with foreign strains that comparatively few in Honolulu can be vouched for as pure bred. According to the latest census, there are less than 30,000 all-Hawaiians in Hawaii Nei, with nearly 8000 hapa-haoles (hah-pah-hah-o-lays—quickly, hah-pah-how-lees), which means half-whites. The total population of Honolulu is around the 40,000 mark, and of these roughly 10,000 only are white.

Not often do I form expectations in a way that lays me open to serious disillusionment. But I had pictured Honolulu differently; and the abrupt evidence of my eyes was a trifle saddening. The name Honolulu is said to mean "the sheltered," and it would not inaptly refer to the population of far-drifted nationalities that shelters in its sweetly hospitable confines.

Soon, however, all temporary dash to hopes of beholding a Hawaiian city became absorbed in the types that had given rise to disappointment, and in the unfolding of the quaint town itself, with its bright shop windows, and sidewalks where real, unmistakably real, Hawaiian wahines sat banked in a riot of flowers for sale, themselves crowned with *leis* (lay'ees—wreaths), and offering others to passers. Besides, something happened that awoke in me a revolutionizing emotion, or concept, or whatever it may be called, that I had never known of myself, nor been brought up to consider. Born and reared in the ultimate West, where the Negro problem troubleth not, the darky gardener (who was half Cherokee Indian), to say nothing of the vegetable-and wash-Chinamen, honest as the long day, were my childhood friends, conspicuously generous and benevolent on Oriental holidays. This emotion, or concept, it would seem was born of the instant need, as probably vital concepts are most often brought into being. And it shook me to the foundations. Do not confuse this with race *hatred*. My respect and admiration for Japan are profound. It is a different thing altogether. And this was the way of it:

Mr. Rowell and Jack were walking together, talking busily, and I had wandered well ahead on the narrow sidewalk of a winding lane, where blossoming trees hung over old walls and fences, and there was barely room for vehicles to pass. I was dreaming along, when suddenly I found myself confronted by a bristle-headed, impudent-eyed Japanese coolie who had stepped out from a doorway close to the pavement. Even at my leisurely pace it would have been only seconds when I should have come up to him, and, for some of those seconds, it looked as though he were not going to give room. Without consciously reasoning I knew that I, a white woman, should rather have died than step around this coolie Asiatic. In his own country ... perhaps; in mine, or any other than his, decidedly no. For an instant I was "seeing red," and when I briefly "came to," my hands were fists, and I felt as if the Jap's last-instant sidestep into his doorway had saved me from an exhibition of Jack's coaching in boxing tactics. Even then I came within a wise ace of slapping the insolent grin my furious side-glance did not miss. I can only hope I looked more pugilistic than a slap.

This man, like many others we saw today, is of a totally different breed from the familiar Japanese in the cities of California—the refined, student house-boy s like our Tochigi of the gentle voice and unfailing courtesy. These coolies are of bigger, sturdier frame and coarser features, with a masculine, aggressive expression in their darker-skinned faces. Jack's practiced eye leads him to think that a large proportion of them is from the rank and file that served in the Japanese-Russian War three years ago. He watched me rather curiously the while I was telling him the incident at lunch, and I knew I was flushing to the memory of my racial upset, when he said, "Why, the poor kid! She's learning the world!" But he made no further comment. Neither he nor Mr. Rowell had observed the quiet happening, and "mad" though I was at the time, I cooled down almost immediately, and soon forgot everything in a comical experience we all three shared when we tried to lunch in the Alexander Young Hotel—a modest skyscraper of gray stone, at the top of which a cafe is conducted. Thither we repaired, and, it being a good half-hour before noon when we stepped out of the elevator, a flaxen-haired woman behind the cashier's desk was the only person visible.

In lack of steward or waiter, Jack led the length of the cool room to a table in a window corner, where we could look over the city. Here an angle in the room brought us to the notice of a waiter, who lost no time in whispering over Jack's white-shirted shoulder to the effect that no gentlemen without coats were admitted to the chaste precincts of the cafe. I was alert to hear Jack ask him for the loan of a coat, as he had done one sparkling early morning at the Titchfield in Port Antonio, Jamaica, when we went for breakfast before starting on a two-days horseback trip across the mountains to Kingston. Oh, indeed, and Jack did not fail to ask this Honolulu waiter for the coat; and the man was so flustered that he compromised with his own dignity by suggesting that he place us at a little less conspicuous table, some twenty feet nearer the elevator. We did not exactly see how it was less conspicuous, and I looked for Jack to demur on principle; but for once he was more interested in luncheon than quizzing the waiter. Furthermore, we had a guest; and the guest already had raised Jack's appetite for an alligator-pear "cocktail"—a relish made of the pear cut in cubes and seasoned in catsup and lemon and salt.

I am sure the fair-tressed cashier with her desk telephone was the guilty one, for presently, the brassy elevator commenced to deliver a steady stream of Honolulans, each unit of which addressed her and then followed her nod toward our "less conspicuous table." Jack, as an old Irish-woman once told him, looks more like his photographs than they look like him, and is often recognized by strangers who have only seen his face in the newspapers; so there was no taking of Mr. Rowell by mistake, or of any one else in the rapidly filling tables, and I think the management should be grateful for the unwonted early-luncheon crowd Jack so innocently drew. The steward, who had until now worn an exceedingly detached expression, waxed assiduous in suggestions for a true Honolulu repast. With a grin and a "what's the use anyway!" Jack let him order for us at his own sweet will. I have to thank him for introducing me to guava ice cream, the deliciously flavored crushed fruit staining the cream salmon pink. Jack's final comment about the affair was:

"Well, I leave it to any one if it isn't silly that in a tropic city, like Honolulu, the conventions of altogether different climates should make slaves of men!"

On the streets many go about in the ordinary business suits of the mainland; but thank goodness all are not so foolish. At least, thank goodness that *we* don't have to follow their example, but may happily be counted with the "white-robed ones" who compose the fitting majority.

Pasadena with all its riot of roses is not more beautiful than lovely Honolulu glowing with wonderful flowering vines as well as large trees that vie with the vines in gorgeous abandon of bloom. And Honolulu has her own roses as well.

Inside Mr. Rowell's gate, I sat me down, breathless with the astounding mantle of color that lay over house and barns and fence. I had heard carelessly of the poinciana regia, and bougainvillea, and golden shower, and was already familiar with the single red and pink hibiscus, which won my affection in the West Indies. And again we must register complaint that either the globe trotters we have met have short memories or little care for these things, for we were quite unprepared for the splendor of them.

"There ain't no such tree," Jack broke our silence before the poinciana regia, the "flame tree," and *flamboyante* of the French. It was named in honor ("Some honor," Jack observed) of Poinci, Governor General of the West Indies around the middle of the seventeenth century, who wrote upon their natural history. I have never seen anything so spectacular growing out of the ground. It might have been manufactured in Japan—like the papaia—for stage property. The smooth gray trunk expands at the base into a buttress-like formation that corresponds to the principal roots, with an effect on the eye of an artificial base broad enough to support the gray pillar without underpinning. The tree grows flat topped, not unlike the monkey-pod, and the foliage of fine pinnate leaves, superimposed horizontally layer upon layer, carries out the "made in the Orient" fantasy. But the wonder of wonders is the burst of flaming bloom covering all the green with palpitating scarlet. Clearly red in the flowering mass, it is another marvel to examine the separate blossoms, one of which covered the palm of my hand. How can one describe it! In form it was more suggestive of an orchid than anything I could think of, and there were one or two small, salmon-yellow petals. The petals were soft and crinkly as those of a Shirley poppy, fine and delicate fairy crêpe.

Under this colorful shelter, Mr. Rowell raises orchids for the market, and I thought I never could tear myself from the lovely butterfly things. I was sorry I could not carry on horseback the ones freely proffered.

In the rambling garden, one could but turn from one bursting wonder to another. The most ramshackle house, chicken coop, fence, or barn is glorified by the bougainvillea vine, named after the early French navigator. In color a bright yet soft brick-red, or terra cotta, like old Spanish tiling, it flows over everything it touches, sending out showers and rockets that softly pile in masses on roof and arbor. Close to the flowers, I discovered they were not exactly flowers, these painted petals, but more on the order of leaves, or half-formed petals. It is the bracts themselves, which surround the inconspicuous blossoms, that hold the color—as with the poinsettia. We had already noticed, in other gardens, great masses of magenta vine, which Mr. Rowell told us is also bougainvillea, and is of two varieties, one a steady bloomer, season upon season. There are other colors, too—salmon-pink, orange, and scarlet. And speaking of the poinsettia, which, even in California, we cherish in pots, here in magical Hawaii it grows out of doors, sometimes to a height of fifteen or twenty feet—as do begonias on some of the islands; but I, for one, want to see to believe.

We are willing to accept anything about the guava, be it tree or shrub, and it is both in this sunset land, for to-day we feasted on its yellow globes—dozens of them. Ripe, they were better far than the ice cream, with soft edible rind inclosing a heart of pulpy seeds crushed-strawberry in tint, which, oddly enough, taste not unlike strawberries—stewed strawberries with a dash of lemon. Before I realize it, I am breaking that vow not to try describing flavors.

At length we must tear rudely from this Edenic inclosure, and saddle the little bay mares. It was good to feel the creaking leather and the eager pull on bits, although in the case of Jack's mount, Koali (Morning Glory), that eager pull was all in a retrograde direction when we attempted to leave town. City limits were good enough for the Morning Glory, and her rider had a perilous time on the slippery quadruped, who had evidently been not too well broken. My heart was in my mouth at her narrow escapes from electric cars, and from sliding sprawls on wet tracks. Finally she capitulated, and all went smoothly once we struck the fine stretch of road to the peninsula, which leads through the famous Damon gardens, that are like an enchanted wood. This is the way to travel, intimately in touch with the lovely land and sea and sky, without having to crane our necks out of car windows or after vanishing views on the wrong side of the coach. For the most part we went leisurely, as the horses were soft, and found it very warm, with that heavy, moist, perfumed air that more than all the scenery makes one feel the strangeness of a new country. Tall sugar cane rustled in the late fan of wind, and a sudden brief shower, warm as milk, wet our coatless shoulders. Little fear of catching cold from a drenching in this climate where it is always summer.

The owner of the mares assures us that all they need be fed is the sorghum that grows outside our fence along the roadway, balanced by a measure of grain twice daily. We are also at liberty to pasture them in a handy vacant lot, and Tochigi will feed the grain which he has stored in the tiny servant house where he sleeps.

"They're used to outdoors day and night, so the sky is sufficient stable roof," Mr. Rowell praised the climate. And so our possession of the horses is all pleasure and slight responsibility.

Little as I really saw of Honolulu on this flying trip, enough it was to fill my head to overflowing with pictures; while that resplendent garden of *flamboyante* and bougainvillea and orchids and golden guavas stays with me like a dream.

PEARL HARBOR, Tuesday, May 28, 1907.

One old-time sojourner on this coral strand fitly wrote: "When all days are alike, there is no reason for doing a thing to-day rather than tomorrow." Whether or not he lived up to his wise conclusion I do not know; but the average hustling white-skin, filled with unreasonable ambition to visit other shores, does not live up, or down, to any such maxim. Maybe it is a mistake; maybe we should pay more heed to the lure of *dolce far niente*. Even so, for us it is not expedient and we may as well put it by. Jack does not regard it seriously, anyway. His deep-chested vitality and personal optimism, together with his gift of the gods, sleep under any and all conditions, if he but will to sleep, quite naturally render him intolerant of coddling himself in any climate under the sun, no matter how inimical to his supersensitive white skin. And I decline to worry. It is so easy to acquire the habit of worrying about one's nearest and dearest, to the ruin of all balance of true values. Nothing annoys and antagonizes Jack so much as inquiries about his feelings when he himself has not given them a thought. Time enough when the thing happens, is his practice, if not his theory; but in justice I must say that he applies this unpreparedness only to himself, and has ever a shrewd and scientific eye for the welfare of those dependent upon him, although never will he permit himself to "nag." "I'm telling you, my dear," once, twice, possibly thrice—and there's an end on't.

Everything is freshening in the cool trade wind that is commencing to wave the live-palm-leaf fans, and on the slate-blue horizon soft masses of low trade wind clouds pile and puff and promise refreshment—"wool-packs," sailors call them, which "listens rather too warm," as Albert Waterhouse would say. The past few days of variable weather have roasted us one minute, and steamed us the next when the un-cooling rains descended. But it is all in the tropic pattern, and it is nice never to require anything heavier than summer "pretties," as Jack loves to name them.

"Now, don't stint yourself, whatever you do, Mate," he urged this morning, half-apprehensive lest I do so in face of the "Iron Heel" disaster. "Get a lot of things—lots of those loose ruffly things—and some evening dresses. You'll need evening things when we go up to stay in Honolulu."

"Hello, Twin Brother!" he greeted me yesterday, when, booted and trousered, I was bridling Lehua. "I wish you didn't have to put on the skirt, you look so eminently smart and appropriate!"

"Be patient," I told him. "We'll all be riding this way in a few years, see if we aren't. You wait."

But the cheery prophecy of public good sense could not stifle a sigh as I blotted out the natty boyish togs with the long, hot black skirt. What a silliness to put the "weaker sex" to such disadvantages—as if we did not manifest our bonny brawn by surviving to fight them!

To the village we galloped to have Koali and Lehua shod at the blacksmith's, and odd enough it was to see a Japanese working on their hoofs, for somehow one does not readily associate the thought of horses with the Japanese.

This one did a fair piece of work, however. But for a succession of violent downpours, we should have taken a long ride. There is inexpressible glory in this broken weather; one minute you move in a blue gloom under a low-hanging sky, and the next, all brilliance of heaven bursts through, gilding and bejeweling the vivid-green world.

This date marks a vital readjustment in ship matters. Two of the *Snark*'s complement are to return to the mainland, and Jack has cabled to Gene to come down by first steamer and take hold of the engines. Not to mention many other details of incomprehensible neglect aboard by the undisciplinary sailing master, the costly sails have been left to mildew in their tight canvas covers on the booms in all this damp weather, with deck awnings stretched *under* the booms instead of protectingly above. And no bucket of water has been sluiced over the deck since our arrival eight days ago, necessitating the not inconsiderable expense of recalking thus early in the voyage. The appearance of the deck can be guessed; and otherwise no effort has been put forth to bring the yacht into presentable order, nor any interest nor headwork displayed in forwarding repairs. If a salaried master will let his valuable charge lapse, there is no cure but to get one who will not. As for the machinery, Gene had begged for a chance to sail as engineer, and now that Bert has concluded that, after all, adventure is not what he wanted, Gene shall be given opportunity to show what he knows about gasoline.

Last Sunday we lunched with the Waterhouses and their rollicking weekend crowd from town, who showed what *they* thought of conventional restrictions in tropic cities, by spending the day in light raiment and bare feet, resting or romping over house and grounds. Mrs. Gretchen's German papa, Mr. Kopke, who is superintendent of the Honolulu Iron Works, was also there, and came back with us to take a personal look-see at our wrecked engine. To-day he made a special trip from the city, bringing an engineer, and the upshot was a more encouraging report than Mr. Kopke had deemed possible from his first inspection. "Anyway," he cheered our dubiousness, "you're a whole lot better off than the little yacht that piled ashore on the reef outside yonder this morning." They decided that the repairing can be done aboard the *Snark* here at Pearl Harbor, instead of our suffering the nuisance of taking her to Honolulu, and curtailing our time in this green refuge.

So Jack's face, that had been fairly downcast for two or three days, cleared like an Oahu sky after a thunder-shower; and later he said to me, with a familiar little apologetic smile:

"Mate Woman, you mustn't mind my getting a little blue sometimes. I can't help it. When a fellow does his damndest to be square with everybody, buys everything of the best in the market and makes no kick about paying for it, and then gets thrown down the way I've been thrown down with the whole building and running of this boat, from start to finish—why, it's enough to make him bite his veins and howl. A man picks out a clean wholesome way of making and spending his money, and every goldarned soul jumps him. If I went in for race horses and chorus girls and big red automobiles, there'd be no end of indulgent comment. But here I take my own wife and start out on good clean adventure . . . . Oh, Lord! Lord! What's a fellow to think! . . . Only, don't you mind if I get the blues *once* in a while. I don't very often.—And don't think I'm not appreciating your own cheerfulness. I don't miss a bit of it, my dear, and I love you to death for it.—And you and I are what count; and we'll live our life in spite of them!"

Other persons have their troubles, too. Bert, for instance, who is the recipient of much gratuitous sympathy from all hands. He does not think the occasion at all funny, and one can hardly blame him. With blood in his eye, he is looking for a certain reporter on one of the local sheets. The reporter had happened upon the fact that Bert's father, who years ago was a sheriff on Kauai, the "Garden Island," was shot and killed by a native leper, a wild free spirit of his race who fled to the mountain fastnesses to escape deportation to the settlement on Molokai. It was a tragic episode, heaven knows; but the bright young reporter, who cannot have been long in the Islands, rendered Bert's situation quite desperate by airily stating that Bert was the *son* of the famous leper of Kauai!

Again referring to that beloved scrap heap, the *Snark*, there's a comedian in our own small tragedy, although he doesn't know it. His sweet and liquid name is Schwank, assumably Teutonic, and, with hands eloquent of bygone belaying pins, "every finger a fishhook, every hair a rope yarn," he tinkers about the boat in the capacity of carpenter. With his large family, he lives on the other side of the peninsula, and bids fair to be a great diversion to us all. Belike he has of old been a sad swashbuckler, for he hints at dark deeds on the high seas, of castaways and stowaways, of smuggled opium and other forbidden sweets; and he gloats over memories of gleaming handfuls of pearls exchanged for handfuls of sugar in the goodly yesteryears. Why did he not make it pailfuls of pearls while he was on the subject? In my own dreams of pearl-gathering in the Paumotus and Torres Straits far to the southwest, I never allow myself to think in less measure than a lapful. But pondering upon this theatrical old pirate's vaunted exchange, I cannot help wishing I had been a sugar planter, for I care more for pearls than for sugar.

Late this afternoon we took out the horses for a few red miles over the roads of Honolulu Plantation. The rich, rolling country recalled rides in Iowa, its high green cane, over our heads, rustling and waving like corn of the Middle West. And everywhere we turned were the stout and gnarly Japanese laborers, women as well as men. Female field laborers may be picturesque in some lands; but I am blest if these tiny Japanese women, with their squat, misshapen bodies and awful bandy legs, and blank, sex-less faces, look well in ours. Their heads are bound in white cloth, while atop, fitting as well as Happy Hooligan's crown, sit small sun-hats of coarse straw. From under bent backs men and women alike lowered at us with their slant, inscrutable eyes. Tony, who claims a smattering of their language, tells us: "I think Americans no lika-da talk those Japanese I hear on my train and Pearl City." And there are 56,000 of them by now in this covetable Territory—prolific, and averse to intermarrying with any of the many other adopted bloods in Hawaii.

Sunday night, after Mr. Kopke left, we went up by train to Honolulu, to fulfill a dinner engagement with Mr. and Mrs. Charles L. Rhodes, to whom we had been introduced in the lobby of the Alexander Young the day of our "conspicuous" luncheon upstairs. Mr. Rhodes is editor of the evening paper, *The Star,* and Mr. Walter Gifford Smith, editor of the *Pacific Commercial Advertiser*, whom Jack had met here in 1904, was also a guest. The others were Brigadier-General John H. Soper and his family. General Soper is the first officer ever honored by the Hawaiian Government—by any one of the successive Hawaiian Governments—with the rank and commission of General. He had been in charge of the police during the unsettled days of the Revolution, and later on was made Marshal of the Republic of Hawaii, in effect previous to her annexation by the United States.

Mr. and Mrs. Rhodes live in a roomy, vine-clambered cottage, set in a rosy lane tucked away behind an avenue clanking with open electric cars; such a pretty lane, a garden in itself, closed at one end, where a magnificent bougainvillea flaunts magenta banners, and a slanting coconut palm traces its deep green frondage against the sky.

This was a most pleasant glimpse into a Honolulu home, and our new friends further invited us to go with them to a reception Wednesday evening. Now, be it known that neither of us is overfond of public receptions; but this one is irresistible, for Prince Jonah Kuhio Kalanianaole and his royal wife are to receive in state, in their own home, with the Congressional party now visiting the Islands from Washington, on the Reception Committee. Also, there is a possibility that Her Majesty, Liliuokalani, the last crowned head of the fallen monarchy, may be there. In these territorial times of Hawaii, such a gathering may not occur again, and it is none too early for us to be glad of a chance to glimpse something of what remains of the incomparably romantic monarchy that died so courageously.

Wednesday, May 29, 1907.

Heigh-O, palm-trees and grasses! This is a lovely world altogether, and we are most very glad to be in it. But it has its small drawbacks, say when the honored Chief Executive of one's own United States of America makes an error quite out of keeping with his august superiority. This placid gray-and-gold morning, arriving by first train from town, and before we had risen from our post-breakfast feast of books at the jolly little outdoor table, a perfectly nice and affable young man, whose unsettled fortune—or misfortune—it is to be a newspaper reporter, invaded our vernal privacy. In his hand no scrip he bore, but a copy of *Everybody's Magazine*, portly with advertising matter, his finger inserted at an article by Theodore Roosevelt on the subject of "nature-fakers."

In this more or less just diatribe, poor Jack London is haled forth and flayed before a deceived reading public as one of several pernicious writers who should be restrained from misleading the adolescent of America with incorrect representation of animal life and psychology. An incident in Jack's "White Fang," published last fall, companion novel to "The Call of the Wild," is selected for damning illustration of the author's infidelity to nature. Our Teddy, oracle and idol of adventurous youth, declares with characteristic emphasis that no lynx could whip a wolf-dog as Jack's lynx whipped Kiche, the wolf-dog. But the joke is on the President this time, as any one can see who will take the trouble to look up the description in "White Fang." And lest you have no copy convenient, let me explain that Jack never said the lynx whipped the wolf-dog. Quite to the contrary—

"Why, look here," he laughed, running his eye rapidly down the magazine column, "he says that the lynx in my story killed the wolf-dog. It did nothing of the kind. That doesn't show that Mr. Roosevelt is as careful an observer as *Everybody's* would have us believe. My story is about the wolf-dog killing the lynx—and eating it!"

"I hope he'll get it straight," he mused after the departing form of the reporter with a "good story." "I can see myself writing an answer to Mr. Roosevelt later on, in some magazine."

Jack's hope that his response to the charge of "nature-faking" would be honestly reported, was a reflex to the relentless treatment he has suffered from the press of the Pacific Coast. It would seem as if the newspaper proprietors from the Canadian to the Mexican borders had filed standing orders to give him the worst of it wherever easiest to do so, and to go out of the way to do so whenever possible. This is undoubtedly due to the menace of his socialistic utterances; but what a distorted civilization it is that makes a man, who has unaided fought his way up from nether levels of circumstance, pay so bitterly for his stark humanitarian politics. "Lots of the newspaper men do not dislike me, and like my work, I know; and I hate to see them have to sacrifice their own convictions and consciences to the policies of their employers—or starve. And reporters, in common with the general run of men, don't like to starve."

(1) Damon Gardens, Honolulu.   (2) "And then Martin must snap us."

What did he himself do when he was a newspaper man? The answer is, that even when he was nearly starving, he held himself back from the temptation to do any work for the dailies except very occasional, special, *signed* articles. I look for him to begin, at the first favorable moment, a novel that will be very autobiographical of his struggles to gain recognition. He has often spoken of his desire to do this.

The newspapers of Honolulu, this Farthest West of his own country, have shown toward him no influence of the unkindness of his natal State, but have been all that is hospitable, and this in face of the rebuff put upon their city when we sailed calmly by to the suburbs. From various sources again we hear of the welcomes that were waiting along the wharves, the garlands that were woven for our necks.

It must be forgiven that I jump from theme to theme in more or less distracted manner; for if the way of my life is one of swift adjustments, so must be the honest way of my chronicle. And so, from Presidents, and reporters, wolf-dogs, and politics, lynxes, and ethics, and histories of author-husbands, I shift to fripperies, and gala gardens, and Polynesian princes.

My party-gown (not a new one, for thus far I have not obeyed the gentle mandate to "buy lots of them") hangs on a line across a corner of the big room, faultlessly pressed by the aesthetic Tochigi, with yards and yards of Spanish lace, souvenir of Santiago de Cuba, about the shoulders, arranged with unerring taste by fair Gretchen. It is always a pleasure to hear her benevolent "How are you people?" and Albert's cheery "Zing!" at the red gate. Often he and the Madonna stroll over in the dusk, in their hands slender red-glowing punks to ward off mosquitoes—the "undesirable immigrants" that have infested Hawaii's balmy nights these eighty years, ever since the ship *Wellington*, last from San Bias, Mexico, unwittingly discharged them in her otherwise empty water barrels at Lahaina, on Maui. It was a sad exchange for unpolluted drinking water. Fortunately the days are free of the pests; but woe to the malihini who kens not deftly how to tuck his bobinet under the edges of his mattress.

The enchantment of our lovely acre and the novel way of living, it would seem, are being challenged by the varying temptations of the Capital. Tonight we attend the reception, and tomorrow ride to Waikiki to spend a few days on the Beach.

PEARL HARBOR, Thursday, May 30, 1907.

Jack preceded me into town to keep a business engagement with the Iron Works people, who are taking the kindest interest in *Snark* repairs.

I took the five o'clock train to Honolulu, where Jack met me, and we drove in a funny little one-horse carriage to the Royal Hawaiian Hotel for dinner. Ever since Jack's letters to me from Hawaii three years ago, I have longed to see this noted tropic hostelry with its white tiers of balconies and its Hawaiian orchestra, and the red and green lights which its foreign guests execrate and adore. Last evening, however, the hotel was quiet—no music, no colored lights, no crowd. But the gardens were there, and the fairy balconies, on the lowest of which we dined most excellently, with an unforeseen guest. Before the "American-plan" dinner hour, we were sitting in a cool corner talking of our visit to the Beach, when a bearded young man stepped briskly up, with:

"You're Jack London, aren't you?—My name is Ford."

"Oh, yes," Jack returned, quickly on his feet. "—Alexander Hume Ford. I heard you were in Honolulu, and have wanted to see you. I've read lots of your stuff—and all of your dandy articles in *The Century*."

Mr. Ford could hardly spare time to look his pleasure, nor to be introduced to me, before rushing on, in a breathless way that made one wonder what was the hurry:

"Now look here, London," in a confidential undertone. "I've got a lot of whacking good material—for stories, you understand. *I* can't write stories—there's no use my trying. My fiction is rot—rot, I tell you. I can write travel stuff of sorts, but it takes no artist to do that. You *can* write stories—the greatest stories in the world—and I'll tell you what: I'll jot down some of the things I've got hold of here and everywhere, and you're welcome to them . . . . What d'you say?"

Jack suggested that he make three at our table, and he talked a steady stream all through—of information about everything under the sky, it would seem, for he has traveled widely. At present he is interested in reviving the old Hawaiian sport of surf-boarding on the breakers, and promised to see us at Waikiki later on, and show us how to use a board. When he left, we were able to draw the first long breath in two hours. In his atmosphere one had the sense of being *speeded up*; but his generous good nature was worth it.

On the electric car bound for Waikiki, we found ourselves part of a holiday crowd that sat and stood, or hung on the running-boards—a crowd that convinced me Honolulu was Honolulu after all. The passengers on the running-boards made merry way for the haole wahine, while a beaming Hawaiian, a gentleman if ever was one, gave me his seat, raising a garlanded hat. The people made a kaleidoscope of color—white women in evening gowns and fluffy wraps, laughing Hawaiian and hapahaole girls in gaudy holokus and woolly crocheted "fascinators," the native men sporting brilliant *leis* of fresh flowers, the most characteristic being the *ilima*, which, strung on thread, forms an orange-colored inch-rope greatly affected for neck garlands and hat bands. Like ourselves, they were all making for the gardens of their Prince.

Some three miles from the center of town, we alighted at the big white Moana Hotel, where, in a lofty seaward *lanai*, overlooking a palmy carriage court, with her husband waited Mrs. Rhodes—a picture in the subdued light, her gown of soft white cloaked with a Chinese mandarin mantle of rose and green and gold. A caressing manner, and her gift of making one feel pleased with oneself, all went to perfect our first hour at Waikiki, spent in sipping from cool glasses while we rested in large rattan chairs, for none but a malihini moves quickly here. Lovely indeed was this first glimpse of Hawaii's celebrated watering place, as we lounged in the liquid night-breeze from over rolling star-tipped waters that broke in long white lines on the dim crescent beach.

Strolling across broad Kalakaua Avenue, we entered a park where great looming trees were festooned high and low with colored lights— Prince Cupid's private gardens thrown wide to his own people as well as to his foreign guests. A prodigious buzz and hum came from over by a lighted building, and we stepped across the lawns to the measure of a fanfare of martial music from Berger's Royal Hawaiian Band. From an immense open tent where many were sitting at little tables, the lilting of a Hawaiian orchestra of guitars and *ukuleles* (oo-koo-lay'lees) blended into the general festive din; and then, threading purely the medley of sound, was heard a woman's voice that was like a violin, rising high and higher, dominating the throng until it lapsed into absolute silence. It was the sweetest of Hawaiian singers, the famous Madame Alapai, and a prodigious gale of applause went up from all over the grounds when she had finished, ceasing instantly at the first crystal tone of her willing encore.

Like a child at a fair, I had no attention for the way of my feet in the grass, and Jack laughed paternally at my absorption as he piloted me by the elbow, with a "Dear Kid—it's a pleasure to take you anywhere, you do have such a good time!"

A pretty Hawaiian maid at the dressing-tent greeted us haole wahines with a smiling "Aloha," and led to where we could shed wraps, and dust noses and pat coiffures; after which the four of us picked a way through the company of women, lovely in their trailing gowns, and men in black and white evening attire or glittering army and navy uniforms, while all around under the trees in the background hundreds of Hawaiians looked on, their dusky faces and beautiful eyes eloquent with curiosity and interest. Up a green terrace we paced, to the broad encircling lanai of what looked to be an immense grass house. And grass house it proved, in which the royal owners dwelt before the building of the more modern mansion.

This particular entertainment, including as it did the Congressional party, was unique in its significance. To the right of the receiving line stood the delegate, Prince Jonah Kuhio Kalanianaole, affectionately called Prince Cupid, a well-known figure in Washington, D. C, a dark, well-featured, medium-sized man in evening dress, handsome enough, but in my eyes quite eclipsed by the gorgeous creature at his side, pure Hawaiian like himself, his wife, the Princess Elizabeth. The bigness of her was a trifle overwhelming to one new to the physical aristocracy of island peoples. You would hesitate to call her fat—she is just big, sumptuous, bearing her splendid proportions with the remarkable poise I had already noticed in Hawaiian women, only more magnificently. Her bare shoulders were beautiful, the pose of her head majestic, piled with heavy, fine, dark hair that showed bronze lights in its wavy mass. She was superbly gowned in silk that had a touch of purple or lilac about it, the perfect tone for her full, black, calm eyes and warm, tawny skin. For these of chief blood are many shades fairer than the commoners.

Under our breath, Jack and I agreed that we could not expect ever to behold a more queenly woman. My descriptive powers are exasperatingly inept to picture the manner in which this Princess stood, touching with hers the hands of all who passed, with a brief, graceful droop of her patrician head, and a fleeting, perfunctory, yet gracious flash of little teeth under her small fine mouth. Glorious she was, the Princess Kalanianaole, every inch a princess in the very tropical essence of her. Always shall I remember her as a resplendent exotic flower, swaying and bending its head with unaffected, innate grace.

One and all, they filed by, those of her own race, proud and humble alike, kissing the small, jeweled brown hand, while the white Americans merely touched it with their own. And what came most sharply to me, out of the conventionality, out of the scene so wrapped about with state and pomp, was a fleeting, shifting glint of the wild in her great black eyes, shining through the garmenture of her almost incredible culture and refinement—a fitful spark of the passing savage soul of her, one of a people but lately clothed in modern manners.

To the left of the deposed Princess, in a deep armchair, sat an even more interesting, if not so beautiful, personage—no less than Queen Lydia Kamakaeha Liliuokalani, the last sovereign of the Kingdom of Hawaii, sister and successor to the far-famed and much-traveled King Kala-kaua. The Queen is rarely on view to foreigners, especially Americans, for she loves us not, albeit her consort, Governor John Owen Dominis, dead these sixteen years, was the son of a Massachusetts captain. I was glad to be well down the line, as I had more time to watch her, for the vigor of her great fight of but yesterday to preserve the Crown of Hawaii is to me one of the most interesting dramas in history—bleeding tragedy to her.

Photographs and paintings do not flatter Queen Liliuokalani. All I have seen depict a coarseness and heaviness that is entirely absent. I was therefore surprised, brought face to face with Her Majesty, to find that face rather thin, strong, and pervaded with an elusive refinement that might be considered her most striking characteristic, if anything elusive can be striking. But this evasive effect, in a countenance fairly European in feature, was due, I think, to the expression of the narrow black eyes, rather close-set, which were implacably savage in their cold hatred of everything American. And who can blame her? As near as I can figure it, she was tricked and trapped by brains for which her brain, remarkable though it be, was no match. Imagine her emotions, she who received special favor from Queen Victoria at the Jubilee in London; she who then had the present Kaiser for right-hand courtier at royal banquets, and the royal escort of Duke This and Earl That upon public occasions, now sitting uncrowned, receiving her conquerors.

It is easier for the younger ones; but the old Queen's pretense is thin, and my sympathy, for one, is very warm toward her. There is no gainsaying that truism, "the survival of the fittest," in the far drift of the human, and the white indubitably has proved the fittest; but our hearts are all for this poor old Queen-woman; although I could not help wondering if she would have liked us any better had she known. Most certainly, when our eyes met in the short contact of glances there was nothing of the tender suavity of the Hawaiian, only abysmal dislike. Taking my cue from those preceding, I offered a dubious paw, which she touched gingerly, as if she would much prefer to slap it. It was a distinct relief to meet the prankish eye of Acting Governor "Jack" Atkinson, my Jack's old friend (who stood next the Queen's chair, murmuring in her ear the names of strangers), and surrender my timorous hand to his hearty clasp. "How are you, old man?" he whispered to Jack.

And thence on, down one side of the long lanai, and off to the lawn, we ran the gantlet of a bowing, embarrassed, amused string of Congressmen with their wives and daughters, all smiling uncomfortably in the absence of introductions, since they formed the Reception Committee in this stranger city. We undoubtedly looked quite as foolish, when the tension was immeasurably let down by a jolly young Congressman who blurted out:

"*That* Jack London! Why didn't somebody tell us? Great Scott!"

A subdued titter went up, and I said to the grinning Jack: "That's how you pay for your 'Dream Harbor' seclusion!"

Now we were free to mingle with the charming throng, and it was "Aloha" here and "Aloha" there, lovely and all-loving salutation, employed alike by white and native. We happened upon old acquaintances from the States, and were introduced to many Honolulans. Some of these were Hawaiian or part-Hawaiian, who met us with a half-bashful, affectionate child-sweetness that was altogether irresistible. There is that in their beautiful eyes which is a golden trumpet call for a like honesty and good will and well-meaning.

Every one shakes hands—men, women, children—at every friendly excuse of meeting and parting. Smiles are one with the language, and there is a pretty custom of ending a remark, or even a direction, or command, with a pleasant "eh!"—the *e* pronounced *a*, with an upward inflection. Jack is especially taken with this gentle snapper, and goes about practicing on it with great glee.

You might have thought yourself at a social fair at home, what of the canopies, refreshments, and familiar faces of countrymen—but for the interspersing of brown Hawaiians, so soft and so velvet in face and body, voice and movement, "the friendliest and kindest people in the world." A learned New Englander over forty years ago eulogized: "When the instinct of hospitality which is native to these islands gets informed and enriched and graced by foreign wealth, intelligence, and culture, it certainly furnishes the perfection of social entertainment. Of course there are in other lands special circles of choice spirits who secure a brilliant intercourse all to themselves of a rare and high kind, but I question if anywhere in the whole world general society is more attractive than in Honolulu. Certainly nowhere else do so many nationalities blend in harmonious social intercourse. Natives of every well-known country reside there, and trading vessels or warships from America and the leading countries of Europe are frequently in port. A remarkable trait of these foreign-born or naturalized Hawaiians is that interest in their native land seems only intensified by their distant residence. The better Hawaiians they are, the better Americans, English, French, or Germans they are. And thus it happens that you meet people fully alive to the great questions and issues of the day all the world over. Their distance from the scene of these conflicts seems to clear their view, and I have heard some of the wisest possible comments upon American affairs, methods, and policies from residents of the islands. Besides, they have in small the same problems to solve in their little kingdom which engage us. All the projected reforms, social, moral, civil, or religious, have their place and agitators here."

The residence of the Prince and Princess was open to the public, and through a labyrinth of handsome apartments we roamed, now up a step into a big drawing-room furnished in magnificent native woods and enormous pots of showering ferns, the walls hung with old portraits in oil of the rulers of Hawaii; now down three steps into a pillared recess where, in a huge iron safe, unlocked for the evening, we were shown various trophies of the monarchies. Near by were several tremendously valuable old royal capes woven of tiny bird-feathers, some red, some of a rich deep yellow, and others of the two colors combined in a glowing orange. In still another apartment, a glass-front cabinet displayed shelf after shelf of medals and trinkets pertaining to the past régime, including the endless decorations received by King David Kalakaua in the lands visited in his progress around the world in the early '80s. Some one remarked that he had possessed more of these royal decorations than any known monarch. But this is not so surprising as the fact that he was the only known reigning monarch who ever circumnavigated the globe.

A space in the fascinating cabinet was devoted to the Crown of the Realm, a piece of workmanship at once formal and barbaric, with its big bright gems, most conspicuous of which, to me, were the huge pearls. One diamond had been stolen, and the large gaping socket was a pathetic reminder of the empty throne in the old Palace which is now the Executive Building.

Many and barbaric were the objects in this modern home, mere "curios" should the uncaring gaze upon them in a museum; but here in

Hawaii they breathed of the pomp of a vanishing race whose very hands we were pressing and whose singers' living voices caressed the heavy, fragrant air; the while across a lawn that had been carpet for Hawaii Nei festivities of many years sat the rebellious deprived Queen under the eaves of a grass house.

When, we wonder, in our westward traverse, shall we see another queen, or a prince, or a princess—even shadows of such as are these of Hawaii? Not soon enough, I swear, to fade the memory of this remarkable trio; for nothing can ever dim the picture that is ours. And the Princess Elizabeth Kalanianaole has set an example, a pattern, that will make us full critical of royal women of any blood.

SEASIDE HOTEL, WAIKIKI BEACH,
HONOLULU, May 31, 1907.

"Waikiki! there is something in the very name that smacks of the sea!" caroled a visitor in the late '70s. Waikiki—the seaside resort of the world, for there is nothing comparable to it, not only in the temperature of its effervescent water, which averages 78° the year round, but in the surroundings, as well as the unusual variety of sports connected with it, surf-canoeing in the impressively savage black-and-yellow dug-outs, surf-boarding, the ancient game of kings, fishing, sailing; and all on a variously shallow reef, where one may swim and romp forgetful hours without necessarily going out of depth on the sandy bottom. The cream-white curve of beach is for miles plumed with coconut palms, and Diamond Head, "Leahi," that loveliest of old craters, which rounds in the southeastern end of the graceful crescent, is painted by every shifting color, light, and shade, the day long, on its rose-tawny, serrated steeps. And many's the sail comes whitening around the point, yacht or schooner or full-rigged ship, a human mote that catches the eye and sets one a-dreaming of lately hailed home harbors and far foreign ports with enchanting names.

Waikiki! Waikiki! We keep repeating the word, for already it spells a new phase of existence. Here but a scant twenty-four hours, and already Jack's Dream Harbor seems faint and distant, slipping into a mild and pleasant, not imperative memory, for the spirit of storied Waikiki has entered ours. The air seems full of wings, I am so happy making home, this time a tent. We two can pitch home anywhere we happen to light: a handful of clothes-hangers, some paper and a supply of Jack's chubby ink-pencils—and other details are mere incidentals, for home is in our hearts. After all, perhaps the art of living, greatest of arts, may be partially summed up in this wise:

> " . . . to inhabit the earth is to love that
>   which is; to catch the savor of things."

This domicile is a brown tent-house, comprising three rooms separated by thin portieres, with an accessory bath-house and servant room, also of tenting, and is the last of a scattered row of detached accommodations belonging to the Seaside Hotel, some of them weathered old cottages whose history one would love to know. A short distance *mauka*, as every one says for "mountainward," or away from *makai* (toward the sea), on a lawn pillared with sky-brushing coconut palms, still stands a true old grass house of romantic association. It was created for the seaside retreat of King Lot, Kamehameha V, during his reign in the decade commencing 1863, and each Wednesday was devoted to the fashioning of it, from *Lama* wood inside and pandanus leaves outside. It was named Lama House, for the wood was of custom sacred to the temples and construction of idols in the older days. The King left no issue, and upon his death the estate went to the Princess Ruta (Ruth) Keelikolani, and at her demise to Mrs. Bernice Pauahi Bishop, the last descendant of Kamehameha the Great.

To the south we are separated from the big Moana Hotel with its tiers of green roofs, which is fairly empty and quiet between steamer arrivals, by a sand-banked stream fed from the mountains, with, beyond, a lavender field of lilies. Kalakaua Avenue runs so far away across the hotel gardens that the only sound from that quarter is an occasional rumble of electric trams crossing a bridge over the stream, fitting into our bright solitude like distant thunder from the black range that we glimpse through a grove of palms and algaroba.

Not twenty feet in front, where grass grows to the water's edge at highest tide, the sands, sparkling under blazing sunrays, are frilled by the lazy edges of the surf; and the flawed tourmaline of the reef-waters, pale green, or dull pink from underlying coral patches, stretches to the low white line of breakers on the barrier reef some half-mile seaward, while farthest beyond lies the peacock-blue ribbon of the deep-sea horizon.

In the cool of morning, we skipped across the prickly grasses for a dip, accompanied by a frisking collie neighbor. The water was even more wonderful than at the Lochs, invigorating enough at this early hour, full of life and movement. Jack gave me lessons in diving through the mild breakers, and it was hard to tear ourselves away, even for the tempting breakfast tray that a white-suited Filipino was bearing to the tent-house.

While I write, Jack, in his beloved old blue kimono, sits working in a drafty space he has hunted in the front room. As for the kimono, it is limp and shabby from many launderings. "But I love the old thing," he says, "although, if you'll buy me a new one next time you're in town, I promise to wear it." He is commencing an article on amateur navigation, for *Harper's*, which he calls "Finding One's Way About." This is the second article of a series for *Harper's* on the *Snark* venture. The first, written at sea and entitled "The Inconceivable and Monstrous," deals with the building of his much-sinned-against craft. The name of the article should be an incitement to read! He declares that these articles will be the only ones concerning the actual voyage, handling the various striking phases of the experience; otherwise he will devote his energies to fiction—his creative man-work,—while I am to keep the diary.

One reason why Jack has concluded to limit his writing upon the voyage itself, is because the eastern magazine that first contracted to buy the same immediately started a pernicious advertising to the effect that it was sending the *Snark* around the world. This naturally incensed Jack, who was paying dearly out of his own pocket with deadly hard work, in the chaotic conditions succeeding the earthquake, to prepare the vessel for sea. The magazine tried to get back at him for his prompt stand against such advertising by attacking his good faith in arranging with a woman's magazine for a set of land articles on domestic customs of women and children in the islands we should visit; whereupon Jack, a bonny fighter, perfectly clear in his own mind as to his intent and integrity, refused to do any voyage articles whatever. To fulfill the contract, in place of the mooted yachting articles, he offered a string of autobiographical studies of his tramping days across the United States; and these were indignantly but avidly accepted by the editor, who was "in wrong" and knew it, and who had to make good to his magazine. Jack is still giggling over the fury of the editor, who was so altogether out of sorts that in an inexplicable humor he offered a higher price for the substitute work—which, not surprisingly, was accepted before he had a chance to catch his breath. The autobiographical sketches are now running under the title of "My Life in the Underworld," although Jack's caption was "The Road," which will be the name of the book when issued.

Mayhap I have been trying to do too much in this unaccustomed climate, for the long ride yesterday from Pearl Lochs left me very tired. The trade wind has died again, and the only breeze was what our speed might afford; and speeding for breeze on a Kona day is enervating for man and beast. But we enjoyed the ride, for the two small mares, with regular use, have become very docile to wrist and heel.

Mr. Fred Church, manager of the Seaside, is a really- truly acquaintance of Jack's Yukon days. There are so many claimants who are not really-truly—although Jack has never "given away" a mother's son of them, on occasion when they have been dragged up by fond relatives to make good their assertions. "Let 'm have their fun," he laughs; "it doesn't hurt me any. It's awful to be called down in front of one's women-folk!" There are instances when I cannot quite approve of the length to which he carries this policy, for very nasty tales have based upon his easy indulgent, "Oh, sure, I remember!" to some perfect stranger who has bragged, "Don't you remember that time you and I . . .?" when Jack and I together were elsewhere at the dates mentioned. But little he cares for the opinions except of a close few—very few. Large-mindedly he lays himself open to all sorts of criticism and revilement—and gets it. "These aren't the things that count, Mate Woman," he reasons. "What you and I think and know are the big things.—Besides," he usually sums up, "I have to sleep with myself, and I sleep well." So much for *his* good conscience.

But I was talking about this genuine Klondiker, Fred Church, our big, good-looking, breezy host, who, ably aided and abetted by his little beauty wife, makes the guest feel as if entertained in their private home—the very genius of hotel management. Mr. Church was full as cordial as the letters he had been sending from the day of our arrival, in which he had urged us to be his guests for all the privileges of the Beach. Pleasure in the Beach itself was doubled by the welcome of these two and their discerning choice of this sequestered little house of brown canvas and wire-screening, swept by every wind that blows, from mauka or makai. Tired and warm as we were, their suggestion for a swim before dinner was just as exactly inspired as Gretchen Waterhouse's invitation to a hot tubbing.

Besides our cottage row, the Seaside Hotel comprises one large frame house of many rooms, half over the water, reached by a winding driveway from the main avenue through a grove of lofty coconut palms, under which stray large cottages belonging to the hotel. In a rambling one-storied building are the kitchen, the bar, an oriental private dining room, and a reception hall, also furnished in Chinese carved woods and splendid fittings, that belong to the estate. This hall opens into a circular lanai with frescoed ceiling—a round dining and ballroom open half its disk. Beyond the curving steps, on the lawn toward the sea, grow two huge gnarled *hau* trees, each in the center of a round platform where drinks are served. The hau is a native of the Islands, and is nearly related to the hibiscus. The limbs snarl into an impenetrable shade, and are hung with light yellow bells formed of eight to ten lobes, which turn to mauve and then to ruddy brown when they fall.

Dinner, served in the private room, was given by the Churches for us to meet some of Honolulu's young married pairs. They formed a glowing ring about the table, which Mrs. Church had decorated in poinsettia and red-shaded candles. Each woman present was distinctly handsome in her own way, and all were beautifully gowned and essentially "smart." Several of their husbands wore white-and-gold uniforms. But no one was more attractive than little Mrs. Church—pretty as a child or a doll, with the dignity of carriage that can make a small woman the stateliest in the world.

After the dinner, the dance—"Transport Night Dance." While the first word is appropriate for the bewitchment of dancing in a Hawaiian night to the music of Hawaii, it is here used to designate the entertainment on arrival of a United States Army transport, when the officers and their ladies come ashore midway in the long passage to or from the Coast and the Philippines.

The immense half-open circle of the lanai was cleared of dining equipment, and the shining floor dusted with shavings of wax. Many-hued Chinese lanterns were the only lighting here and out among the trees, where dancers rested in the pauses of the music.

And the music. It was made entirely by a Hawaiian orchestra of guitars and ukuleles, with a piano for accent, and all I had heard and dreamed of the glamour of "steamer night in Honolulu" came to pass. It seemed hardly more real than the dream, gliding over the glassy floor to lilt of hulas played and sung by these brown musicians whose mellow, slurring voices sang to the ukuleles and guitars because they could not refrain from singing. Only one regret was mine that Jack did not dance. Jack never dances. "I never had time to learn," he says, "and now I'm too old! I'd rather keep cool and watch you dance."

One of our party at dinner was Mrs. A. G. Hawes, whose name, Francesca Colonna, is no more gorgeously Italian than her great black eyes and gold-banded black hair. Between two dances, she carried me off to a group at a table under a hau tree, where I found Jack talking with Princess David Kawananakoa and her husband, who is brother to Prince Cupid, and whom he resembles. This princess, Abigail, was a Campbell, and is only about an eighth Hawaiian. And oh, she is a beauty!—no more splendid in carriage than her sister-in-law, but much more European in coloring and feature. Doubtlessly she could be quite as regal upon occasion; but this evening she was charmingly vivacious, and I caught myself looking with affection born of the instant into her beautiful eyes that smiled irresistibly with her beautiful mouth—"a smile of pearls."

During a dance with an army officer, I quite fittingly and very slightly cut my hand upon a sword in a sheath of swords decorating the central column. My partner was greatly distressed and apologetic, but I assured him that my first military ball could not have been complete without this sword scratch.

An interesting incident of the evening was the meeting with Mrs. Francis Gay, of Kauai. Years ago, I used to see her and her sister, now Mrs. Jordan, traveling to and from Berkeley and San Francisco, music-rolls in hand, both daughters of Judge C. F. Hart, who had married a lady of Hawaii. Mrs. Gay is very handsome, with the eyes and mouth of her mother's people—sweet and caressing and gracious.

The lovely ball closed with "Aloha Oe," Love to You, in waltz measure, while the dancers joined in singing. The last, slow, dying cadence left one with a reposeful sense of fulfillment, and none broke this dreamy repose by clapping for an encore.

WAIKIKI, Saturday, June 1, 1907.

Yesterday, after a luncheon that included our first *yam* (little different from and no better than a fried potato-patty), we rode to Diamond Head, where at last I gazed into my first crater. The way led through Kapiolani Park, where the little sleeping volcano formed a painted background for the scattered trees and blossoming lotus ponds. Once out of the shady driveways, we sweltered on the rising white road in a windless glare.

It was a mud volcano, this Leahi, and upon its oblong steep sides remain the gutterings of age-ago eruptions. While less than eight hundred feet high, at a distance it appears much higher. We had had a never-to-be-forgotten view of it on our first ride to Honolulu, when, through a gap, we looked across the tree-embowered city, and the low red crater of Punchbowl—Puowaina; and far Diamond Head rose too ethereal in the shimmering atmosphere to be of solid earth thrown up by ancient convulsions.

Skirting the south side of the Head, we tethered our dripping horses, and on foot climbed the light-colored, limy wall, seething hot under the midday sun. I arrived at the edge of the crater sans heart and lungs, muscles quivering, and eyes dim. But what I there saw brought me back in short order to my normal state of joy at being alive. Compared with other wonders of Hawaii Nei, probably this small hollow mountain should be sung without trumpets. But I have not seen Haleakala and Kilauea, Mauna Kea or Hualalai, and lacked no thrills over my first volcano, albeit a dead one. The bowl is a wonderfully symmetrical oval, and may be half a mile long—we could not judge, for the eye measures all awry these incurving walls of tender green, cradling, far beneath, the still green oval mirror of a lakelet.

We rested our burned eyes well on the soft green shell of earth before retracing the scorching way down to the horses, and decided that small-boat travel is ill training for mountain scaling anywhere near the Southern Cross. Around Diamond Head we continued, gazing off across blue bays and white beaches to Koko Head, very innocent seen from the land by light of day, but full of omen by night when winds blow hot and small *Snarks* drift too near wicked reefs. To-day the road led close by Diamond Head lighthouse and the signal station that telephoned our approach to Honolulu; and we learned that it was wirelessed from the city to the island of Maui, where the Congressional party hung 10,000 feet, on the lip of Haleakala's twenty-three-mile crater. How different from times when the only way of messages was by the watery miles separating the islands, in small sloops and schooners or outrigger canoes, and telephones had never been dreamed of.

On the way to return Mr. Rowell's mares, Jack took me aside to the transport wharf that I might see the departure of a vessel from Honolulu, for never, since his own experiences, has he spoken without emotion of this beautiful ceremonial. There is nothing like it anywhere else in the world.

The steamer decks were bowers of fragrant color, as was the wharf, for the shoulders of the departing congressmen and their womenfolk were high-piled with wreaths, of ilima, of roses, of heliotrope, carnations, lilies, and scented green things, while the dense throng ashore was hardly less garlanded, and streams of flowers flowed back and forth on the gangways. A great humming of voices blent with the quivering strains of an Hawaiian orchestra on the upper deck, and now and again all lesser tuneful din drowned in a patriotic burst from Berger's Royal Hawaiian Band ashore. An impressive scene it was, not alone for beauty, but in a human way, for the myriad faces of the concourse shaded from white through all the browns to yellow skins, mingling in good fellowship and oneness of spirit in this hour of farewell to the lawmakers of their common cause. And none of these wishing godspeed were more imposing nor charming than the Hawaiians, from the two Princes and their splendid consorts to the humblest of their people. *Humblest* is wrong—there is no humility in the breed. Their eyes look only an innocent equality of sweet frankness, and their feet step without fear the soil they can but still feel is their dearest own.

Prince Cupid, the delegate, received round after round of cheers from the passengers as the deep-mouthed siren called the parting moment, and at the last, the native orchestra, descending the gangway, joined with the wind instruments in Queen Liliuokalani's own song, composed during her eight months' imprisonment, sweetest of farewells and hopes for a returning, "Aloha Oe." The human being did not live whose heart was not conscious of a nameless longing for he knew not what. One ached with burden of all the good-bys that ever were and ever will be, of all the sailings of all the ships of all the world. I looked up into Jack's face, and his eyes were shining moist as he pressed my hand, knowing I was as moved as he could wish.

"O warp her out with garlands from the quays,"

went through my mind when the vessel glided slowly past the wharf, and the ropes of living blossoms and network of wild-hued serpentine parted and fell into the water. Flowers filled the air as they were tossed to and from the gay tiers of the ship, many falling into the stream, until she moved upon a gorgeous tapestry.

As the huge black transport cleared, suddenly her surface seemed flying to pieces. A perfect fusillade of small dark objects in human form sprang from her sides, rails, rigging, from every height of ringbolt and sill, and disappeared in almost unrippling dives through the swirling blossomy carpet of the harbor.

"Look—look at them!" Jack cried, incoherent with the excitement of his joy in the little kanaka imps who entered the water so perfectly and came up shaking petals from their curly heads, white teeth flashing, their child faces eloquent with expectation of a lucrative shower from the passengers. A bountiful day it was for them, and little their bright eyes and brown hands lost of the copper and silver disks that slowly fell through the bubbling flood. We wished we were down there with them, for it is great fun to pick a coin from the deep as it filters down with a short, angled, tipping motion.

"Do you wish you were aboard, going back?" Jack asked, as we turned for the last time to look at the diminishing bulk of the transport, bannered with scarves and handkerchiefs and serpentine. I did not. I want to go home only from east to west. Who knows? It may be through the Panama Canal!

In our tent household, Jack is the only one who works. My typewriter was left behind at Pearl Lochs, and I do not allow myself to think of the hot, if interesting hours of copying upon returning Such content is ours here at Waikiki, that Jack says it is a shame to press it all into one life, for it could be spread over several incarnations. We sleep like babies, in the salt night airs wafting through the mosquito canopies. Before breakfast, it is into the blissful warm tide, diving through bubbling combers, coming up eyes level with tiny sails of fishermen beyond the barrier reef. The pretty, pretty strand! All hours one hears the steady, gentle boom and splash of the surf—not the big disturbing, ominous gnashing and roaring of the Pacific Coast rollers, nor the distant carnivorous growlings off the rock-jagged line of New England. And under sun or moon, it is all a piece of beauty. Toward Diamond Head, when the south wind drives, the swift breakers, like endless charges of white cavalry, leap and surge shoreward, flinging back long silver manes. The thrill of these landward races never palls at Waikiki. One seems to vision Pharaoh's Horses in mighty struggle against backwashing waters, arriving nowhere, dying and melting impotent upon the sand.

Jack, to whom beauty is never marred by knowledge of its why and wherefore, has explained to me the physics of a breaking wave.

"A wave is a communicated agitation," he says. "The water that composes a wave really does not move. If it moved, when you drop a stone in a pool and the ripples widen in an increasing circle, there should be at the center an increasing hole. So the water in the body of a wave is stationary. If you observe a portion of the ocean's surface, you will see that the same water rises and falls endlessly to the agitation communicated by endless successive waves. Then picture this communicated agitation moving toward shore. As the land shoals, the bottom of the wave hits first and is stopped. Water is fluid, and the upper part of the wave not having been stopped, it keeps on communicating its agitation, and moves on shoreward. Ergo," says he, "something is bound to be doing, when the top of a wave keeps on after the bottom has stopped, dropped out from under. Of course, the wave-top starts to fall, forward, down, cresting, overcurling, and crashing. So, don't you see? don't you see?" he warms to his illustration, "it is actually the bottom of the wave striking against the rising land that causes the surf! And where the land shoals gradually, as inside this barrier reef at Waikiki, the rising of the undulating water is as gradual, and a ride of a quarter of a mile or more can be made shoreward on the cascading face of a wave."

Alexander Hume Ford, true to promise, appeared to-day with an enormous surf-board, made fun of the small ones that had been lent us, and we went down to the sea to learn something of *hee-nalu*, sport of Hawaiian kings. The only endeaver of fish, flesh, and fowl, which Mr. Ford seems not to have partially compassed, is that of the feathered tribe—undoubtedly from lack of time, for his energy and ambition seem tireless enough even to grow feathers. Jack, who seldom stops short of what he wants to accomplish, finds this man most stimulating in an unselfish enthusiasm to revive neglected customs of elder islands days, for the benefit of Hawaii and her advertisement to the world. Although we have seen a number of natives riding the breakers, face downward, and even standing upright, almost no white men appear to be expert. Mr. Ford, born genius of pioneering and promoting, swears he is going to make this islands pastime one of the most popular on earth, and, judging by his personal valor, he cannot fail.

The thick board, somewhat coffin-shaped, with rounded ends, should be over six feet long for adults. This plank is floated out to the breaking water, which can be done either wading alongside or lying face-downward paddling, and there you wait for the right wave. When you see it coming, stand ready to launch the board on the gathering slope, spring upon it, and—keep on going if you can. Lie flat on your chest, hands grasping the sides of the large end of the heavy timber, and steer with your feet. The expert, having gauged the right speed, rises cautiously to his knees, to full stature, and then, erect with feet in the churning foam, makes straight for the beach, rides up the sparkling incline, and steps easily from his arrested sea-car.

A brisk breeze this afternoon, with a rising surf, brought out the best men, and we saw some splendid natives at close range, who took our breath away with their reckless, beautiful performance. One, George Freeth, who is only one quarter Hawaiian, is accounted the best surf-board rider and swimmer in Honolulu.

When a gloriously bodied kanaka, naked but for a loin-cloth carved against his shining bronze, takes form like a miracle in the down-rushing smother of a breaking wave, arms outstretched and heels winged with backward-streaming spray, you watch, stricken of speech. And it is not the sheer physical splendor of the thing that so moves one, for lighting and informing this is an all dominating spirit of joyful fearlessness and freedom that manifests an almost visible soul, and that lends a slow thrilling of awe to one's contemplation of the beauty and wonder of the human. What was it an old Attic philosopher exclaimed? "Things marvelous there are many, but among them all naught moves more truly marvelous than man."

And our journalist friend, malihini, white-skinned, slim, duplicated the act, and Jack murmured, "Gee! What a sport he is—and what a sport it is for white men too!" His glowing eyes, and a well-known firm expression about the jaw, told me he would be satisfied with nothing less than hours a day in the deep-water smokers. As it was, in the small surf, he came safely in several times. I accomplished one successful landing, slipping up the beach precisely to the feet of some stranger hotel guests, who were not half so surprised as myself. It took some while to learn to mount the board without help, for it is a cumbrous and unruly affair in the heaving water.

The rising tide was populous with Saturday afternoon bathers, but comparatively few women, except close in-shore. A fleet of young kanaka surf-boarders hovered around Ford and his haole pupils, for he loves children and is a great favorite with these. Often, timing our propelling wave, we would find a brown and smiling cherub of ten or so, all eyes and teeth, helpfully timing the same wave, watching with altruistic anxiety lest we fail and tangle up with the pitching slice of hardwood. Not a word would he utter—but in every gesture was "See! See! This way! It is easy!"

(1) Working Garb in Elysium.   (2) Duke Kahanamoku, 1915.

Several times, on my own vociferous way, I was spilled diagonally adown the face of a combing wave, the board whirling as it overturned and slithering upended, while I swam to bottom for my very life, in fear of a smash on the cranium. And once I got it, coming up wildly, stars shooting through my brain. And once Jack's board, on which he had lain too far forward, dived, struck bottom, and flung him head over heels in the most ludicrous somersault. His own head was struck in the ensuing mix-up and we were able to compare size and number of stars. Of course, his stars were the bigger—because my power of speech was not equal to his. It seems to us both that never were we so *wet* in all our lives, as during those laughing, strenuous, half-drowned hours.

Sometimes, just sometimes, when I want to play the game beyond my known vitality, I almost wish I were a boy. I do my best, as to-day; but when it comes to piloting an enormous weighty plank out where the high surf smokes, above a depth of twelve to fifteen feet, I fear that no vigor of spirit can lend my scant five-feet-two, short hundred-and-eleven, the needful endurance. Mr. Ford pooh-poohs: "Yes, you can. It's easier than you think—but better let your husband try it out first."

Late in the day there came to the tent-house a solid, stolid sailor-man of fifty or so, giving his name as Captain Rosehill, and asking for a berth in the *Snark*. Jack talked with him at some length, and finally advised him to look over the *Snark* carefully before making up his mind, giving him to understand that there is more than mere navigating to do aboard so small a vessel, and that before we are able to sail from Hawaii he will be sure to find plenty of work in the matter of making her ready. Rosehill evidently knows Schwank, for when that worthy's name was mentioned, he gave a prodigious sniff which died in a grunt. The only time the man smiled was at leaving. Upon inquiry, we find that his melancholy is not without justification, for beyond discussion he is "king" of Marcus Island, a small guano principality that he discovered in 1889 somewhere between Bonin Islands and the Carolines. Jack was interested in the facts for themselves, and also because he himself landed in that section of the world during his voyage in the *Sophie Sutherland*, which made a call at Bonin Islands. Through a mix-up with the Japanese government, Rosehill was deprived of indefinite millions that he might have harvested from the guano deposit. They say he knows the South Seas like a book, and is a good navigator. Nothing would make Jack happier than to be free to devote himself to the navigation of his own boat, for if there is one place above all others where he is more contentedly at home, it is at sea. But a sailing master he must have, and the right man will lift a world of responsibility from his shoulders.

WAIKIKI, Sunday, June 2, 1907.

An eventful day, this, especially for Jack, who is in bed thinking it over between groans, eyes puffed shut with a strange malady, and agonizing in a severe case of sunburn. I can sympathize to some extent, for, in addition to a considerable roasting, my whole body is racked with muscular quirkings and lameness from the natatorial gym nasties of the past forty-eight hours. Our program to-day began at ten, with a delirious hour of canoe riding in a pounding surf. While less individual boldness is called upon, this game is even more exciting than surf-boarding, for more can take part in the shoreward rush.

The great canoes are themselves the very embodiment of royal barbaric sea spirit—dug whole out of hard koa logs, long, narrow, over two feet deep, with very slightly curved perpendicular sides and rounded bottoms; furnished with steadying outriggers on the left, known as the "i-a-ku"—two long curved timbers, of the light tough hardwood, with their outer ends fastened to the heavy horizontal spar, or float, of wili-wili, called the "a-ma." The hulls are painted dull, dead black, and trimmed by a slightly inset, royal-yellow inch-rail, broadening upward at each end of the boat, with a sharp tip. There is an elegance of savage warlikeness about these long sable shapes; but the sole warfare in this day and age is with Neptune, when, manned by shining bronze crews, they breast or fight through the oncoming legions of rearing, trampling, neighing sea cavalry.

It required several men on a side to launch our forty-foot canoe across sand into the shoring tide, and altogether eight embarked, vaulting aboard as she took the water, each into a seat only just wide enough. Jack wielded a paddle, but I was placed in the very bow, where, both out and back, the sharpest thrills are to be had. As the canoe worked seaward in the high breaking flood, more than once breath was knocked out of me when the bow lunged right into a stiff wall of green water just beginning to crest. Again, the canoe poised horizontally, at right angles to the springing knife-edge of a tall wave on the imminence of overcurling, and then, forward-half in midair, plunged head-into the oily abyss, with a prodigious slap that bounced us into space, deafened with the grind of the shore-going leviathan at our backs. I could hear Jack laughing in the abating tumult of sound, as he watched me trimming my lines so as to present the least possible surface to the next briny onslaught. He knew, despite my desperate clutches at the canary streak on either hand, and my uncontrolled noise, that I was having the time of my life, as, from his own past experience, he had told me I would have.

It was more than usually rough, so that our brown crew would not venture out as far as we had hoped, shaking their curly heads like serious children at the big white water on the barrier reef. Then they selected a likely wave for the slide beachward, shouting strange cries to one another that brought about the turning of the stern seaward to a low green mounting hill that looked half a mile long and ridged higher and higher to the burst.

"'A hill, a gentle hill, Green and of mild declivity.' . . . It is not!" Fred Church quoted and commented on his Byron and the threatening young mountain, with firm hands grasping his paddle, when, at exactly the right instant, he joined the frantic shrill *"Hoë! Hoë!" (Paddle! paddle like—everything!*) that sent all paddles madly flying to maintain an equal speed with the abrupt, emerald slope. Almost on end, *wiki-wiki, faster—faster, and yet faster*, we shot, ever the curl of white water behind, above, overhanging, menacing any laggard crew. Once I dared to look back. Head above head I glimpsed them all; but never can fade the picture of the last of all, a magnificent Hawaiian sitting stark in the stern, hardly breathing, curls straight back in the wind, his biceps bulging to the weight of canoe and water against the steering paddle, his wide brown eyes reflecting all the responsibility of bringing right-side-up to shore his haole freight.

And then the stern settles a little at a time, as the formidable seething bulk of water dissipates upon the gentle up-slope of the land before the Moana, while dripping crew and passengers swing around in the backwash and work out to repeat the maneuver.

Few other canoes were tempted into the surf to-day, but we saw one capsize by coasting crookedly down a wave. The yellow outrigger rose in air, then disappeared in crashing white chaos. Everything emerged on the sleek back of the comber, but the men were unable in the ensuing rough water to right the swamped boat. We lost sight of them as the next breaker set us zipping inshore, but on subsequent trips saw them swimming slowly in, towing the canoe bottom-upward, like a black dead sea monster, and apparently making a picnic of their disaster.

An hour of this tense and tingling recreation left us surprisingly tired, as well as cold from the strong breeze on wet suits and skins. Mr. Ford, with a paternal "I-told-you-so" smile at our enthusiasm over the canoeing, was prompt for the next event on our program, which was a further lesson in surf-boarding. After assisting me for a time, I noticed he and Jack were sending desireful glances toward the leaping backs of Pharaoh's Horses, and I knew they wanted to be quit of the pony breakers inshore—the *wahine* surf, as the native swimmers have it, and manful-wise ride the big water. Our friend had a thorough pupil in Jack, who with characteristic abandon never touched foot to bottom in four broiling hours.

Nursing my own reddened skin in the cool tent-house, I saw a weary figure dragging its feet across the lawns, which it was hard to recognize for Jack until he came quite near. Face and body, he was covered with large swollen blotches, like hives, and his mouth and throat were closing painfully. Rather against his wish, I sent Tochigi to summon a doctor, for his condition was alarming. Despite full knowledge of his extremely sensitive skin, he had not given a thought during those four hours, face-downward on the board, to the fact that under the vertical rays of a tropic sun a part of him never before so exposed was being cooked through and through. Shoulders and back of neck were cruelly grilled, goodness knows; but the really frightful damage had been wreaked on the backs of his legs, especially the tender hind-side of the knee joints, which were actually warping from the deep burning so rapidly that in a few moments he could not stand erect because the limbs refused to straighten. Between us we managed to get him into bed, and later on, restless with the intolerable pain of his ruined surfaces, and thinking my room might be cooler, he could progress there only on *heels and palms, face upward.* "Don't let me laugh—it hurts too much," he moaned through swollen lips, realizing the preposterous spectacle.

Little aid could be rendered, either of diagnosis or practice, by the physician, Dr. Charles B. Cooper. From his six-feet-odd of height he bent wide, black eyes upon the piteous mass on my bed, that indisputably required all known sun-burn remedies; but the extraordinary swollen blotches were plainly beyond him. He had observed cases of mouth and throat swelling, though never one so bad as this, from fruit poisoning in the tropics; but this patient had eaten nothing that he had not been living on for weeks. And also there was the blotched body.

"Just my luck!" this from the sufferer. "I'm always running into something no one ever saw or heard of! Although this is something like the shingles I had on the *Sophie Sutherland*."

Dr. Cooper left some medicine, and later his filled prescription came from a druggist, to relieve the torturing burn. Meantime I kept up a steady changing of cool, wet cloths on the warped legs, while Jack's "It can't last forever!" was the best cheer under the circumstances, until the blotches began to subside and the throat could swallow grateful drafts of cold water, and a supper of long, iced poi-cocktail—"Such beneficent stuff," he dwelt upon it.

You! All whiteskins who would learn Ford's rejuvenescent royal sport, take warning that the "particular star" which illumes our world, despite its insidiousness, is particularly ardent in Hawaiian skies.

PEARL LOCHS, Tuesday, June 6, 1907.

Home in our Dream Harbor, after a full week away—for of course Jack could not return on Monday as planned. The burning hours were beguiled with cool cloths and reading aloud, Jack taking his turn when I grew nervous with my own distressed cuticle and an aching ear from diving. Out of his grip of varied reading matter, he had selected Lilian Bell's "The Under Side of Things"—I wonder if with reference to his fried-and-turned-over condition! A Bulletin reporter lightened a half hour in an interview upon our unplotted future around the globe, and told us that our erstwhile sailing master, leaving yesterday for the Coast on the Sierra, had given the impression that he considered the *Snark* unsafe.

"He built her!" was Jack's only comment.

"And sailed over two thousand miles in her," the newspaper man grinned.

On Tuesday, waiving all discussion, Jack got into his clothing, the operation (not an unappropriate word) accompanied by running commentary on things as they were, which would be both interesting and instructive in a biographical sense, did one dare the editorial censor. Neither of us was this day "admirin' how the world was made," and my widest sympathy was with his fevered sentiments concerning astronomy, geology, the starry hereafter, mid-Pacific watering places—and Alexander-Hume-Fords.

"But I warned you, and warned you!" fended poor Ford, suppressing an involuntary snicker as the fervid cripple, now on his feet, essayed a step or two. "And you're luckier than I was the first time I got burned—worse than you are—and by mistake used capsicum vaseline on my skin!—And anyway, I really did think you had become toughened a bit on your month at sea."

With stiff-crooked legs, for he could neither unbend nor further bend the knees, and feet pitched some twenty inches apart, Jack's action was perforce unlike that of any known biped. So enamored did he become of the wonder of it that he insisted upon employing it to progress to the lanai for luncheon, where his most pitying acquaintances failed to keep back their mirth. Be assured he enjoyed it all as much as they, for the lessening hurt made him very happy. An hour face-downward on the beach that fateful afternoon had not improved my own carriage, but I was not unwilling to risk it on a short trip along Kalakaua Avenue to the Aquarium, which Jack, from his memories, had pronounced a world-wonder. With many jibes at his remarkable gait, the Churches helped him aboard a car, and in the cool many-roomed grotto, built of quarried coral, we forgot all earthly dole, spellbound before the incredible forms and colors of the sentient rainbows.

It is impossible to communicate any adequate idea of these color organisms. If anything could be laughably lovely, any one of these would serve: Striped Roman scarf effects showed behind the glass as if in a shop window display; polka-dot patterns in color schemes beyond imagining; against the glass lay figured designs that manufacturers would make no mistake in copying. And all were possessed of an iridescent quality that made one expect them to melt into the shifting greens of their element, as they dimmed in the farther spaces of the tanks. But presently they would intensify, coming on larger and brighter like marine headlights in Elfland.

One fish was an aquatic bird-of-paradise for hues, with a long spine like an aigrette springing from midway of a body almost as round as a coin and not much larger, with golden-brown beak and bold black eye. His name was the kihi-kihi. The hamaleanokuiwi was a turquoise-blue, five-inch shuttle, terminating in a peacock-blue wisp of tail, with fins like ruffles tipped with stripes of yellow and black, and a long blue needle for beak. The little fins back and below its beaded eyes were tiny azure butterflies striped two ways with purple and gold; and on each side the turquoise body a splotch of opaque gold lay like a sunbeam. Around this bright blue marvel slowly wove one of a magenta as vivid, and half as long, of familiar shape but with the bulging eye of a frog shaded by a thick ruby lid, two pale-pink fins shaped like center-boards, and a dorsal fin with five smartly raked masts.

The kikakapu did not look his bristly name at all, but was a shape-less handful of pigments—pale green as a parrot, with birdlike head of harlequin opal and parrot eye of black and yellow. Half of the dorsal was a black-velvet spot rimmed with gold, his tail two shades of gray with a root of scarlet. I haven't patience to spell the name of an almost perfect oval of blue black, with a flaming autumn leaf on each side, a narrow dorsal of shaded rose and salmon-yellow bearing a dotted line of red, and a gray and red flag for tail, while two sapphire-blue feath-ers trailed underneath. Next him flaunted a canary-yellow fish that had patently been scissored midlength and grown a stiff mauve tail in the middle of its vertical rear, to match a mauve-velvet, long-beaked face. A canary-wing formed this one's dorsal fin, and two absurd back-slanted spikes and a ribby trailer decorated its horizontal base.

The opule and the luahine were both meant to be normally formed,—the first, speckled on top like a mountain trout, its frills red and black and blue, jaw crimson spotted, with grass-green gills and tiny gilt fins, and on its dark sides three parallel rows of larger dots, and one dropped below, of startling blue, each with an electric light behind! The second, all brown save for a scarlet headlight on the tall dorsal, was similarly lit up, all over, fins as well, the head zigzagged with lightning streaks of the same electric blue. The akilolo wore these cold blue jewels set on plum satin, with electric-green stripes on its head, crimson and green fins and sharply demarked rudder of bright yellow.

One was a lovely thing, and would have been a little heart of gold, if its white-and-gilt tail had not transformed it into a perfect ace of spades. Another, modestly shaped, bore pink fins socketed in emerald like the head and tail, a yellow stomach, seal-brown back, with three broad downward bands of the emerald joining a wide lateral band of the same, decorated in hollow squares of indigo! I'm telling you, as Jack would say. There were also dainty mother-of-pearl forms, and gorgeous autumnal petals of the ocean drifting among the jeweled swimming things, with little rainbow crabs lying on the bottom of sand and shells, among other crannied creatures.

An imaginative child could spin unending day dreams about these living pictures in the cool grottoes of the Honolulu Aquarium; and for nightmares, there are excellent specimens of the octopus family. These squid we have on the Pacific Coast, but there is no way of observing them. Mr. Potter, the superintendent, said his were unusually active to-day, and we saw them displaying all their paces—a very useful spectacle for those who may venture among the more unfrequented coral hummocks at Waikiki. A wader can be made very uncomfortable by their ugly ability to attach to a rock and a victim at one and the same time. They showed their fighting colors through the glass, coming straight at us, their little devil's-heads set with narrow serpent-eyes glinting maliciously, and sharp turtle-beaks, all their tentacles—awful constricting arms covered with awful suckers—cast behind in the lightning dart.

When attacked, the squid opens an "ink bag," fouling the water to the confusion of its enemy. A native in trouble with one tears right into this ink bag with his own teeth, and to this mortal wound the pediculate marine dragon gives up the ghost. The only thing about the squid that is not unpleasant, to say the mildest, is its color—in action a rosy tan; but when curled in the rock crevices, protective tinting makes it hard to detect. Mr. Potter dropped some tiny crabs into the tank from behind the scenes, which caused an exhibition not soon to be forgotten. The almost invisible squid, watching with one bright eye, unwreathed its eight flexile, trailing limbs, rose swiftly, swooped, and enfolded the prey as with a swirl of grey net or veiling. When the monster presently unwound, the mites of crabs had been entirely absorbed.

"And the Creator sat up nights inventing that," Jack observed with sacrilegious gravity, slowly shaking his curly poll. The superintendent looked appropriately startled, but not unappreciative.

This Honolulu Aquarium, though small, is said to surpass in the beauty of its exhibit anything in the world, not excepting the Italian; and fancy our surprise to learn that it is not maintained by the Territory, nor yet by the city, existing solely by the enterprise of the electric railway company. The "colored" fish are recruited from the chance catch in nets of native fishermen. It is not easy to understand why Honolulu is lukewarm with regard to this, one of her greatest attractions. Mr. Ford should be spoken to about it!

And Hawaii is a paradise for the visiting fisherman, where can be hooked anything from a shark to small fry of various sorts, whether "painted" or otherwise. Among the many game salt-water fish may be named black sea bass, barracuda in schools, albacore, dolphin, swordfish, yellow-tail, amber fish, leaping tuna and several other kinds of tuna—all these fish of unthinkable weight and size. And flying fish may be picked off with rifle or shotgun—or netted, as with the old Hawaiians.

Ever keen on the trail of Why and Wherefore, Jack has left no stone of research unturned as to the cause of the violent swelling that succeeded his sunburning, and has finally diagnosed it as urticaria.

Glad are we to rest once more in our Sweet Home, in sight of that bright reminder of the long voyage yet to be, the *Snark* and her un-wonted clatter of active repairs. For Captain Rosehill has accepted the commission, and "dry bones are rattling," as Jack chuckled a moment ago from the hammock. The sad old sea-dog has taken hold with a ven-geance, but professes little respect for all the modern "fol-de-rol of gew-gaws" that he found lying around, costly labor-saving gear, unavailing only because of the ruinous mishandling it received in the post-earth-quake days of building. He scoffs any notion that the vessel will refuse to heave to under proper conditions, contending that we could not have had enough wind that puzzling night she balked. Standing with huge, limp-hanging arms, he *almost* half-smiled at our big sea anchor—an article he has always yearned to possess. Clearly it is the one thing aboard with which he is satisfied.

Jack finds endless source of amusement in his skipper and the irre-pressible Schwank, who, it seems, once sailed together. The experience evidently has not endeared one to the other, and all our gravity is taxed when the pair display their divergent ways of showing mutual dislike and contempt. Rosehill is a man of few words; but words are not needed when Schwank's name is mentioned. The sound of that raucous proper noun curdles the old sailor's sober and asymmetrical features. On the other hand, Schwank is voluble and expressive. Never in his wildest tales of that ill-starred voyage with Rosehill has he hinted that he was ship's cook under Rosehill. When he recounts how the vessel was wrecked, one would conclude that Schwank had been in command instead of the other, and, in giving this intentional twist to verity, he loses sight of the fact that it looks much as if he, Schwank, must be responsible for the loss. "I told Rosehill to brace up," he will roar pompously, throwing a mighty chest. He always appears about to rise triumphant from the solid earth. Nor has he lost all of his piratical tendencies. From his acre of fruitful soil, he sells produce at extortionate prices. And he is clever enough to vend these commodities through his most beautiful offspring. When Maria-of-the-Seraph-Smile or Ysabel-of-the-Divine-Gaze stands before me in the very artistry of colorful tatters, proffering a scraggly pineapple or an abortive tomato, valued at Israelitic sums, they are not to be gainsaid. The pleasure is mine to be robbed.

Martin finds quite a crowd to cook for, although he reports that the captain eats little, and acts as if he thinks less of the cook. We have an inkling that the old man nurses a crusty disposition, for the boys have already metamorphosed his pretty name into "Raisehell"—not within his hearing, I'll warrant. Soon or late there is going to be a clash with Schwank—that is plain. "They're too good to be true—they're classic sailormen. May the best man win! Rosehill has the hiring and firing to do now," and Jack complacently lights a cigarette—he has again taught himself to smoke—and listens to the welcome music of orders and prompt response to same that come on the shoreward breeze.

PEARL LOCHS, Friday, June 7, 1907.

When you come to Hawaii, do not fail to visit one of the big sugar plantations, to see the working of this foremost industry of the Territory, for nowhere in the world has it been brought to such perfection. Mr. Ford had arranged a trip to the Ewa Plantation, a short distance by rail southwest of the Lochs. With him came an interesting young South African millionaire, who was much more bent upon discussing socialism with Jack London than inspecting sugar mills—although in the varied nationalities among the laborers he might find a rare mine of sociological data.

The railroad traverses a level stretch of country dotted with pretty villages peopled by imported human breeds. In my mind's eye lingers one wee hamlet like a jewel in the sun—a group of little Portuguese shacks covered with brilliant flowering vines and hedged with scarlet hibiscus, all imaged in a still stream that brimmed even with its green banks. Not for nothing were these sunny-blooded children of Portugal blessed with wide and beautiful eyes; for they can see no virtue in a dwelling that is not surrounded and entwined with living color. No matter how squalid their circumstance, they do not rest until growing things begin to weave a covering of beauty.

Our station lay in the center of the Plantation, which embraces nearly 50,000 acres. It was the far-sighted father of Princess Kawananakoa, Mr. Campbell, who ten years ago bought this property for one dollar an acre. Last year its output of sugar was over 29,000 tons. One alone of the underground pumping plants which we wandered through, cost $180,000; and every day 70,000,000 gallons of water are pumped on this Plantation.

Mr. H. H. Renton, the manager, devoted his day to our party. It must be more or less of a satisfaction, however, to a man of his patent capabilities, lord over the complicated affairs of such a project and its horde of workers, to display his achievement to men who can comprehend its enormousness and possibilities.

In comfortable chairs on a flat car drawn by a small locomotive, over a network of tracks that intersect the property, we rode from point to point, meanwhile simmering gently in the moist hot air thick with odor of growing cane, or, near the huge mill, of sugar in the making. The land reminded us of Southern California in springtime, with tree arbored roads and flower-drifted banks and fine irrigating ditches. We want to spend a day on horseback at Ewa, in the lanes and byways with their lovely vistas. Judging from Mr. Renton's own leisurely enjoyment of the occasion and frequent halting of the car that we might gather wildflowers and wild red tomatoes the size of cranberries, one would not have dreamed how busy a man he is.

It is hard, in the peaceful heart of this agricultural prospect, to realize that not long ago it was a place dark with pain and blood and terror. For here, a hundred and eleven years ago, Kamehameha the Great dedicated a temple, *heiau*, with human sacrifices, preparatory to sailing for Kauai on conquest bent.

Sugar cane is classified as a "giant perennial grass," but, unlike most members of the grass family, has solid stems, and grows from eight to twenty feet high. The origin of cane in these islands is unknown, although it is thought to have been introduced from the South Sea Islands by early native navigators in their questing canoes. It was used as an article of diet at the time white men first set foot in Hawaii, but not made into sugar until about 1828; and less than a decade afterward the first exportation of sugar was shipped. Primitive stone rollers pressed out the sweet juice, which was boiled in crude iron vessels. Present-day processes have been brought to a high state of scientific excellence, and probably no plant in the world has been so exhaustively exploited. The red lava soil, decomposed through the ages, has been found through experimentation to be the most productive, and the irrigation scheme of one of these large plantations, with its artesian wells and mountain reservoirs whence water is carried great distances, is a colossal feat of engineering.

A man once wrote that agriculture in the tropics consisted of not hindering the growth of things. But the raising and converting into sugar of these vast areas of rustling sugar-in-the-stem is not such smooth luck. He who would manufacture sugar has many formidable if infinitesimal foes to success, among which Mr. Renton named the nimble leaf hopper, the cane borer, the leaf roller, the mole cricket, the mealy bug, the cypress girdler, and the Olinda bug. To discover the natural enemies of these pests requires an able corps of entomologists seeking over the face of the globe, as well as working sedulously in the Experiment Station in Honolulu.

The mill itself, with its enormous processes, I shall not attempt to describe further than to assure you that it is a place of breathless interest and wonder. One sees and tastes the sugar in its successive phases of manufacture, up to the point where it is shipped to the States for the last stage of refining.

And more absorbing than these technicalities of the Plantation were the human races represented among the workers who live and labor, are born, are married, and die within its confines. Through a bewilder of foreign villages we wandered on foot—Japanese, Chinese, Portuguese, Norwegian, Spanish, Swedish, Korean; even the Russians were here but lately. Porto Ricans were tested, but proved a bad lot, always ready with a knife from behind. One cannot fail to note the scarcity of Hawaiian laborers—and rejoice in it, for they are proud and free creatures, and it would seem pity to bind them on their own soil. On the other hand, there is no gainsaying that they are capable toilers when they will. Indeed, it is said that they accomplish twice the work that a Japanese is willing to do in a day; but when pay day comes, the Hawaiian is likely not to appear again until all his money is gloriously squandered. He is strong and trustworthy, and makes an excellent overseer, or *luna*, as well as teacher; for he is not merely imitative, but intelligent in applying what he has learned.

Mr. Renton led us into schools and kindergartens maintained for the scores of children, and presided over for the most part by white women. In one room we found a Japanese-Hawaiian teacher—a sweet and maidenly young thing, her Nipponese strain lending an elusive delicacy to the round warm native features. In faultless English she explained the duties of her schoolroom, showing great pride in a sewing class then in session, and pointing through the window to where the boys of her class could be seen putting the yard to rights.

I thought we could never leave the kindergartens, with their engaging babies of endless colors and variety of lineaments, pure types and crossbred. Most beautiful of all were the Portuguese, with only one drawback to their childish charm—the grave maturity of their faces. Bella, however, two-years-tiny, golden-eyed and gold-tawny of skin, forgot her temperamental soberness and coquetted shamelessly from her absurd chair in the circle on the bright floor, when she should have been attending to Teacher. But even Bella came to grief. Like some other coquettes she was winningly familiar at a distance; and when I tried to cultivate a closer acquaintance with the young pomegranate blossom, and take a picture of her loveliness, she fell victim to a panic of embarrassment and terror that ended in violent weeping in Teacher's lap.

Homeward bound, it seemed as if we had been transported to and from a foreign land for the day, although what land was the problem, in view of the manifold types we had walked among.

Once more within our red wicket, we found Gene just arrived from the Coast steamer, and were informed by the evening paper that he was to accompany the *Snark* voyage for the purpose of illustrating Jack London's books!—If only he will illustrate that he can take care of the engines, he will do more for Jack than could the best black-and-white artist who ever drew.

In the soft black evening, some of our neighbors drifted across the yielding turf under the ancient trees, the women taking form in the velvet dark like tall spirit vestals trailing dim draperies and swirling incense. We lay out in the cool grass, the lighted ends of our scented punks flitting and darting like fireflies, and listened to Peer Gynt from the Victor indoors, and Mascagni's orchestral paradises of sound, Patti's rippling treble, and Emma Eames's clear fluting of "Still as the Night," floating upward to the sighing obligato of a rising wind from across the rustling reef-waters.

Sweet land of palms and peace, love and song—and yet, those who knew her in days gone by would walk sadly now in remembered haunts. Old faces are missing, and faces resembling them are few. The Hawaii of yesterday passes, and it makes even the stranger very pensive to see the changing. To one who views her from the height of his heart, a bright commercial future is cold compensation for the irreplaceable loss of the old Hawaii.

PEARL LOCHS, Tuesday, June 11, 1907.

A bit of real Hawaii was ours last night—Hawaii as she is, with more than a trace of what she has been. It came about through an invitation from one of our neighbors, Mr. Moore, who owns the cemetery near Pearl City, to accompany his wife and himself to a native *luau* (loo-ah-oo—quickly, loo-ow), meaning feast. We four had the honor of being the only white guests, for in these latter days the natives are chary of including foreigners in their more intimate entertainments. But for Mr. Moore's confidential and sympathetic relation toward them, nothing would have induced them to consent to our intrusion.

The feast was a sort of "benefit," given at the christening of the baby of one of Mr. Moore's men, one "Willie," this being a familiar custom among the people. Mr. Willie and his pretty, giggly wife were in a small fine frenzy of hospitality and embarrassment at receiving a man who writes books, and ran out to the gate calling "Come in! Come in! Come in!" in rapid sweet staccato.

We should have preferred to remain outdoors in their garden inclosure, which was decorated with palm fronds and flowers. But we were ushered to the cottage, where one glance into the hot little parlor, fainting with heavy-scented bouquets, every window sealed tight as if in a Maine winter, taught us that it was the pride of their simple, generous lives, with its neat furniture and immaculate "tidies" on chair, sofa, and exact center-table. Head and neck and shoulders, we were garlanded with ropes of buff ginger blossoms twined with maile, and sat around straight-backed in delighted discomfort, praying for fans. Admiring unstintedly the handsome slumbering infant who was the object and beneficiary of all the festival, we strove the while to express to our host and hostess how glad and proud we felt to be with them.

From the cool twilight lanai floated in the most bewitching, sleepy, sensuous music, rippled through with gurgles of lazy laughter. Presently, left to wander at will, whom should we discover in the happy huddle of musicians but Madame Alapai herself, not at all the grand prima of her Prince's gardens, but a warm, benevolent, smiling wahine, robed simply like all the rest in spotless white holoku, and unaffectedly ready, once her sudden, laughing bashfulness was conquered, to warble anything and everything she knew.

The coyness of these winsome brown women is only skin deep, for
to smiles and sincerity they warm and unfold like their own tropic
blossoms to the morning sun. Deliciously they laugh at everything or
nothing, with an abandon that does not tire, but draws the becharmed
malihini fervently to wish he were one of them for the nonce—a product
of sunshine and dew and affection, without painful responsibility, with
no care for the moment of aught but the living, loving present.

Madame Alapai accompanied the first American tour of the Royal
Hawaiian Band, and the story runs that she was prepared to go on the
second, but her husband, foolishly jealous of her successes and advantages, decided he needed a change of air and scene, and made the manager of his song-bird a proposition the prompt rejection of which cost
the band its prima donna. This proposition was that he travel with the
troupe and be paid a salary for the honor of his mere company, since he
possessed no marketable talent. It seemed sufficient to his limited vision that he should allow his wife to earn *her* salary. Be it credited the
amiable lady that the facts were made public without her assistance,
for she remains guiltless of shaming her life-companion by ridicule or
criticism. When asked why she did not go to the Coast the second time,
she replies, with a slightly lofty air that is without offense, what of its
childlikeness: "Oh, they wanted me to go, but I refused."

She sang for us without reserve, out of her very good repertory.
Her voice is remarkable, and I never heard another of its kind, for it is
more like a stringed instrument than anything we can think of—me-
tallic, but sweetly so, pure and true as a lark's, with falls and slurs that
are indescribably musical and human. The love-eyed men and women
lounging about her with their guitars and ukuleles, garlanded with
drooping roses and carnations and ginger, were commendably vain of
showing off their first singer in the land, and thrummed their loveliest
to her every song. None can touch strings as do these people. Their fingers bestow caresses to which wood and steel and cord become sentient
and tremulously responsive.

The ukulele is the sweetest thing in the world—the petite guitar-
shape, with its four slender strings, that seems a part of the native at
every merrymaking. It hailed originally from Portugal, but one seldom
remembers this, so native has it become to the Islands. Primitive Hawaiians played on a crude little affair that was a mere stick from the
wood of the *ulei*, a sturdy flowering indigenous shrub. The tuneful stick
was cut eighteen or twenty inches long and three or four wide, strung

across with goat-gut, and was held in the teeth like a Jew's-harp, while the strings were swept with a fine grass-straw. Lovers thus whispered through their teeth an understood language of longing and trysting, the light wood vibrating the voice to some distance in the still night.

From temporary arbors broke the clatter of busy wahines making ready the feast, and new guests laughed their way into the garden. Our nostrils twitched to unknown but appetizing odors. We expected as a matter of course that we should sit cross-legged on grass-mats while eating, and were disappointed to find a table prepared for the more distinguished of the company. At least I was disappointed; and Jack did not dare say he was glad of the white-man's chair, but chuckled when I caught his eye from where he sat across the narrow board with Madame Alapai. Jack's friends know well his way of speaking of his "broken knees," or wrists, or ankles; for, despite his glorious physique—deep chest and well-muscled shoulders and limbs—his hands and feet are small, and his small-boned frame has ill withstood the severe strain put upon it in his youth, on sea and plain, river and lake and mountain—to say nothing of railroad, in his tramping days. Consequently, he cannot tie himself into convenient knots or roll into bundles as can I, and an hour on floor or ground, no matter how cushioned with banana and coconut leaves, where he must sit cramp-legged, or crouch, is little short of agonizing.

And the luau! At every place was a heap of food so attractive that one did not know which mysterious packet to open first. Each had at least a quart of poi, of the approved royal-pink tint, in a big shiny goblet carved from a coconut thinned and polished and scalloped around the brim, and this substance as usual formed the pièce de résistance. There are varying consistencies of poi. The "one-finger" poi is thick enough to admit of a sufficient mouthful being twirled at one twirl upon the forefinger; two-fingered poi is thinner, requiring two digits to carry the required portion. I do not know whether or not three-fingered poi is ever exceeded; but if it is, I am sure no true Hawaiian or kamaaina would hesitate to apply his whole fist to it.

It appeared etiquette to sample every delicacy forthwith, rather than to finish any one or two until all had been tasted. And we depended solely upon our fingers in place of forks and spoons. A twist of poi on the forefinger is conveyed neatly to the lips, followed by a pinch of salt salmon, for seasoning, or of hot roast fish or beef or fowl steaming in freshly opened leaf-wrappings; for this is the excellent way roast foods are prepared, then laid in the ground among heated stones, and covered with earth. Thus none of the essential flavor is liberated until the clean hot leaves of the ti-plant, or the canna in absence of the ti, are removed at table.

There was also chicken stewed in coconut milk, sweet and tasty, and, for relishes, outlandish forms of sea life, particularly the *opihis* (o-pe'hees), salt and savory, which we think we might come to prefer to raw oysters. Mullet is eaten raw, cut in tempting little gray cubes and dusted with native coarse red salt; but while Jack pronounced it one of his favorite articles of diet henceforth whenever obtainable, I could not quite make the experiment. I may in time acquire a liking for well-seasoned raw fish, which in all logic is less offensive to the mind than live raw oysters and razorback clams; but fairly certain am I that never shall I assimilate *ake* (ah-kay)—which is raw liver and chile peppers, and a pet dish here.

Some small clams, *alamihi*, were very good, but I moved askance at the pinkish round tidbits from squid tentacles, although my lord and master smacked his lips over them and urged me on. I contented myself with little parboiled crabs and lobsters.

One toothsome accompaniment to a Hawaiian meal is the *kukui*, or candlenut, the meat of which is baked and broken up fine, and mixed with native salt. Pinches of this relish are eaten with poi and other viands, and it is sometimes stirred in to season a mess of raw mullet. The kukui tree, a comparatively recent introduction from the South Seas, has nearly as many uses as the coconut palm, for aside from the gustatory excellence of its nut, a gum from the bark is valuable, and a dye found in the shell of the nut was formerly used to paint the intricate patterns of the tapa that served for clothing. This dye also formed a good waterproofing for tapa cloaks, and with it tattoo artists drew fashionable designs into the flesh of their patrons, who also rubbed their bodies with oil pressed from the nut, especially in making them slippery for wrestling and fighting.

For the drinking there was choice of a mild beer and "pop" (soda-water of various colors), and coconut water in the shell; and for dessert, the not unpleasant anti-climax of good old vanilla ice cream to remind us that Hawaii has long been in the grasp of Jack's "inevitable white man."

And then the dancing. Mr. Moore had promised us a *hula*; but a hula, except by professional dancers, is more easily promised than delivered. The native must be in the precise right humor of acquiescence

(1) Seen from Nuuanu Pali: Jack London, Lorrin A. Thurston, J.P. Cooke. (2) The
Sudden Vision   (3) The Mirrored Mountains (Painting by Hitchcock)

before any performance is forthcoming for the malihini. Our pleasant task was to overcome the panicky shyness that whelmed both men and wahines when we coaxed them to show their paces. Few, very likely, had ever danced before strangers. Indeed, for the most part, the hula is forbidden by law. And the majority of these were simple rural folk with a terror of possible wrong-doing. I think the Hawaiians are quick to detect a meretricious gayety or any patronizing, overdone familiarity; and to make them feel one's genuine interest in their customs is the only means by which to establish a basis of social intercourse. Left to themselves, they will dance anywhere at any time. Tochigi witnessed his first hula on Toby's train! He did not comment upon it; but after seeing Americans dance, each couple following its own method, he respectfully observed that he thought we danced more for our own pleasure than for that of onlookers.

At length a bolder or more persuadable spirit, yearning to express the real general desire to please, broke through the crust of reserve and began a series of body convolutions to the endless two-step measure of guitars and ukuleles that had throbbed in a leafy corner of the grass shelter during the luau.

Arch faces lighted, hands clapped and feet kept time, eyes and teeth flashed in the dim light of lanterns and lamps, and flower-burdened shoulders swung involuntarily to the irresistible rhythm. One after another added the music of his throat to an old hula that has never seen printer's ink, while the violin threnody of the Alapai raised the plaintive, half-savage lilt to something incommunicably high and haunting.

Jack seemed in a trance, his eyes like stars, while his broad shoulders swayed to the measure. Discovering my regard, caught in his emotion of delight in this pregnant folk dance and song, he did not smile, but half-veiled his eyes as he laid a hand on mine in token of acknowledgment of my comprehension of his deep mood. For in every manifestation of human life, he goes down into the tie ribs of racial development, as if in eternal quest to connect up the abysmal past with the palpable present.

A pause, full of murmurs and low laughter, then a strapping young wahine with the profile of Diana seized an old guitar, and with a shout to another girl to get on her feet, leaned over and swept the strings masterfully with the backs of her fingers, at the same time setting up a wanton, thrilling hula song that was a love cry in the starlight, each repeated phrase ending in a fainting, crooning, tremulous falsetto which trailed off into a vanishing wisp of sound. She could not sit quietly, but swung her body and lissom limbs in rhythm like a wild thing possessed, seeming to galvanize the dancers by sheer force of will, for one by one they sprang to the bidding of her voice and magnetic fingers, into the flickering light where they swayed and bent and undulated like mad sweet nymphs and fauns. Now and again a brown sprite separated from the moving group, and came to dance before the haole guests, the dance a provocation to join the revelry. Sometimes the love appeal was unmistakable, accompanied by singing words we wotted not of, but which were the cause of much good-natured merriment from the others. Then suddenly the performer would become impersonal in face and gesture, and melt back into the weaving group.

After a while the dancing lagged, and we felt it was time for us to relieve these kind people of our more or less restraining presence. They had done so much, and to wear out such welcome would have been a crime against good heart and manners.

Having neglected to ask the obliging Tony to wait his dummy for our returning, down the track we footed, listening to small noises of the night, among which could be detected the sighing of water buffalo, those grotesque gray shapes that patiently toil by day in the rice fields.

PEARL LOCHS, Friday, June 14, 1907.

Eleven days after Jack's broiling at Waikiki, yesterday the largest blisters began forming on his scarlet limbs—rising and running into one another until a combined blister would be a foot long. His interest in the phenomenon helps him pass the irritating hours. I shall be happy indeed for both our sakes when he is once more comfortable, for his condition keeps me in a nervous shudder of sympathy. But time slips by very entertainingly, with a heated rubber of cribbage mornings after breakfast of papaia and coffee, and hot crabs which Jack, in a reclining chair on the terrace, watches his industrious fish-wife pull in from the jetty. Then we read aloud until work time, just now having finished Brand Whitlock's "The Turn of the Balance," and begun on a course of George Moore's novels.

At lunch to-day Miss Johnson introduced us to a girl friend from Maine, and it was a unique experience to sit in the hot-house air, gazing out upon the hot-house vegetation, the while we conversed in "downeast" colloquialisms, among other incidents recalling one when Jack and I, on our honeymoon, drove for the first time in a cab on runners over the crackling streets of Bangor after a freeze-up. "Did you see her jump at the sound of that falling leaf!" Jack laughed on the way home, for the young lady from Maine had been not the only one startled when a twenty-foot frond let go its parent palm and crashed to earth.

Our captain of the roseate name is painting the *Snark*, and she floats, a boat of white enamel, in the still blue and silver of the morning flood, while for frame to the fair picture a painted double-rainbow overarches, flinging the misty fringes of its ends in our enraptured faces. From the shell-pink dawn, through the green and golden day, to sunset and purple twilight and starshine, we move in beauty. "What a lot of people must have been shanghaied here by their own desire!" Jack ruminates. And truly, Hawaii is sufficient excuse for never going home.

Mr. Scott, of the Iron Works, sailed over from Honolulu last Sunday in his fast yacht, the *Kamehameha*, and she was a lovely sight slanting about on the crisp water in a fresh whiff of wind, her owner doing some fancy sailing around the *Snark*, apparently trying to see how close he could dare without touching. With him came a corps of engineers who had offered to give their holiday for the fellow who wrote "The Game" and "The Sea Wolf." Jack was quite overwhelmed by this tribute, to the shame of his own state and her lukewarm workmen. He was especially pleased over the liking of these young men for "The Game," which is a favorite of his own, few Americans seeming to care for it, although England and her colonies "eat it up."

Gene has coaxed our launch into action, and in it we rode to the yacht. Jack is overjoyed, for it has been useless ever since the time in San Francisco when it was allowed to lie for weeks full of salt water, well-nigh ruining the little engine. While Jack talked business aboard, I swam back alone to shore with the launch in attendance. "I never thought I should marry a woman who could swim like that!" he shouted after me. "You didn't," the woman puffed; "you taught her to swim like that!" And now we look forward to days when together we shall swim for hours beyond the breakers at Waikiki, and anywhere in the world.

Jack London is a devoted card-player who seldom finds chance to sharpen his wits on a good game; but he finds sport these evenings in playing four-handed hearts, or whist, with Martin, Gene, and myself. I am not at all talented in the direction of games; but because of my husband's fondness for cards I make a supreme effort to be at least an average player, finding much enjoyment in the contest. There is pleasure and profit in almost anything one undertakes to learn of "the other fellow's game" in this world, if one but employs a little selfless understanding.

Last evening there were no cards, for we had opportunity again to come in contact with the Hawaiians, receiving a party in our sylvan drawing-and music-room. Miss Johnson had told us that Judge Hookanu (Ho-o-kah-noo), the native district judge at Pearl City, wished to bring his wife to call. To our prompt invitation they responded with the immediate family as well as more distant relatives. One of these, who dislikes Americans, during a conversation with Miss Johnson concerning the Londons, remarked: "Oh, yes, the English are always very nice." "But the Londons are American—very American!" Miss Johnson straightened her out. However, the dusky lady was cordial enough when our meeting took place, as were all the party. The Judge proved an intelligent and kindly soul, and Mrs. Hookanu, whom we had long admired at a distance, is a magnificently proportioned woman with the port of a queen, always attired in stately lines of black lawn or silk.

None of our visitors had heard the records of Hawaiian music which we played for them, and clapped their hands over the hulas like joyous children. But those merry hands folded meekly and devoutly when the Trinity Choir voices rose on the night air, and all joined in singing the harmonies of "Lead, Kindly Light" and the several other beautiful hymns, especial favorites of my irreligious philosopher. The spirit of these folk is so sweet, so guileless, I know I shall love them forever. Manners among them are gentle and considerate, so courteous in every conventional observance, prompted by their simple, affectionate hearts. Hookanu means *proud*, and these who bear the name demonstrate a blending of pride and gentlehood that is altogether aristocratic.

While Jack manipulated the talking-machine, I lay happily with head in a friendly lap while satin-brown fingers caressed face and hair, looking high through the lacy foliage to where big stars hung like bright fruit in the branches. Jack wound up with the Hawaiian National Anthem, and the Judge removed his hat and stood, the others rising about him. Then we cajoled them into contributing their own music, and after some hesitation, untinged by the faintest unwillingness, they settled dreamily to singing their favorite melodies—brown velvet maids with laughing, shining eyes, who warbled in voices thin and penetrating as sweet zither-strings, softly, as if afraid to vex the calm night with greater volume.

At parting we walked to the gate, arms around the willing shoulders of our new friends, their own Aloha nui on our lips. And every aloha spoken or sung in Hawaii is the tender tone-fall of a dying bell, tolling for the old Hawaii Nei.

Then, arms-around, we two paced back across the grass, and stood for a moment on the edge of our bewitching garden, looking at the slender sliver of a new moon of good omen dipping low above the shadowy hills.

WAIKIKI, Tuesday, June 25, 1907.

Once more in the brown tent-cottage at Waikiki, as the hub for many spokes of exploration in the Islands. I mistrust we shall never again pursue our idyllic life at the peninsula. Unfortunately, no way has been devised to live in two or more places simultaneously—except in the imagination, and that we can richly do.

Many jaunts are in the air: an automobile journey around Oahu; a yacht race girdling the same island, on which "Wahine Kapu," no woman, is writ large upon the visages of the yachtsmen; a torchlight fishing expedition fifty miles distant with Prince Cupid, under the same rules; a wonderful trip to Maui, to camp through the greatest extinct crater in the world, Haleakala, said to surpass Etna, in extent and elevation; and Jack has been deftly pulling wires to bring about a visit for us both to the famous Leper Settlement on Molokai, which is said to occupy one of the most beautiful sites in the Islands. Lucius E. Pinkham, president of the Board of Health, has been our guest to dinner, and not only has he put no obstacles in our way, but seems anxious for us to see Molokai. There has been considerable misrepresentation of the Settlement, and he evidently believes that Jack will write a fair picture. Mr. Pinkham seems to have the welfare of the lepers close at heart; and I have heard that when he fails to obtain from the Government certain appropriations for improvements, he draws on his own funds.

Thus, the air is brimful of glamour and interest, which helps to offset a tender regret for the lovely Lochs and for our neighbors who have been so lavish in neighborliness. One night before we departed, the Hookanu young folk arranged a crabbing party, and sang the hours away under the light of a half-moon; another time, at sunset, we fished off Mr. Schwank's premises on the lee shore of the peninsula, where we landed a mess of "colored fish" like a flock of wet butterflies. On his own soil we found our lusty ship carpenter most cordial, plying us with fruit and coconuts, laughing with childlike joy at our praise of his tiny farm garden, and bridling with pride over our admiration of his handsome Portuguese wife and their children.

Here at the Beach life is so gay there is hardly chance to sleep and work, what with arrivals of transports and their ensuing dinners and dances in the hotel lanai, swimming and surf-boarding under sun and moon—very circumspectly under the sun! One fine day we essayed to ride the breakers in a Canadian canoe, and capsized in a wild smother exactly as we had been warned. I stayed under water such a time that Jack, alarmed, came hunting for me; but I was safe beneath the overturned canoe, which I was holding from bumping my head. He was so relieved to find me unhurt and capable of staying submerged so long that promptly he read me a lecture upon swimming as fast as possible from a capsized boat, to avoid being struck in event of succeeding rollers flinging it about.

One night, with Mr. and Mrs. Hawes we attended a moonlight swimming party at the seaside home of Mr. and Mrs. C. Hedemann, longtime Danish residents of Honolulu, and became acquainted with more of the white Islands' people. A lovely custom prevails here among the owners, who, in absences abroad, allow friends the use of their suburban places for occasions of this kind. Across the hedges we peeped into the next garden, where Robert Louis Stevenson lived during his visit to Honolulu.

After a military dance at the hotel last evening, tables were carried out on the lawn to the sands-edge, where a supper was served by silent, swift Japanese in white. It was like a dream, sitting there among the trees hung with soft rosy lights, our eyes sweeping the horizon touched by a low golden moon, and across the effervescing foam of an ebbing tide at our feet, and the white sea horses charging the crescent beach, to Diamond Head purple black against the star-dusted southern sky. "Do you know where you are?" And there was but one answer to Jack's whisper—"Just Waikiki," which tells it all. The charm of Waikiki—it is the charm of Hawaii Nei, "All Hawaii."

WAIKIKI, Friday, June 28, 1907.

To Mr. Ford we owe a new debt of gratitude. And so does Hawaii, for such another promoter never existed. All he does is for Hawaii, desiring nothing for himself except the feverish, unremitting pleasure of sharing the attractions of his adopted land. The past two days have been spent encircling Oahu, or partly so, since only the railroad continues around the entire shoreline, the automobile drive cutting across a tableland midway of the island. Oahu comprises an area of 598 square miles, is trapezoidal in shape, its coast the most regular of any in the group. Another notable feature is that it possesses two distinct mountain chains, Koolau and Waianae, whereas the other islands have isolated peaks and no distinct ranges. Waianae is much the older of the two. The geology of this volcanic isle is a continual temptation to diverge.

The two machines carried ten of us, including the drivers, two young fellows who, it was plain to see, hung upon every word of Jack— oyster pirate, tramp, war correspondent, and what not. The party was composed of men whom Mr. Ford wanted Jack to know, representing the best of Hawaii's white citizenship. There was Mr. Joseph P. Cooke, dominating figure of Alexander & Baldwin, which firm is the leading financial force of the Islands (it was Mr. Cooke's missionary grandparents, the Amos P. Cookes, who founded and for many years conducted what was known as the "Chiefs' School," afterward called the "Royal School," which was patronized by all of the higher chiefs and their families); Mr. Lorrin A. Thurston, descended from the first missionaries, and associated conspicuously with the affairs of Hawaii, both monarchical and republican—and incidentally owner of the morning paper of Honolulu; and Senior A. de Souza Canovarro, Portuguese Consul, an able man who has lived here twenty years and whose brain is shelved with Islands lore.

The world was all dewy cool and the air redolent with flowers when, after an early dip in the surf, we glided down Kalakaua Avenue between the awakening duck ponds with their lily pads and grassy partitions. Leaving the center of town by way of Nuuanu Avenue, along which an electric car runs for two miles, we headed for the storied heights of the Pali (precipice), and presently began climbing toward the converging walls to the pass through the Koolau Range. This Nuuanu Valley is a wondrous residence section, of old-fashioned white mansions of bygone styles of architecture, still wearing their stateliness like a page in history. The dwellers therein are cooled by every breeze—not to mention frequent rains. It is a humorous custom for a resident to say, "I live at the first shower," or the second shower, or even the third, according to his distance from wetter elevations in the city limits. The rainfall in Nuuanu, and Manoa, the next valley to the southeast, is from 140 inches to 150 inches annually. Many of these old houses stand amidst expansive lawns, the driveways columned with royal palms—the first brought to the Islands. One white New England house was pointed out as the country home of Queen Emma, bought with its adjoining acres by the Government and turned into a public park. The old building contains some of the Queen's furniture, and other antiques of the period. "The Daughters of Hawaii," an organization of Hawaii-born women of all nationalities, has the care of the whole premises.

I promised myself an afternoon in the cemetery, where quaint tombs show through the beautiful trees and shrubbery, and where, in the Mausoleum, are laid the bones of the Kamehameha and Kalakaua dynasties. King Lunalilo, who succeeded the last of the Kamehamehas and preceded Kalakaua, rests in the mausoleum of Kawaiahao Church in town.

Up we swung on a smooth road graded along the hill-sides, the flanks of the valley gradually drawing together, the violet-shadowed walls of the mountains growing more sheer until they seemed almost to overtop with their clouded heads breaking into morning gold—Lani-huli and Konahuanui rising three thousand feet to left and right. From a keen curve, we looked back and down the green miles we had come, to a fairy white city lying suffused in blue mist beside a fairy blue sea.

Four miles from the end of the car-track, quite unexpectedly to me, suddenly the machine emerged from a narrow defile upon a platform hewn out of the rocky earth, and my senses were momentarily stunned, for it seemed that the island had broken off, fallen away beneath our feet to the east. On foot, pressing against a wall of wind that eternally drafts through the gap, and threading among a dozen small pack-mules resting on the way to Honolulu, we gained the railed brink of the Pali. In the center of a scene that has haunted me for years, since I beheld it in a painting at the Pan-American Exposition at Buffalo, I looked down a thousand feet into an emerald abyss over the awful pitch of which Kamehameha a century ago forced the warriors of the King of Oahu, Kalanikupule —a "legion of the lost ones" whose shining skulls became souvenirs for strong climbers in succeeding generations. Some one pointed to a ferny, bowery spot far below, where Prince Cupid once kept a hunting cabin; but there was now neither trace of it nor of any trail penetrating the dense jungle.

To the left, lying northwest, stretch the perpendicular, inaccessible ramparts of the Koolau Range, which extends the length of the island, bastioned by erosions, and based in rich green slopes of forest and pasture that fall away to alluvial plains fertile with rice and cane, and rippled with green hillocks. Where we stood, a spur of the range bent in a right-angle to the eastward at our back; and off to the right, the great valley is bounded by desultory low hills, amid which an alluring red road leads to Kailua and Waimanalo by the sapphire sea, where we are told the bathing beaches and surf are wonderful.

A reef-embraced bay on the white-fringed shore caused me to inquire why Honolulu had not been builded upon this cool windward coast of Oahu, with its opulent and ready-made soil. "Any navigator could tell you that," Jack chided. "Honolulu was begun when there was no steam, and the lee side of the island was the only safe anchorage for sailing vessels."

The sun was now burning up the moving mists below, and through opalescent rents and thinning spaces we could trace the ruddy ribbon of road we were to travel. If I had dreamed of the majestic grandeur of these mountains, of the wondrous painted valley to the east, how feebly I should have anticipated other islands until first learning this one. Jack keeps repeating that he cannot understand why it is not thronged with tourists, and calls it the garden of the world. We have seen nothing like it in America or Europe. And yet Oahu is not spoken of as by any means the most beautiful of the Hawaiian Islands. Instead, both residents and visitors rave over the "Garden Isle," Kauai, the Kona coast of Hawaii and that Big Island's gulches, the wonders of Maui with its Iao Valley and Haleakala, "The House of the Sun." What must they all be, say we, if these persons have not been stirred by Windward Oahu!

After clinging spellbound to our windy vantage for half an hour (Jack meanwhile not forgetting to calculate how many times Kalani-kupule's unfortunate army bumped in its headlong fall), we coasted the intricate curves of a road that is railed and reenforced with masonry, fairly hanging to a stark wall for the best part of two miles. I noticed that Mr. Cooke preferred himself to negotiate his White Steamer on this blood-tingling descent, until we rounded into the undulating floor of the plain, where we stared abruptly up at the astonishing way we had come, with its retaining walls of cement, some of them four hundred feet in length.

One stands at the base of an uncompromising two-thousand-foot crag, an outjut of the range, and it appears but a few hundred feet to its head. For there is an elusiveness about the atmosphere that makes unreal the sternest palisades, the ruggedest gorges. Everything is as if seen in a mirror that has been dulled by a silver breath. That is it—it is all a reflection—these are mirrored mountains and shall always remain to me like something envisioned in a glass. "Do you know where you are?" But I shook my head and hand to Jack's call. Never did I imagine Oahu was like this on its other side.

I for one was commencing to realize how early I had breakfasted, when the machines turned aside from the road on which we had been running through miles of the Kahuku sugar plantation into a private driveway that led to Mrs. James B. Castle's sea-rim retreat, The Dunes. Having been called unexpectedly to Honolulu, she had left the manager of the plantation, Mr. Andrew Adams, to do the honors, together with a note of apology embodying the wish that we make ourselves at home, and a request that we write in her guest book. After luncheon the men insisted that I inscribe something fitting for them to witness. Warm and tired and dull, I wrote the following uninspired if grateful sentiment:

"With appreciation of the perfect hospitality—and deep regret that the giver was absent."

The others followed with their signatures; and when Mr. Ford's turn came, his eye read what I had written, but his unresting mind must have been wool-gathering, for he scribbled:

"Hoping that every passerby may be as fortunate."

A chorus of derision caused him to bend an alarmed eye upon the page, which he carefully scanned, especially my latter phrase. And then out came the page. Mr. Cooke unavailingly assured him that Mrs. Castle enjoyed a good joke, but the scarlet-faced Ford was not to be induced to replace the sheet. I then prepared another, to which our friend affixed his autograph. This is the first time we have ever seen that irrepressible gentleman crestfallen in the least degree; and he remained subdued for the rest of the day. "Man, man, why don't you relax once in a while?" I had said to him earlier in the day. "You'll wear yourself out before you're forty. You should dwell at length upon words like Eternity, Repose, Rome—" but I was interrupted by an "Oh, fudge!" as he saw what difficulty I was having to preserve a grave countenance.

Mr. Adams showed us over the labor barracks, neat settlements of Japanese and Portuguese, in which he seems deeply interested, especially as concerns the future of the younger element—the swarms of beautiful children that we saw rolling in the grass. The Portuguese flocked around the Consul, who was apparently an old and loved friend.

Several miles farther, we came to the Reform School, where the err-ing youth of Oahu are guided in the way they should go, by Mr. Gibson, a keen-faced, wiry man, who has made splendid showing with the boys, these being largely of the native stock. There was not a criminal face among them, and probably the majority are detained for temperamen-tal laxness of one sort or another. Emotional they are, and easily led, and inordinately fond of games of chance—but dishonest never. A small sugar plantation is carried on in connection with the school, which is worked by the boys.

Our last lap was from the Reform School to Waialua, which lies at the sea edge of the Waialua Plantation. Haleiwa means "House Beautiful," and is pronounced Hah-lay-e-vah. There is so much dis-sension as to how the "v" sound crept into the "w," that I am going to keep out of it, and retire with the statement that Alexander, in his splendid "History of the Hawaiian People," remarks that "The letter 'w' generally sounds like 'v' between the penult and final syllable of a word."

House and grounds are very attractive, broad lawns sloping to an estuary just inside the beach, and in this river-like bit of water pictur-esque fishing boats and canoes lie at anchor. A span of rustic Japanese bridge leads to the bath-houses, and here we went for a swim before dinner. We would not advise beginners to choose this beach for their first swimming lessons, for it shelves with startling abruptness, while the undertow is more noticeable than at Waikiki. But for those who can take care of themselves, this lively water is good sport and more brac-ing than on the leeward coast.

We strolled through the gardens and along green little dams be-tween duck ponds spotted with lily pads, and the men renewed their boyhood by "chucking" rocks into a sumptuous mango tree, bringing down the russet-gold fruit for an appetizer. I may some day be rash enough to describe the flavor of a mango, or try to; but not yet—al-though I seem to resent some author's statement that it bears a trace of turpentine.

Leaving Haleiwa next morning, we deserted the seashore for very different country. For a while the motor ascended steadily toward the southwest, on a fine red road—so red that on ahead the very atmosphere was roseate. Looking back as we climbed, many a lovely surf-picture rewarded the quest of our eyes, white breakers ruffling the creamy beaches, with a sea bluer than the deep blue sky.

At an elevation of about eight hundred feet one strikes the rolling green prairieland of the "Plains," where the ocean is visible northwest and southeast, on both sides of the island. Such a wonderful plateau, between mountain-walls, swept by the freshening northeast trade—miles upon miles of rich grazing, and hill upon hill ruled with blue-green lines of pineapple growth. At one pineapple plantation we stopped that Jack might take a look around at the fabulously promising industry. Mr. Kellogg, the manager, gave an interesting demonstration of how simple is the cultivation of the luscious "pines," and held stoutly that a woman, unaided, could earn a good living out of a moderate patch. "So you see, my dear," Jack advised me, "when I can't write any longer, you can keep both of us at Wahiawa!"

Although like prairie seen from a distance, we discovered that this section of Oahu is serrated by enormous gullies, in character resembling our California barrancas, but of vastly greater proportions. A huge dam has been constructed for the purpose of conserving the water for irrigation.

Something went wrong with Mr. Cooke's machine, and he was obliged to telephone from Wahiawa to Honolulu for some fixtures. Think of this old savage isle in the middle of the Pacific Ocean, where, from its high interior, one may talk over a wire to a modern city, for modern parts of a "horseless carriage," to be sent by steam over a steel track! It is stimulating once in a day to ponder the age in which we live.

And on one of these ridges near Wahiawa, not so long ago, there preyed a sure-enough ogre, a robber-chief whose habit it was to lie in wait in a narrow pass, and pounce upon his victims, whom he slew on a large, flat rock.

WAIKIKI, June 29, 1907.

"Have you seen the Cleghorn Gardens?" is a frequent question to the malihini, and only another way of asking if one has seen the gardens of the late Princess Victoria Kaiulani, lovely hybrid flower of Scottish and Polynesian parentage, daughter of a princess of Hawaii, Mirian Likelike (sister of Liliuokalani and Kalakaua) and the Honorable Arthur Scott Cleghorn. We are too late by twenty years to be welcomed by Likelike, and eight years behind time to hear the merriment of Kaiulani in her father's house—Kaiulani, who would now be of the same age as Jack London. King Kalakaua died at the Palace Hotel in San Francisco on January 20, 1891, and when his remains arrived in Ho-

nolulu from the U.S.S. *Charleston* nine days later, and his sister Liliuokalani was proclaimed his successor, the little Princess Kaiulani, their
niece, was appointed heir apparent. And now her venerable father's
acquaintance we have added to our vital impressions of Hawaii.

The famous house, Ainahau, is not visible from the Avenue. Here
the bereft consort of Likelike lives in solitary state with his servants,
amid the relics of unforgotten days. He receives few visitors, and we
felt as if breaking his privacy were an intrusion, even though by invitation. But the commandingly tall, courtly old Scot, wide brown
eyes smiling benevolently under white hair and beetling brows, paced
halfway down his palm-pillared driveway in greeting, and led our
little party about the green-shady ways of the wonderland of flowers
and vines, lily ponds and arbors, "Where Kaiulani sat," or sewed, or
read, or entertained—all in a forest of high interlacing trees of many
varieties, both native and foreign. I was most fascinated by a splendid
banyan, a tree which from childhood I had wanted to see. This pleased
the owner, whose especial pride it is—"Kaiulani's banyan"; although
he is obliged to trim it unmercifully lest its predatory tentacles capture the entire park.

Into nurseries and vegetable gardens we followed him, and real
grass huts that have stood untouched for years. Another pride of Mr.
Cleghorn's is his sixteen varieties of hibiscus, of sizes and shapes and
tints that we would hardly have believed possible—magic puffs of exquisite color springing like miracles from slender green stems that are
often too slight, and snap under the full blossom-weight.

And the house. The portion once occupied by the vanished Princess is never opened to strangers, nor used in any way. Only her father wanders there, investing the pretty suite of rooms with recollection of her tuneful young presence. For she was little over twenty
when she died.

But we were made welcome in the great drawing-room, reached by
three broad descending steps, and containing works of art and curios
from all the world: old furniture from European palaces that would be
the despair of a repulsed collector; tables of lustrous Hawaiian woods
fashioned to order in Germany half a century ago; rare oriental vases
set upon flare-topped pedestals ingeniously made from inverted tree
stumps of beautiful brown *kou* wood, polished like marble; a quaint and
stately concert grand piano; and, most fascinating of all, treasures of
Hawaiian courts, among them some of the marvelous feather work. In

the dim corners of the immense room, *kahilis* stand as if on guard—barbaric royal insignia, plumed staffs of state, some of them twice the height of a man. The feathers are fastened at right angles to the pole of shining hardwood, forming a barrel-shaped decoration, somewhat like our hearse-plumes of a past generation. But the kahili is only sometimes of funereal hue, more often flaming in scarlet, or some grade of the rich yellows loved of the Islanders. Originally a fly-brush in savage courts, the kahili progressed in dignity through the dynasties to an indispensable adjunct to official occasions, sometimes exceeding thirty feet in height. To me, it and the outrigger canoe are the most significantly impressive of royal barbaric forms.

The walls of the room are solidly ranged with books for some two thirds of their height, and above the books hang fascinating old portraits of bygone Hawaiian royalty as well as famous personages of the outer world. Jack's eyes snapped as he fingered the old volumes—I can see his face now, avid as always to read every word between the covers of every book ever made by man. Not because these were rare old editions in rare old bindings was he wooed, but just because they were books, old books with their chronicles of the minds and hearts, hazards and achievements of mankind.

Francesca Colonna Hawes, with whom we had come, opened her incredible black eyes in astonishment, the while we sat at tea in a narrow red-tiled room overlooking a court of flowers, when our host remarked in his grave voice:

"Why can you not write in my gardens, Mr. London? It would please me. You are very welcome to come every day. And you would be entirely undisturbed. Why not, now?"

According to Mrs. Hawes, this is an unheard-of consideration in these times of Mr. Cleghorn's seclusion. "Why don't you?" I queried of Jack, on the way home. "Maybe I shall," he replied. But I think he will not, for he is curiously timorous about availing himself of favors.

Mr. Cleghorn also suggested that he could arrange a private audience with Queen Liliuokalani at her residence in town, if we desired. Which reminds me that Jack holds a letter of introduction to her from Charles Warren Stoddard, who knew her in the days of her tempestuous reign. He and Jack have called each other Dad and Son for years, although acquainted only by correspondence. But we have little wish to intrude upon the Queen, for it can be scant pleasure to her to meet Americans, no matter how sympathetic they may be with her changed state.

Upon a carven desk lay open a guest book, an old ledger, in which we were asked to leave our hand. The first name written in this thick tome is that of "Oskar, of Sweden and Norway," and, running over the fascinating yellowed pages, among other notable autographs we read that of Agassiz.

Here, there, and everywhere, in photograph, in oil portraiture, on wall and upon easel, we met the lovely, pale face of the bereft father's Kaiulani, in whose memory he seems to exist in a mood of adoration. Every event dates from her untimely passing. "When Kaiulani died," he would begin; or "Since Kaiulani went away," and "Before Kaiulani left me—" was the burden of his thought and conversation concerning the past of which we loved to hear. Pictures show her to have been a woman possessing the beauty of both races, proud, loving, sensitive, spirituelle, with the characteristic curling mouth and great luminous brown eyes of the Hawaiian, looking out wistfully upon a world of pleasure and opportunity that could not detain her frail body. Flower of romance she was—romance that nothing in the old books of South Sea adventuring can rival; her sire, a handsome roving boy ashore from an English ship back in the '50's; her mother a dusky princess of the blood royal, who loved the handsome white-skinned youth and constituted him governor of Oahu under the Crown, that she might with honor espouse him.

And now, the boy, grown old—his Caucasian vitality having survived the gentle Polynesian blood of the wife who brought him laurels in her own land,—having watched the changing administrations of that land and race for nearly threescore years, abides alone with the shadow of her and of the pale daughter with the poet brow who did honor to them both by coming into being. To this winsome child-woman, previous to her voyage to England's Court, Robert Louis Stevenson, living where we peeped into the garden but a few nights gone, sent the following:

"[Written in April to Kaiulani in the April of her age; and at Waikiki, within easy walk of Kaiulani's banyan! When she comes to my land and her father's, and the rain beats upon the window (as I fear it will), let her look at this page; it will be like a weed gathered and pressed at home; and she will remember her own islands, and the shadow of the mighty tree; and she will hear the peacocks screaming in the dusk and the wind blowing in the palms; and she will think of her father sitting there alone.—R. L. S.]

(1) L. G. Kellogg and Jack London at Wahiawa, 1907.   (2) The Brown Tent Cottage at Waikiki—Jack at corner.   (3) A Pair of Jacks—Atkinson and London   (4) Ahuimanu

"Forth from her land to mine she goes,
   The island maid, the island rose,
Light of heart and bright of face:
   The daughter of a double race.

"Her islands here, in Southern sun,
   Shall mourn their Kaiulani gone;
And I in her dear banyan shade,
   Look vainly for my little maid.

"But our Scots islands far away
   Shall glitter with unwonted day,
And cast for once their tempests by
   To smile in Kaiulani's eye."

Aboard the *Noeau*, bound for Molokai,
Monday Evening, July 1, 1907.

Noeau (No-a-ah-oo—quickly No-a-ow)—the very name has a mournful, ominous sound; *Noeau*, ship of despair, ferry of human freight condemned. We are not merry, Jack and I, for what we have witnessed during the past two hours would wring pitying emotion from a graven image. And just when we would cheer a trifle, it not being our mutual temperament long to remain downcast, our eyes are again compelled by the huddle of doomed fellow-creatures amidst their pathetic bundles of belongings on the open after-deck of the plunging interisland steamer bound for Molokai.

None of it did we miss—the parting and the embarkation of the banished; and never, should I live a thousand fair years, shall I forget the memory of that strange, rending wailing, escaping bestiality by its very deliberateness, for, no matter how deep and true may be the grief, this wailing expression of it constitutes a ceremonial in this as in other countries where it survives as a set form of lamentation. Shrill, piercing, it curdled the primitive life-current in us, every tone in the gamut of sorrow being played upon the plaintive word *auwe* (ah-oo-way'— quickly ow-way'), *alas*, in recurrent chorusing when each parting took place and the loved one stepped upon the gangplank, untouched by the officers and crew of the small steamer.

"Clean" passengers were taken aboard first, the vessel picking up at another wharf those who bore no return ticket to the land of the clean. As the *Noeau* came alongside, the crowd ashore appeared like any other leave-taking gathering of natives, even to the flowers; but suddenly Jack at my elbow jerked out, "*Look*—look at that boy's face!" And I looked, and saw. It was a lad of twelve or so, and one of his cheeks was so swollen that the bursting eye seemed as if extended on a fleshy horn. Beside him a woman hovered, her face dark with sorrow. Our eyes were soon quick to detect the marks and roved from face to face, selecting more or less accurately those who proved later to be passengers for the dark fifty-odd miles across Kaiwi Channel and along the north coast of Molokai to the village of Kalaupapa that is their final destination and home on this earth.

But one can only see what one can see, and there were men and women among these who bore no apparent blemish; and yet, this moment we can distinguish these among the disfigured company on the lurching after-deck.

The ultimate wrench of hearts and hands, the supreme acme of ruth, came when, separated by the widening breach between steamer and dock, the lost and the deserted gazed upon one another, and the last pitiful offerings of leis fell into the water. No normal malihini could stand by untouched; it was utterly, hopelessly sad—a funeral in which the dead themselves walked.

For one white child, a blonde-haired little German maid, we felt especial solicitude. Her bronze companions all had dear ones to wail for them and for whom to "keen." But she stood quite apart, with dry eyes old before their time, watching an alien race deliver its woe in ways she had not learned. Whose baby is she? To whom is she dear? Where is the mother who bore her? And the answer was just now volunteered by the Superintendent of the Leper colony, returning from a vacation, Mr. J. D. McVeigh. The child's mother is already in Kalaupapa, far gone with a rapid form of leprosy; and this little daughter, who had been left with a drunken father who treated her ill, has been found with the same manifestation, and will live but a few years. So she is going to her own, and her own is waiting for her, and it is well. But think of the whole distorted face of the dream of life . . . dear Christ!

. . . Now the white child has fallen asleep in a dull red sunset glow, her flaxen head in the lap of a beautiful hapa haole girl who carries no apparent spot of corrosion. She looks down right motherly upon the tired face of the small Saxon maid. Hawaiian women eternally "rock cradles in their hearts," which are so expansive that it is said to matter little whose child they cradle—bringing up one another's offspring with impartial loving-kindness. This practice extended even into high-est circles, as Liliuokalani attests in her own entertaining book, "Ha-waii's Story by Hawaii's Queen." She herself was "given away" at birth, wrapped in the finest tapa cloth, to Konia, a grand-daughter of Kame-hameha the Great, wedded to a high chief, Paki. Their own daughter, Bernice Pauahi, Liliuokalani's foster-sister, was afterward married to C. R. Bishop, Minister of Foreign Affairs in 1893 under King Lunali-lo, Kalakaua's predecessor. The Queen writes that in using the term foster-sister she merely adopts one customary in the English language, there being no such modification recognized in her own tongue. As a matter of fact, in childhood she knew no other parents than Paki and Konia, no other sister than Pauahi. Her own father and mother were no more than interesting acquaintances. For this custom she offers only the reason that the alliance by adoption cemented ties of friendship be-tween chiefs, which, spreading to the common people, doubtless encour-aged harmony—a harmony that would have delighted King Solomon, to say nothing of white men's courts of law!

They forget quickly, these Hawaiians, one hears; and one must be-lieve, I suppose—and, believing, thanks whatever gods may be; for this blissful latitude never was created for the harboring of grief. But the ability or tendency to forget pain has little to do with its momentary poignancy. The passionate Hawaiian suffers with all the abandon of the blood that keeps him always young. The sorrow is real, and the weep-ing. If these people could not recover speedily from despair, they would die off faster than they are already perishing from their arcadian isles.

On our deck, observing the dolorous scene aft, is a young native girl, round and ripe and more lovely than any we have yet seen. Clean and wholesome, unsullied by any blight, a happy body, she stands be-side her father, a handsome gray-haired Hawaiian with lofty mien; and one wonders what are the young girl's thoughts as she gazes upon these wrecks of her kind. And yet, she herself might have to be sought in Molokai another year. As well seek her underground, is the next thought. Poor human flesh and blood!

KALAUPAPA, MOLOKAI,
Tuesday, July 2, 1907.

We are endeavoring to reconstruct whatever mind-picture we have hitherto entertained of that grave of living death, Molokai. But it is no use, and we would best give it up. Eye and brain are possessed of the be-wildering actuality, and having expected Heaven knows what lugubrious prospect, we are all at sea. Certain it is that all preconceptions were far removed from the joyous sunny scene now before us, as I rock in a hammock on the Superintendent's lanai, shaded from the late sunshine by a starry screen of white jasmine. Jack stretches at length on a rattan lounge, cigarette in one hand and long cool glass in the other; and what we see is a peaceful pasture of many acres, a sort of bulging village green, in the center a white bandstand breathing of festivity. Around the verdant semi-hemisphere, widely straggling as if space and real estate values were the least consideration of mankind, dot the flower-bedecked homes of the leprous inhabitants. Breaking rudely into this vision of repose, a cowboy on a black horse dashes furiously across the field and whirls out of sight. A leper. Two comely wahines in ruffly white holokus, starched to a nicety, stroll chatting by the house, looking up brightly to smile Aloha with eyes and lips. Lepers. Jack looks at me. I look at Jack. And this is Molokai the dread; Molokai, isle of despair, where Father Damien spent his martyrdom.

The Settlement lies on a triangle, a sort of wide-based peninsula, selected by Dr. Hutchinson in 1865, shut effectively off as it is from the rest of the island to the south by a formidable wall rising four thousand feet into the deep-blue sky—a wall of mystery, for it is well-nigh unscalable except by the bands of wild goats that we can discover only by aid of Mr. McVeigh's telescope. Every little while, as a sailor sweeps the horizon, he steps to the glass, hidden from the community by the jasmine screen, and studies the land of his charge, keeping track of the doings of the village.

The only trail out of or into this isolated lowland zigzags the bare face of the pali near its northern end, at the sea-girt extremity of the Settlement reserve. A silvery-green cluster of kukui trees marks the beginning of the trail not far up from the water's edge. Thus far and no farther may the residents of the peninsula stray; and the telescope is most often trained to this point of the compass. That trail does not look over-inviting; but we have set our hearts upon leaving Kalaupapa by this route, albeit Mr. McVeigh, who knows what is in our thought, warns that it is undergoing repairs and is unsafe. Indeed, he has gone so far as to say that it is out of the question for us to ascend it in its dilapidated condition.

In view of the pleasant reality of the island, yesternight's racking experience seems a nightmare. Over and above pity for the stricken exiles, we were none too comfortable ourselves, for in the tiny stuffy staterooms it was impossible to sleep, and except for coolness the populous deck was scarcely less disturbing. Besides the Superintendent, the other passengers were hapa haoles and a white Catholic father with his Bishop, bound for the Settlement to inspect their institutions.

We turned in early on deck-mattresses, after listening to some thrilling yarns from the captain and mate of the sorry little steamer, to say nothing of those of Mr. McVeigh, who sparkles with Hibernian wit. As the miles and time increased between the lepers and the harbor of farewells, they searched out their ubiquitous ukuleles and guitars, and rendered us all happier for their presence, poor things. All would have been well, and the music and murmuring voices soon have had us drowsing, but for a tipsy native sailor who chipped in noisily with ribald song and speech that was loudly profane.

At intervals the captain and mates issued from their unrestful cubbies on the short strip of plunging deck (these interisland channels have a reputation equal to the passage between Dover and Calais), and conversed at length in unmuffled accents. To cap my sleepless discomfort, Jack, who had been fighting all night, he avers unconsciously, to wrest away the soft pillow he had insisted upon my using, finally appropriated the same with a determined "pounding of the ear" in hobo parlance. And poor I, lacking the meanness to reclaim it at price of rousing the tender soul from his troubled slumber, languished upon a neck-wrenching bolster stuffed, I swear, with scrap-iron. It has since occurred to us that it may have been a life-preserver.

At the dim chill hour of four, all passengers for Kalaupapa were landed in a rough-and-ready life-boat through breakers which, to our regret, were the reverse of boisterous. We had looked forward to making through a breach of surf like that shown in photographs of Kalaupapa Landing. But it was novel enough, this being let down the lurching black flank of the ship where she rolled in the unseen swell, into an uncertain boat where muscular arms eased us into invisible seats. The merest fitful whisper of air was stirring, and there was something solemn in our progress, deep-dipping oars sending the heavy boat in large, slow rhythm over a broad swell and under the black frown of a wall of darker darkness against the jeweled southern sky.

The landing is a small concrete breakwater, into the crooked arm of which we slipped, trusting in the lantern gleam to dark hands of natives that reached to help. We wondered, entirely without alarm, if they were leprous fingers we grasped, but rested upon fate and climbed our best.

The wall was rimmed with sitting figures, and when our twenty-five leper passengers set foot on the cement, some were greeted in low, hesitant Hawaiian speech as if by acquaintances. In the flicker of the swinging lanterns we glimpsed a white woman's anxious face and two pale hands stretched out. And tears were in my eyes to see the German mother and child united, even in their awful plight.

A quiet Japanese man took charge of me and my suitcase, and I was carried in a cart up a gentle rise to this cottage smothered in garden trees, the door of which is reached by way of a scented, vine-clasped arbor. The night was almost grewsomely still, and I tried to pierce the gloom to judge how near was that oppressive wall to the south, but could form no idea in the velvet black.

The Japanese turned me over to his wife, a small motherly thing who fluttered me into a bright white room with canopied bed, into which she indicated I was to plump forth-with; that the bath was just across the lanai; breakfast at eight; and could she do anything for me?

In a few moments Jack arrived, and we slept well into the new day. After breakfast the official "clean" members of the colony dropped in, Doctors Goodhue and Hollmann, the pioneer resident surgeon and his assistant, with their wives, as well as the German-Hawaiian parents of Mrs. Goodhue, who had tramped down the pali the previous day from their ranch in the highlands "beyond the pale," to visit their daughter. And Jack and I promptly registered the thought that if they could negotiate that trail, why not we?

Never have we spent such a day of strange interest. Before luncheon, Mr. McVeigh drove us to within two or three hundred yards of the foot of the pali, to see the Kalaupapa Rifle Club at practice. And would you believe? Quite as a matter of course we sat on benches side by side with the lepers, and when our turns came, stood in their shooting boxes, and with rifles warm from their hands hit the target at two hundred yards. Oh, I did not quite make the bull's-eye, but there were certain drawbacks to my best marksmanship the heavy and unfamiliar gun that I had not the strength to hold perfectly steady, and the audience of curious men whose personal characteristics were far from quieting to malahini wahine nerves. Both of us were duly decorated with the proud red badge of the Club, bearing "Kalaupapa Rifle Club, 1907," in gilt letters.

But fancy watching these blasted remnants of humanity, lost in the delight of scoring, their knotted hands holding the guns, on the trig-

gers the stumps of what had once been fingers, while their poor ruined
eyes strove to run along the sights . . . .

It took all our steel, at first, to avoid shrinking from their hideous-
ness; but, assured as we were of the safety of mingling, our concern was
earnestly to let them know we were unafraid. And it made such a touching difference. From out their watchful silence and bashful loneliness
they emerged into their natural care-free Hawaiian spirits.

For, you must know, all leprosy is not painful. There is what is
termed the anaesthetic variety, which twists and deforms but which
ceases from twinging as the disease progresses or is arrested, and the
nerves go to sleep. Another and inexpressibly loathsome form manifests
itself in running sores; but Dr. Goodhue now takes prompt action on
such cases, his brave, deft surgery producing marvelous results. Tuber-
cular leprosy makes swift inroads and quick disposal of the sufferer.
But it should make the public happier to know that here the majority
of the patients come and go about the business of their lives as in other
villages the world over, if with less beauty of face and form.

In the afternoon, Mr. McVeigh being much occupied after his vacation, Dr. Hollmann took us in charge, and showed us first the Bishop (Catholic) Home for Girls, presided over by Mother Marianne, the
plucky aged Mother Superior of Hawaii Nei. Here she spends most
of her life, two sisters living with her. Like a tall spirit she guided us
across the playground and through schoolrooms and dormitories. In
one of the latter we recognized a young girl who came on the *Noeau* last
night. Standing in a corner talking with two old friends whose faces
were almost obliterated, this latest comer neither looked nor acted as if
there was anything unusual about them. She has a rare sense of adjustment, that girl—or else is mercifully wanting in imagination.

It seems that women are more susceptible to the ruin of disease,
mental or physical, than their brothers—at least they show it more ru-
inously. I have noticed in feeble-minded and insanity institutions that
the eclipse of personality is more complete among the females. Perhaps
it seems this way because we are used to especial comeliness in women,
and to see a vacant or disfigured countenance above feminine habili-
ments instead of the sweet flower of woman's face, is dreadful beyond
the dreadfulness of man's features under similar misfortune.

"Would you like to hear the girls sing?"

Like was hardly the word; I would have fled weeping from what
could only be an ordeal to every one. But we could not refuse good

Mother Marianne the opportunity to display the talents of her pupils, and a Sister was dispatched to summon them.

Draggingly enough they came, unsmiling, their bloated or contracted features emerging grotesquely from the clean holokus. Every gesture and averted head showed a piteous shame over lost fairness—a sensitive pridefulness that does not seem to trouble the male patients.

Clustered round a piano, one played with hands that were not hands—for where were the fingers? But play she did, and weep I did, in a corner, in sheer uncontrol of heartache at the girlish voices gone shrill and sexless and tinny like the old French piano, and the writhen mouths that tried to frame sweet words carolled in happier days. They gazed dumbly at the white wahine who grieved for them—indeed, for some moments it would have been difficult to say who was sorrier for the other. Out of their horrible eyes they watched us go, and I wonder if Jack's sad face and my wet cheek were any solace to them. But they called Aloha bravely as we went down the steps, as did a group of girls under a hau tree—one of whom, a beautiful thing, crossing the inclosure with the high-breasted, processional carriage of the Hawaiian, showed no mark of the curse upon her swart skin where the young blood surged in response to our greeting.

The Bay View Home was our next objective, in which are kept the most advanced cases of the men. Nothing would do but Jack would see everything to be seen—and where he goes and can take me, there does he wish me to go to learn the face, fair and foul, of the world in which we live. And here we came across several of our own race, with whom we talked, and who appeared quite cheerful—let us say philosophical. One in particular, a ghastly white old man whose eyes hung impossibly upon his cheeks, spoke with the gentlest Christian fortitude, trying to smile with a lip that fanned his chest—I do not exaggerate. Only one there was who seemed not in the slightest resigned—he who led us among his brother sufferers in this house of tardy dissolution.

"Do any of them ever become used to their condition?"

His terrible eyes came down to my face with a look of utter hopelessness.

"I have been here twenty-five years, Mrs. London, and I am not used to it yet."

Glancing back from the gate, we saw him still standing on the lanai, straight and tall, gazing out over the sea; a man once wealthy and honored in his world—a senator, in fact. And now there remains noth-ing before him after his two and a half disintegrating decades of exile, but long years of the same to follow, at the end of which he sees himself, an unsightly object, laid in the ground out of the light of heaven.

There is one hope, always, for those of the lepers who think—the shining hope that blessed science, now aroused, may discover at any illuminated moment the natural enemy of the *bacillus lepra* which has been isolated and become thoroughly familiar to the germ specialists. Jack, visiting the Kalihi Detention Home and Experiment Station, in Honolulu, in company with Mr. Pinkham, was shown the *bacillus lepra* under the microscope. Plans are under way for a federal experiment laboratory and hospital on Molokai for the study of the evil germ, "The dirty beast!" Jack mutters under his breath. The Settlement itself is a territorial care, managed by the Board of Health.

In another building we inspected the little dispensary, and here met Annie Kekoa, a half-white telephone operator from Hilo, on Hawaii, daughter of a native minister. One of her small hands is very slightly warped; otherwise she is without blemish, and very charming—edu-cated and refined, with the loveliest brown eyes and heart-shaped face. Being a deft typewriter, she is employed in the dispensary to fill her days, for she is entirely unreconciled to her changed condition. Little she spoke of herself, but was eager for news of Honolulu and our own travels. We told her of a resemblance she bears to a friend at home, and she said in a shaken voice: "When you see your friend again, tell her she has a little sister on Molokai." At the moment of parting, a sud-den impulse caused us both to forget the rules, and we reached for each other's hands. I know I shall never be sorry.

"Major" Lee, one-time American engineer in the Inter-Island Steamship Company, demonstrated the workings of a newly installed steam poi factory. He was in the gayest of humors, and ever so proud of his spick-and-span machinery. "We're not so badly off here as the Outside chooses to think," he announced, patting a rotund boiler. And then, with explosive earnestness: "I say, Mr. London—give 'em a breeze about us, will you? Tell 'em how we really live. Nobody knows—nobody has told half the truth about Molokai and the splendid way things are run. Why, they give the impression that you can go around with a basket and pick up fingers and toes and hands and feet. They don't take the trouble to find out the truth, and nobody seems to put 'em straight. Why, leprosy doesn't work that way, anyhow. Things don't *fall off:* they *take up*—they absorb. We've got our pride, you know, and we don't like the wrong thing believed on the Outside, naturally. So you give the public a breeze about us, Mr. London, and you'll have the gratitude of the fellows on Molokai."

And I thought I saw, in Jack's active eye, a hint of the fair breeze to a gale that he would set a-blowing on the subject of "the fellows on Molokai."

When "Major" Lee sailed his last trip on the old Line, the luckier engineers of the *Noeau*, taking him to Kalaupapa, said: "Come on down to our rooms, and be comfortable." Lee protested—No, it would not be right; it wouldn't be playing the game; he was a leper now, a leper, do you hear?—and things were different, old fellows . . . . "Different, your granny!" and with friendly oaths and suspicious movements of shirt-sleeves across eyes, the chief and his men had their old comrade into their quarters and gave him the best they had, even to a stirrup-cup— an infringement of orders, as alcohol is the best accomplice of leprosy.

Leaving Kalaupapa, we drove to the elder village, Kalawao, across the mile of the rolling peninsula, a pathway of beauty from the iron-bound, surf-fountained sea line, to the grandeurs of the persistent pali to the south, which is beyond word-painting, unfolding like a giant panorama even along that scant mile. Such crannied canyons, crowded with ferns; such shelves for waterfalls that banner out in the searching wind; such green of tree and purple of shadow. Midway of the trip, Dr. Hollmann turned to the left up a short, steep knoll, from the top of which our eyes dropped into a tiny crater—deep, emerald cup jeweled with red stones, a deeper emerald pool in the bottom, fringed with clashing sisal swords. We came near having a more intimate view of the inverted cone, for a sudden powerful gust of the strong trade that sweeps the peninsula caught us off guard and obliged us to lean sharply back against the blast. Descending the outer slopes of the miniature extinct volcano, we poked around for a while amidst some nameless graves, the old cement mounds and decorations crumbling to dust. The place was provocative of much speculation upon human destiny.

In Kalawao we called at the Catholic Home for Boys, presided over by Father Emmerau and the Brothers, and met up with Brother Dutton, veteran of the Civil War, Thirteenth Wisconsin, who later entered the priesthood, and has immolated himself for years among the leper youth. We found him very entertaining, as he found Jack, with whose career he proved himself well acquainted.

And then across the road to a little churchyard, we stood beside the tombstone of Father Damien—name revered by every one who knows how this simple Belgian priest came to no sanitary, law-abiding, well-ordered community such as to-day adorns the shunned triangle of low-land. He realized his destination before he leaped from the boat; and, once ashore, did not shrink nor turn back from the fearful duty he had imposed upon himself. A life of toil and a fearful lingering death were the forfeit of this true martyr of modern times. We have seen photographs of him in the progressing stages of his torment, and nothing more frightful can be conjured.

Never did we think to stand beside his grave. Just a little oblong plot of carefully tended green, inclosed in iron railing, with a white marble cross and a foot-stone—that is all; appropriately simple for the simple worker, as is the Damien Chapel alongside, into which we stepped with the Bishop, our fellow passenger on the *Noeau*, and Fathers Emmerau and Maxime, to see the modest altar. Standing there before the plain shrine in the subdued light, it seemed as if there could have been no death for the devoted young foreign priest who came so far to lay down his life for his friends.

After dinner, cooked by the pretty Japanese Masa and her husband, during which I learned to like the sweet, dried squid, the other household came over to our lanai. And while we talked, in through the twilight stole vibrations of swept strings, and the sob of a violin, and voices of the men's "Glee Club" that wove in perfect harmonies—voices thrilling as the metal strings but sharpened and thinned by the corroded throats of the singers. Think—think—there we sat in plenitude of health and circumstance, while at the gate, through which none but the clean may ever stray, outside the pale of ordinary human association, these poor pariahs, these shapes that once were men in a world of men, sang to us, the whole, the fortunate, who possess return passage for that free world, the Outside—lost world to them.

They sang on and on, the melting Hawaiian songs, charming "Ua Like No a Like," and "Dargie Hula," "Mauna Kea" beloved of Jack, and his more than favorite, Kalakaua's "Sweet Lei Lehua," with tripping, ripping hula airs unnumbered. At the end of an hour bewitched, to Mr. McVeigh's low "Good night, boys," their last Queen's "Aloha Oe," with its fadeless "Love to You," that has helped to make Hawaii the Heart-Home of countless lovers the world over, laid the uttermost touch of eloquence upon the strange occasion. The sweet-souled musicians, who in their extremity could offer pleasure of sound if not of sight to us happy ones, melted away in the blue starlight, the hulaing of their voices that could not cease abruptly, drifting faint and fainter on the wind.

KALAUPAPA, Wednesday, July 3, 1907.

"Quick! First thought! *Where are you?*" Jack quizzed, as through the jasmine we peered at a score of vociferous lepers running impromptu horse races on the rounding face of the green. Remote, fearsome Molokai, where the wretched victims of an Asiatic blight try out their own fine animals for the prize events of the Glorious Fourth! "Some paradox," murmurs Jack. And all forenoon we listened to no less than four separate and distinct brass bands practicing in regardless fervor for the great day. Laughing, chattering wahines bustled about the sunny landscape, carrying rolls of calico and bunting; for they, too, will turn out in force on the morrow to show how the women of Hawaii once rode everywhere in the kingdom—following upon that gift of the first horse by Captain Cook to Kamehameha—astride in long, flowing skirts of bright colors—the *pa'u* riders of familiar illustrations.

Mr. McVeigh, satisfaction limned upon his Gaelic countenance at all this gay preparation, is much occupied, together with his *kokuas* (helpers), in an effort to forestall another brand of conviviality that is unendingly sought by the lepers on their feast days; and, denied all forms of alcohol, they slyly distil "swipes" from anything and everything that will ferment—even potatoes.

But the lusty Superintendent was not too busy to plan our entertainment for the afternoon, which took the shape of a ride to the little valleys of the pali. There was an odd assortment of mounts—every one of which, despite the appearance of two I could name, was excellent in its way. Mr. McVeigh's solid weight was borne by a big dapple-gray, while Dr. Hollmann bestrode a stocky bay; and Miss Kalama Myers, the strapping handsome sister of Mrs. Goodhue, sat a tall, black charger. Jack's allotment was a stout, small-footed beastie little larger than a Shetland, and to me fell a disappointingly undersized, gentle-seeming white palfrey. To my observant eye, Jack *looked* more than courtesy would allow him to express, for his appearance was highly ridiculous. Although of medium height, five feet nine inches, his feet hung absurdly near the ground, and his small Australian saddle nearly covered the pony's back.

We ambled along for a short distance, when our host's huge gray suddenly bolted, followed by the others, and I as suddenly became aware that my husband was no longer by my side. The next instant I was in the thick of a small stampede across country, the meekness of the milk-white palfrey a patent delusion and snare, while Jack's inadequate scrap, leaping like a jackrabbit, had outdistanced the larger horses. Every one was laughing uproariously, and Jack, now enjoying the practical joke played on us both, waved an arm and disappeared down Damien Road in a cloud of red dust.

Pulling up to a decorous gait through Kalawao, we left the peninsula and held on around the base of the pali till the spent breakers washed our trail, where a tremendous wall of volcanic rock rose abruptly on the right. The trail for the most part was over bowlders covered with seaweed, and we two came to appreciate these pig-headed little horses whose faultless bare hoofs, carried us unslipping on the precarious footing.

Skirting the outleaning black wall, we looked ahead to a coast line of lordly promontories that rise beachless from out the peacock-blue deep water, between which are grand valleys inaccessible except by boat and then only in calm weather. Two of these valleys, Pelekunu and Wailau, contain settlements of non-leprous Hawaiians, who live much as they did before the discovery of the Islands, although they now sell their produce to the Leper Settlement.

Turning into the broad entrance of a swiftly narrowing cleft called Waikolu, we rode as far as the horses could go, and some pretty problems were set them on the sliding, crumbling trail; and we overheard the Superintendent's undertone to Dr. Goodhue: "No malihini riders with us to-day!" which is encouragement that we may be permitted to travel the coveted zigzag out of the Settlement. Then tethering them in the kukui shade, we proceeded on foot up a steep, muddy path where the vegetation, drenched overnight with rain, in turn drenched us and cooled our perspiring skins. Except for the trail—and for all we knew that might have been a wild-pig run—the valley appeared innocent of man; but presently we gained to where orderly patches of water taro with its heart-shaped leaves terraced the steep, like a nursery of lilies, and glimpsed idyllic pictures of grass-houses built on ferny ledges of the mountain side, shaded by large-leaved banana and breadfruit trees, and learned that in these upland vales live certain of the lepers who, preferring an agricultural life, furnish the Settlement with vegetables and fruit. And we tried some "mountain apples," the *ohia'ai*, as distinguished from the *ohia lehua* which furnishes a beautiful dark hard-wood. This fruit is pear-shaped, red and varnished as cherries, and sweet and pulpy like marshmallows. Here were also many *lauhala* trees, from the flat and pointed leaves of which mats and hats are woven, while the orange-colored flowers were an old favorite for the making of leis.

Jack's imagination went a-roving over the possibilities: "Why, look here, Mate Woman," he planned, "we could, if ever we contracted leprosy, live here according to our means. I could go on writing and earning money, and we could have a mountain place, a town house down in the village, a bungalow anywhere on the seashore that suited us, set up our own dairy with imported Jerseys, and ride our own horses, as well as sail our own yacht—within the prescribed radius, of course—and let Dr. Goodhue experiment on our cure!—Isn't it all practical enough?" this to the grinning "Jack" McVeigh, who was regarding him with unconcealed delight, and who assured us he wished us no harm, but for the pleasure of our company he could almost hope the plan might come to pass!

Hours Jack spends "cramming" on leprosy from every book on the subject that the doctors have in their libraries. And literally it is one of the themes about which what is not known fills many volumes. The only point upon which all agree is that they are sure of nothing as regards the means by which the disease is communicated. The nearest they can hazard is that it is *feebly* contagious, and that a person to contract it must have a predisposition. Thus, one might enter the warm blankets of a leper just risen, and, by hours of contact with the effluvia therein, "catch" the disease. The same if one slept long in touch with a victim—and then only if one had the predisposition. And who is to know if the predisposition be his? Certain theories as to the mode of contagion were given us as settled facts by the authorities of the Lazar Hospital in Havana, where we first became interested in leprosy; but that there is little dependence to be placed on these opinions is borne out by at least two known cases on Molokai: one, a native who has remained "clean" though living with a wife so far gone that she attends to her yearly babies with her deft feet; and the other, a woman who has buried five successive leprous husbands, and has failed to contract the disease.

We recall that in Havana we were assured that no attendant, no white person living for years within the confines of the institution, had ever become afflicted; and the same is held on Molokai—which reports make us, as visitors, feel secure. On the other hand, several of the few white men here assert that they are absolutely ignorant as to the means of their own contagion, not having, to their knowledge, been exposed. One of these is a village storekeeper, a healthy, hearty fellow whom we have seen riding about in smart togs on a good horse. He possesses but one spot—on one foot—which to date has neither increased nor diminished. When he discovered the "damned spot," promptly he reported himself to the Board of Health; and here he makes the splendid courageous best of his situation.

No cure of leprosy has ever been discovered. But occasionally some patient is found upon bacteriological examination to have no leprosy in him—never having had leprosy. Such are discharged from the Settlement. And nine times out of ten, they do not want to go, and will practice any innocent fraud to retain residence in the place that has become a congenial home.

In some ways the inhabitants of this peninsula are the happiest in the world. Food and shelter are automatic; pocket-money may be earned. Several private individuals conduct stores. The helpers, kokuas, are in the main lepers, and earn their salaries. The Board of Health carries on agriculture, dairying, stock-raising, and the members of the colony are paid for their labor, and themselves own many heads of cattle and horses which run pasture-free over some 5000 acres. The men possess their fishing boats and launches, and sell fish to the Board of Health for Settlement consumption. Sometimes a catch of 4000 pounds is made in a night. It is not an unhappy community—quite the reverse. And their religions are not interfered with, which is amply shown by the six different churches that flourish here. Also there is a Young Men's Christian Association.

Long we rested on the Goodhue lanai to-night, and long the shadowy leper orchestra serenaded beyond the hibiscus hedges, while some one recalled a story of Charles Warren Stoddard's "Joe of Lahaina," in which a Hawaiian boy, bright companion of other days, crept to the gateway in the dusk, and there from the dust called to his old friend. Forever separated, they talked of old times when they had walked arm in arm, and arms about shoulders, in Sweet Lahaina.

KALAUPAPA, Thursday, July 4, 1907.

This morning we were shocked from dreams by noises so strange as to make us wonder if we were not struggling in nightmare—unearthly cackling mirth and guttural shoutings and half-animal cries that hurried us into kimonos and sandals to join our household at the gate where they were watching a scene as weird as the ghastly din. Only a little after five o'clock, the atmosphere was fittingly vague, and overhead we heard the rasping cry of a bosun bird, *puae*. In the eery whispering dawn there gamboled a score or so "horribles," men and women already horrible enough, God wot, and but thinly disguised in all manner of extravagant costumings. They wore masks of home manufacture, in which the makers had unwittingly imitated the lamentable grotesquerie of the accustomed features of their companions—the lopping mouth, knobby or almost effaced noses, flapping ears; while, equally correct in similitude, the hue of these false-true visages was invariably an unpleasant, pestilent yellow. Great heaven!—do our normal countenances appear abnormal to them?

Some of the actors in this serio-comic performance were astride cavorting horses, some on foot; and one, an agile clown in spots and frills, seemed neither afoot nor horseback, in a way of speaking, for he traveled in company with a trained donkey that lay down peaceably whenever it was mounted. One motley harlequin, whose ghostly white mask did not conceal a huge bulbous ear, exhibited with dramatic gesture and native elocution a dancing bear personified by a man in a brown shag to represent fur.

And all the while the crowd kept up a running fire of jokes and mimicry that showed no mean originality and talent.

In the silvering light across the dewy hemisphere a cavalcade of pa'u riders took shape, coming on larger and larger with a soft thunder of thudding hoofs, wild draperies straight out behind in the speeding rush, and drawing up with a flourish, horses on haunches, before the Superintendent's house. The vivid hues of the long skirts began to grow in the increasing daylight—some of them scarlet, some blue, or orange, while one proud equestrienne sued for favor with a flaunting panoply of Fourth of July red, white, and blue.

Many of the girls were mercifully still comely, even pretty, and rode superbly, handling their curvetting steeds with reckless grace and ease, and I could hear Jack's kodak, the same that he used in the Japanese-Russian War three years ago, clicking repeatedly despite the early hour.

All forenoon these gala-colored horsewomen trooped singing and calling over the rises and hollows of the countryside, to incessant blaring of the bands of both villages combined. The whole was a picture of old Hawaii not to be found elsewhere in the Territory, and certainly nowhere else in the world. For no set reproduction of the bygone customs could equal this whole-souled exhibition, costumed from simple materials by older women who remembered days of the past, carried out in the natural order of life in one of the most beautiful spots in the Islands, if not on the globe. No description can depict the sight that was ours the forenoon long. Jack was wordless so far as concerned his work, and gave up to the enjoyment of the experience.

To our distress, we were appointed, along with Mrs. Myers, to award prizes at the race track. We feared "getting in wrong," as Jack put it, by injudicious choices among the contestants, with whom we wanted to leave a fair impression. But Jack McVeigh pooh-poohed our diffidence, and insisted that we serve on the committee. Horseback we went to the races, and found the track like any other, with its grand stand, its judges, its betting and bickering—the betting running as high as $150—its well-bred horses, and wild excitement when the jockeys came under the wire.

Jack tied his fractious pony, and I saw him on foot over by the judges' stand, waving arms and cowboy hat and yelling himself hoarse, just as crazy as the crowd of lepers he jostled, who were as crazy as he. I knew he was having the time of his life, close to life as it is lived on Molokai oversea. Later, he was conversing soberly with a Norwegian and his wife, both patients, who told us we had no idea what it meant to them all for us to come here and mingle among them as friends, and that people were very happy about it. This was sweet tidings, for the lepers are so little forward in manners that invariably we must accost them first, whereupon they break into the smiling Aloha of their land.

Between heats, there were footraces, and screaming sack races, and races to the slowest, in which Jack McVeigh figured on the rump of a balking donkey, and won; then followed a wahine contest of speed, and a wahine horse race.

But the most imposing event of the afternoon, as of the morning, was enacted by the pa'u riders, who paced leisurely in stately procession once around the course, then circled once in a swinging canter, and, finally, with mad whoopings, broke into a headlong stampede that swept twice and a half around before the Amazons could win control of their excited animals. A truly gorgeous spectacle it was, the flying horses with their streaming beribboned tails, the glowing riders, long

(1) Princess Likelike (Mrs. Cleghorn).   (2) Princess Victoria Kaiulani.
(3) Kaiulani at Ainahau. (4) "Kaiulani's Banyan."

curling hair outblown, and floating draperies painting the track with brilliant color—all mortal decay a thing forgot of actors and onlookers alike, in one grand frolic of bounding vitality and youth.

"Can you beat it! Can you beat it!" Jack panted ecstatically.

The three prizes were for $5, $3, and $2, and it would not be guessing widely to say that they came out of the private pocket of McVeigh, along with numerous other gifts during the day. He is not the man to go about with his heart's good intentions pinned on his sleeve—indeed, a supersensitive character would be out of place as manager of such an institution; but hand in hand with iron will and executive ability, he carries a heart as big as the charge he keeps, and a keen gray eye quick to the needs of his children, as he calls them.

The three beaming winners galloped abreast once around the track, and then rode out; but suddenly the buxom wahine, bright and bold of eye and irresistible of smile, who had taken second, wheeled about and came to attention before the judges' stand with the request, to our great surprise, that I ride once around with her. "Oh, do, do!" Jack under his breath instantly prompted, fearing I might hesitate to make myself so conspicuous. Of course I mounted forthwith, and together we pranced the circuit, to deafening cheers from hundreds of throats.

But I was not riding with a leper, as we had thought, for it turned out that this inviting girl is a kokua, an assistant at the surgery, from whom the bid to ride with her was in the best Kalaupapa social usage.

The Superintendent's big dinner was a signal triumph, and he handled the mixed company with rare tact, several factions being represented. But even the grave and gentle Bishop Liebert and the Fathers warmed to his kindly and ready humor, and soon all were under the spell of Kalama's perfumed garlands and the really sumptuous feast that Masa and her husband, aided by the ladies, had prepared. Jack and I were in still raptures over Mrs. Goodhue, whose sparkling beauty, crowned with a scarlet carnation lei, was something to gladden the heart.

Following several merry toasts, Mr. McVeigh rose and raised his glass to "The Londons—Jack and Charmian, God bless them!" And went on to confess to a warm regard that touched us deeply. For he has given us his confidence during the past day or two in a way that has mightily pleased us. At the end of the little speech, breaking into his engaging smile of eyes and lips, he announced that he knew all present would wish us well upon our departure, which was approaching all too soon, etc., etc., and which would be via the pali trail; and that Mrs. London should ride the best horse on Molokai—his mule Makaha!

By the time we arrived at Beretania Hall for the evening entertainment, it was crammed to suffocation with a joyful crowd of lepers, orchestra in place, resting on their violins, banjos, guitars and ukuleles. After they had opened with Star-Spangled Banner and several Hawaiian selections, a willowy young woman, graceful as a nymph but with face as horrible as her body was lovely, rendered a popular lightsome song in tones that had lost all semblance to music. Half-caste she is, traveled and cultured, once a beauty in Honolulu, whose native mother's bank account is in seven figures. And this girl, in the blossom-time of life, with death overtaking in long strides, bereft of comeliness, awful to behold, and having known the best that life has to bestow, rises superior to life and death, and, foremost in courage, surpasses the gayest of her sisters in misfortune. What material for a Victor Hugo!

At the end of an hour, we left the fantastic company dancing as lustily as it had sung and laughed and ridden the gladsome day through. No one, listening outside to the unrestrained merrymaking, could have guessed the band of abbreviated human wrecks, their distorted shadows monstrous in the flickering lamplight, performing, unconcernedly for once, their Dance of Death.

KALAUPAPA, Friday, July 5, 1907.

Let none say that great men, capable of noble martyrdom, have ceased from the earth in this day and age. And Dr. William J. G. Goodhue, with his exceeding modesty, would be the first to protest any association of his pleasant name with such holy company. But no outsider, entering upon the scene of his wonderful and precarious operations in tissue and bone diseased with the mysterious curse of the ages, could doubt that he had come face to face with one who spares himself not from peril of worse than sudden death.

Ungloved, his sole protection vested in caution against abrading his skin, and an antiseptic washing before and after his work, the man of empirical science waded elbow-deep into the unclean menace upon the operating table. He was assisted by two women nurses, one Hawaiian, one Portuguese, and both with a slight touch of anaesthetic leprosy.

The first subject to-day was a middle-aged wahine, jolly and rolling fat, who was borne in laughing and borne out laughing again. In between were but a few self-pitying moans when she raised her head to watch the doctor. We had every proof that she knew no pain, nor even discomfort; but the sight of copiously flowing blood caused her to weep and wail "Auwe!" until one of the nurses said something that made her laugh in spite of herself. The sole of her foot had thickened two inches, and she had not stepped upon it for a couple of years. Into this dulled pad, lengthwise, the cool surgeon cut clean to the diseased bone, which he painstakingly scraped, explaining that the blood itself remains pure, only the tissues and bone being attacked by the *bacillus lepra*.

But the second patient, a good-looking lad who came on the *Noeau* with us, was victim of a terrible case of the most loathsome and agonizing sort, which made it necessary to anaesthetize him—Dr. Hollman using the slow and safe "A. C. E." (Alcohol, one part; Chloroform, two parts; Ether, three parts). The only visible spot was a running sore forward of and below the left shoulder; but what appeared on the surface was nothing to that which the knife divulged.

Although the details are not pretty, and I shall not harrow with more of them, I wish I could picture the calm, pale surgeon, with his intensely dark-blue eyes and the profile of Ralph Waldo Emerson, whose kinsman he is, working with master strokes that cleansed the deep cavity of corruption; for it was an illustration of the finest art of which the human is capable.

And now this boy may possibly be quite healthy for the rest of a natural life, and die of some other malady or of old age. Again, the bacillus at any time may resume its destructive inroads elsewhere in his system. There are myriad unknown quantities about leprosy. All Dr. Goodhue, with his sad and charming smile, can say about it with finality, is:

"The more I study and learn about leprosy, the less assurance I have in saying that I know anything about it!"

By this evening all troubadour spirit was quenched, and no minstrelsy greeted our postprandial lolling on the lanai. No voice above a night-bird's disturbed the quiet of tired Kalaupapa. And we also were weary, for seeing the operations, although not our first, claimed a certain measure of nervous energy; besides, we had ridden hard to another rugged valley in the late afternoon, goat-hunting on the crags, and were ready for early bed. In passing, I must not forget to relate that we were shown some black-and-white-striped mosquitoes up-valley, the proper carriers of yellow fever—though Heaven forbid that they ever have a chance to carry it!

Mr. and Mrs. Myers, those delightful souls, to-day ascended the baking pali on foot, to prepare for our coming on the morrow, when we shall have accomplished the hair-raising path of the long-forbidden exit from Kalaupapa. Now that permission has been graciously accorded, the witty Jack McVeigh enlarges continually upon the difficulties and dangers of the route.

WAIKIKI, Sunday, July 7, 1907.

At eleven o'clock yesterday, on our diminutive animals, we bade farewell to our friends under the cluster of kukuis where they had accompanied us on the beginning of the ascent, and proceeded to wage the sky-questing, arid pathway, for this section of the pali is almost bare of vegetation. Short stretches as scary we have ridden; it is the length of this climb that tries—angling upon the stark face of a 2300-foot barrier.

They told me, when I bestrode the short strong back of the little mule Makaha, to "stay by her until the summit is reached. She never fails. "Implicitly I obeyed, for the very good reason that I would have been loath to trust my own feet, let alone my head. Never a stumble did her tiny twinkling hoofs make, even where loose stony soil crumbled and fell a thousand feet and more into the sea that wrinkled oilily far below; and the hardy muscle and lungs of her seemed to put forth no unusual effort. But Jack and the Hawaiian mail carrier, who led the way, were obliged several times to dismount where the insecure vantage was too much for the quivering, dripping ponies, although they are accustomed to the work. Once, from the repairing above, some rubble fell, fortunately curving clear. Makaha, who has a few rudimentary nerves of her own, shied, but instantly recovered, only to shy again at a bag of tools by the trailside.

Sometimes an angle was so acute that our beasts were forced to swing on hind legs to reach the upper zigzag, where poised front hoofs must grip into sliding stones or feel for hold amidst large, fixed rocks, and the rider lay himself on the horse's neck. A miss meant something less than a half mile of catapultic descent through blue space into the blue ocean. Once Jack glimpsed destruction from the guide's horse that slipped and scrambled and almost went off the zigzag immediately overhead. I, at a turn below, saw the peril to Jack, and knew my first real anxiety. But the gray pony regained his feet amid flying gravel. There were places where it seemed incredible that anything less agile than a goat could stick.

"Gee! I don't wonder McVeigh won't let malihinis go out this way," Jack called down, craning his neck to see the base of the sea-washed rampart, and failing. "It is worse than its reputation!"

The Settlement lay stretched in the noonday sun, like the green map of a peninsula in a turquoise sea. And we amused ourselves, while resting the animals, picking out landmarks familiar to us.

"There's McVeigh's house, and the Doctor's, where you see that bunch of trees," Jack pointed, "and I'll bet he's following us every inch with that telescope of his. Let's wave our arms for luck."

A short distance from the summit we joined the rebuilt portion of the trail, and passed the time of day with the stolid Japanese laborers and their bright-eyed foreman. Six feet wide, some parts railed, to our pinched vision it appeared a spacious boulevard. Our sensations, now speedily at the top and looking over, must have been something like those of Jack of Beanstalk fame when he found a verdant level plain at the end of his clambering. Here was a prairie of green hillocks browsed by fat cattle, and threaded by a red road. A roomy family carriage waited, driven by a stalwart son of the Myers', and we parted from the guide, patting our little beasts before he led them back to the "falling-off place." A mule of parts, that canny small Makaha. I shall not see her like again.

The restful drive of a couple of miles through rich pasture land dotted with guava shrub brought us to the home of the Myers family, in the midst of a 60,000-acre ranch. There are no hotel facilities whatever on Molokai, which is forty miles long by ten in breadth, and the visitor without friends and friends of friends on the island will see little unless equipped for camping. The climate in these islands is mild and cool, the hills and ruggeder mountains interspersed with meadows, where spotted Japanese deer have become so numerous that shooting them is a favor to the ranchers. Kalama, that fine all-round sport, had begged us to come sometime and go with her for a week's hunting.

High Molokai should be a paradise for sportsmen, and it is surprising the Territory does not get together with the owners and try to develop facilities at Kaunakakai for housing, and transportation into the back country, which is surpassingly beautiful and interesting. Somewhere on the coast there is an old battlefield where countless human bones still whiten; and on the rocky coast to the south can be seen in shallow water the ruins of miles of ancient fish ponds equaled nowhere in the group. On the northwest one glimpses Oahu, cloud-capped and shimmering in the blue, while Haleakala bulks ten thousand feet in air on Maui to the east.

This ranch home is buried in flowers, and my unbelief in begonias a dozen feet high underwent rude check. A fairy forest of them surrounds the guest cottage, casting a rosy shadow on window and lanai. I should have been content to remain here indefinitely. Little Miss Mabel, sweet sixteen, entertained us charmingly, and during luncheon, served by a butterfly maid of Japan, the telephone jingled, and Kalama down in Kalaupapa was telling us to be sure to swim in the cement irrigation reservoir before starting for the hot drive to the steamer. Which we did, and many thanks.

On the ten-mile rolling descent to the port, Kaunanakai, there was ample chance to observe this side of the supposedly melancholy isle, and Jack, noticing dry creeks and the general thirsty appearance of the lower foothills, descanted upon its rich future when irrigation schemes are worked out and applied. As it is now, only in the rainy season do the streams flow.

Dashing native cowboys, bound for a wedding luau, passed us on the road, teeth and eyes flashing, gay neckerchiefs about their singing brown throats, and hat-brims blown back from their vivid faces, out-Westing the West.

Kaunanakai itself is not especially attractive, and during two hours' waiting for the *Iwilani*, we occupied ourselves keeping as comfortable as possible, for July is hot on the leeward sides of the "Sandwich Islands."

Once aboard, and our luggage, taken on at Kalaupapa, safely located, we watched the loading of freight and live-stock on the little steamer. Between the deep rolling of the ship and the din and odor of seasick swine for'ard, there was little rest the night. And the Steamship Company has a very unceremonious way of dumping its passengers ashore in Honolulu at the most heathenish hours. The car lines had not yet started when we stood yawning and chill beside our bags and saddles on the wharf, and Jack was obliged to wake a hackman to drive us to Waikiki. The city lay dead but for an occasional milk-wagon, and after all we did not grudge ourselves the dawning loveliness of the morning—an unearthly gray-silver luminance wherein a large lemon-tinted moon melted in a pale lilac sky. It was like a miracle, this swift awakening of the growing earth. Birds stretched into song, the water-taro rustled in a fitful wind, young ducks stirred and fluffed their night-damp feathers on the edges of the ponds, where lilies opened to the brightening waves of light, while the broken slaty mountains in the background shifted their graying curtains of shimmering rain. Diamond Head developed slowly into the scene, like a photographed mountain in a dark-room, and took opalescent shades of dove and rose. Creation might have been like this! And we recalled Mascagni's "Iris," for it seemed as if all living things burgeoned visibly on the warm awakening earth.

Tochigi had to be roused at the brown tent, and despite drowsiness Jack plunged into an accumulation of mail and other work before breakfast. "We have to work hard for our outings, don't we, Mate Woman?" he called to me, his smile broadening into a yawn. "But it makes us appreciate them the more!"

And all through the busy morning hours, and the surf-boarding and swimming and romping of the afternoon, of all the remarkable impressions of that astounding week on Molokai, the pali endured. Again and again we seem to cling to the impossible face of it, creeping foot by foot, alert, tense, unafraid except for each other . . . . [1]

WAIKIKI, Thursday, July 11, 1907.

In a fine frenzy to give a just presentation of the Leper Settlement, Jack has lost no time finishing the promised article, "The Lepers of Molokai."

In it he gives a picture of himself having a "disgracefully good time," yelling at the track-side with the lepers when the horses came under the wire, and presently branches off into a serious consideration of the situation, interspersed with bright items of life in the Settlement. The article is highly approved by Mr. Pinkham, and Mr. Thurston avers it is the best and fairest that has ever been written. Jack is modestly elated, because he has succeeded in pleasing both these men who happen to be far from friendly in the general affairs of the Territory. And, best of everything, to Jack, in all honest enthusiasm he has pleased himself.

Although the President of the Board of Health is entirely satisfied with himself and with the article, as well as with Jack's press interviews regarding the trip, several prominent citizens have expressed themselves to the official as highly indignant that we should have been allowed in the Settlement. But the imperturbable Pinkham has told

[1] A few weeks after our ascent, one of the Japanese laborers fell 1500 feet in the clear.

them with asperity that it does not profit them or Hawaii to imitate ostriches and simulate obliviousness of the fact that the world knows of leprosy in Hawaii. And why should Hawaii be supersensitive? Leprosy is not unknown in the large cities even of America; and Hawaii should be proud to advertise her magnificent system of segregation, unequaled anywhere in the world, and be glad to have it exploited by men of conscience and intelligence.

WAILUKU, MAUI, Sunday, July 14, 1907.

Two evenings gone, in company with Mr. and Mrs. Thurston, we boarded the *Claudine*, which, though much larger than the *Noeau*, pitched disgustingly in the head-sea of Kaiwi Channel, and took more than spray over the upper deck for'ard where were our staterooms. Jack and I fell unexpectedly sick, and our friends likewise, although not unexpectedly. Lorrin Thurston has traversed these channels since boyhood, and never does he cease from acute suffering during frequent crossings.

A swarm of Japanese sailed steerage and outside on the lower deck, each bearing a matted bundle exactly like his neighbor's, the women carrying their possessions wrapped in gorgeously printed challies in which a stunning orange was most conspicuous among vivid blues and greens and intermediate purples. Early in the trip all were laid low in everything but clamor, and from our deck we could see the poor things in every stage of disheartened deshabille, pretty matron and maiden alike careless of elaborate chignon falling awry, the men quite chivalrously trying to ease their women's misery in the pauses of their own.

Kahului, our destination, is on the northern shore of the isthmus connecting West Maui with the greater Haleakala section of this practically double island; but Mr. Thurston's emotions were of such intensity that around midnight he crept weakly to our latticed door and suggested we disembark at Lahaina, the first port, finish the night at the hotel, and in the morning drive around the Peninsula of West Maui to Wailuku.

Nothing loath to escape the roughest part of the passage, doubling that disturbing headland, we dressed and gathered our hand-luggage; and at half past one in the morning dropped over the *Claudine's* swaying black side. As we clung in the chubby, chopping boat, manned by natives with long oars, dimly we could make out dark towering heights against the starry sky, and on either side heard the near breakers swish and hiss warningly upon the coral. And all about, near and far, burned the slanting flares of fishermen, the flames touching the black water with elongated dancing sparkles. Voices floated after, from the anchored steamer, and ghostly hoof-beats clattered faint but distinct from the invisible streets of the old, old town. As at Molokai, shadowy hands helped us upon the wharf—and the tender witchery of the night fled before the babble of hackmen, stamping of mosquito-bitten horses, a lost and yelping dachshund pup that insisted on being trod upon, and the huge red-headed hotel proprietor of an unornamental wooden hostelry, its dingy entrance lighted with smoking kerosene lamps.

"Beautiful Lahaina," warbles Isabella Bird Bishop, in her charming book "Hawaii"; "Sleepy Lahaina," she ecstatically trills—and she is not the only writer who has sung the praises of this town of royal preference, once the prosperous capital of the kingdom, and the oldest white settlement, where touched the whaling ships that sometimes anchored fifty strong off shore. But this prosperity entailed disease and death, since the adventurous sailors were given free run by their unscrupulous captains. The village dwindled to less than a wraith of its former opulence, much of the original site now being planted to cane. A little distance above, the old Lahainalua Seminary, founded in 1831, still flourishes, maintaining its reputation as an excellent industrial school. At the start the scholars supported themselves by cultivating land granted by the chiefs to the school, and were obliged to build the schoolhouse and their own lodgings. Later on a printing press and book bindery were established, and the institution did much of the printing of text books in use. The very first Hawaiian sheet, *Lama Hawaii*, was published here, preceding the *Kumu Hawaii*, at Honolulu.

And the reader of Isabella Bird yearns for Lahaina above all bournes; he cannot wait to test for himself Lahaina's spell of loveliness and repose. But this repose must belong to the broad day, or else the gallant lady's mosquito net was longer than ours, which cruelly refused to make connection with the coverlet. Jack's priceless perorations will ever be lost to posterity, for I shall repeat them not.

In the morning, Mrs. Thurston peeped laughingly in and asked if I knew my husband's whereabouts; and I, waking solitary, confessed that I did not, although I seemed to recall his desertion in a blue cloud of vituperation against all red-headed hotel hosts and stinging pests. Mrs. Thurston, viewing the blushing morn from the second-story veranda, had come upon the weary boy fast asleep on the hard boards, blanket over head and feet exposed, and led me to where he lay. But none more vigorously famished than he, when we sat in an open-air breakfast-room, table spread with land fruit and sea fruit; for Mr. Thurston had been abroad early to make sure the repast should be an ideal one after our hard night—fish from the torchlight anglers, alligator pears dead-ripe out of the garden, and the famous luscious mangoes of Lahaina, the best in the Islands.

"And me for the good coffee!" Jack appreciated, for he suspicioned that the quiet but efficient man had been also in the kitchen, and he loves his coffee when it is coffee. Rather reticent upon first acquaintance, Mr. and Mrs. Thurston have blossomed into the most cordial and witty of comrades, ready for anything.

Mrs. Bishop, in the seventies, spoke of Lahaina as "an oasis in a dazzling desert." The dazzling desert has been made to produce the cane for two great sugar mills whose plantations spread their green over everything in sight to the feet of the sudden mountains rent by terrific chasms rising 6000 feet behind the village. Once this was a missionary center as well as the regular port of call for the devastating whale ships. The deserted missionary house, fallen into decay these long years, is still landmark of a Lahaina that but few live to remember.

The streets of the drowsy town are thickly shaded by coconuts, breadfruit with its glossy truncated leaves and green globes, monkey-pod, kukui, bananas, and avocados; and before we bade farewell to Lahaina, Mr. Thurston drew up beside an enormous mango tree, benefactor of his boyhood, where an obliging Hawaiian policeman, in whose garden it grows, with his pretty wife threw rocks to bring down a lapful of the ripe fruit—deep yellow, with crimson cheeks, a variety known as the "chutney" mango.

It is some twenty-three scenic miles from Lahaina to Wailuku, and the road runs for a distance through tall sugar cane, then begins an easy ascent to where it is cut into the sides of steep and barren volcanic hills above the sea. There was a glorious surf running, and for miles we could gaze almost straight down to the water, in some places catching glimpses of shoals of black fish in the blue brine where there was no beach and deep ocean washed the feet of the cliffs.

Jack has blue-penciled my description of the capital luncheon arranged in advance by Mr. Thurston, holding that although I write best on the subject of food, my readers may become bored. So I shall pass on to Iao Valley (E-ah-o—quickly E-ow) where we drove in the afternoon, following the Wailuku River several miles to the valley mouth.

Iao has been pronounced by travelers quite as wonderful in its way as Yosemite. I should not think of comparing the two, because of their wide difference. The walls of Iao are as high, but appear higher, since the floor, if floor it can be called, is much narrower. Most gulches in Hawaii draw together from a wide entrance; but in Iao this is reversed, for, once the narrow ascending ingress is passed, the straight walls open like the covers of a book which Doré might have illustrated, the valley widening into an amphitheater of unsurpassable grandeur. On the ferned and mossed walls of the entrance hang festoons of deep-trumpeted, blue convolvulae between slender dracena palms and far-reaching branches of silvery kukuis, quivering or softly swaying in passing airs.

It is ridiculous to try to give any impression of the prodigious palisades, with their springing bastions, the needled peaks, shimmering tropical growth of tree and vine, bursting, sounding falls of watercourses rushing headlong over mighty bowlders, the swift-rolling glory of clouds, casting showers of gold upon joyous green pinnacles or with deep violet shadow turning these into awful fingers pointing to the zenith; nor can one fitly characterize the climate—the zephyrs warm and the wind-puffs cool that poured over us where we lay on a table-land, reached by trail through a sylvan jungle of ferns, in matted grass so deep and dense that we never felt the solid earth.

Long we rested and marveled, surrounded by impregnable fastnesses, speaking little, in an ecstasy at this superlatively grand and beautiful cleft, at its head, lord of all lesser peaks and spires and domes, Puu Kukui springing nearly 6000 feet into the torn sky. There are other valleys back of Puu Kukui, as beautiful as Iao, but more difficult of access. It is said by the few who have ascended, that the view from the top of Puu Kukui is away and beyond anything they have ever seen.

There is but one way out of Iao, as usual in these monster gulches of Hawaii, and that is the way in. Old warriors learned this to their rue, caught by Kamehameha in the sanguinary battle that completed his conquest of Maui, when their blood stained the waters of the stream as it flowed seaward, which henceforth bore the name of Wailuku, "Red Water."

From our high vantage, looking seaward, down past the interlacing bases of emerald steeps eroded by falling waters of aeons, the vision included the plains country beneath, all rose and yellow and green with cultivated abundance, bordered at the sea-rim by white lines of surf inside bays and out around jutting points and promontories, the sapphire deep beyond, and upon the utmost indigo horizon pillowy trade clouds low-lying—all the splendor softened into tremulous, glowing mystic fairyland. "Hawaii herself, in all the buxom beauty, roving industry . . . with all the bravery and grace of her natural scenery."

One pursues one's being in Hawaii within an incessant atmosphere of wonder and expectation—ah, I have seen Yosemite, the Grand Canyon, the Alps, the Swiss lakes; but Hawaii is different, partaking of these, and still different, and more elusively wonderful. Even now, as I write of what our eyes have gloried in, they behold mighty roofless Haleakala, ancient House of the Sun, its ragged battlements piercing two miles into the ether, above the cloud-banners of sunset.

HALEAKALA RANCH, MAUI, Monday, July 15, 1907.

Believe except one be deaf, dumb, and blind, there is no boredom in these Islands. Indeed, one must avoid bewilderment among the myriad attractions that fill the days to overflowing. Little opportunity was ours to become acquainted with the old town of Wailuku, with its picturesque population of natives and immigrants, for yesterday's program included a private-car trip over the Hawaii Commercial and Kihei Sugar Companies' vast plantations. We were the guests of Mr. J. N. S. Williams, superintendent of the Kahului Railroad Company, who entertained us at Kahului, where we went aboard the car. There was a bustling air of activity and newness about the port town—track-laying, boat-loading, house-building; and in the harbor swung at anchor a big freighter of the American-Hawaiian Line, unloading on lighters and receiving sugar by the same means.

Waving fields of cane occupy practically all the lowland between the two sections of Maui, spreading into the slopes of Haleakala's foothills and extending well around to the "windward" side of the island. The trip included a visit to one of the mills and a descent some four hundred feet into the shaft of Kihei's pumping station, where we were conducted by a young football giant from Chicago, Paul Bell, who was regretting that his work would prevent him from accepting an invitation to accompany our party through the crater.

At the village of Paia, with its streetful of alluring Japanese shops, we transferred to carriages for an eight-mile drive to this stock ranch

2000 feet up Haleakala. Seen from afar, the mountain appears simple enough in conformation, smooth and gradual in rise. At closer range the rise is gradual, to be sure, but varied by ravines that are valleys, and by level pastures, and broken by ancient blow-holes and hillocks that are miniature mountains as symmetrical as Fujiyama. It is almost disappointing—one has a right to expect more spectacular perpendicularity of a 10,000-foot mountain. Even now, from where we sit on a shelf of lawn, under a tree with a playhouse in its boughs, it is impossible to realize that the summit, free for once of cloud, is still 8000 feet above, so lazily it leans back. And looking downward, never have our eyes taken in so much of the world from any single point.

Louis von Tempsky, English-Polish, son of the last British officer killed in the Maori War, handsome, wiry, military of bearing and discipline, is manager of this ranch of sixty thousand-odd acres. He came to Hawaii years ago on a vacation from his New Zealand bank cashiership, and he never went back—"Shanghaied," says Jack. One cannot blame the man. Here he is able to live to the full the life he loves, with those he loves—the big free life of saddle and boundless miles, with his own fireside (and one needs a fireside up here of an evening) at the end of the day. His wife, Amy, was born in Queen Emma's house in Honolulu, of English parentage. Her father, Major J. H. Wodehouse, was appointed English Minister to Hawaii about three years before annexation to the United States took place, and now, home in England, is retired upon a pension.

And such a family they are—the beautiful home-queen of a mother with the handsome father of their sturdy brood, two daughters in their early teens, who are boys in the saddle and cowboys at that; and a small maid of four, Lorna, who rides her own pony. And lastly, a small precious son who is not quite old enough to cross a saddletree.

The climate is much like California's in the mountains, and very refreshing after the sea-level midsummer heat. This bracing air makes one feel younger by years. Life here is ideal—a rambling old house, with a drawing-room that is half lanai, hung with good pictures, furnished with a good library and piano, and fine-matted couches deep in cushions; a cozy dining-room where one comes dressed for dinner, and a commodious guest-wing where Jack and I have two rooms and bath, and he can work in comfort.

The lawn is in a two-sided, sheltered court, intersected with red-brick walks, and lilies grow everywhere. From our books on the lawn beside a little fountain under tall trees where birds sing and twitter, we rise and step past the lilies to the edge of the garden, where the world falls sloping from our feet to the ocean. Standing as if in a green pavilion, we seem detached from the universe while viewing it. Terrace upon terrace of hills we see, champaigns of green speckled with little rosy craters like buds turned up to sun and shower; and off in the blue vault of sea and sky, other islands, dim and palpitating like mirages. One hears that Maui, the second largest island, contains 728 square miles and that it is 10,000 feet high; but what are figured confines when apparently the whole world of land and sea is spread before one's eyes on every hand! Hand in hand, we look, and look, and try to grasp the far-flung magnitude, feeling very small in its midst. "Beautiful's no name for it," breathes Jack; and through my mind runs a verse of Mrs. Browning's, a favorite of my childhood at Auntie's knee:

> "We walk hand in hand in the pure golden ether,
>   And the lilies look large as the trees;
>   And as loud as the birds sing the bloom-loving bees—
> And the birds sing like angels, so mystical-fine,
>   While the cedars are brushing the Archangel's feet.
> And Life is eternity, Love is divine,
>   And the world is complete."

This morning early we were out looking over our mounts and seeing that our saddles, brought from home, were in good shape. "I love the old gear!" Jack said, caressing the leather, well worn on many a journey these two years. A cattle-drive and branding, with colt-breaking to follow, were the business of the day. At ten we galloped away from the corrals, and Jack and I went right into the work with Mr. Von Tempsky and his girls, Armine and Gwendolen, and the native cowboys, to round up the cattle. Oddly enough, although born and raised in the West, we two have sailed over two thousand miles to experience our first *rodeo*.

To my secret chagrin, I was doomed to be tried out upon an ambitionless mare, albeit Louisa is well-gaited and good to the eye. But I dislike to spur another person's animal, so took occasion to look very rueful when my host, coming alongside, inquired: "Are you having a good time?" He could see that I was not, and sensed why; so he advised me not to spare the spur, adding: "There isn't a better cattle pony, when she knows you mean business!"

And oh, these "kanaka" horses, with their sure feet! And oh, the wild rushes across grassland that has no pit-falls—gophers are un-

known,—thudding over the dust-less, springing turf, hurdling the
higher growth, whirling "on a cowskin" to cut off stray or willful
steers, and making headlong runs after the racing herd. All the while,
with Armine and Gwendolen, taking commands from General Daddy,
and sitting tight our eager horses, fairly streaking the landscape in
ordered flight to head off the runaways, the young girls with hair flying, sombreros down backs, cheeks glowing, eyes sparkling, utterly
devoted to the work in hand—striving their best for ultimate praise
from Daddy.

Miles we covered, doubling back and forth, searching out and driving the bellowing kine; up and down steep ravines we chased them,
along narrow soft-sliding trails on stiff inclines, turning to pathless
footing to keep them going in the right direction. And the farther
afield we rode, the farther stretched the limitless reaches of that de-
ceiving mountain.

At last the herds were converged toward a large gate not far from
the outlying corrals, and after a lively tussle we rounded up all but
one recalcitrant—a quarter-grown, black-and-white calf that outran a
dozen of us for half an hour before we got him.

Promptly followed the segregation of those to be marked; the
throwing of calves in the dusty corral, and their wild blatting when
the cowboys trapped them, neck and thigh, with the lasso; the restless
circling of the penned beasts waiting their turns; the trained horses
standing braced against lariats thrown from their backs into the seething mass; the rising, pungent smoke of burning hair and hide as the
branding irons bit; then the frantic scrambling of the released ones to
lose themselves in the herd.

Together with several neighbors who had ridden over, we sat fence-
high on a little platform overlooking the strenuous scene, and when
the branding was finished, the colt-breaking began, in which the Von
Tempsky children took the most intense interest, as did we. Their father superintended his efficient force of native trainers in their work
of handling three-year-old colts that had never known human touch
nor feel of rope, which made a Buffalo Bill show seem tame indeed.
For breathless hours we watched the making of docile saddlers, all being finally subdued but one, which threatened to prove an "outlaw."
After the "buck" has been taken out of the young things, they are tied
up all night to the corral fence, and in the morning are expected to be
tractable, with all tendency to pull back knocked out of them forever.

"And some are sulky, while some will plunge,
(So ho! Steady! Stand still, you!)
Some you must gentle, and some you must lunge,
(There! There! Who wants to kill you!)
Some—there are losses in every trade—
Will break their hearts ere bitted and made;
Will fight like fiends as the rope cuts hard,
And die dumb-mad in the breaking-yard."

UKULELE, ON HALEAKALA, Tuesday, July 16, 1907.

Thirteen strong, we rode out from the ranch house this morning, on the second phase of our week's trip in the crater and on around through the Nahiku "Ditch" country. Besides the cowboys, gladsome brown fellows, overjoyed to go along, there were seven in the party, with a goodly string of pack animals tailing out behind. And bless my soul! if there wasn't Louisa, meekly plodding under a burden of tent-poles and other gear. For Mr. Von Tempsky had now allotted me his own Welshman, "the best horse on the mountain," he declared.

Fifty-four hundred feet above sea level, our initial stop was here at Ukulele, the dairy headquarters of the ranch. Why Ukulele, we are at loss to know, for nothing about the place suggests that diminutive medium of harmony. However, there is a less romantic connotation, for the definition of ukulele is literally "jumping flea." But, as Jack says, "Let us hope the place was called after the instrument!"

The ascent we found steeper than below the ranch house, but it worked no hardship on horse or rider. We were in good season to "rustle" supper, and went berrying for dessert. Of course, there had to be a berry-fight between Jack and the two husky girls, who soon became weird and sanguinary objects, plastered from crown to heel with the large juicy *akalas*, which resemble our loganberries. Jack asserts that they are larger than hens' eggs; but lacking convenient eggs, there is no proving him in error. Nothing does him more good than a wholehearted romp with young people, and Armine and Gwen were a match that commanded his wary respect. "I love to have my girls romp with Mr. London," once I heard a mother say. "He is like a clean-minded, wholesome boy, and never too rough."

After supper, we reclined upon a breezy point during a lingering sunset over the wide, receding earth, lifted high above the little affairs of men, and, still high above, the equally receding summit. We felt light, inconsequential, as if we had no place, no weight, no reality—motes poised on a sliver of rock between two tremendous realities.

Louis von Tempsky, resting his lithe, strong frame for once, recounted old legends concerning the House of the Sun, and the naming thereof, and the fierce warfare that is ever going on about its walls, between the legions of Ukiukiu and Naulu, the Northeast Trade and the Leeward Wind; and until we were driven indoors by the chill, we lay observing the breezy struggle beneath among opposing masses of driven clouds.

And now, after a game of whist between Jack and Mrs. Thurston on the one side, and Messrs. Thurston and Von on the other, we are going to rest upon our *hikie* (hik-e-a), the same being a contrivance of hard boards, some seven feet square, covered with lauhala mats and quilts made to measure.

PALIKU, CRATER OF HALEAKALA,
Wednesday, July 17, 1907.

And it's ho! for the crater's rim, to look over into the mysterious Other Side from the tantalizing skyline that promises what no other horizon in all the world can give. Hail, Haleakala! largest extinct crater in existence! It's boots and saddles for the unroofed House of the Sun. What will it be like? ("Nothing you've ever seen or dreamed," this from the Thurstons.) Shall we be disappointed? ("Not if you're alive!" contributes Von Tempsky.) Jack gives me a heaving hand into the saddle, and a kiss by the way, and my Welshman strikes a swinging jog-trot that plays havoc with the *opu*-full—opu being stomach—with which my terrible mountain appetite has been assuaged.

Now rolling grasslands give place to steep and rugged mountain, with sparse vegetation. Here and there, relieving the monotony, gleams a sheaf of silver blades, the "silver-sword," with a red brand of blossoms thrusting from the center; or patches of "silver verbena," a pretty velvet flower that presses well and serves as *edelweiss* for Haleakala. Stopping to breathe the horses, we nibble *ohelo* berries, which look much like cranberries, but have a mealy-apple flavor. There is wild country up here, where sometimes cattle and ranging horses are pulled down by wild dogs; and back in the fastnesses, even mounted cowboys, rounding up the stock, have been attacked.

And somebody is singing all the time. If it is not Mr. Von's tenor, one hears Mr. Thurston's pleasant voice on the breeze, essaying

(1) Landing at Kalaupapa, 1907.   (2) The Forbidden Pali Trail, 1907.
(3) Coast of Molokai—Federal Leprosarium on shore.   (4) Jack in the
Leper Settlement, 1907.   (5) Father Damien's Grave, 1907

a certain climacteric note that eludes his range at the end of "Sweet Lei Lehua." A strong and engaging character is Mr. Thurston, nervous, alert, under his firm-lipped smile; a body quick to steel into action; hair grayed in service to his Islands; keen black eyes shaded by thoughtful brows, and eyes whose very color frowns at uncleanness or hypocrisy—eyes that reflect and absorb humor at every turn. And there is something imperious in his carriage and backward fling of head, that savors of courts and kings and halls of statesmanship.

Over the sharp, brittle lavas of antiquity our horses, many of them barefooted, their hoofs like onyx, scramble with never a fall on the panting steeps; on and on, up and up, we forge, with a blithe, lifting feel in the thin and thinner air, while the great arc of the horizon seems ever above the eye-level. And then rings a thrilling call from ahead that the next rise will land us on the jagged edge of the hollow mountain. I am about to join the charge of that last lap when a runaway packhorse—none other than Louisa—diverts my attention to the rear. When I turn again, the rest are at the top—all but Jack, who faces me upon his Pontius Pilate, until I come up. "Dear Kid, I wanted to see it with you," he explains, and together we follow to Magnetic Peak—so-called what of its lodestone properties. And then . . .

More than twenty miles around its age-sculptured brim, the titantic rosy bowl lay beneath; seven miles across the incredible hollow our gaze traveled to the glowing mountain-line that bounds the other side, and still above . . . we could not believe our sight that was unprepared for such ravishment of beauty. Surely we beheld very Heaven, the Isles of the Blest, floating above clouds of earth—azure, snow-capped peaks so ineffably high, so ungraspably lovely, that we forgot we had come to see a place of ancient fire, and gazed spellbound, from our puny altitude of ten thousand feet, upon illimitable heights of snow all unrelated to the burned-out thirsty world on which we stood.

It was only Mauna Kea—Mauna Kea and Mauna Loa, on the Big Island of living fire, half again as high as our wind-swept position; but so remote and illusive were they, that our earthborn senses were incapable of realizing that the sublime vision was anything more than a day-dream, and that we looked upon the same lofty island, the highest on earth, that had greeted our eyes from the *Snark*.

"It never palls," Armine whispered solemnly, tears in her forget-me-not-blue eyes. And her father and Mr. Thurston, who had stood here unnumbered times, soberly acquiesced. Jack and I knew, with certitude birthed of the magic moment, that our memory, did we never repeat our journeying, would remain undimmed for all our days.

"But we are coming back some day!" Jack voiced his thought; and then we devoted ourselves to hanging upon the glassy-brittle brink and peering into the crater's unbelievable depths, that are not sheer but slope with an immensity of sweep that cannot be measured by the eye, so deceptive are the red and black inclined planes of volcanic sand.

Pointing to a small ruddy cone in the floor of the crater, Mr. Thurston said: "You would hardly think that that blowhole is higher than Diamond Head, but it is!" And before there was time to gasp and readjust our dazzled senses, he was indicating an apparent few hundred feet of incurving cinder-slope that looked ideal for tobogganing, with the information that it was over a mile in length. A dotted line of hoof prints of some wayward wild goat strung across its red-velvet surface, and presently we were tossing bits of lava over-edge upon unbroken stretches immediately below, to watch the little interrupted trails they traced until the wind should erase them. Only when the men loosened large bowlders into the yawning chasm, and we saw them leaving diminishing puffs of yellow ocher dust as they bounded upon the cinder-sweeps, could we begin to line up the proportions of the immediate crater-side, for whole minutes were consumed, and minutes upon minutes, for those swift stones to pass beyond sight.

"And why," queried Jack, "are we the only ones enjoying this incomparable grandeur? Why aren't there thousands of people climbing over one another to hang all around the rim of 'the greatest extinct crater in the world'? Such a reputation ought to be irresistible. Why, there's nothing on earth so wonderful as this! I should think there wouldn't be ships enough to carry the tourists, if only for Iao and Haleakala. Perhaps Hawaii doesn't want them, or need them . . . . Personally," he laughed, "I'm glad my wife and I are the only tourists making a racket here to-day.—And we're not tourists, thank God!"

Two broad portals there are into the House Built by the Sun, and through them march the warring winds, Ukiukiu and Naulu. In at the northern portal, Ukiukiu drives the trade clouds, mile-wide, like a long line of silent, ghostly breakers, only to have them torn to shreds, as to-day, and dissipated in the warm embrace of the rarefied airs of Naulu. Sometimes Ukiukiu meets with better luck, and fills the castle with cloud-legions; but ours was the luck this day, for the crater was cleared of all but remnants of floating cloud-stuff, and our view was superb.

At last, tearing from the absorbing spectacle, we descended a short way to a stone-walled corral, where the bright-eyed, sweet-mannered cowboys had lunch waiting—a real roughing-it picnic of jerked beef and salt pork, products of the ranch; and hard-poi, called *pai'ai*, thick and sticky, royal pink-lavender poi, in a big sack. Into this we dug our willing fists, bringing them out daubed with the hearty substance. It came to me, blissfully licking the pai'ai from my fingers, that this promiscuous delving for poi into one receptacle that obtains among the natives, and which the real kamaaina hesitates not to emulate, is far from the unfastidious custom it is sure to appear upon first sight. "Why, sure—" Jack caught the idea, "you stick your finger into a thick paste, and the finger is withdrawn coated with it. Ergo, your finger has touched nothing of what remains in the pot—or sack.—Hooray for the Kid-Woman! I salute!"

After lunch we climbed a disgorged litter of bowlders and sharp lava, to inspect the meager crumbling ruins of fortifications built by Kamehameha the Great into the side of the mountain; then, overtopping the dizzy verge, slowly we sank into the ruddy depths, by way of the cinder declivities we had speculated upon from our lofty perch. Closer acquaintance proved them entirely too rough with loose rubble for tobogganing. The horses left sulphurous yellow tracks as they pulled their pasterns out of the bottomless burnt sands, and a golden streamer flew backward from each hoof-fall. So swift was our drop that riders strung out ahead speedily grew very, very small, though distinct, as if seen through the wrong end of a telescope. In the marvelously pure atmosphere each object stood out clean-cut, while an insidious sunburn began to make itself felt on lips and cheeks and noses. Apart from slightly shortened breathing at the summit, we had felt no inconvenience from the elevation.

And so our caravan straggled into the depths of Haleakala, sometimes a horseman galloping springily across a dark cinderslope in a halo of tawny sun-shot dust, then dropping steeply, his mount nearly sitting; while overhead and behind, on the evanescent trail of our making, came the picturesque pack horses and cowboys, and one small patient mule laden with camp comforts. From farthest below rose quaint reiterative chants of hulas, as Louis von Tempsky rode and sang, loose in the saddle, reins on his cow-pony's neck, debonair and tireless, with a bonny daughter to either side.

Strange is the furnishing of this stronghold of the Sun God. And few are the spots in it that would invite the tired and parched wayfarer to tarry. For all the beauty of its rose and velvet of distance, there reigns intense desolation everywhere, with something sinister in the dearth of plant or animal life. Passing an overtoppling crimson Niagara of dead lava frozen in its fall, we reinvested the silent bleakness with fire and flow and upheaval, until, suddenly whooping into a mad race up the flanks of a big blowhole that had earlier presented its dry throat to our downward scrutiny, we hesitated to look over into the soundless pit, half expecting we knew not what. No such luck, of course, although dead volcanoes have been known to stir into life; and we slanted back into the floor of the House, and went on our burning, arid course.

It gives an odd sensation to realize that one is traversing miles literally inside a high mountain. We thought of friends we should have liked to transport abruptly into the unguessable cavity. Strangely enough, as we progressed, it turned out that the warm color, so vivid from the summit, flushes only one side of the cones, like a fever not burned out; although ahead, on the opposite wall, there is a giant scar of perfect carmine.

At length we commenced to wind among little crateresque hillocks, clothed with rough growths by the healing millenniums, until, far on, we could just glimpse the Promised Rest of verdure—clustered trees and smiling pasture, where our tents were to be pitched for two nights, while the beasts should graze. But the distance was as deceptive as a mirage, and we had still to endure many a sharp trail across fields of clinking lava, black and fragile as jet, swirled smoothly in the cooling, and called *pahoehoe*; while the *a-a* lava, twisted and tormented into shapes of flame, licked against the blue-crystal sky above our heads. I never cease to feel a sense of aghastness before these stiff, upstanding waves of the slow, resistless molten rock, flung stark and frozen like the still waters of the Red Sea of old; and here, at the bases of these carven surges, are smooth sandy levels, dotted with shrubs, where one may gallop in and out as if on the floor of a recessant ocean.

Involved in a maze of wayward lava-flows among little gray cones, the vast aspect of the crater was lost, although, turning, we could yet discern Magnetic Peak. In every direction the views changed from moment to moment; and wonder grew as we tried to grasp the immensity of the old volcano and its astounding details. Once we halted at the Bottomless Pit itself—a blowhole in the ground that had leisurely spat liquid rock, flake upon flake, until around its ugly mouth a wall accumulated, of material so glassy light that large pieces could easily be broken off. And one must have a care not to lean too heavily, for judged by its noiseless manner of swallowing dropped stones, a human body falling into the well would never be heard after its first despairing cry.

There is but one chance to water animals until campground is reached, and we found the pool dry—auwe! But the kanakas, carrying buckets, scaled the crater wall to a higher basin, from which they sent down a stream. One by one the horses drank while we rested in an oasis of long grass, cooling our flaming faces in the shade.

A mile or two more, and we reined up to the cracking of rifle-shots under the cliff at Paliku, a fairy nook of a camping spot, where Mr. Von and the cowboys, having beaten us in, were bringing down goat-meat for supper. I was guilty of inward treacherous glee that only one was hit, as that was plenty for our needs; and the spotted kids looked so wonderful clambering a wall on which we could see no foothold.

Camp had been planned in a luxuriant grove of *opala* and *kolea* trees close to the foot of the pali; but the ground being soggy from recent rains, we found better tent-space in the open, where sleek cattle grazed not far off, getting both food and drink from the lush grass that grows the year round in this blossoming pocket of the desert.

This reminds me that there are sections on the "dry" side of Maui where herds subsist entirely upon prickly cactus, having no other food or moisture. Only a few weaker ones succumb to the spines of the cactus, and it is said that there are no finer cattle on the islands than the survivors.

All took a hand in the task of settling camp, we women filling interminable sacks with ferns, to serve as mattresses. The change of exercise was the best thing that could happen to us malihinis, else we might have stiffened from the many hours in saddle.

And what a starved company it was that smacked its lips at smell of the untiring Von's jerked beef broiling on a stick over a fire at the open tent-flap, behind which the rest of us sat and made ready the service on a blanket. For it is right cold of an evening, nearly 7000 feet in the air—a veritable refrigerating plant in the mansion of the Sun.

I hope, if ever I land in heaven, and it is anything half as attractive as this earth I go marveling through, that it will not be incumbent upon me to keep a journal. Seeing and feeling are enough to keep one full occupied. And yet, some one in my family of two, it would seem, must chronicle the details of its colorful existence.

PALIKU, TO HANA, MAUI, Thursday, July 18, 1907.

Too burned and tired to fancy goat-hunting in a steady rain, Mrs. Thurston and I spent yesterday resting, reading, sleeping, and playing cards in the dripping tent, while our men went with Mr. Von and the girls. The drenching clouds drifted and lifted on the pali, where the sun darted golden javelins through showers until the raindrops broke into a glory of rainbows. Then the brief splendor waned, leaving us almost in darkness at midday, in an increasing downpour.

Our hunters returned in late afternoon, wet and weary, but jubilant and successful, eager for supper and a damp game of whist on the blankets. After we had tucked under those same blankets, with shrewdly placed cups to catch the leaks in our soaked tent-roof, we listened to the mellow voices of the Hawaiians singing little hulas and love-songs and laughing as musically.

This morning it was down-tent, and boots and saddles once more; but ere we made our six o'clock getaway, I found a half hour to go prowling to the feet of the pali, to an alluring spot that had been in my eye since the day before—a green lap in the gray rock where a waterfall had been. Winning through a nettly wet thicket, I peeped into a ferny, flowery corner of Elfland at the base of a vertical fall down which the water had furrowed a shining streak on the polished rock amid clinging, fanning ferns and grasses and velvet mosses—a grotto fit for childhood's loveliest imaginings to people with pink and white fairy-folk and brown and green gnomes.

They were treacherous and slippery trails that led out of the crater and down through Kaupo Gap, chill with Naulu's drafty onslaught, where Pélé, Goddess of Fire, broke through the wall of the crater and fled forever from Maui to take up her abode on Mauna Loa's wounded side; but soon out of the clouds we rode and went steaming in the horizontal rays of a glorious sunrise. Again there were glimpses of Mauna Kea and Mauna Loa, supernal in the morning sky, although a trifle more plausible seen from this lesser level.

Down our sure-footed animals dropped into lush meadows, where fat cattle raised their heads to stare; up and down, across crackling lava beds, like wrecked giant stairways balustraded by the cool gray-and-gold walls of the Gap, from between which we could make out the surfy coast line. Once we had struck the final descent, there were no ups, but only downs, for 6000 feet; and several times our saddles, sliding over the necks of the horses, obliged us to dismount and set them back.

On a brown, rocky bluff above the sea we found an early lunch ready and waiting, at the house of a Portuguese-Hawaiian family named Vieira, and by eleven were loping easily along green cliffs, past old grass-houses still occupied by natives—a sight fast becoming rare. From one weirdly tattered hut, a nut-brown, wrinkled woman, old, but with fluffy black hair blown out from wild black eyes, rushed flinging her arms about and crying "Aloha! Aloha!" with peal upon peal of mad sweet laughter.

For several miles the coast was much like that of Northern California, with long points running out into the ocean; but soon we were scrambling up and down gulch-trails. In olden times these gulches were impassable on account of the tremendous rainfall on this eastern shore, averaging two hundred inches yearly. (Three years ago it registered as high as four hundred and twenty inches.) So the wise chiefs, somewhere around the sixteenth century, with numerous commoners at their command, had the curt zigzags paved with a sort of cobblestone, without regard to ease of grade, and the rises and falls of this slippery highway are nothing short of formidable, especially when one's horse, accustomed to leading, resents being curbed midway of the procession and repeatedly tries to rush past the file where there is no passing-room.

But the animals quickly proved that they could take perfect care of themselves and their riders, and we advantaged by this welcome assurance to look our fill upon the beautiful coast and forested mountain. Tiny white beaches dreamed in the sunlight at the feet of the gulch-valleys, where rivers flowed past coconut palms that leaned and swayed in the strong sea breeze, and brown babies tumbled among tawny grass huts, while gay calicoes, hung out to dry, furnished just the right note of brilliant color.

Some of the idyllic strands were uninhabited and inviting; and we spoke of the tired dwellers of the cities of all the world, who never heard of Windward Maui, where is space, and solitude, and beauty, warm winds and cool, soothing rainfalls, fruit and flowers for the plucking, swimming by seashore and hunting on mountain side, and Mauna Kea over there a little way to gladden eye and spirit. Then, "Mate, are you glad you're alive?" broke upon my reverie as Jack leaned from his horse on a zigzag above my head.

It would not have seemed like Hawaii if we had not traversed a cane plantation, and halt was made at the Kipahulu Sugar Mill, while Gwen's horse must have a shoe reset. It would appear that the onyx feet of the unshod horses, that have never worn iron in their lives, stand the wear and tear of the incalculably hard travel over the ripping lava better than the more pampered animals.

All the eager train knew from experience that at Hana waited their fodder; and we, in like frame of mind, restrained them not. We had done thirty-five miles when we pulled up before the small hotel—and such miles! Mr. Cooper, manager of Hana Plantation, called upon us with extra delicacies to eke out the plain hotel fare—avocados, luscious papaias, and little sugary bananas. "Gee!" murmured Jack from the buttery depths of a big alligator pear, "I wish we could grow these things in the Valley of the Moon!"

This village of Hana lies high on the horseshoe of a little blue bay embraced by two headlands, and is fraught with warlike legend and history. In the eighteenth century, King Kalaniopuu, of the old dynasty, whose life was one long bloody battle with other chiefs of Maui for the possession of these eastern districts, held the southern headland of the bay, Kauiki, for over twenty years; then the great Kahekili deprived the garrison of its water supply, and retook the fort, which is an ancient crater. In the time of Kamehameha, this fort withstood his attacks for two years, after the remainder of Maui had been brought to his charmed heel.

Tonight, I know, I shall fall unconscious with the ringing of iron hoofs on stony pathways and the gurgle and plash of waterfalls in my ears.

HANA, To KEANAE VALLEY, MAUI,
Saturday, July 20, 1907.

The Ditch Country—this is the unpoetical, unimaginative name of a wonderland that eludes description. An island world in itself, it is compounded of vision upon vision of heights and depths, hung with waterfalls, of a gentle grandeur withal, clothed softly with greenest green of tree and shrub and grass, ferns of endless variety, fruiting guavas, bananas, mountain-apples—all in a warm, glowing, tropical tangle; a Land of Promise for generations to come. For all who can sit a Haleakala horse—the best mountain horse on earth—must come some day to feast their eyes upon this possession of the United States whose beauty, we are assured of the surprising fact, is unknown save to perhaps a hundred white men. This of course is exclusive of the engineers of the trail and ditch and those financially interested in the plantations of Windward Maui. And undoubtedly no white foot ever previously trod here.

The Ditch Country—untrammeled paradise wherein an intrepid engineer yclept O'Shaughnessy overcame almost unsurmountable odds and put through a magnificent irrigation scheme that harnessed the abundant waterfalls and tremendously increased the output of the invaluable sugar plantations. And to most intents it remains an un-trammeled paradise, for what little the pilgrim glimpses of the fine achievement of the Nahiku Ditch itself is in the form of a wide concrete Waterway running for short, infrequent distances beside the grassy trail before losing itself in Mr. O'Shaughnessy's difficult tunnels, through which most of its course is quarried.

All manner of Hawaiian timber goes to make up the incomparable foresting of this great mountain side whose top is lost in the clouds. Huge koa trees, standing or fallen, the dead swathed in vines, the quick embraced by the ie-ie, a climbing palm that clings only to living pil-lars, its blossoming arms hanging in curves like cathedral candelabra; the ohia ai, lighting the prevailing green with its soft, thistle-formed, crimson-brushed blossom, and cherry-red fruit; the ohia lehua, prized for its splendid dark-brown hardwood, but bearing no edible fruit; and the kukui, silver-green as young chestnuts in springtime, trooping up hill and down dale. Especially ornamental are the luxuriant tree ferns on their chocolate-brown, hairy pedestals, and many of the ground ferns were familiar—even the gold-and silver-back grow in Hawaii. Indeed, a fern collector would be in his element in these Islands. Maui alone has all of a hundred and thirty-odd varieties.

We nooned on a rubber plantation in which Mr. Thurston is finan-cially interested. Indeed, we have yet to learn of any Hawaii enterprise of importance in which he is not, including, which we have but lately learned, the Haleakala Ranch, in which he, James B. Castle, and H. B. Baldwin each own one third. Mr. and Mrs. Anderson entertained us at a hospitable luncheon, served by two kimono'd Japanese maids—little bits of pictures off a fan, Jack observed. He, by the way, well-nigh disgraced himself when, replying to a query from his hostess whether or not he liked foreign dishes, he assured her he enjoyed all good foods of all countries, with one exception—"nervous" pudding, which he de-clared made him tremble internally. The words and accompanying gestures were still in the air when a maid entered bearing the dessert—a trembling, watermelon-hued dome of gelatine! A horrified silence was broken by Mr. Anderson's shout of laughter, in which every one joined with relief. But Jack consistently declined any part of the "nervous" confection, saying that he always preferred coffee alone for his dessert.

Armine, to the surprise of her father and sister, and my speechless delight, offered to let me ride her superb Bedouin for the afternoon, a young equine prince with gait so springy that he seemed treading in desert sand. We had traveled nearly all day in heavy showers, and were convinced of the accuracy of the figures of Windward Maui's annual rainfall, for no saddle-slicker was able to exclude the searching sky-shot water. But the discomfort of wet-clinging garments was lost in our rapt attention to the increasing splendor of the landscape. Rightly had our guides assured us that yesterday's scenery was as nothing compared to this, where the waterfalls ever increased in height and volume, thundering above and sometimes clear over the trail quarried into a wall of rock that extended thousands of feet over our heads and a thousand sheer below the narrow foothold. Our brains swam with the whirling, shouting wonder of waters, the yawning depths that opened below our feet, filled with froth of wild new rivers born of the fresh rains. Jack's warning was true: I have saved no words for this final stunning spectacle.

We reached Keanae Valley tired in body, in eye, in mind—aye, even surfeited with beauty. But once in dry clothing weariness fell from us, as we disposed ourselves in reclining rattan chairs on a high porch of the little house, and leisurely counted the cataracts fringing the valley amphitheater, upon whose turrets the sunset sky, heavy with purple and rose and gold, seemed to rest. All together we made out thirty-five, some of them dropping hundreds of feet, making hum the machinery in great sugar mills elsewhere. Commercialism in grand Keanae! And yet, it is not out of the way of romance to associate the idea of these tremendous natural forces with the mighty enginery that man's thinking machinery has evolved for them to propel in the performance of his work.

KEANAE VALLEY, TO HALEAKALA RANCH,
Sunday, July 21, 1907.

Mr. Von had us stirring by half-past six, after ten hours in bed. So soundly had we been sunk in "the little death in life," that even a violently driven rain which thoroughly soaked our dried riding togs, hanging on chairs in the middle of the room, failed to disturb. We experienced the novel sensation of shivering in a tropic vale, the while pulling on water-logged corduroy and khaki, even hats being soggy.

Our amiable host and hostess, Mr. and Mrs. Tripp, after serving a breakfast of wild bananas, boiled taro, poi, broiled jerked beef, and fresh milk, bade us Godspeed with tiaras and necklets of ginger-blossoms, and we fared forth out of the wondrous mist-wreathed valley and up-trail on horses spurred with knowledge of this last stretch to home stables. The air was ineffably clear, as if from a cleansing bath, with only light clouds in the sunny sky to rest the eyes.

More ditch trails and jungle of unwithering green, sparkling wet, and steaming rainbows in the slanting sun-gold of the morning; more and still more wonderful gulches, to make good Mr. Von's overnight prophecy. And we traversed a succession of makeshift bridges that called for the best caution of the horses who knew the every unstable inch. Jack, pacing behind on many-gaited Pontius Pilate, told me afterward that his heart was in his throat to see the slender spans give to the weight and swinging motion of my stout charger, who, never ceasing to fret at being withheld from the lead, pranced scandalously in the most unwise places.

At length we approached a promised "worst and last gulch," a flood-eroded, lofty ravine of appalling beauty, down the pitch of which we slid with bated breath, to the reverberation of great falls on every hand. Obeying Mr. Von's serious behest, we gathered on the verge of a roaring torrent overflung by a mere excuse for a bridge, not more than four feet wide, roughly fifty feet long, and innocent of railing. To our left the main cataract sprayed us in its pounding fall to a step in the rocky defile where it crashed just under the silly bridge, thence bursting out in deafening thunder to its mightiest plunge immediately below, cascading to the sea.

"Now, hurry and tell Von what you want," Jack shouted in my ear above the watery din. And what I wanted was to be allowed to precede the others over this bridge;—oh, not in bravado, believe—quite the contrary. I was in a small terror of the thing, but, since it had to be crossed, I was determined if possible to cross it by the least risky method. Fact was, I feared to trust the Welshman, justly intolerant of his enforced degradation to the ranks, not to make a headlong rush to overtake his rival, Mr. Von's horse, should he lead, for a single rider at a time was to be permitted on the swaying structure.

Without discussion, Mr. Von appreciated and consented; and when the order of march was arranged, the Welshman proved his right to leadership, without hesitation, wise muzzle between his exact feet, sniffing, feeling every narrow plank of the unsteady way. It was an experience big with thought—carrying with it an intense sense of aloneness, aloofness from aid in event of disaster, trusting the vaunted human of me without reserve to the instinct and intelligence of a "lesser animal." The blessed Welshman!—with chaos all about and little foundation for security, trembling but courageous, he won slowly step by step across the roaring white destruction and struck his small fine hoofs into firm rising ground once more.

With brave, set face Harriet Thurston, who was little accustomed to horses, came next after Mr. Von, and her ambitious but foolhardy steed, midway of the passage, began jogging with eagerness to be at the end, setting up a swaying rhythm of the bridge that sent sick chills over the onlookers, and it was with immense relief we watched him regain solid earth. Pontius Pilate bore Jack sedately, followed by the little girls.

It may give some faint conception of the scariness of this adventure, to tell an incident related by Mr. Von. One of his cowboys, noted on Maui for his fearlessness, always first in the pen with a savage bull, and first on the wildest bucking bronco off range, absolutely balked at riding this final test of all our nerve: "I have a wife and family," he expostulated; then dismounted and led his horse across.[1]

KALEINALU, MAUI, Tuesday, July 23, 1907.

Kaleinalu, "Wreath of Billows," the seaside retreat of the Von Tempskys, is but another illustration of the ideal chain of conditions that marks existence in these fabulous isles. Jack is almost incoherent on the subject of choice of climates and scenery and modes of living to be found from mountain top to shore. One may sleep comfortably under blankets at Ukulele and Paliku, with all the invigoration of the temperate zone; enjoy mild variable weather at 2000 to 3000 feet, as at the Ranch; or lie at warm sea level, under a sheet or none, blown over by the flowing trade wind. "Watch out, Mate," he warns me; "I'm likely to come back here to live some day, when we have gone round the world and back—if I don't get too attached to the Valley of the Moon." And he ceases not to marvel that the shoreline is not thronged with globe trotters bickering for sand lots. It is a wonderful watering place for old and young,

[1] Ours was the last party that ever crossed that bridge. A new one was hung shortly afterward.

1 Ours was the last party that ever crossed this bridge. A new one
was hung shortly afterward. with finest of sand for the babies to play
in, and exciting surfing inside protecting reef, for swimmers.

And here we malihinis are resting, after one day of tennis and
colt-breaking up-mountain, from our six days in the saddle. Nothing
more arduous fills the hours than swinging in hammocks over the
sand in a shady ell of the beach-house, reading, playing whist, swimming in water more exhilarating than at Waikiki, romping, sleeping—and eating, fingering our poi and kukui-nut and lomi'd salmon
with the best.

Tomorrow we bid good-by to these new, fine friends, who must have
sensed our heart of love for them and their wonderland, for they beg
us to return, ever welcome, to their unparalleled hospitality. By now
we have proudly come into our unexpected own, with a translation of
our name into the Hawaiian tongue, worked out by Kakina and Mr.
Von, who speak like natives with the natives, and sometimes with each
other, while the speech of the lassies abounds in the pretty colloquialisms of their birth-land.

Always they say *pau* for connotation of "finish," or "that will do,"
or "enough"; *kokua* for help, noun or verb—or, in the sense of approval,
or permission; *hapai* is to carry; *hiki no*, as we should say "all right,"
"very well"; *hele mai*, or *pimai*, come here, or go there; one oftenest
hears *pilikia* for trouble, difficulty, or *aole pilikia* for the harmonious
negative; the classic *awiwi*, hurry, has been superseded by that expressive and sharply explosive slang, *wikiwiki*; and when this loveliest of
hostesses orders a bath prepared, she enunciates *auau* to the Japanese
maids. Most commands, however, are given in mixed English-Hawai-
ian. The old pure word for food, and to eat, *paina*, is never heard, for the
Chinese kowkow—*kaukau* in the Hawaiian adaptation—has likewise
come to stay.

Von's most peremptory commands often trail off into the engaging
eh? that charmed our ears the first day at Pearl Lochs. And so, as I say,
upon us has been bestowed the crowning grace of all the gracious treatment accorded upon Maui—the Hawaiian rendering of London, which
is *Lakana*; although how London can be transmuted into Lakana is as
much a mystery as the mutation of Thurston into Kakina. At any rate,
my pleased partner struts as Lakana Kanaka (kanaka means literally
man), while meekly I respond to Lakana Wahine.

Aboard *Claudine*, Maui to Honolulu,
Wednesday, July 24, 1907.

One felicitous fact about our travel in this year of grace and happy circumstance is that Jack and I are together experiencing many things novel to both. Each has hitherto seen a bit of the world; but we start anew in a mutual learning of long-desired knowledge of other races and countries.

From Kahului the passengers were towed on a big lighter to the *Claudine* rocking well offshore; and, watching Louis von Tempsky's lean, military figure growing smaller on the receding wharf, we felt a surge of emotion at parting. "He's all man, that Von," Jack said, hastily turning away and lighting a cigarette. "He's pure gold," Harriet Thurston murmured from long acquaintance. And in my ears still rang the quaint cadences of his voice, rising from the cinder-slopes of Haleakala, or heard from smoking corral, or hammock on the beach, in little hulas of his own devising. Aloha, Von, and all Von's own; *aloha nui oe*—which spells all the love in the world, now and always.

From the deck we saw his fine beef-cattle being towed swimming out to the steamer, and crowded in the main-deck forward, bound for the Honolulu market. And when the *Claudine* swept out of the roadstead, we gazed our last, through daylight into dark, upon old Haleakala, whose stern head only once looked out from a rosy sunset smother.

The moon came up like a great electric globe, spilling pools of brilliant light in the inky water. At Lahaina the steamer lay off to take aboard a few passengers, and we glimpsed the infrequent lights of the little quiet town that had been our unexpected first port on the island which had proved so undisappointing in all its phases. We could have wished nothing better than to disembark again at Sleepy Lahaina, mosquitoes, wet tenting, reckless bridges, burned faces and all, and repeat the whole realized holiday planned so splendidly by our good genius, Lorrin Thurston, who is ever too steeped in affairs to spend adequate leisure in these lands of his own devoted love. While a man is accumulating the means of ultimate opportunity, the precious years and blood of youth flow by into the limbo of lost things. Long ago I entreated Jack to hold before his mental eye a time not too far distant when he might rest brain and hand. But from what I have learned of his dynamic temperament and boundless energy, and that brain that seems forever unsatisfied and that must always be reaching for attainable and unattainable, I am sure he will, as he says, "never rust out."

"There is so much to do," he will repeat, his great eyes full of visions, "so much to learn, to read. The days and nights of a thousand years are not long enough."

NUUANU VALLEY, Thursday, August 1, 1907.

It seems that we are to know many homes in Hawaii Nei. Now it is with Mr. and Mrs. Thurston, and their family of one daughter and two sons, who have lifted us, bag and baggage, from the August fervency of Waikiki to a cooler site within the "first shower" level of Nuuanu. Here, at the end of a short side street, their roomy house juts from the lip of a ferny ravine worn by a tumultuous watercourse from the Koolau Mountains. And here, on the edge of the city, from the windows of our second-story rooms, over the banks of the stream, we can see, across fertile plains broken with green hillocks, the blue, velvet masses of the Waianae Range, and, below, can pick out Pearl Lochs and the silvered surf-line of the coast around to Honolulu Harbor.

From a broad lanai, at table, morning, noon, and night, can be observed the life of the port, the movement of ships and steamers arriving from and departing for the storied harbors of all the world. Even Waikiki is visible, with its eternally lovely headland, Diamond Head. Jack, at work, must needs sit with back resolute against the distracting windows that set him dreaming and talking to me of the future of the *Snark*.

"Think, think where we are bound—the very names stir all the younger red corpuscles in one!—Bankok, Celebes, Madagascar, Java, Sumatra, Natal—oh, I'll take you to them all; and your lap shall be filled with pearls, my dear, and we shall have them set in fretted gold by the smiths of the Orient."

Whereupon, with sudden severity, he breaks off with: "There— don't talk to me any more, woman! How am I going to get my thousand words done, to pay for those pearls we're going to buy in the Paumotus and Torres Straits, and all that turtle shell from Melanesia, if you keep me from work now!"—Poor me, speechless, with clasped hands of transport in his own rapturous imaginings! But, since this youngling philosopher, who always dreams with his two feet upon solid earth, seldom fails to bring his intentions to pass, safely enough may I count upon the gleaming sea-seeds and polished turtle-scales, the adventuring for which is seven eighths of the prize.

In the shady spaces of this big house, the Thurstons accord us the perfect entertainment of freedom to come and go at our own sweet will, for they are as busy as we. At table, and afterward lounging in hanging-couches and great reclining chairs, we listen rapt to Kakina's fascinating memories of the old regime, from his missionary childhood on through the variable fortunes of the doomed monarchies, in which he bore his important part. And he, wisely reticent except with those he knows are deeply appreciative of the romance and tragedy of the Hawaiian race and dynasties, delves into his mine of information with never a palling attention from us. "If I only had inside my own head what he knows so well," mourns Jack, "how I could write about these Islands.—Just listen to this:" and he reads to me from notes he has made, or relates some incident of unparalleled romance in the annals of the kingdom.

Of a late afternoon, Mrs. Thurston and I drive down the palmy avenue into the architectural jumble of the business center, picturesque despite its intrinsically unbeautiful buildings, what of foreign shops and faces and costumes. Here we abstract her husband from the *Advertiser* editorial sanctum, and Jack from the barber's shop; afterward driving for an hour in the bewilder of old wandering hibiscus byways and narrow streets, where hide, in a riot of foliage, the most exquisite little old cottages of both native and foreign elements. Thus, on the way to and fro, we become acquainted with the city known and loved until death by travelers like Isabella Bird, whose book still holds place, with me, as the sweetest interpretation of the Hawaii we have thus far seen.

One evening we left behind the homes that stray over the lower slopes of the purple-rosy, worn-down crater of Punch Bowl, Puowaina; wound up past the Portuguese settlement that hangs, overgrown with flowers, on haphazard rough-quarried terraces, and ascended through a luxuriant growth of blossoming, fruiting cactus, to the height of five hundred feet, where we stood at the mouth of the perfect crater basin that had suggested the name of Punch Bowl. This lesser cone, blown out by a comparatively recent, final upheaval between the spurs of the older peaks and the Pacific, standing isolated as it does, we can now see should be visited early in one's sojourn in Honolulu, for it is a remarkable point from which to orient oneself to the city's topography. And lo, a white speck on the waterfront, we could make out the *Snark*, moored opposite a leviathan black freighter. From the mauka edge of the Bowl we looked up Pauoa, one of the wooded vales that rend Honolulu's matchless background, flanked with blade-sharp green ridges.

For the present, although we miss the convenient swimming of Waikiki, welcome indeed is this chance to acquaint ourselves with other phases of this Paradise at the cross-roads of the Pacific.

Sunday, August 4, 1907.

"Mate, you know, or I think you know, how little figure fame cuts with me, except in so far as it brings you and me the worthwhile things—the free air and earth, sky and sea, and the opportunities of knowing worthwhile people." Thus Jack, descanting upon some of the rare privileges that money cannot buy but which his work has earned him in all self-respect. Which leads to the observation that in this community composed of groups of the closest aristocracies in the world, bar none, to quote Jack's sober judgment, mere wealth cannot buy the favor of their hospitality. It is a well-recommended tourist who ever sees behind the malihini social atmosphere of Honolulu. And of all the exclusive spirit manifested by the kamaainas, none is more difficult to conquer than that of the elder Hawaiian and part-Hawaiian families.

So it was with quiet gratification that we two, in company with the Churches, set out day before yesterday for the out-of-town retreat of Mr. and Mrs. Henry Macfarlane, members of the same family with whom we have come in contact from time to time, since the day we first shook the Commodore's hand in Pearl Lochs.

Over the Pali we went, and this second view lost none of the glamorous memory of the former. Now that I have seen other glories of Hawaii, I find that no comparison can be made. The wonder of the Nuuanu Pali stands unique.

Descending the Pali zigzags to the main road, we soon turned off to the left and rolled over the red loops of a branch drive to the very base of the Mirrored Mountains, where nestles Ahuimanu, "Refuge of Birds." It is a beauteous spot, more than faintly Spanish in suggestion, where an old house, in sections connected by arbors, rambles about a court of green lawn that terraces down to the hospitable gate. The Spanish-mission effect of the low architecture with its arbors is enhanced by the fact that it occupies the site of an old Catholic institution, built by the first French Bishop of Honolulu as a place where he might retire for meditation and prayer. A short distance behind the present buildings the precipitous

(1) Hana.   (2) The Red Ruin of Haleakala.   (3) Von and Kakina.

mountain rises until its head is lost in the clouds. Somewhere on its face, reached by a stiff trail, hides a pocket, a small, green solitude, called the Bishop's Garden. From this the trail climbs so steeply that it is said none but the olden natives could surmount it, and one young priest lost his life making the attempt.

Adown the terraced walk, with this background of romance and stern beauty, stepped our part-Hawaiian hostess with the inimitable stately bearing of her chiefly race, clad in ample-flowing white holoku; and a little behind walked her daughter, Helen, as stately and graceful if more girlishly slender. Our welcome was of a warmth and courtesy that still further bore out the Spanish air of the place. But Hawaiian manners and hospitality were never patterned upon the Spanish or any other; they are original, and as natural to these gracious souls as the breath of their nostrils.

In a few moments we all emerged from our rooms in bathing attire, and walked barefoot along a grassy pathway wet with a fresh rain shot from the near clouds that hid the upstanding heights, to a large cement pool fed from a waterfall. The sun had fallen untimely behind the valley wall, while the air was anything but summery in this nook where daylight is of short duration; but the crisp shock of cold water sent blood and spirit a-tingling. Before we had finished a game of water-tag, there was a merry eruption of young cousins from the city, several of whom we greeted as acquaintances. Boys and girls, all in swimming suits or muumuus, they turned the tranquil late-afternoon into a rollicking holiday, some making directly for the pool, some playing hand ball, and all wasting no moment of their youth and high spirits while the light lasted.

In the absence of her husband, Mrs. Macfarlane presided at the head of a long table that nearly filled the low-ceilinged, oblong room in a wing of the old house, and the more racket the hungry swarm raised, the more benignly she beamed upon our funning. The greater the number of guests and their appetite, the greater the content of the Hawaii-born.

Following dinner, we sat or lay about in the soft-illu-mined living-room, into the past blown all the bashful reserve that unknowing ones mistake for superciliousness in the Hawaiian. Mrs. Macfarlane we coaxed from smiling confusion to talk of her family's interesting present and past, members of whom, Cornwells and Macfarlanes, served in honored capacities under the crowned heads of her country, as late as Queen Liliuokalani's reign.

In a comprehensive corner window seat some of the young men sprawled reading magazines, and a quartet at the card-table was oblivious to all comforts of deep easy-chairs, pillowed floor-nooks, and indoor hammocks. One golden-eyed boy on a scarlet hassock strummed an ukulele to a low song to his lady-love, who gazed back languorously out of great soft Hawaiian eyes, from the cushioned recess of a hanging-chair—lovely as an exotic blossom, in her long, clinging holoku of rose-flowered silken stuff. Oh, we were very Spanish this night—and all-Hawaiian.

And yet, there is but a trace of the Hawaiian stock in any of these—like Jack's French, or my own Spanish strain—an eighth, perhaps, a sixteenth, a thirty-second; but the modicum of golden-brown blood that they are heir to lends them their delicious lack of sharp edges. Among them one is gentled and loved into thinking well of oneself and all mankind.

"I love them, I love them, Mate. I have *Aloha nui loa* for them, forever," Jack murmured as we pattered over the brick-flagging of the fragrant arbor to a quaint bedroom whose small-paned windows might have looked out upon a New England landscape.

At six we were roused by the shouting clan trooping to the pool, and the indefatigable Jack rose to write for a couple of hours before breakfast, on his Maui article, "The House of the Sun." By nine, with dewy-sweet cables of roses about our shoulders, unwillingly we bade farewell to the charming household, and drove under a lovely broken sky to the foot of the Nuuanu Pali. Here, as much for the experience of climbing the upended ridges as to ease the burden of the horses, three of us left the carriage for Mrs. Church to drive, we to meet her at the pass. Except for a short climb I once made at Schynige Platte in Switzerland, this wet and slippery path, lying straight up an extremely narrow hogback, was the steepest and most difficult of my life. The ground drops with startling suddenness on either hand—or foot; and for me it was not infrequently both hand and foot. But we won over the horses, and had leisure at the drafty platform once more to feast our unsatiated eyes on the wide beauty of the scene that never can pall.

My husband, who holds that it is a waste of valuable effort to shave himself when he might be enjoying the soothing ministrations of a specialist, went to the barber in town while I shopped in the fascinating Japanese, Chinese, Portuguese, and East Indian stores, always with an eye to the fine Filipino and other embroideries, pina or pineapple cloth, of all exquisite tints, and unusual and gorgeous stuffs worn by the oriental women in Honolulu—stuffs of silk and wool and mysterious fibers impossible to buy in the States, as there is no demand. And the heart feminine thrills not in vain over kimonos and mandarin coats, for the prices are absurdly cheap, and the colors food for the eye, with untold possibilities for household as well as personal decoration.

From little houses and huts on the rolling fields, parties of natives, men, women, old and young, and naked brown imps of children, gather to bathe in a rocky basin of the ravine; and from the balconies of the big house often we watch them sporting, in gaudy, wet-clinging muumuus, unaware of any haole observer—their natural, carefree selves, splashing, diving, laughing and singing, laundering their hair, and calling to one another in wild, sweet gutturals. This afternoon we were struck with a new note—a strange, savage chanting. In it there was distinct, accentuated rhythm, but no music as we understand the term—only the harsh, primitive voicing of a man with the noble, grayed head of the old Hawaiians. Listening to the curious untamed note, the like of which we had never heard, Mr. Thurston said: "You are lucky to hear that under these circumstances—when the old fellow thinks no one but his own people are listening. He is probably intoning the *oli*, or genealogy, of one of the swimmers. There *was* no music, what we would call music, until the missionaries brought it here."

In the sudden transition from the ancient tabu system to an entirely changed order that came with the death of Kamehameha I in 1819, followed by the arrival from Boston a couple of years later of the first missionaries, the old "singing" became obsolescent. The new music, with its pa, ko, li, conforming to our do, re, mi, was taken up by every one, soon becoming universal with these people who learned with such facility; and out of the simple, melodious Christian hymning, the natives evolved a music inoculated with their old rhythms, that has become uniquely their own. Captain James King, who sailed with Captain Cook on his disastrous last voyage, makes the interesting statement that the men and women chanted *in parts*.

The predominance of vowel and labial sounds lends a distinct character to the tone-quality of Polynesian language, lacking as it does our consonants *b, c, s,* and *d, f, g, j, q, x,* and *z,* so that the upper cavities of the throat are not called into full play. Therefore the voice, with its Italian vowels, developed a low and sensuous quality that, when strained for dramatic or passional expression, breaks into the half-savage, barbaric tones that stir the ferine blood lying so close to the outer skin of the human. Sometimes there is a throaty musical gurgle that seems a tone-language out of the very tie-ribs of the human race.

Jack, listening with all of him, seems lost in another world. The phrasing was made by old Hawaiians to suit the verse of the mélé, a sort of chanted saga, and not to express a musical idea. The cadencing was marked by a prolonged trilling or fluctuating movement called i'i, in which the tones rose and fell, touching the main note that formed the framework of the chant, repeatedly springing away for short intervals—a half-step or even less. In the hula the verses are shorter, with a repetitional refrain of the last phrase of each stanza. That full-throated, lissom-limbed girl at the christening feast on the peninsula illustrated some of the foregoing when she sang for the dancers.

With a pleasant thrill I looked forward to meeting Alice Roosevelt Longworth at a dinner and dance given this evening at the Seaside by Mr. and Mrs. Church. In one's imagination she seems the epitome of the American Girl, and I found her far more beautiful than her pictures, with eyes wide apart, unafraid and level, looking golden as topazes from across the table in a glow of yellow candleshades upon yellow roses. And when "Princess Alice" smiles, she smiles, with eyes as well as lips. There is inner as well as outer poise about her brown-golden head, and she is straight as a young Indian and fair as a lily—a slender, jeweled thing in clinging blue brocade, her slim throat clasped by a sparkling collar of diamonds.

She and Jack were in no time cheek-by-jowl in a heated argument upon "nature-faking" that would have delighted, by proxy, her illustrious father, with whom Jack has all these weeks been tilting in the press; and I heard him offering to back a bulldog against the Colonel's wolf-dog, in the latter's back yard!

As for me, I sat between Nicholas Longworth and my Jack's old friend "Jack" Atkinson. And I found the latter solid, square, looking true in body and spirit; blue-eyed and sure, by all repute too busy being himself, and working for the other selves of his Islands, ever to find time for marrying or for accumulating gold either from business or from the abundant red soil of Hawaii. Mr. Longworth is a solid sort of man, too—agreeable and humorous in the bargain; and our talk at table—strange subject for a banquet—was largely concerned with the welfare of the Leper Settlement, in which both he and Mr. Atkinson are extraordinarily interested.

The Longworths were scheduled to serve on the committee receiving Secretary Strauss and his party from Washington; and while Jack and I first begged off from attending the formal occasion, when we learned it was to be in the old throne room of the Palace, "I suppose you'd like to see it all—and it *will* be worth seeing," Jack suggested. And so, after a few dances in the lanai to the melting orchestra, Mr. Atkinson whirled us away in his machine for the Executive Building, standing in its illuminated gardens. Soon we were passing along the dignified line of those receiving, out of which Mrs. Longworth, who is refreshingly unbound by convention, temporarily strayed to bombard Jack with a new argument in favor of the wolf-dog she had essayed to champion against his imaginary bull-pup.

But what snared our fancy on this occasion was not the gathering of august American statesmen and their European-gowned, bejeweled ladies, nor the impressive meeting between Secretary Strauss from Washington and Governor Carter of Hawaii. Our eyes were most often with the throng of high-caste Hawaiians in the lofty hall, more especially the splendid women, gowned in their distinguishing and distinguished white holokus, standing proud-bosomed, gazing with their beautiful eyes of brown at the white-and-gold girl who is the daughter of their alien ruler, President Theodore Roosevelt. And we wondered what memories were playing in their brains as they unavoidably recalled other brilliant occasions when they had filed by the imposing crimson throne yonder, to bow kissing the hands of their hereditary kings, and their last queen. She, H. R. H. Liliuokalani, has resolutely declined all invitations whatsoever to this house of her royal triumph and her humiliating imprisonment, since 1895, the year of her formal renouncement of all claim to the crown, and her appeal for clemency to those who had taken part in the insurrection.

HONOLULU, Tuesday, August 6, 1907.

A few kamaainas of Honolulu have long since discovered the climatic and scenic advantages of Tantalus, Puu Ohia, one of the high, wooded ridges behind the city, more particularly in the sultry summer months. Tantalus is ideal for suburban nests, overlooking as it does the city and Waikiki District, well-forested, with opportunity for vigorous exercise on the steep sides of Makiki and Pauoa valleys, and to their rustic eyry at the head of Makiki Valley, the Thurstons carried us by saddle.

One afternoon, while I languished with a headache, Jack gleefully returned from a tramp with his host, bringing me some of the wild fruits and nuts of the mountain, among them water-lemons and rose-apples. The first are round balls of about two-inch diameter, with greenish-brown, crisp rind full of tart, pulpy, spicy seeds. Although quite different in flavor and color, the formation reminds one of pomegranates and guavas. But the rose-apple!—evergreen native of the West Indies, it is too good to be true, for the edible shell has a flavor precisely like the odor of attar of roses, which is my favorite perfume. Almost it makes one feel native to the soil of a strange country, to nourish the blood of life with its vegetation.

Last night, back in town, Jack, at the request of Mr. Thurston and the Research Club of which he is a member, delivered his much-bruited lecture, "Revolution," at the home of Mr. and Mrs. Clinton G. Hutchins, a most cordial pair.

This paper of Jack's, an arraignment of the capitalist class for its mismanagement of human society, was originally a partly extempore flare of the spirit, several years ago before an audience of nearly five thousand at the University of California, where he himself had studied during part of a Freshman year. President Benjamin Ide Wheeler, who had for some time been after Jack to lecture, "And choose your own subject," was appropriately aghast at what he had made himself responsible for, and there was great subsequent pilikia in both college and press.

The capitalist dailies, as was their wont, deliberately misreported, *without the context*, the speaker's *quotation* of Lloyd Garrison's notorious "To hell with the Constitution," and credited the treasonable utterance of the famous agitator of bygone days to our twentieth century humanitarian.

Subsequently, in 1905, Jack, who had been elected President of the Intercollegiate Socialist Society, launched the same speech in Harvard Annex, without unduly shocking intellectual Massachusetts; but when Woolsey Hall, the fabulous "million dollar hall" at Yale, rang with the address, New Haven banished all of Jack's books from the chaste shelves of its public libraries, with somewhat disastrous results to his book-sales. A great weekly purchased the article (which is no more or less than a mere statement of provable facts, and the position and intention of the Socialist Party), but has never yet had the courage to publish it.

But to return: Hawaii knows little of socialism, for she lacks the problems that confront the United States and other great countries. Sugar is her backbone, labor is almost entirely imported, and handled in a patriarchal way that makes for contentment, especially in so rigor-less a climate. Feudal Hawaii is; but the masters are benevolent.

And Jack, who stepped before the Research Club with the blue fire of challenge in his eyes, his spirited head well back, and a clarion in his beautiful voice, found these gentlemen to be their own vindication of the name they had chosen for their Club. For with open minds they hearkened to this passionate youngster, insolent with righteous certi-tude of his solution of the undisputed wrongs of the groaning old earth; and presently, as if catching the unmistakable, unexpected atmosphere of intelligent and courteous attention, Jack muted his golden trumpets.

The frank, interested discussion lasted into the small hours, and Lorrin Thurston, no mean antagonist with his lightning-flash argu-ments, who laid every possible gin and pitfall for Jack's undoing, beamed upon the rather startling guest he had introduced among his tranquil contemporaries, and whispered to me:

"That boy of yours is the readiest fellow on his feet in controversy that I ever laid eyes upon!"

HONOLULU, Wednesday, August 14, 1907.

Tomorrow we embark once more upon our Boat of Dreams, for the Big Island, whence, if the engines prove satisfactory, and our new skipper, Captain James Langhorne Warren of Virginia, measures up to Jack's judgment, we shall sail from Hilo in earnest for the South Seas. Captain Rosehill and the crew failed to assimilate, and a change had to be made.

And now, a few notes upon these latter days on Oahu for—how long? Jack's "Hawaii's one of the very few places I care to repeat," would seem assurance that we have not looked our last upon Diamond Head, the Mirrored Mountains, and many another unforgetable vision.

No one interested should fail to visit the Entomological and Sugar Cane Experiment Station, where the clear-eyed and sometimes tired-eyed scientists are glad to explain the remarkable work being done in coping with all pestiferous enemies of profitable agriculture in the Ter-ritory. Mr. "Joe" Cooke, midway in a drive to the polo field, allowed us a fascinating hour or two with our eyes glued to wondrous microscopes that showed us an undreamed world of infinitesimal life.

In the open air once more, we set out for Moanalua Valley, to see the polo ponies that were being conditioned for the great game, which we attended two days later. The players of Hawaii cherish a widespread and enviable reputation for their keen, clean game.

Saturday dawned clear and fine, after a hard rain. The beautiful course around the wet and slippery field was lined with automobiles, while an upper terrace furnished the parked carriages an unobstruct-ed view. Miss Rose Davison, astride a mighty red roan, officer of the S.P.C.A., and a splendidly efficient character, marshaled the crowd, with the assistance of a staff of mounted Hawaiian police— magnifi-cent fellows all. Every one loves the Hawaiian police for their ability, courtesy, and distinguished appearance.

Miss Davison asserted her authority in several instances, letting down a checkrein, examining a harness, criticizing the condition of a horse, whether from overdriving or under-feeding, or a dozen other misfortunes—sparing nor high nor low of the public that flocked to the green terrace in every sort of vehicle, from faultlessly appointed victorias and smart traps to the humblest carts and buggies. When the sturdy and determined Rose first went into action on Oahu, she put out of business every Japanese stage-line over the Pali, the teams of which had long been a scandal.

Mr. and Mrs. Longworth, in Jack Atkinson's machine, next to Mr. Cooke's, declared that this tournament, set in the exquisite little val-ley, and played so inimitably, was quite the most exciting they had ever witnessed anywhere.

"Do you realize, my dear," Jack remarked that night, return-ing at twelve from a Press Club dinner, "that this and the night on the Kamehameha are the only two I have been out without you in the three months we've been here?—Not such a bad little husband, *eh*?" he grinned; then roguishly spoiled the implied compliment by adding, as he picked up the morning paper which he had had no leisure to scan, "I guess I'm lazy!" A moment later he added; "But sure as you're born, I'm going to be credited with some of the pranks of the boys from the *Snark*, for one or another of them is taken for me at every turn—and there are lots of people who'll make the most of it!"

"Let 'm: what do we care?" And I fell asleep to dream of a sublimat-ed and radiant Rose Davison, clad in bronze chain-mail, tilting, upon

Gwen von Tempsky's golden polo pony Jubilee, at hordes of Japanese stages drawn by nightmare-toiling, skeleton horses.

We had heard of the Bishop Museum as being one of the world's best, embracing exhibits that cover exhaustively every phase of the islands of the Pacific Ocean, historical, geographical, ethnological, zoological; and hither Robert, elder son of Mr. Thurston, took us one afternoon. Despite the exalted repute of this storehouse of antiquity, we had passed it by, for the idea of wandering through a stuffy public building on a hot day, concerning ourselves with lifeless relics, when we might be out in the open-air world of the quick, had never appealed.

Once inside the portals of koa wood, as ornamental as precious marbles, we knew no passing of time until the hour of their closing for the day. The building alone is worthy of close inspection, finished as it is throughout with that incomparable hardwood. In the older sections, the timber has been fantastically turned, much of its splendid grain being lost in convolutions of pillar and balustrade; but modern architects have utilized the wood in all its glory of rich gold, mahogany-red, maple-tints, and darker shades, with sympathetic display of its remarkable traceries that sometimes take the form of ships at sea, heads of animals, or landscapes.

The Curator of the Museum, Dr. William T. Brigham, spends his learned years in the absorbing work of sustaining and adding to the excellence of his famous charge, and we were sorry not to have a glimpse of him. But, for what reason we know not, he entertains a violent prejudice against Jack London, and on this day refused point-blank when he heard we were within his sacred precinct, to make an appearance. Surely, a peculiar attitude for a scientist; and quite at variance with our friends of the Research Club.

Of all the invaluable treasures behind glass, we lingered most enchanted before the superb feather cloaks, or capes, long and short, of almost unbelievable workmanship, as well as helmets, fashioned of wicker and covered with the same tiny feathers, yellow or scarlet, of the *oo*, *mamo*, *iiwi* and *akakane*, birds now practically extinct, and modeled on a combined Attic and Corinthian pattern. The cloaks, robes of state, called *mamo*, were the costly insignia of high rank. A wondrous surface of feathers, black, red, red-and-black, yellow, yellow-and-black, upon a netting of *olona*, native hemp. Some notion of the wonder of these magnificent garments may be gained by the statement that nine generations of kings lapsed during the construction of one single mantle, the greatest of all these in the Bishop Museum, that fell upon the god-like shoulders of the great Kamehameha. Among the others, beautiful though they be, this woof of *mamo*, of indescribable glowing yellow, like Etruscan gold, stands out "like a ruby amidst carrots."

All this royal regalia, blood-inherited by Mrs. Pauahi Bishop, together with the kahilis, formed the starting point for the great Museum. And the kahilis! Their handles are inlaid cunningly with turtle shell and ivory and pearl, some of them ten to thirty feet in height, topped by brilliant black or colored cylinders of feathers fifteen or eighteen inches in diameter.

No tapa is made in Hawaii to-day, although these people formerly excelled all Polynesia for fineness of the almost transparent, paper-like tissue, which was worn, several deep, for draping the human form. Now, for the most part, Hawaiian tapa can be seen only in the Museum, where it is pasted carefully upon diamond-paned windows. There is little resemblance between this delicate stuff and the beautiful but heavy modern tapas of Samoa, with which one grows familiar in the curio shops of Honolulu.

A painstakingly correct replica of the volcano Kilauea claimed especial attention, in view of our visit in the near future to the real vent in Mauna Loa's 14,000-foot flank; and we lingered over a remarkable model, worked out in wood and grass and stone, of an ancient temple and City of Refuge, or *heiau*, with its place of human sacrifice at one end of the inclosure. A gruesome episode took place shortly after this model was installed. A young Hawaiian, repairing the roof, lost balance and crashed through, breaking a gallery railing directly above the imitation sacrificial altar, where his real blood was spilled—Fate his executioner, *ilamuku*.

One more of the countless exhibits, and I am done. Here and there in the building, stages are set with splendid waxen Hawaiians engaged in olden pursuits, such as basket-weaving and poi-pounding. The figures, full-statured, are startlingly lifelike, except in the unavoidable deadness of the clever coloring. It is impossible to imitate the living hue, of which the natives say, "You can always see the blood of an Hawaiian under his skin." The model for one of the best of these figures died some time ago; and to this day his young widow comes, and brings her friends, to admire the beautiful image of the lost one.

No matter how the very thought of a museum aches your feet, and back, and eyes, do not pass by the Bishop Museum.

It was our good fortune to be bidden, with the Thurstons, to a New England breakfast at the Diamond Head seaside residence of Judge and Mrs. Sanford B. Dole. Judge Dole, who was President of the Provisional Republic (often called the Dole Republic) that followed the downfall of the monarchy, is an exceedingly busy man; and so, rather than visit and be visited during the week, at eleven of a Sunday he and Mrs. Dole welcome their friends to déjeuners that have become famous.

Imposingly tall, benignant and patriarchal, blue-eyed and healthy-skinned, with silver-white hair and long beard, the Judge is unaffectedly grand and courteous, making a woman feel herself a queen with his thought for her every comfort—here a cushion, now a footstool, there a more yielding chair or lounge, or a broad palm-leaf fan. He must have been another of the courtly figures of the old régime, and Jack always warms to the instance of the gallant resistance made by him and another stripling, holding the Palace doors against an infuriated mob during an uprising incident to a change of monarchs. "Can't you see them? Can't you see the two of them—the glorious youth of them risking its hot blood to do what it saw had to be done!" he cries with glowing appreciation of the sons of men.

Anna Dole, the Judge's wife, is a forceful, stately woman of gracious manners, with handsome eyes rendered more striking by her beautiful white hair and snowy garb—a diaphanous holoku of sheerest linen and rare lace. Jack could not keep his eyes from the pleasant sight of her, as she sat across from her reposeful husband at table. "I could hardly help being rude," he said afterward.

And groaning board is just what it was, from alligator pears (it is Mrs. Dole's own garden pears which have been ravishing the palate of my husband at the Thurstons' these many days), and big spicy Isabella grapes, papaias, enormous luscious Smyrna figs, mangoes, pineapples, and "sour-sop," a curious and pleasant fruit, of the consistency of cotton or marshmallow, and of a taste that can be best described as a mixture of sweet lemonade and crushed strawberries.

Also we sampled our first breadfruit, roasted over coals, although not at its best in this season. Jack and I concluded that upon closer acquaintance we should like it as well as taro or sweet potatoes, for it resembles both potato and bread, broken open and steaming its toothsome soft shellful of large tender seeds.

But this exotic menu was not the half. We were expected to partake, and more than once, of accustomed as well as extraordinary breakfast dishes—eggs in variety, crispy bacon, and delicious Kona coffee from Leeward Hawaii—and, to bind us irrevocably to New England tradition, brown-bread and baked pork and beans!

And all this leisurely breakfasting was done to the animated conversation of two of the most representative of kamaainas, who talked unreservedly of their vivid years and their ambitions for the future of the Islands. Always and ever we note how devoted are the "big" men of the Territory, old and young alike, above all personal aggrandizement, to the interests of Hawaii. It is an example of a truly benevolent patriarchy.

Following the repletion of this justly famous matin banquet, which, it scarce need be urged, one should approach sans at least one meal, we reclined about the awninged lanai, talking or listening to the phonographic voices of the world's great singers, the while a high tide, driven by the warm Kona wind, broke upon coral retaining walls in a deep rhythmic obligato.

"THE DOCTORAGE," HOLUALOA, HAWAII,
Wednesday, August 21, 1907.

Long ago, when the building and purpose of the *Snark* were first reported in the press, Dr. E. S. Goodhue, brother of our noble Dr. Will Goodhue on Molokai, wrote to Jack, bidding us welcome when we should put in at Kailua, in the Kona District of the west coast of Hawaii. Subsequent correspondence made us more and more pleased with the prospect of knowing the physician. And here we are, surrounded with the loving-kindness of his little family, in their home nested a thousand feet up the side of Hualalai, "Child of the Sun," a lesser peak on this isle of mounts—merely eight thousand feet in height, and an active volcano within the century.

There was a touchingly kind gathering of Honolulu acquaintance on the 15th, to bid the *Snark* Godspeed for the Southern Seas, by way of Kailua and Hilo on Hawaii. Jack's eyes were a trifle dim when, piled with sumptuous leis, he waved farewell while the little white yacht, under power, moved out in response to the new skipper's low, decisive commands—a very different craft, or so we thought, from the floating wreck that, praying to be unnoticed of yachtsmen, slipped by the same harbor four months earlier.

With the exception of Nelson, a Scandinavian deep-water sailor, we all fell seasick in the rough channel; and next day, in a dead calm of which we had been warned, in Auau Channel between Maui and the low island of Lanai, the big engine was started, with high hopes of reaching Kailua by nightfall. But auwe! Something went immediately wrong, despite the months of expensive repair, and Jack's face was a study as we exchanged glances. "Seems as if I had been expecting it all along," he said finally; "but it does make one feel a little sore in the old worn place." However, we called upon our reserve of patience and made the best of it. The break, which was in the original casting, occurred in the circulating-pump that keeps the engine cool when running, and of course the engine was useless. "The original bed-plate had a flaw, too," Jack did not need remind me. "Why couldn't this flaw show on the trial trips at Honolulu?" And there was no answer except "the monstrous and inconceivable" that marked all the building of the beautiful vessel.

Haleakala vouchsafed occasional glimpses of its lofty head at sunset, and on Sunday we sighted Hawaii above a cloud-bank. Crippled as we were, with neither engine nor wind-power, we could only wonder when the few remaining miles would be covered; for still in our ears sounded tales of schooners long becalmed off the Kona coast, and of one that drifted offshore for a weary month.

Monday night, four days from Honolulu, the *Snark* wafted into Kailua, where Kamehameha died in 1819, at the age of eighty-two, his searching brain to the last filled with curiosity about the world in which he lived, even to an interest in rumors of the Christian religion, which had found their way from the Society group. Three years after his death, his widow, Kaahumanu, his favorite, a remarkable woman whose career would make a great romance, together with her second husband, Kaukualli, held a grand midsummer burning of idols collected from their hiding places.

Kailua is the first port into which our boat has made her own way under sail. It was an occasion of sober excitement, in a moonless night lighted softly by great stars that illumined the shifting cloud vapors. The enormous bulk of the island appeared twice its height against the sparkling night-blue sky, and a few unblinking lights midway of the darkling mass hinted of mouths of caverns in a savage mountain.

When at last the searchlight was manned, fed by the five-horsepower engine that had been driving our blessed electric fans, we discovered the low-lying, palm-clustered village, and, sweeping the water with the shaft of radiance, made out a ghostly schooner in our own predicament.

"Do you know where you are?—do you like it?" Jack breathed in the almost oppressive stillness, where we sat in damp swimming-suits, in which we had spent the afternoon, occasionally sluicing each other with canvas bucketfuls of water from overside. Ah, did I like it! I sensed with him all the wordless glamour of the tropic night; floating into a strange haven known of old to discoverer and Spanish pirate, the land a looming shadow of mystery; our masts swaying gently among bright stars so low one thought to hear them humming through space, and no sound but the tripping of wavelets along our imperceptibly moving sides, and a dull boom of breakers not too far off the port bow. As we drew closer in the redolent gloom dimly could be seen melting columns and spires of white, shot up by the surf as it dashed against the rugged lava shore line.

Little speech was heard—the captain alert, anxious, the searchlight playing incessantly to the throbbing of the little engine, anchor ready to let go at instant's notice. Suddenly the voice of Nelson, who handled the lead-line, rang out sharply its first sounding, and continued indicating the lessening depth as we slid shoreward in a fan of gentle wind, until "Twelve!" brought "Let her go!" from the skipper. Followed the welcome grind of chain through the hawse pipe, and the yacht swung to her cable as the fluke laid hold of bottom, the breakers now crashing fairly close astern; and we lay at anchor in a dozen fathoms in Kailua Bay, all tension relaxed, half-wondering how we had got there.

Hardly could we compose ourselves to sleep, for curiosity to see our first unaided landfall in broad daylight. And it was not disappointing, but quite the tropic picture we had imagined, simmering in dazzling morning sunlight. One could not but vision historical scenes that had been enacted in the placid open bay, say when the French discovery-ship *Uranie* put in, the year of Kamehameha's death, and was received by a white man, Governor Adams, "Kuakine"; and, later, the brig *Thaddeus*, long months from Boston Town with her pioneer missionaries, greeted by the welcome tidings that the tabus were abolished, temples and fanes destroyed, and that peace reigned under Kamehameha the Second, Liholiho, who, among other radical acts, had broken the age-long tabu and sat down to meat with his womenkind.

Among these missionaries were Mr. and Mrs. Thurston, grandparents of our Kakina. All must have suffered outlandish inconveniences, to say the least, in this primitive environment; and I am minded of having read how, on one occasion, those early Thurstons made a passage from Kailua to Lahaina in a very small brig that hardly furnished standing room for its four hundred and seventy-five passengers and numerous live stock—which was not considered an unusual overcrowding.

A good five-mile pull it is from the village to the "Doctorage," through quaint Kailua, past Hackfeld's old store, and the formal little white Palace where, Dr. Goodhue's young son Marion told us, Prince Kalanianaole and his princess are staying; on, higher and higher, across a sloping desert of cactus blooming white and red and yellow, and laden with juicy-sweet "prickly pears," in which, with care for the prickles, we quenched a continuous thirst in the sapping noonday heat.

Shortly after quitting Kailua in the Goodhue surrey, Marion pointed out a tumbledown frame dwelling, the home of the original Thurstons, which is now almost disintegrated by *termites*, borers, inaccurately termed "white ants," whose undermining must ceaselessly be fought in the Islands. This house is a dreamfully pathetic reminder of those long-dead men and women who voyaged so courageously to a far land where, oh, savage association! a conch shell was the bell for the afternoon session of school. Their special interest in the Hawaiian people had been awakened in the New England missionaries by the acquaintance of several kanaka sailors brought to New Haven by Captain Brintnall in 1809, more especially one Opukahaia, whom they dubbed Obookiah. In 1817 the "Foreign Mission School" was instituted at Cornwall, Connecticut, for heathen youth, and five Sandwich Islanders were among the first pupils. Obookiah died the following year, but three of his countrymen embarked with the missionaries in 1819, in the brig *Thaddeus*, Captain Blanchard.

Presently we began to enjoy a cooler altitude, in which the vegetation changed to a sort of tropical orchard—a wilderness of avocado, kukui, guava, and breadfruit trees burdened with their shining knobby globes of emerald, like those of Aladdin's jeweled forest. And coffee—Kona coffee; spreading miles of glossy, green shrubbery sprinkled with its red, sweet berry inclosing the blessed bean.

At 1000 feet elevation we struck a variously level winding highway which we pursued to the post office of Holualoa, and from which we turned down an intricate lane between stone walls overhung with blossomy trees, that with sudden twist delivered us into an unguessed verdant shelf of the long seaward lava slope. Here the Goodhues live and work and raise their young family of two in this matchless equable climate. Miss Genevieve Lynch, a niece of the Doctor, presides over the education of the children.

(1) Prince Cupid. (2) Original "Monument." (3) The Prince's Canoe. (4) At Keauhou, Preparing the Feast. (5) Jack at Cook Monument. (6) Jack at Keauhou (7) Kealakekua Bay—Captain Cook Monument

Dr. Goodhue's Emersonian head and face recall old New England portraits, with dark-blue eyes contrasting to a clear ivory complexion; and his wife, a talented woman who has studied art in the eastern cities, welcomed us twain as if we had been long-expected kinfolk.

Jack has located a shady corner for his work, out of range of the distracting landscape, and is swinging along on that autobiographical novel he has so long contemplated. The hero is "Martin Eden," and the author cannot make up his mind whether to use the euphonious name for title, or call the book "Success."

"Now, this is what I call a white-man's climate," he pronounces with satisfaction. "Few of us Anglo-Saxons are so made as to thrive in tropic spots like Kailua yonder," indicating the far-distant and just-visible thumb-sketch of that storied hamlet, "no matter how beautiful they may be to the eye."

Dr. Goodhue agrees to this; but Jack will not follow him in the contention that, under the Hawaiian sun, even in this semi-temperate climate, said Anglo-Saxon should rest more and work less feverishly than do we. "I wish you'd heed what I am advising you," almost wistfully the good Doctor urges. "You'll last longer under the equator and have a better time on your voyage.—If I did not have such sweet responsibilities," he smiled upon his wife and Marion and Dorothy, "I'd beg the chance to go along as ship's physician! ... And as for myself," he added, "I *have* to work too hard—largely prescribing for people like you and myself, who have not heeded my own warnings."

There is small need for residents of Kona to plan special entertainment for guests, provided those guests have eyes to see. First, one's imagination is set in motion by this unheard-of sloping vastness of lava so ancient that it has become rich soil covered, in the higher reaches, with swaths of bright sugar cane and coffee, ferns and trees. Below this belt of vegetation, barren seamy lava stretches to the coast line, lost in distance to right and left, all its miniature palm-feathered bays marked by a restless edge of pearly surf in dazzling contrast to the vivid turquoise water inshore. Off to the south, the last indentation to be seen is historic Kealakekua Bay, where Captain Cook paid with his life for stupid mishandling of a people proud beyond his comprehension of the Polynesian race. We have never seen anything like this azure hemisphere of sea and sky. For there is no horizon seen from the Kona Coast. The water lies motionless as the sky—a frosted blue-crystal level, no longer a "pathless, trackless ocean," for over its limitless surface run serpentine paths, coiling and intermingling as in an inconceivable breadth of watered silk. Ocean and sky are wedded by cloud masses that rear celestial castles in the blue ether, which in turn are reflected in the "windless, glassy floor"; and the atmosphere and vaporous consummation is best described as a *blue flush*. The very air is blue.

We can just make out our small house-upon-the-sea, tiny pearl upon lapis lazuli, beyond the slender, white spire of Kailua's church. And fair little Dorothy, her eyes the all-prevalent azure, slips white-frocked and cool to our side and lisps her father's child-verse:

> "There Jack London's coming, see!
> In a little white-speck boat;
> He will wave his hands to me,
> Then he'll float and float and float;
> So he said last time he wrote—
> He is such a man of note!"

HOLUALOA, Thursday, August 22, 1907.

This forenoon we spent in the manner so disapproved by our wise host, catching up with work that had fallen behind in those blistering four days from Honolulu. Our industry was rewarded by a tonic horse-back trip with the Doctor and Marion, and Mr. Conant, manager of a large sugar plantation.

For some three miles we loped or trotted south along the fine road skirting this mighty slope at varying altitudes of 1000 to 1500 feet. On our saddles were tied rain-coats, for smart, air-clearing rains are frequent of an afternoon, filling one's nostrils with the smell of the good red earth.

"Oh, look—look! Mate! Look at your yacht!" Jack suddenly cried; and sure enough, there was she, the "white-speck boat," in a whisper of wind crawling out across the level blue carpet of the open roadstead, growing dimmer and dimmer in the Blue Flush, bound for Hilo, our port of departure for the Marquesas.

We turned down a trail through guava and lantana shrubbery sparkling from the latest shower. Lantana, one of the most considerable vegetable pests of the Islands, a native of South America, was introduced in 1858 as an ornamental garden flower, and a pretty shrub it is, with small, velvet blossoms of richest tones of orange, yellow, and rose. But the friendly mynah bird found its aromatic blue-black berries delicious fodder, and the rest is plain: he spread the prolific plant over thousands of acres of valuable pasture-land, that became choked with the rank growth, and even in the lower forests it grew several feet in height, forming almost impenetrable jungle, of great beauty except to the landowner. The experiment station was kept busy searching for its natural enemy, and of several discovered, the Lantana Seed-Fly proved the most destructive; so that by now, large tracts of lantana in the islands present an appearance of having been burned, so thoroughly has the seed-fly done its work.

Marion bestrode a ridiculous dun ass, a family pet that for the most part wreaked its own determined will upon its young rider, especially when its large braying, "a sound as of a dry pump being 'fetched' by water and suction," elicited like responses from the "bush" where these Kona Nightingales, as they are known throughout the Islands, breed unchecked and are yours for the catching. These, if not a favorite, are an inexpensive and popular means of travel among the poorer natives and the long-legged *pakés* (Chinese) on the roads of the District.

Winning through the belt of shrubbery, we traversed a desert of decomposed lava, our path edged pastorally with wild flowers, among them the tiny dark-blue ones of the indigo plant. Across and down this stretch undulates the ruin of the prehistoric *holualoa*—a causeway built fifty feet wide of irregular lava blocks, flanked either side by massive, low walls of lava masonry several feet thick. This amazing slide extends from water's edge two or three miles up-mountain, and its origin, like the ambitious fish ponds, is lost in the fogs of antiquity. Its probable use was for the ancient game of *holua*—coasting on a few-inches-wide sledge—*papa holua*—with runners over a dozen feet long and several inches deep, fashioned of polished wood, hard as iron, curving upward in front, and fastened together by ten or more crosspieces. The rider, with one hand grasping the sledge near the center, ran a few yards for headway, then leaped upon it and launched headforemost downhill. Ordinarily, a smooth track of dry *pili* grass was prepared on some long descent that ended in a plain; but this holua*loa* (*loa* connotes *great*), is supposed to have been sacred to high and mighty chiefdom, whose papa holuas were constructed with canoe-bottoms. Picture a grand chief of chiefs, and his court of magnificent warriors, *alii*, springing gloriously upon their carved and painted sledges, flashing with ever increasing flight adown this regal course until, at the crusty edge of the solid world, they breasted the surf of ocean!

The ancients of Hawaii were keen sportsmen—and gamblers. One historian asserts that many of their games were resorted to largely for the betting, which was pursued by both sexes, and often culminated in impromptu pitched battles. Jack, who loves a well-matched prizefight, which he calls a "white-man's game" (he repeatedly swears that if he could choose he would rather be world's champion boxer than the greatest of writers), has had his admiration of the Hawaiians augmented by learning that boxing, *moko-moko*, regulated by umpires who rigidly enforced strict rules, was the favorite national sport, often attended by spectators numbering as high as ten thousand.

Then there was wrestling, *hakoko*, and the popular *kukini*, foot-racing. Disk-throwing, *maike*, was played with a highly polished stone disk, *ulu*, three or four inches in diameter, slightly convex from edge to center, on a track half a mile long and three feet broad. The game was either to send the stone between two upright sticks fixed but a few inches apart at a distance of thirty or forty yards, or to see which side could bowl it the greater length. The champions would sometimes succeed in bowling upward of a hundred rods.

They also knew a complicated game of checkers, played with black and white pebbles upon a board marked with numerous squares. And oh, joy—these irrepressible sports raised cocks for fighting, and wagered hotly around the ringside! Jack declares Mr. Ford will have to resurrect some of the games, as he has done with surf-boarding, not only amongst the natives, but for the delectation of haole residents and visitors.

This monster scenic railway of Polynesian forefathers lies in flowing undulations like our modern ones, showing the engineers to have been men of calculation. One old Hawaiian told us the pretty story that the terrific toil of building the holualoa was performed by amorous youths contesting for a single look at the loveliness of a favorite of the *moi*, king.

Despite the fact that wahines existed under severe and sometimes heartless tabus and punishments for the infringement thereof, they played the usual important role of femininity among superior races. They were exempt from sacrifice; and the rank of children was inherited chiefly from the maternal parents. War canoes were named after the loved one of the chiefs, as evidenced by Kamehameha, whose sentiment for Kaahumanu caused him to rename for her the brig *Forester*, bought from Captain Piggott in exchange for sandalwood. And after Kamehameha II, Liholiho, had removed the ban of Adam-less feasting, woman's further emancipation went on apace. When, in the past century, the "people" were called by their white government to vote, there was no murmur from the husbands, fathers, and brothers, if report be true, at having their womenkind accompany them to the polls to cast their own ballot. The haole lawmakers, however, not ripe to tolerate woman suffrage, and equally unwilling to cause hurt, got around the embarrassing difficulty by merely neglecting to count the feminine names![1]

The "free life of the savage" is a myth, so far as concerns the old Hawaiians. Almost every act was accompanied by prayer and offering to the tutelar deities. Every vocation had its patron gods, who must be propitiated, and innumerable omens were observed. A fisherman could not use his new net without sacrifice to his patron fane, more especially the shark-god. A professional diviner, *kilokilo*, had to be called in for advice as to the position of a house to be erected; and no tree must stand directly before the door for some distance, lest bad luck be the portion of the householder. Canoe-building was a ceremonial of the strictest sort; while, most important of all, the birth of a male child was attended with offerings to the idols, with complicated services.

Again am I lost in the labyrinth of Hawaii's tempting history, for between the lines one may find the utmost romance, in abundance pressed down and burgeoning.

The Kona coast is said to be as primitive in its social status as anywhere in Hawaii to-day, but we saw none but wooden dwellings, tucked in the foliage of the high bank behind Keauhou's miniature crescent beach with its rippling miniature surf—a mere nick in the white coastline, where small steamers call at a little roofed pier. In a small lot, inclosed by a low stone wall, gravely we were shown by the natives a large sloping rock, upon which, we were informed, Kamehameha V, grandson of the Great Ancestor, was born. Queen Liliuokalani has lately caused the wall to be built around the sacred birthplace.

HOLUALOA, Friday, August 23, 1907.

This perfect day, in high balmy coolness, found us driving twenty miles over the shower-laid pavement of the highway. Once more we glimpsed the *Snark*, still holding to westward in order to lay her proper

---

[1]   In a late *Pacific Commercial Advertiser*, I notice the following cable:

"WASHINGTON, August 13, 1917:

Favorable report was made to the Senate to-day on the bill to empower the Hawaiian Legislature to extend suffrage to women and submit the question to voters of the territory."

slant for the coastwise course—by now a mere flick of white or silver or shadow in the shifting light, sometimes entirely eluding sight in the cloud-dimming blue mirror.

The road swings along through forest of lehua and tree-ferns, the larger koa flourishing higher on the mountain; and on some of the timbered hillsides Jack and I exclaimed over the likeness to our home woods.

At intervals, up little trails branching from the road, poi-flags fluttered appetizingly in the breeze—a white cloth on a stick being advertisement of this staple for sale. I longed to follow these crooked pathways for the sake of a peep at the native folk and their doubtlessly primitive huts.

"I wish I had miles of these stone walls on my ranch," quoth Jack, on the broad top of one of which he sat, munching a sandwich in the kukui shade. Everywhere one sees examples of this splendid rock-fencing, built by the hands of bygone common people to separate the lands of the aristocracy.

The return twenty miles were covered in a heavy rain that the side-curtains could not entirely exclude, and we stopped but once—to make a call upon a neighbor, a hale and masterful man of eighty-odd years, whose fourth wife, in her early twenties, is nursing their two-months-old babe. "Gee!" Jack said in an awed tone as we resumed our way under a sunset-breaking sky, "the possibilities of this high Kona climate are almost appalling! This is certainly the place to spend one's declining years." And the Doctor added, "They say in this district that people never die. They simple dry up and float away in the wind!"

Jack's admiration for the holoku remains unabated; and so, as have many Americans, I have quite adopted it for housewear as the most logically beautiful toilette in this easy-going latitude. Callers arrive: I am bending over the typewriter, wrapped in a kimono. In a trice, if my husband has not started the back-buttons wrong, I am completely gowned in a robe of fine muslin and lace, with ruffled train, ready for any domestic social emergency.

HOLUALOA, Saturday, August 24, 1907.

To Keauhou again we came this lovely evening, guests of Mr. and Mrs. Thomas White of Kona. After a mad dash, neck and neck, on the bunched and flying horses, with heavy warm rain beating in our hot faces, Guy Maydwell, who with his charming French wife, "Brownie," are old acquaintances, led the riot makai on the wettest, slipperiest, muddiest trail he knew through the slapping wet lantana, and we arrived at the jewel of a bay drenched to the skin, our feet squashing unctuously in our boots.

Red calico muumuus had been brought for us malihini haoles, that we might be entirely Hawaiian in the water, and at last I was able to demonstrate to my own skepticism that it is more than possible to keep from drowning in a flowing robe. A bevy of brown water-babies were already bobbing blissfully in the sunset-rosy flood that was warm as new milk.

In the water I was seized with almost a panic when a distressful stinging sensation began spreading over my body like flame. Simultaneously, Genevieve cried out, and others began to make for the beach with little shrieks of pain and laughter. The brown mer-babies tried with wry, half-smiling faces to explain, but it took an older native to make plain that in the twilight we had blundered into a squadron of Portuguese men of war, whose poisonous filaments are thrown out somewhat as spiders cast their webs over victims. A man of war has been known to lower these filaments many feet, say into a shoal of sardines, whereupon the sardines become paralyzed from the poison at the instant of contact and the enemy is able to hoist them to the surface. No wonder our tender skins felt the irritation. Never again shall I be able to look upon the fairy fleets of Lilliputian blue ships with quite the same unalloyed pleasure in their pretty harmlessness.

Robust appetites we brought to Mrs. White's luau, spread on the little wharf. Although we did sit on the floor, in approved native posture, it was a trifle disappointing to note the forks, spoons, and knives, together with many haole dishes. Jack considerately forestalled any comment from me by whispering "They do not know us well enough to realize that we would appreciate the strictly Hawaiian customs."

Some of the Keauhou folk sat with us, but were extremely shy, for few strangers find their way to the little village by the sea; and at the shore end of the pier a group of brown singers stared at us out of their beautiful eyes while their voices blended "with true consent" in older melodies than any we had heard.

Jack and I rode home in the dim misty moonlight, beholding the land and sea in a wondrous new aspect, the Blue Flush all turned to iridescent pearl and the fairy silver sea streaked with dull gold by a low-hanging moon. In the stillness our hoofs rang sharply on the lava steep, or a clash of palm swords in a vagrant puff of wind startled the horses to the side. It was a wild ride, up into the chiller air strata and along the clattering highway, and we enjoyed imagining ourselves half-winged creatures in a dream.

HOLUALOA, Sunday, August 25, 1907.

Jack rose betimes and accomplished his thousand words on the novel, the while I hurried to copy three chapters already written. The surrey was ready to start upon the last stroke of the charmed ink-pencil, and with an eager "I'll be with you in a minute!" Jack flashed into the house for a pack of "Imperiales" and a box of matches, and out again to join us for the long-desired trip to Kealakekua Bay.

Farther than any day yet we bowled along the blithesome highroad, and then dropped into the increasing heat of the shimmering tropic levels, into Napoopoo village under its fruitful palms on the beach. Mr. Leslie, a friend of the Goodhues, had us into his pleasant home to cool off from the hot drive, and led to where two canoes lay ready at the landing to paddle us over the storied waters to the Cook Monument. Weather-grayed little outriggers they were, one of them, propelled by an astonishing person, a full-blooded Hawaiian albino—curious paradox of a white man who was not a white man.

Skimming the lustrous, still water beyond the inshore breakers, on our way to the point of land, Kaawaloa, where stands the white monument pure and silent in the green gloom of trees, our eyes roved the palm-feathered, surf-wreathed shore and beetling cliffs honeycombed with tombs where old canoes still hold tapa-swathed bones of bygone inhabitants. Some of these, undoubtedly, knew the features of the Captain James Cook whom they deified as an incarnation of their secondary god, Lono, previous to slaying him for his misbehavior with a people too decent to countenance methods he had found successful among certain South Sea groups.

And we reinvested the ideal environment with its sturdy old whalers and picturesque adventurers' ships, and garlanded dusky mermaidens swimming out in laughing schools to the strange white men from an undreamed world beyond the blue flush that bounded theirs, while again the friendly natives made high luau beneath the palms of the waterside. Our handsome boatman somewhat shook the mermaid fantasy when he contributed: "*Aole*—no; no swim this place . . . I tell you—planty, planty shark."

No shark could we discern; only, in coral caverns deep below the quaint outrigger, burnished fishes playing in and out like sunbeams. We skimmed a jeweled bowl, the blue contents shot through with broadsides of amber by the afternoon sun, and on the surface shadowy undulations—violet pools in the azure; liquid sapphire spilled upon molten turquoise; and all exquisite hues melting into an opalescent fusion of water and air.

An arm of lava draws in the harbor on the north, and near its end the rocky ruins of a heiau, undoubtedly of Lonomakahiki, where Captain Cook was worshiped, lends an appropriately sacrificial spell, which the irreverent and loud-voiced mynah does everything in his power to desecrate. We landed on the low rocks opposite the white concrete monument, which stands midway of the little cape. The original memorial was a piece of ship's copper, nailed to a coco palm near the site of the present imposing shaft, which is inclosed in a military square of heavy chain-cable supported from posts topped by cannon-balls.

When Captain Cook was slain here, in 1779, his body was borne to a smaller heiau above the pali, where the same night the high priests performed their funeral rites. The flesh was removed from the skeleton, and part of it burned, while the bones were cleansed and tied with red feathers and deified in the temple of Lono. All that the men of his ship, the *Resolution*, could recover of their commander's valorous meat was a few pounds which had been allotted to Kau, chief priest of Lono, which he and another friendly priest secretly conveyed to them under cover of night. Most of the wan framework, distributed among the chiefs according to custom, was eventually restored, and committed with military honors to the deep.

It has been held that the flesh of Captain Cook was devoured, but this rumor has been entirely disproved by the most authentic evidence from written accounts of officers of the *Resolution* and the *Discovery*. What probably gave rise to the false impression of the gustatory propensities of the Hawaiians at that time is the fact that three hungry youngsters, prowling about during the dark ceremonial, picked up the heart and other organs that had been laid aside, and made a hearty lunch, taking them for offal of some sacrificial animal. It is not recorded whether or not these gruesome giblets were already roasted! The three children lived to be old men in Lahaina. There is no proof that the Hawaiians ever were cannibals, whereas there is undisputed evidence that in extremity many Caucasians have eaten their fellows.

Always a rebellious memory will be mine that I allowed myself to be dissuaded by the Doctor and my husband from climbing the avalanched slope at the base of the pali in which those canoe-coffined bones of Kealakekua's dead are shelved. It is even said that Kekupuohe, wife of Kalaniopuu, who was king of Hawaii at the time of its discovery by Captain Cook, is interred here. Such a burial place is rare in the Islands, for more frequently bones were secreted beyond discovery, as in the case of the mighty warrior Kahekili, who died at Waikiki less than twenty years after Cook's passing, and whose white bones were effectively hidden in some cave near Kaloko on the North Kona coast. Mine was a perfectly healthy yearning to brave the face of the cliff and peer into sunless cobwebby recesses to see what I could see. I was ready to go even contrary to the physician's earnest warning about the exhausting heat on that bare rock; but when Jack's heedful eyes said *"Please"* I obeyed the Doctor's advice.

Once back on the lava masonry of the steamboat landing at Napoopoo, in the shade we ate luncheon, dangling our happy heels overside; after which Mr. Leslie carried us off again to his house, where he showed us the original Cook "monument," the famous slab of greenish, sea-worn copper, bearing the old inscription. A man of deep content is the wealthy Mr. Leslie, who declares that he prefers life in this dreamy Polynesian village, with his tranquil-sweet part-Hawaiian wife, to any place on earth. Perhaps his philosophy of happiness is somewhat like that of our Jack, who always comes back to this:

"A man can sleep in but one bed at a time; and he can eat but one meal at a time. The same with cigarettes, drink, everything. And, best of all, he can only love one woman at a time ... a long time, if he is lucky."

HOLUALOA, Monday, August 26, 1907.

Another afternoon in the saddle, this time bound for the timber line of the greater forests on Hualalai. Our rendezvous was at the Whites' home, a delightfully old-fashioned cottage that is largely lanai. The New England parlor, with its upholstered chairs, piano, and little stands, is enriched by rare emblems of Mrs. White's noble Hawaiian ancestors, such as kahilis, feather-leis, and fans; and upon piano and walls are portraits and photographs of Islands royalty. Princess Kaiulani's wonderfully fine, wistful face is everywhere, always the beloved child among her people.

Mr. White, debonair and gay, on a nimble cattle pony, led up a guava-wooded trail that leads to a fair free range of upland, where we could safely give rein to the impatient horses, as on the Haleakala pasture-lands. Higher still, near the edge of the woods we rounded in with a flourish at a picturesque inclosure containing an old, old frame house, or connected group of houses of various periods. Here live Mrs. Roy, Mrs. White's part-Hawaiian mother of chiefly lineage, with another daughter and her husband, Mr. and Mrs. A. S. Wall.

Never was ranch house so quaintly beautiful. The garden is terraced shallowly, its grassy divisions hedged with flowering hibiscus, white and blush and rose, and crimson flame, and all about the rambling structure, bounded castle-like with a great wall of lofty eucalyptus, grows a tended riot of plants—red amaryllis, and glooms of heliotrope; young bananas, their long leaves like striped ribbons; tree-ferns in the deep, short-clipped sod; a sober cypress or two; tawny lilies, with splashes of blood in their hearts; a merry blow of Shirley poppies, white and crinkly and scarlet-edged like bonbons, and double poppies of white and mauve and twilight-purple; steep gables of the dwelling smothered under climbing roses; and rarest roses blooming about the steps; flagged walks bordered with violets white and blue, filling the air with sweet.

And begonias amazingly everywhere. Begonias big, begonias little; begonias in sedate rows, pink and white; begonias in groups, and singly; begonias standing a dozen feet tall swaying like reeds in the wind; and the very entrance to the charmed garden is through a gateway of withy begonias, afire like lanterns dripping carmine, wrist-thick and twenty feet in length, bent and bound into a triumphal arch of welcome. What had seemed the enormity of the Molokai begonias receded before these that were twice their height and girth. And speaking of Molokai reminds me that a guest at the Whites to-day is a relative of the Myers family—a magnificent woman, high-featured, high-breasted, with the form and presence of a goddess and the indefinable Hawaiian hauteur that dissolves before a smile.

The old house seems made of crannied nooks, and contains curious and antique furnishings that fared across the Plains or around Cape Horn; little steps up, little steps down, from room to room; or rooms joined by flagged pavement drifted with flowers.

Later, continuing up Hualalai, we edged along lehua woods that would make a lumberman dream of untold wealth of sawmills; and I for one yearned toward the forest primeval of koa above, which we had not time to penetrate. Once this big mountain was the property of the Princess Ruta Keelikolani, granddaughter of Kamehameha.

"But remember, always," Jack comforted me; "we must, according to Ford's practice, leave *something* unseen and undone, to bring us back."

Native cowboys, with shining eyes and teeth, and gay neckerchiefs, dashed about the pasture, working among the cattle. Upon the backs of detached ruminating cows sat the ubiquitous and impudent mynah birds, devouring pestiferous horn-flies. And we malihinis were amused and edified by the sworn statements of the men of our party, that the scraggly tails of the Kona horses, which had aroused our polite curiosity, are shaped by hungry calves patiently chewing this patently questionable fodder with scant protests from the larger beasts.

One feature of great human interest on this ranch is a remarkable wall, well-built of large stones, four feet high, and more than broad enough to accommodate an automobile. It rose in a single day, by edict of Kamehameha, to inclose four hundred acres of choice cattle land. The people turned out en masse and toiled systematically under the genius of organization and the direction of his lieutenants.

He who has come to believe that the "trade winds make the climate of Hawaii," cannot comprehend why, here in Kona, lying north and south, where the trades are cut off by Mauna Loa's bulk to the east and the dome of Hualalai to the north, this is the most "abnormally healthy" climate in the group. Explanation is found in the frequent afternoon and night rains resulting from the piling up, by a gentle west wind, of banks of cloud against the high lands. Toward sundown, whatever airs have been blowing from the west, die out, replaced by an all-night mountain breeze, chill and refreshing, which makes one draw the blankets close.

HOLUALOA, Tuesday, August 27, 1907.

"The little ship—the little old tub!" Jack fairly crooned, hanging up the telephone receiver. "It was Captain Warren, and they anchored last night in Hilo Bay. He says they ran into a stiff gale as soon as they got out of that Blue Flush calm of yours, and the big schooner that left Kailua the same day had to double-reef, while our audacious little tub weathered the big blow under regular working canvas. The captain's voice was quite shaky with emotion when he said he was more in love with the *Snark* than ever.—Some boat, Mate-Woman, some boat!" And all during the drive to Kailua to call on Prince and Princess Kalanianaole he kept bubbling over with his joy in "the little tub."

Prince Cupid had repeatedly urged Dr. Goodhue to bring us to see them at the Palace; but the meeting was doomed through carelessness of a Japanese servant who failed to deliver the Doctor's telephoned message; and the couple, to our disappointment, were absent.

We tied the team in the broad shade of an old banyan, and proceeded along the garden path between white-pillared royal palms to the mauka entrance, where we knocked and knocked again and again. Peering through the ajar door, we saw, at the farther end of the little reception hall, facing our way, upon its man-high pedestal the marble head of King Kalakaua, heroic size, festooned with freshly made leis of the enamel-green mailé and glowing red roses. Mrs. Goodhue and I, at the Doctor's suggestion, ventured inside and sat upon a quaint haircloth sofa, black and slippery, while Jack took a smoke out the makai door, and the Doctor rapped upon an inner one. A slipshod Japanese finally answered the summons, and reported no one at home.

So I was robbed of my opportunity to wander in the square wooden palace of departed as well as deposed Polynesian royalty, that had superseded the grass habitations of Hawaii's undiscovered centuries. It was on the Kona coast, according to tradition, that the very first white navigators who flushed these Delectable Isles set their feet—the captain of a Spanish vessel that was wrecked at Keei, just below Kealakekua Bay. The only other survivor was his sister, and the natives received them kindly. Intermarrying, these two Castilian castaways became the progenitors of well-known chief families, one of these being represented by Kaikioewa, a former governor of Kauai. There is also small doubt that the Sandwich Islands were discovered by another Spaniard, Juan Gaetano, in 1555, since no other Europeans were navigating the Pacific at that early time.

The Princess's garden is ravishing—a fragrant crush of heliotrope and roses and begonias, with shadowy bowers among vine-veiled high trees. Our mind's eye needed only the flower of all—the tropic presence of the mistress of the Palace.

HOLUALOA, Wednesday, August 28, 1907.

Many letters of introduction were urged upon Jack London when the *Snark* sailed for earth's remote places, civilized and otherwise. For all and sundry of which he was grateful—and laid them in a neat pigeon-hole in his tiny, practical stateroom. The only times he has ever been known to present such introductions have been long after acquaintance has in some other way come about.

"I can't do it," he protests. "I'm a funny sort of fellow, I suppose. But to bludgeon a person with an introductory letter is as good as asking a perfect stranger to put himself out to entertain me and mine."

The residents of Kona, to one or two of whom we bear unpresented letters, have been exceedingly kind in the matter of calling, and equally indulgent about our inability, due to work and sightseeing, to return their courtesy. So the Doctor and his wife conceived the idea, which Jack, who hates formal calling, hailed with acclaim, of inviting them all in for an evening. The Doctor also made the suggestion that Jack read aloud some of his early stories; and Jack, albeit he likes to read only to one or two, or a very few, saw that his host had set heart upon the program, and consented willingly.

The neighborhood gathered, sixty strong, in the paneled rooms that could easily hold twice the number, lighted by colored Chinese lanterns; and following a general reception, the pleasant company settled to listen.

Perhaps the good Doctor considered his young house-guest something of a firebrand, for, with affectionate hand-on-shoulder, in his well-modulated voice he added to his announcement of the stories a brief statement of his misunderstanding of Jack's political views. Jack, who never asks that his uncompromising Socialistic position on economics be in the least glossed over for anybody, anywhere, took occasion to speak briefly, in his bright, swift, eloquent way, on the topic always close to brain and heart, with the more immediate purpose of setting his friend and himself straight in relation to the question. The threescore guests approved his explanation with hearty applause.

Midway in the reading of the three Klondike yarns which Jack had chosen, the family cat waxed unwontedly hospitable and desirous of attention, as is the way of some children and many animals upon public occasions. The unglassed window-casings are not calculated for the keeping-out of cats, and Mrs. Puss returned again and again, threading her mewing progress among the chairs. To the undoing of poor Jack, already irritated and diverted, a large cockroach behind him on the polished floor claimed the lean huntress's notice, which skurrying victim she pursued between the unsuspecting speaker's feet from the rear. Jack, instantly reminiscent of spiders and centipedes, no matter how innocuous, sprang like his own spring-muscled Sea Wolf straight into the air, coming down spiritually somewhat beneath floor-level when he realized the cause of startlement. "I can't help it!" he said, flushed and laughing. "And where was I, anyway, in my 'flight that midmost broke'?" picking up the book he had let go.

The Kona folk dance on all possible occasions except funerals and divine worship; so after the reading, the smooth lehua floors were cleared, and the younger people, to a caressing native orchestra, danced, while others talked with Jack on the lanai, strolled under the needled branches of the ironwood trees, or hung out of broad sills, gazing across the unseen void of lava to the starlit sea and up into the starlit sky.

HOLUALOA, Thursday, August 29, 1907.

Mr. Tommy White, aided and abetted by Mrs. Tommy, making good their determination that Jack London and his wahine should see a real, untarnished-by-haole luau, had us down once more to the jewel-sanded horseshoe of Keauhou waterside, and gave us what bids fair to rival all memories of Hawaiian Hawaii that have yet been ours.

Our one responsibility, at ease on yielding layers of ferns and flowers and broad ti-leaves that brown hands had spread, was to strike the exact right human note with the Keauhou dwellers. The essential thing a foreigner, who would know them, should avoid is the slightest spark of condescension toward the free, uncapturable spirit-stuff of the race. Proud, with fine, light scorn of lip and eye, volatile if you will, they are still unhumiliated by circumstance. Grudges they do not harbor; but pride bulks large in their natures. Affection spent upon them returns in tenfold meed of love and confidence that to forfeit would be one of the few true sins of mankind.

Arriving early enough to observe the bustle of preparation, we peeped into an improvised kitchen over by the bank, near which sucking-pigs were barbecued in native fashion, stuffed with hot stones and wrapped in ti-leaves and laid among other hot roasting-stones in the ground; and wahines sat plaiting individual poi-baskets from broad-ribboned grasses.

The men were approachable, and ready to chat upon the least encouragement. One in particular was an elegantly mannered man, of fine form and carriage and handsome face, hair touched with gray at

(1) and (2) By-ways of Hilo.   (3) and (4) Waiakea, Hilo.   (5) Riding the
Flume: Londons (Center), Baldings (Right).   (6) The Flume across a Gulch.

the temples and corners of eyes sprayed with the kindly wrinkles that come from much smiling through life. Educated at Punahou College in Honolulu, he speaks noticeably correct English. Again tonight we noticed that the elderly men are even more distinguished in appearance than their sons, with unmistakably aristocratic air, something lion-like about their gray-curled heads, the leonine note softened by smile-wrought lines and wonderfully sweet expression of large, wideset, long-lashed eyes. And in their bearing is a slow stateliness of utter serenity, as of souls born to riches of content. Many tend to obesity; but this superior specimen was slim, and clean-limbed, and muscularly graceful as a cadet in marching trim.

Mr. Kawehaweha, a full-blooded Hawaiian who ran for the Legislature last year, was cordial as ever, and entirely at ease, while his pretty hapa-paké wife, amiably non-committal at a former meeting, blossomed out deliciously, talking excellent English and doing much by her unaffected example to draw the other women from their cool aloofness.

One unerasable picture I must give: Upon arrival we had noticed a more than ordinarily large and elegant canoe of brilliant black and yellow, fitted with mast and sail, hauled out upon the sunset-saffron strand. "The Prince's canoe," was the word, and a perfect thing it was in the semi-torrid scene. And then came Prince Cupid, and we knew, for once, why he was so-called. In careless open-breasted fishing-clothes, a faint embarrassment in his calmly aristocratic expression as he regretted his absence the day of our call, he was another creature from the formal Prince of Honolulu. Despite mature years, he looked a beautiful boy as he stood before us, holding his hat in both taper hands, showing a double row of white teeth in a beautiful smile that spread like breaking sunlight to his warm brown eyes. He declined an invitation to remain to the luau, pleading his rough attire as an excuse and saying that he was expected home; and by the time we were taking our places around the feast, the great barbaric canoe floated beside the pier and presently sailed out leisurely, two men resting on their steering-paddles, their graceful, indolent Prince, crowned with red bugles of stephanotis, in the stern sheets.

In the past, the physical difference between the nobility—alii—and the common or laboring people was far more marked than to-day, when practically all Hawaiians are well nourished. "No aristocracy," says one historian, "was ever more distinctly marked by nature." Death was the penalty for the merest breach of etiquette, such as for a commoner to remain on his feet at mention of the moi's (king's) name, or while the royal food or beverage was being carried past. This stricture was carried even to the extent of punishing by death any subject who crossed the shadow of the sacred presence or that of his *halé*, house. Besides the ordinary household officials, such as wielder of the kahili, custodian of the cuspidor, masseur (the Hawaiians are famous for their clever massage, or *lomi-lomi*), as well as chief steward, treasurer, heralds, and runners, the court of a high chief included priests, sorcerers, bards and story-tellers, hula dancers, drummers, and even jesters.

The chiefs were as a rule the only owners of land, appropriating all that the soil raised, and the fish adjacent to it, to say nothing of the time and labor of the makaainana (workers) living upon it—a proper feudal system. The only hold the common people and the petty chiefs had upon the moi was their freedom to enter service with some more popular tyrant; and as wars were frequent, it behooved monarchs not to act too arbitrarily lest they be caught in a pinch without soldiery.

Whenever we dip into the lore of Hawaii, "it makes us sit up," to quote Jack—stirred by the tremendous romance of it all, visioning the conditions of those days, among rich and poor, the people slaving and sweating for their warlike masters, and, after the manner of slaves the world over down the past, worshiping the pageantry supported by their toil—whether priceless feather-mantles, ornaments, weapons of warfare, or red-painted canoes with red sails cleaving the blue of ocean.

Before reclining upon the green-carpeted wharf, we haole guests were weighted with leis of the blumeria, in color deep-cream centered with yellow, in touch like cool, velvety flesh, clinging caressingly to neck and shoulder. The heavy perfume is not unlike that of our tuberose, although not quite so overpowering. Half-breathing in the sensuous air, we were conscious of the lapping of dark waters below, that mirrored the star-hung sky dome.

Our unforced appreciation of their traditional delicacies had much to do with the unbending of the natives, both those who sat with us and those who served. And when Jack and I were seen to twirl our fingers deftly in their beloved poi and absorb it with avidity that was patently honest, the younger women and girls were captured, ducking behind one another in giggly flurry at each encounter of smiles and glances. I wonder if they ever pause to be thankful that they live in the days of *ai noa*, free eating, as against those of *ai kapu*, tabu eating, which obtained before the time of Kamehameha II!

The foods were of the finest, and, half-lying, like the Romans, we ate at our length—and almost ate our length of the endless variety, this time without implements of civilized cutlery. I suppose quite unnecessarily, we pitied those who boast that they have lived so-and-so many years in the Islands and have never even tasted poi—together with most other good things of the land and sea and air.

Jack and I, recalling the christening feast at Pearl Lochs, looked vainly for some sign of desire on the part of the Hawaiians to dance, and finally asked Mr. Kawehaweha about it. The young people appeared unconquerably bashful, but an old man, grizzled and wrinkled, his dim eyes retrospective of nearly fourscore years, squatted before us, reenforced with a rattling dried gourd, and displayed the rather emasculated hula of the Kalakaua reign—an angular performance of elbows and knees accompanied by a monotonous, weird chant, the explosive rattling of the gourd accentuating the high lights. The hoary ancient responded to several encores, and while the "dance" was different from any we had witnessed, it seemed a bloodless and decadent example of motion in which was none of the zest of life that rules the dancing of untrained peoples.

With smiles and imploring looks, and finally, in response to their tittering protestations of ignorance of the steps, declaring that after all we believed they did not know the hula, we touched the mettle of a number of the younger maidens. One white-gowned girl of sixteen disappeared from the line sitting along the stringer-piece of the pier, and presently, out of the dusk at the land-end, materializing between the indistinct rows of her people, she undulated to the barbaric two-step fretting of an old guitar that had been strumming throughout. Instantly the social atmosphere underwent a change, glowing and warming. Wahines with their sweet consenting faces, and their men, strong bodies relaxed as they rested among the ferns, jested musically in the speech that has been likened to a gargle of vowels. Another and younger sprite took form in the shoreward gloom and joined the first, where the two revolved about each other like a pair of pale moths in the lantern light. Fluttering before Mrs. Kawehaweha, they invited her to make one of them; but either she could not for diffidence, or would not, even though her husband sprang into the charmed space and danced and gestured temptingly before her blushing, laughing face. A slim old wahine coaxed by the two girls, whom all the company seemed anxious to show off as their choicest exponent of the olden hula, next stood before us, and held us breathless with an amazing and all-too-short dance. Unsmiling, she seemed without consciousness of our presence—twisting and circling, drawing unseen forms to her withered heart, level eyes and still mouth expressionless, dispassionate as a mummy's. She was anything but comely, and far from youthful. But she could outdance the best and command the speechless attention of all.

Came a pause when the guitar trembled on, although it seemed that the dancing must be done. Just as, reluctantly, we began to gather ourselves and our leis and everyday senses, in order not to outlive the sumptuous welcome, into the wavering light there glided a very young girl, slender and dark, curl-crowned, dainty and lovely as a dryad, who stepped and postured listlessly with slow and slower passes of slim brown hands in the air, as a butterfly opens and shuts its wings on a flower, waiting for some touch to send it madly wheeling into space.

And he came—the Dancing Faun; I knew him the moment he greeted my eyes. Black locks curled tightly to his shapely head, his nose was blunt and broad, eyes wild and wicked-black with fun, and lips full and curled back from small, regular teeth. I could swear to a pointed ear in his curls to either side, and that his foot was cloven. I could not see these things, but knew they must be. His shirt, for even a Faun must wear a shirt in twentieth century Hawaii, was a frank tatter—a tatter and nothing more, over a splendid chest that was brown and glistening. The hands, long and strong, spoke the getting of an easy livelihood from tropic branches.

The listless dryad swayed into quickened life, and the last and most beautiful spectacle of the night was on. I do not try to describe a hula. To you it may mean one thing, or many; to me, something else, or many other things. One may read vulgarity and sordid immorality into it; another infuse it with art and with poetry. And it is the love-poetry of the Polynesian. A poet sings because he must. The Hawaiian dances because he cannot help dancing. Deprived of his mode of motion, he fades away, and is likely to become immoral where before he was but unmoral, as a child may be. The page of the history of this people is nearly turned. Such as they were, they have never really changed—the individuality of their blood, manifested in their features, their very facial expression, is not strong enough to persist as a race, but unaltered endures in proportion to its quantity, so largely mixed as it is with other strains. The pure-bred Hawaiians are now far-apart and few, dying off every year with none to fill their gracious places. The page is being torn off faster and faster, and soon must flutter away.

HOLUALOA, to HUEHUE, Friday, August 30, 1907.

The Doctor, as a final benefaction, waiving inconvenience to himself, sent us and our luggage the whole journey to Waimea on the Parker Ranch, in his own carriage, in charge of the Portuguese coachman, Jose.

The first night we were fortunate enough to spend at Huehue, home of the John Maguires, wealthy Hawaiian ranchers who had extended the invitation at the Goodhues' reception. Lacking such hospitality, the malihini must travel, either by horse or carriage, or the one automobile stage, a very long distance to any sort of hotel. "They don't know what they've got!" Jack commented on the ignorance of the American public concerning the glorious possibilities of this country. "Just watch this land in the future, when they once wake up!"

Mrs. Maguire, one eighth Hawaiian, is an unmitigated joy, compounded as she is of sweet dignity and a bubbling vivacity that wipes out all thought of years and the wavy graying hair that only adds to the beauty of her brown eyes—a merry, sympathetic companion, one decides, for all moods and ages. Her husband is also part haole, but looks a noble example of the Hawaiian type, like the descendant of a race of rulers, strong kings, with commanding brow and eye of eagle, firm mouth, square jaw, and stern aquiline nose, the lofty-featured countenance gentled by a thatch of thick powder-gray hair and a most benevolent expression.

And the pair, we find, have been wedded but a year or two. Aileen, a thirteen-year-old heiress, granddaughter of John Maguire through a former alliance, completes the small family.

The Kona Sewing Guild was in full blast when we drew up in the blooming garden of the rambling house. Mrs. Goodhue, who had come this far on our way, joined the force and left me napping on a hikie in our guest-cottage, tired from a strenuous day of packing, typing—and traveling, even through such beautiful country, in full view of the ravishing Blue Flush of sea and sky.

"I hate to wake my poor tired Kid-Woman," Jack's voice called me from sleep an hour later; "but the most wonderful horse out here is waiting for you to ride him."

"But I've no clothes," as I came back to earth.

"Oh, I've got some for you," he grinned, depositing a bright-red calico muumuu on the hikiè, "and I'm just dying to see you ride in it!—Mrs. Maguire has one on, and looks all right."

Properly adjusted, in the cross-saddle this full garment appears like bloomers, and I can vouch is surpassingly comfortable.

And to me they led one of Pharaoh's horses—no other could it be, so full his eye, so proud his neck, the pricking of his ear so fine; none but a steed of Pharaoh's wears quite such flare of nostril, nor looks so loftily across the plain. Ah, he is something to remember, "Sweet Lei Lehua," and we can never forget his lovely crest, nor the flick of that small pointed ear, and the red, red nostril, blowing scented breath of grass and flowers—sweet as the flower whose name he wears.

Our ride was on the lava-rocky flank of Hualalai and all within the boundaries of the Maguire possessions, which comprise some 60,000 acres. My steed, like the Welshman on Haleakala showing yonder above the clouds, evidenced his sober years only in judgment of head and hoof. We breasted precarious places of sliding stones and slid down others as steep and uncertain, brushing lehua and ferns; into deep, green-grown blowholes of prehistoric convulsions we peered; and finally, descending a verdant pinnacle where Mrs. Maguire led for the viewing of broad downward miles of tumultuous lava to the blue sea, we went most gingerly on a grassy trail beset with snares of lava tinkling like glass, over natural bridges of the same brittle-blown substance, then threaded a sparse lehua wood to the main road.

All the while our hostess, younger hearted than any, even little Aileen, was the spirit of the party, a constant incentive to daring climbs or breathless bursts of speed, just an untired girl in mind and body of her, and one could but join gloryingly in her abandon of enjoyment that comes with swift and easy motion, urging to greater effort, whirling around curves, going out of the way to leap obstacles. And which is better, and what constitutes long life: to sit peacefully with folded hands while the rout goes by a-horse-back with laugh and love and song, walking carefully all one's days, or to live in heat of blood and thrill of beauty and every cell of persisting youth, taking high hazard with sea and sail, mountain and horse, and every adventurous desire? Jack, with his high-hearted exuberance, is my living answer and example.

Spinning an abrupt curve, the animals stopped at a gate like shots against a target, and our gleeful leader spurred at right angles straight up a four-foot stone wall to the next zigzag of road, we following willy-nilly in the mad scramble, marveling how we escaped a spill.

Following the Feast of Horses came the luau—not so-called, for it is the usual dinner of these people who, it seems to us, feed upon nectar and ambrosia. Fancy the young, tender fowl, stewed in coconut cream, and the picked and lomied rosy salmon bellies, with rosier fresh tomatoes, and salmon-pink salt like ground pigeon-blood rubies, and—but the entirely Hawaiian dinner, served with all the elegance of a wealthy *ménage*, cannot be described.

"Go on, play, Mate," Jack said in the twilight, where he lounged on the lanai after dining; "I haven't heard a funeral march on a grand piano for a long time, in this lotus loveland of guitars and ukuleles and their delectable airs."

And so, high upon Hualalai in the Sandwich Isles, I sat me down to the Largo of Handel, and Chopin's and Beethoven's stately processionals. For the man of my heart loves nothing better than these funereal rhythms of the masters. And, for once, in this land of spent fires, we all forewent and forgot the lilt of hulas and threnodies of dusky love songs, in the brave, deep music of our own Caucasian blood.

"I haven't heard those things since I studied in Paris," Mrs. Maguire said, with reminiscence in her sobered eyes; and a "Thank you" for the Largo came through the doorway from a visiting clergyman, while a blithe young judge of the District called for Mendelssohn's Funeral March while I was about it.

But Jack, with cigarette dead between his pointed fingers, lay in a long chair, his wide eyes star-roving in the purple pit of the night sky; for music always sets him dreaming, and many's the time I have momentarily wondered, at concert and opera, if he heard aught but the suggestions of the opening measures, so busily did he make notes upon whatever those suggestions had been to his flying brain.

HUEHUE, to PARKER RANCH,
Saturday, August 31, 1907.

"The sweetest poi is eaten out of the hau tree," "*He mikomiko ka ai'na oka poi o loko oka umeke hau*," say the Hawaiians; and our parting gift from the Maguires was a little treasure of a calabash, polished smooth and shining, of the light-golden wood, out of their cherished hoard.

Then, sped by the warm "Aloha nui oe" of all, and a last farewell from "Mother" Goodhue, we set our faces toward the expanse of lava

that was to be our portion for a day. Our principal impression, geographical as well as geological, of the journey, is of lava, and lava, and
more lava—new lava of 1881, old lava, older lava, oldest lava, and wide
waste of inexpressible ruin upon ruin of lava, lava without end. How
present any conception of this resistless, gigantic fall of molten rock
across which, mid-mountain, our road graded? For the general aspect
of dead, stilled lava is little different from the photographic portrayal
of the living, fluid substance. It cools, and quickly, in the veriest shapes
of its activity, and the traveler who misses the wonder of a moving
mountain side sees fair representation in the arrested flood. It needs
little imagination to assist one's eye to carry to the brain the illusion
of movement in the long red-brown sweep from mountain top to sea
margin. In many places we could see where hotter, faster streams had
cut through slower, wider swaths; and again, following the line of least
resistance, where some swift, deep torrent had burned its devastating
way down between the rocky banks of a gully.

The pahoehoe lava preserves all its swirls and eddies precisely as
they chilled in the longago or shorter-ago; while the a-a rears snap-
ping, flame-like edges against obstructions, or has piled up of its own
coolness in toothed walls. Far, incalculable, shimmering leagues below,
purple-brown lava rivers lie like ominous shadows of unseen menaces
upon plains of disintegrate eruptive stuff of our starry system that has
for remotest ages ceased to resemble lava.

Ribboning this strange, fire-licked landscape our road lay gray
white as ashes, sometimes spanning dreadful chasms where once had
blown great blisters and bubbles which, chilling too suddenly, had collapsed, leaving caverns and bridges of material fragile as crystal, layer
upon layer, that at close range looked to be molten metal, shining like
flaked gold and silver mixed with base alloy.

Often our eyes lifted to the azure summer sea with its tracks like
footprints of the winds, or as if the water had been brushed by great
wings. And with this day, meeting the breezes of Windward Hawaii,
there passed my Blue Flush into the limbo of heavenly memories.

Leaving the later flow, we traversed a land of lava so eternally
ancient that it blossoms with fertile growth. Beautiful color of plant
life springs from this seared dust of millenniums—cactus blossoming
magenta and reddish-gold and snow-white; native hibiscus, flaunting
tawny-gold flames, in high, scraggly trees of scant foliage; lehua's
crimson-threaded paint brushes; blue and white morning-glories and

patches of red flowers, flung about like velvet rugs. And here one comes upon what remains of a famous sandalwood forest that was systematically despoiled by generations of traders from the time of its discovery somewhere around 1790, according to Vancouver. By 1816 the deforesting of sandalwood had become an important industry of the natives, chief and commoner, with foreigners.

The wood was originally exported to India, although said to be rather inferior. Then the Canton market claimed the bulk of the aromatic timber, where it was used for carved furniture, as well as for incense. Even the roots were grubbed by the avaricious native woodsmen, and trade flourished until about 1835, when the government awoke to the exterminating of the valuable tree, and put a ban upon the cutting of the younger growth. But it is not surprising to learn that the tireless forethought of Kamehameha had already protested against the indiscriminate barter, and particularly the sacrifice of the new growth.

Thoroughly we enjoyed our novel holiday, when we grew warm and tired, napping alternately on the back seat on each other's shoulders, Jack, as is his fashion, dropping off suddenly like a child. When awake, he is always either working, talking, or reading; and I love to see his damp, curly head droop to the urge of a drowsy afternoon, for every moment's unconsciousness adds to his strength for the busy task of living that he has set himself. "You must simply *hate* me for the way I can sleep, any time and anywhere," he will sympathize with my insomnia—for he declares he has never yet seen me asleep. "Why, once," I have heard him tell, "when I was a boy, I got to thinking how awful it would be to have insomnia, and I stayed awake all of one night. It *was* awful. But it never happened again to me."

The livelong day we had traveled upon privately owned ranches, and at last found ourselves on Parker Ranch, the largest in the Territory, its variously guessed-at 150,000 acres lying between and on the slopes of the Kohala Mountains to the north, knobby with spent blowholes, and great Mauna Kea, reaching into the vague fastnesses of the latter. This grand estate, estimated at $3,000,000, is the property of one small, slim descendant of the original John Parker, who, with a beautiful Hawaiian maiden to wife, founded the famous line and the famous ranch, which is a principality in itself. Perhaps no young Hawaiian girl, since Kaiulani, has commanded, however modestly, so conspicuous a place as that occupied by the beautiful Thelma Parker.

For all we had gone with humane leisure, the horses fagged as the day wore, and often we walked awhile to rest them and refresh our own cramped members, treading rich pasture like the field of Ardath, starred with flowers we did not know, and keeping an eye to bands of Scotch beef-cattle, some of the 20,000 head with which little Thelma is credited. After the pampering climate of Kona, coats and carriage robes were none too warm at the close of day, when we neared the sizable post-office village of Waimea, headquarters of the enormous ranch.

Never shall be forgotten that approach to Waimea lying under Kohala's jade-green mountains like California's in showery springtime; nor the little craters in plain and valley, like red mouths blowing kisses to the sun; nor yet the softly painted foothills and sunset cloud-rack, and the sweet, cool wind and lowing herds.

"It seems like something I have dreamed, long ago," Jack mused; for, year in and year out, in sleep he often wanders purposefully in a land of unconscious mind that his waking eyes have never seen.

PARKER RANCH, Monday, September 2, 1907.

Jack has always declared that the only accident he feared was a blow on the head from behind that would "addle" his brain. And yesterday morning, while the blow came, not from a garroter but from the solid sod of earth, the dreaded "addle" became one of his experiences of life.

Through the courtesy of Mr. Thurston, we are enjoying the hospitality of the manager, Mr. Alfred W. Carter, and his wife, who dwell in the roomy home of Thelma, now abroad. And right welcome they made us in their quiet, unobtrusive manner.

In the morning Mr. Carter had our saddles put on "perfectly safe" horses that were a striking contrast to the ebullient animals Mrs. Maguire chose for us. Mr. Carter was evidently going to take no risks; nevertheless the most curious thing happened.

The big, stolid-looking gray selected for Jack was a dependable character on which the youngest Carter children were taught to ride— an ideal "family" horse. Jack was in his saddle, and turning to speak to our hostess at the gate, when the gray rose in air and came head-down in an unmistakable and violent "buck." Pitching, rearing, whirling, none but a proper "bronco buster" could have stayed on its back, and Jack, who had never ridden a bucking horse in his life, stuck creditably enough until, after a short plunging run, the beast twisted suddenly and he was thrown clear to the side, striking on left shoulder and back of head.

I was terribly frightened at the thudding impact, but Jack struggled to his feet, bewildered and much put-out, and offered to remount the snorting animal. Mr. Carter, however, now on the ground, would not allow this, and himself made the attempt. At his first touch the spiritless family pet recommenced his performance, while Mrs. Carter begged her husband to desist.

The kanaka cowboy who had brought the horses removed Jack's Australian saddle, threw on his own Mexican one with scant gentleness, and sprang into it, and there was no pilikia whatever. Jack's saddle was gone over by Mr. Carter, but he could find no irritating burr nor anything to account for the extraordinary behavior of the horse.

We thought, Jack and I, that the stalwart cowboys did not look entirely guiltless of practical joking; but their master would not listen to any such aspersion, because, if for no other reason, they would not dare tamper with the family's standby.

The saddle was put on a bay mare, and we carried out the program of visiting the racing stables; and I alone was aware of the pain in Jack's eyes from the rising agony in his head.

That night the ache became maddening, and I worked long hours, kneading his spinal column and the back of his neck, and applying cold compresses when he verged on delirium, meanwhile dreading the worst from the fever that increased till his face was scarlet and his tongue babbled nonsense.

In despair, I decided to reverse the treatment, and went foraging to the silent region of the kitchen for hot water. Immediately this compress was applied to the base of his brain, a change was noticeable, and very soon the sufferer was quietly asleep, to my inexpressible relief. To-day he is still abed, weak from shock of accident and delirium, congratulating himself that his brain was not permanently addled, and laughing over my report of the comical things he said when out of his head.

Judging from even the little we have been able to see of the Parker Ranch, it is reason in itself for a future visit to Hawaii. The glorious country, with its invaluable assets, is handled with all the precision of a great corporation. In our short ride we saw a few of the fine thoroughbred horses which are raised, one of the imported stallions being a son of Royal Flush. Royal Flush, the sire, lives and moves and pursues his golden-chestnut being on the ranch of Rudolf Spreckles, adjoining our own on Sonoma Mountain.

LOUISSON BROTHERS' COFFEE PLANTATION,
HONOKAA DISTRICT, HAWAII,
Thursday, September 5, 1907.

The Carters would not hear of Jack traveling before the end of three days, by which time the worst of the aching soreness was gone from his head. And on Wednesday, in their carriage drawn by a pair of big roadsters driven by a Hawaiian coachman, we proceeded to Honokaa, where we were met by another carriage, sent by the Louisson brothers.

The day's trip demonstrated a still better realization that the Big Island comprises two thirds of Hawaii Nei's area of 6700 square miles, as well as the copiously watered fertility of this windward coast. Leaving Waimea, we continued across the rolling green plains, whose indefinite borders were lost in Mauna Kea's misty foothills. Rain fell soothingly, and often we glimpsed fierce-looking, curly-headed Scotch bulls with white faces, vignetted in breaking Scotch mist into the veriest details of old steel engravings; and Hawaiian cowboys, taking form in the cottony vaporousness, waved and called to our coachman ere swallowed again.

One cannot encompass Hawaii without stepping upon the feet of one lordly mountain or another. If it is not the exalted Mauna Kea, it is surely the hardly less lofty Mauna Loa, or Hualalai.

And everywhere, here as always in these Islands, any moment one may look off to the sea, whether calm or blue-flushed, or, as here, deep-blue and white-whipped, driven like a mighty river by the strong and steady trade wind. One never grows fully accustomed to the startling height of the horizon, which seems always above eye-level, cradling one's senses in a vast blue bowl.

At last the road dipped seaward to the bluffs where lies red-roofed, tree-sheltered Honokaa, headquarters of a great sugar plantation. Jack made all arrangements for our weary team and the driver to be cared for overnight, rather than return the same day; and after luncheon at the little hotel, we set out upon the almost unbroken climb of several miles to Louissons' coffee plantation, where we had been invited by these two indefatigable brothers. Never have I met but one man who could surpass in perpetual motion our dear and earnest friend Alexander Hume Ford, and that man is "Abe" Louisson, who, body and eye and brain, seems animated by a galvanic battery. His brother Henry is correspondingly serene and restrained, but the two are all of a piece of unaffected hospitality.

It was a waving, shimmering land of incalculable breadth and length through which we ascended, of green so fair that there is no other green like it—cane so closely standing that it responds to all moods of the capricious sky, like the pale-green surfaces of mountain lakes; cane that floods its fair green clear to the sudden red verge of cliffs sheering into the blue, high-breaking ocean. And every way we looked, there were the sweat-shining, swart foreigners, Japanese, Portuguese, and what not, in their blue-denim livery of labor, watched and directed by mounted khaki-gaitered *lunas* (overseers), white or Hawaiian, or both, under broad sombreros.

We had not been in the high-basemented cottage half an hour, when the driven enthusiasm of Mr. "Abe" had us out again and among the magnificent coffee plants; and we learned that a coffee plantation can be one of the prettiest places under heaven, with its polished, dark-green foliage, head-high and over, crowded with red jewels of berries, interspersed by a valuable imported shade tree which he calls the *grevillea*. This tree serves the dual purpose of shading the plants—which are kept resolutely trimmed to convenient height—and of fertilizing with its leaves the damp ground under the thick shrubbery. And nowhere have we seen such luxuriant growth of coffee. The after-dinner *café noir* was unequaled in our experience save for a certain magic brew we used to drink at the Francis Plantation in the mountains of Jamaica less than two years gone.

This afternoon, enjoying good saddle horses over the Louisson ground, to us the hilly roads, the woods, the very air, were so like those of our own hill country that a pang of homesickness was felt by both. As if to further the illusion, at dinnertime Nature furnished a violent earthquake, albeit our first of volcanic origin. We were making very jolly over dessert and the thick black coffee, when the house seemed seized in an angry grasp and shaken like a gigantic rat. I never did like earthquakes, and the April eighteenth disaster which we two saw through in Glen Ellen and San Francisco has not strengthened my nerve. Jack, with expectant face, remained in his seat; but I, as the violence augmented, stood up and reached for his hand, vaguely wondering why every one did not run for the outside. The frame building seemed yielding as a basket—purposely erected that way. At the beginning of the tremor, the cook and his kokua had come quietly into the room and held the lamps; and when the second shock was heard grinding through the mountain Mr. Abe, wishing us to have the full benefit of the harmless diversion, rose dramatically, black eyes burning and arms waving, and cried:

"Here it comes! Listen to it! It's coming! Hear it! Feel it!"

And come it did, but more mildly. After we were in bed there was one light shock, accompanied by a distant rumbling and grinding in this last living island of the group.

Of course, our first thought following upon the immediate excitement of the shake was of the volcanoes. Would Kilauea, which had this long time dwindled to a breath of smoke, recrudesce? A telephone to Hilo brought no report of any activity. The initial attempts to use the wire were ludicrous failures, for every Mongolian and Portuguese of the thousands on Hawaii was yapping and jabbering after his manner, and the effect was as of a rising and falling murmur of incommunicable human woe, broken here and there by a sharper or more individual note of trouble. A white man's speech carried faintly in the unseen Babel.

LOUISSONS' TO HILO, Friday, September 6, 1907.

In the perfumed damp cool of morning we bade farewell to the hospitable bachelors, and descended once more from the knees of Mauna Kea to its feet upon the cliffs. The world was all a-sparkle from glinting mountain brow above purple forest and thick shining cloud-ring, down the dewy undulating lap of rustling cane, to the dimpling sea that ruffled its edges against the bold coast. Trees, heavy with overnight rain, shook their sun-opals upon us from leaf and branch, and little rills tinkled across the road that leads to the main drive. The air was filled with bird-songs, and in our hearts there was also something singing for very gladness.

Thus far, in all our junketing, we have relied for the most part upon saddle horses and railroad trains, or private conveyances of one sort or another. Long stretches endured in back seats of wagons have never appealed. But to-day's journeying, in the middle seat of three, luggage strapped on behind the four-in-hand stage, was a unique and profitable experience, furnishing an excellent chance to observe the labor element. For we traveled in company with members of its various branches—Hawaiian, Portuguese, Japanese, and all the other breeds, and no dull moment was ours.

The only seam in the day's pleasant fabric was the unfailing, incomprehensible, heart-rending want of sympathy with animals displayed by the Japanese. Jack, boiling with the stupid blindness of drivers and passengers, spluttered and fumed and made most uncomplimentary remarks when we overtook a heavy vehicle, packed ten-strong with placid Asiatics, male and female, which a pair of half-starved, undersized horses were unable to budge, on a steep ascent hub-high in a muddy landslide caused by the earthquake. It had not occurred to one single immobile-faced human of them to ease the load. But when Jack, with much expressive arm-flailing of the air, had relieved his just exasperation, all but the women were on the ground, and the pitiable team was able to forge ahead.

Needless to say, the sons of Nippon did not relish this interference, and there was glowering in our direction. "Scowls don't buy them anything!" Jack settled back in his seat, feeling much calmer. "What they need on this island is Rose Davison!" For all his admiration of the Japanese, he is in a state of eternal protest against their thoughtless incomprehension of animals; and in reminiscences of days with General Kuroki's army in Korea, the treatment of horses seems to remain his most vivid memory, especially in the matter of leaving to die by the roadside those which broke their legs on the icy march, or were otherwise injured, instead of putting them out of their misery. Fortunately for the pleasure of his journey to-day, one of our relay drivers was a genial Portuguese, who proved a very good whip as well as an interesting guide through the country.

The overcrowding was ludicrous. At some stop on the way, a bevy of Japanese would swarm into the stage without first a "look-see" to find if it was already full, literally piling themselves upon us. Jack, determinedly extricating them and holding firmly to his seat, would say with laughing eyes and smiling-set lips, while he thrust his big shoulders this way and that: "Gee! I like to look at them, but they'd camp on us if we'd let them!"

Ever a good "mixer," he is yet almost finicky about undue familiarity from what he chooses to term "lesser breeds," although his association with them is entirely without offense. There is a streak in him, not of snobbery, but of a sort of physical aristocraticness founded upon a well-considered philosophy. Very exclusive in the matter of personal articles, he thinks it a waste of valuable time to perform any menial office for himself when he can employ some one else to do it, and is seldom without a body-servant, at home or abroad.

"I'd rather be learning from the books than tying shoelaces or pressing trousers," elucidates he; and he likes me to apply the same reasoning. "How can you and I be continually sharing the endless books and ideas, if you are going to spend your time with feather-dusters and brooms and cookery? There are specialists for everything. You and I are joysmiths, and we specialize in ideas; let others specialize in their chosen fields.—No, I am not going to carve. I am never going to carve. I prefer to talk, and listen. I pay the servants in the kitchen to do the carving. *I* carve, *I* wash the dishes, *I* cook—by earning the money, through my own specialty, which I have chosen, to pay others to do that branch of my work."

He has come to appreciate that a growing sprig of French embroidery in my fingers does not interfere with my mental development the while I sit beneath his teaching (and he is always teaching—it is the breath of his body), and has ceased to regard with disfavor my scrap of fine linen and weaving needle—because, forsooth, he loves my fine raiment, and is ever impatient of any coarseness in its texture or workmanship. Ah, well, an attempt to set down his kaleidoscopic personality can result only in seeming paradox. He is so many, infinitely many, things; and there is no paradox in him, to one fortunate enough to be able to divine the just whole of his rounded universality.

The only compromise he made with the overreaching coolie tide was to take into our seat a sad little Porto Rican cripple, a mere child with aged and painwrought face, whom the passengers, of whatsoever nationality, shunned because of the bad repute of his blood in the Islands; and also a sunny small daughter of Portugal, glorious-eyed and bashfully friendly. When presented with a big round dollar, "a cartwheel," Jack called it, she answered maturely, to his query as to how she would squander it, a laconic:

"School shoes."

Shades of striped candy! How did her mother accomplish it? Now, the shrinking Porto Rican lad hobbled straight into a fruit store at the next halt, reappeared laden with red-cheeked imported apples, and with transfigured face of gratitude, held up his treasure for us to share. Jack, with moist eyes, bit his lip. So much for one Porto Rican in Hawaii. One would like to know *his* mother, too.

Jack, whose mind grasps the scheme of a cooperative commonwealth above all need for humbling charity from easeful lords of capital, nevertheless has a right hand that expresses the tenderness of his heart, and lets not his left hand know. The happiest thing in his happy, interesting journey was the turning inside-out of his loose-silver pocket; and I am not sure that the thong was not pulled on that long slender chamois gold-sack he has carried since Klondike days. Even I, somewhat in the relation of his left hand, do not know all he gave to the beatific babies who accompanied us this long day's ride.

Isabella Bird Bishop has painted an immortal word-picture of the gulches of Windward Hawaii in the Hilo District—giant erosions of age-old cloud-floods, their precipitous sides hidden in a savage riot of vegetation, heavy with tropic perfume. And this day, swinging through and beyond the coffee and cane of the Hamakua District that adjoins the Kona, following the patient grades along the steep faces of these stupendous ravines, descending to bridges over glorious streams that began and ended in waterfalls (" Build the road and bridge the ford!" Jack quoted rapturously), we remembered how she, long before any bridging of these, forded on horseback these same turbulent watercourses, swollen by freshets, at the risk of her precious life. For she was possessed of the joy of existence, that woman, as, unescorted in a period when few women braved traveling alone, she ventured ocean and island and foreign continent, writing as vividly as she lived.

Only fleeting glimpses we had of the coast—sheer green capes overflung with bursting waterfalls that dropped rainbow fringes to meet the blue-and-white frills of surf. "Bearded with falls," to quote Robert Louis Stevenson, is this bluffwise coast of the Big Island, and we envied the *Snark*'s crew who from seaward had viewed the complete glory, from surf to mountain head.

Laupahoehoe, "leaf of lava," in the simple poesy of the ancient Hawaiian, is the name of a lovely native village on a long low outthrust at the mouth of a wide ravine. Weather-softened old houses as well as grass huts stray its dreamy length, under coco palms etched against the horizon; and the natives seem to have no business but to bask beneath the blue-and-gold sky. One lovely thumb-sketch we glimpsed, where a river frolicked past a thatched hut under a leaning coco palm, near which a living bronze stood motionless—a rare picture in modern Hawaii.

Laupahoehoe, Hakalau, Onomea—we passed them all, and toward the end of day our absurd four-in-hand of gritty little mules trotted

(1) Waikiki, 1915: Mr. and Mrs. London (Center); Mr. A. H. Ford (Right)
(2) A Fragment of Paradise—Coconut Island, Hilo.   (3) Jack.   (4) Rainbow Falls, Hawaii

into a splendid red boulevard. Just as we had settled our cramped limbs to enjoy the unwonted evenness of surface, the driver pulled up in Wainaku, a section of suburban Hilo, before a seaward-sloping green-sward terrace fanned by a "Travelers' palm" under which grazed a rain-wet, golden-coated mare. Here, upon a word sent ahead by mutual friends, this time the Maydwells, we were again to know the hospitality of perfect strangers—an unequaled hospitality combined of European and Polynesian ideals by the white peoples who have made this country their own.

On the steps of an inviting lanai room stood a blue-eyed lady-woman, sweet and cool and solicitous, with three lovely children grouped about her slender, blue-Princess-gowned form—a Chicago girl whose husband, William T. Balding, holds an important position with the Waiakea Sugar Company, whose mill purrs all hours at Wainaku by the sea.

Refreshed by a bath, and arrayed in preposterously wrinkled ducks and holoku out of tight-packed suit cases, we dined exquisitely in an exquisite dining-room hung with fern baskets, the table sparkling with silver and cut-glass, the napery worthy of a glass show-case, and served by the ever-lovely adopted butterfly-maid of Japan. Will Balding, blue-eyed, clear featured, and dark-haired, is the perfect complement of his fair-tressed wife, and Jack's last words, as he fell asleep early under the snowy netting, were:

"A pair of thoroughbreds."

SHIPMANS' VOLCANO HOME, HAWAII,
Saturday, September 7, 1907.

Away back in 1790 or thereabout, an American fur-trader named Metcalf, commanding the snow *Eleanor*, visited the Sandwich Islands on his way to the Orient, his son, eighteen years of age, being master of a small schooner, *Fair American*, which had been detained by the Spaniards at Nootka Sound.

A plot was hatched by some of the chiefs to capture the *Eleanor*, and was frustrated by Kamehameha, who himself boarded her and ordered the treacherous chiefs ashore. Following this, a high moi of Kona was insulted and thrashed with a rope's-end by Captain Metcalf for some trifling offense, and vowed vengeance upon the next vessel that should come within his reach.

The snow *Eleanor* crossed the Hawaii Channel to Honuaula, Maui, where a chief of Olowalu with his men one night stole a boat and killed the sailor asleep in it, afterward breaking up the boat for the nails. Metcalf set sail for Olowalu, where, under mask of trading with the natives, he turned loose a broadside of cannon into the flock of peaceful canoes surrounding the *Eleanor*, strewing the water with dead and dying.

After this uncalled-for, wanton massacre of innocent islanders, Metcalf returned to Hawaii, and lay on and off Kealakekua Bay waiting for the *Fair American*, which had by now arrived off Kawaihae, on the sea-boundary of the present Parker Ranch, which we had glimpsed when we passed through.

Chief Kameeiamoku went out with a fleet of canoes as if to trade, and when the eighteen-year-old skipper of the *Fair American* was off his guard, threw him outboard and dispatched the crew with the exception of Isaac Davis, the mate.

Simultaneously, John Young, the original Young of Hawaii, found himself detained ashore, and all canoes under tabu by orders of Kamehameha, in order that Metcalf should not hear of the loss of his son and the schooner. The *Eleanor* continued lying off and on, firing signals, for a couple of days, and finally sailed for China.

John Young and Isaac Davis were eventually raised by Kamehameha to the rank of chiefs, endowed with valuable tracts of land, and they in turn lent the great moi their service of brain and hand in council and war, although carefully guarded for years whenever a foreign vessel hove in sight.

Small cannon, looted from the *Fair American* as well as other vessels which had been "cut out," were of priceless value in the experienced hands of the white men in enabling Kamehameha eventually to win his war of conquest, especially over the Maui armies under the sons of Kahekili.

All of which is preamble to the pleasant fact that we are enviable guests of Mr. and Mrs. W. H. Shipman, of Hilo, at their volcano house, and Mrs. Shipman is the grand-daughter of the gallant Isaac Davis. Also we find she is half-sister to our friend Mrs. Tommy White. Such a healthy, breezy household it is; and such a wholesome, handsome brood of young folk, under the keen though indulgent eye of this motherly, deep-bosomed woman whose three fourths British ancestry keeps firm vigilance against undue demonstration of the ease-loving strain of wayward, sunny Polynesian blood she has brought to their dowry. And the tropic wine in her veins has preserved her from all age and decay of spirit. During this day and evening I have more than once failed to resist my desire to lay my tired head upon her breast, where it has been made amply welcome.

A social and domestic queen is Mrs. Shipman, and right sovranly she reigns over her quiet, resourceful Scotch spouse, whose pride in her efficient handling of their family twinkles in his contented blue eye. And though models of discipline and courtesy, their offspring are brimming with hilarious humor, while of ttimes their mother's stately, silken-holokued figure is the maypole of their dancing, prancing romp. Those holokus are the care of the two elder daughters, who never tire of planning new variations of pattern and richness, with wondrous garniture of lace and embroidery.

Mrs. Shipman—and again we are in Kakina's debt—had telephoned Mrs. Balding to extend an invitation to this suburban home near the volcano; and according to arrangement Jack and I met her on the up-mountain train from Hilo to the terminal station, where the Shipman carriage and splendid team conveyed us ten miles farther to this high house in a garden smothered in tree-ferns.

Jack preceded me into town, as he had *Snark* business—as well as difficulties—to attend to; and Mrs. Balding drove me up later for my first glimpse of Hilo, the second city of the Territory, on its beautiful site at the feet of Mauna Loa, one of the prettiest island towns one could wish to see, divided by two rivers, the Wailuku tearing its way down a deep and tortuous gorge. Nothing could be more impressive than Hilo's background of steadily rising mountain of cane and forested and twisted lava-flow. The rivers are spanned by steel bridges, and the main streets are broad and clean and shaded by enormous trees, with many branching lanes overarched by blossoming foliage and hedged with vines and shrubbery. Captain Vancouver, that thoroughgoing benefactor of Polynesia, saw the possibilities of this port (once called after Lord Byron, brother of the poet, who nearly a century ago dropped the anchor of his frigate Blonde in the offing, and surveyed the bay as well as the Volcano Kilauea), for he wrote:

"Byron Bay will no doubt become the site of the capital of the island. The fertility of the district of Hilo, . . . the excellent water, and abundant fish pools which surround it, the easy access it has to the sandalwood district, and also to the sulphur, which will doubtless soon become an object of commerce, and the facilities it affords for refitting vessels, render it a place of great importance."

At the second station out of Hilo, near the main wharf, where we could just see the dear little *Snark* moored, the train was boarded by the dwindling *Snark*ites, the captain and Martin—and our disgruntled engineer, who could not conform to ship discipline, who came to bid me goodby. Tochigi, unable to overcome his relentless seasickness, already sorely missed by us, had sailed for San Francisco.

The little observation-car was filled with well-to-do Hilo residents bound for the weekend at their volcano lodges, and I could see Jack planning two more homes on his lengthening list.

To Kilauea, at last, at last—my first volcano, albeit a more or less disappointing Kilauea these days, without visible fire, the pit, Halemaumau, only vouchsafing an exhibition of sulphurous smoke and fumes. But live volcano it is, and much alive or little, does not greatly matter. Besides, one may always hope for the maximum, since Kilauea is notoriously capricious.

For eighteen miles the track up from Hilo slants almost imperceptibly, so gradual is the ascent through dense, tropical forest, largely of tree ferns, and, latterly, dead lehua overspread with parasitic ferns and creepers. There seems no beginning nor end to the monster island; and despite the calm, vast loveliness of many of its phases, one cannot help thinking of it as something sentient and threatening, and of the time when it first heaved its colossal back out of the primordial slime. And it is still an island in the making.

The carriage, sent up the day before from Hilo, was driven by one Jimmy, a part-Hawaiian, part-Marquesan grandson of Kakela, the Hawaiian missionary to the Marquesas group, whose intervention saved Mr. Whalon, mate of an American vessel, from being roasted and eaten by the cannibals of Hivaoa. Jimmy's grandfather was rewarded by the personal gift of a gold watch by Abraham Lincoln, in addition to a sum of money from the American Government. "And don't forget, Mate," Jack reminded me, "your boat is next bound to the Marquesas!"

It was a hearty crowd Mrs. Shipman served at dinner; and imagine our smacking delight in a boundless stack of ripe sweet corn-on-the-cob mid-center of the bountiful table! Among all manner of Hawaiian staples and delicacies, rendered up by sea and shore, we found one new to us—stewed ferns. Not the fronds, mind, but the stalks and stems and midribs. Served hot, the slippery, succulent lengths were not unlike fresh green asparagus. The fern is also prepared cold, dressed as a salad. Jack thinks we might utilize our California brakes when we are home again.

The father of his flock rode in late from his own great cattle ranch, Puuoo, on Mauna Kea. The flock as well as its maternal head rose as one to make their good man comfortable after his long rough miles in the saddle. In a crisp twilight, the men smoked on the high lanai, and the rest of us breathed the invigorating mountain air. It was hard to realize the nearness of this greatest of living volcanoes. Presently Jack and I became conscious of an ineffably faint yet close sound like "the tiny horns of Elfland blowing." Crickets, we thought, although puzzled by an unwontedly sustained and resonant note in the diminutive bugling. And we were informed, whether seriously I know not, that the fairy music proceeded from landshells (Achatinella), which grow on leaves and bark of trees, some 800 species being known. Certainly there *are* more things in earth and heaven—and these harmonious pixie conches, granting it was they, connoted the loftier origin. Jack's eyes and mouth were dubious:

"I ha'e ma doots," he softly warned; "but I hope it *is* a landshell orchestra, dear Kid, because the fancy gives you so much pleasure."

Sunday. September 8. 1907.

Kilauea, "The Only," has a just right to this distinguished interpretation of its name, for it conforms to no preconceived idea of what a conventional volcano should be. Not by any stretch of imagination is it conical; and it fails by some nine thousand feet of being, compared with the thirteen-odd-thousand-foot peak on the side of which it lies, a mountain summit; its crater is not a bowl of whatsoever oval or circle; nor has it ever, but once, to human knowledge, belched stone and ashes—a hundred and fifty years ago when it wiped out the bulk of a hostile army moving against Kamehameha's hordes, thus proving to the all-conquering chief that the Goddess Pélé, who dwells in the House of Everlasting Fire, Halemaumau, was on his side.

Different from Mauna Loa's own lofty crater, which has inundated Hawaii in nearly every direction, Kilauea, a vent in Mauna Loa's side, never overflows, but holds within itself its content of molten rock. The vertical walls, from 100 to 700 feet high, inclose nearly eight miles of flat, collapsed floor containing 2650 acres; while the active pit, a great well some 1000 feet in diameter, is sunk in this main level.

In the forenoon we visited the Volcano House on the yawning lip of the big crater, and sat before a great stone fireplace in the older section, where Isabella Bird and many another wayfarer, including Mark Twain, once toasted their toes of a nipping night in the yesterdays.

From the hotel lanai we looked a couple of miles or so across the sunken lava pan to Halemaumau, from which a column of slow, silent, white smoke rose like a genie out of underworld Arabian Nights, and floated off in the light air currents. No fire, no glow—only the ghostly, vaporous smoke. And this inexorable if evanescent banner of the sleeping mountain has abundant company in myriad lesser streamers from hot fissures all over the red-brown basin surrounding it, while the higher country, green or arid, shows many a pale spiral of steam.

Rheumatic invalids should thrive at the Volcano House, for this natural steam is diverted through pipes to a bath-house where they may luxuriate as in a Turkish establishment; and there is nothing to prevent them from lying all hours of the day near some chosen hot crack in the brilliant red earth that sulphurous steam has incrusted with sparkling yellow and white crystals.

Having arranged with the genial Mr. Demosthenes, Greek proprietor of this as well as the pretty Hilo Hotel, for a guide to the pit later on, Mrs. Shipman directed her coachman farther up Mauna Loa—the "up" being hardly noticeable—to see living as well as dead koa forest, and the famous "tree molds." Some prehistoric lava-flow annihilated the big growth, root and branch, cooling rapidly as it piled around the trees, leaving these hollow shafts that are exact molds of the consumed trunks.

The fading slopes of Mauna Loa, whose still active crater is second in size only to Kilauea's, beckoned alluringly to us lovers of saddle and wilderness. One cannot urge too insistently the delusive eye-snare of Hawaii's heights, because an elastic imagination, continuously on the stretch, is needful to realize the true proportions. To-day, only by measuring the countless distant and more distant forest belts and other notable features on the incredible mountain side could we gain any conception of its soaring vastitude.

For a time the road winds through green, rolling plains studded with gray shapes of large, dead trees, and then comes to the sawmills of the Hawaii Mahogany Company. Here we went on foot among noble living specimens of the giant koa, which range from sixty to eighty feet, their diameters a tenth of their height, with wide-spreading limbs—beautiful trees of laurel-green foliage with moon-shaped, leaf-like bracts. It was in royal canoes of this acacia, often seventy feet in length, hollowed out of these mighty boles, that Kamehameha made his conquest of the group, and by means of which his empire-dreaming mind planned to subdue the Society Islands. As a by-product, the koa furnishes bark excellent for tanning purposes.

Great logs, hugely pathetic in the relentless grasp of man-made machinery, were being dragged out by steel cable and donkey-engine, and piled in enormous and increasing heaps. Jack, who is inordinately fond of fine woods if they are cut unshammingly thick and honestly, left a good order with Mr. Kant, the manager on the ground, for certain generous table-top slabs to be seasoned from logs which we chose for their magnificent grain and texture.

In addition to their flourishing koa business, these mills are turning out five hundred ohia lehua railroad ties per day, and filling orders from the States. But one can easily predict a barren future for the forests of Hawaii if no restraint, as now, is enforced in the selection of trees.

In the bright afternoon, mounted on the Shipmans' saddle horses, with our Hawaiian guide we made descent into Kilauea, accompanied by Mr. Bruce Cartwright, Jr., a Honolulan acquaintance whom Jack greatly admires—a big, frank-eyed young fellow, whose clean ambition is to attend Yale University, particularly for the forestry courses.

The morning's cursory view had been no preparation for the beautiful trail, on which we were obliged to brush aside green tree-branches and ferns and berry bushes in order to see the cracking desolation of the basin. Abruptly enough, however, we debouched upon its floor, under the stiff wall we had descended, now towering hundreds of feet overhead. Before us lay a crusted field of reddish dull-gold, where whiffs and plumes of white steam rose near and far from awesome fissures—a comfortless waste without promise of security, a treacherous valley of fear, of lurking hurt, of extermination should a foot slip.

On a well-worn pathway, blazed in the least dangerous places, we traversed the strange, hot earth-substance. The horses, warily sniffing, seemed to know every yard of the way as accurately as the tiny Hawaiian guide. But we recalled Christian in the Valley of the Shadow, for at every hand yawned pitfalls large and small and most fantastic—devilish cracks issuing ceaseless scalding menace, broken crusts of cooled lava-bubble, jagged rents over which we hurried to avoid the hot, gaseous breath of hissing subterranean furnaces.

Now and then the guide requested us to dismount, leading, crawling, into caverns of unearthly writhen forms of pahoehoe lava—weirdly beautiful interiors—bubbles that had burst redly in the latest overflow of Halemaumau into the main crater. On through the uncanny, distorted lavascape cautiously we fared under a cloud-rifted sky, and finally left the horses in a small corral of quarried lava, thence proceeding afoot to the House of Fire.

Perched on the ultimate, toothed edge, we peered into a baleful gulf of pestilent vapors rising, forever rising, light and fine, impalpable as nightmare mists from out a pit of destruction. Only seldom, when the slight breeze stirred and parted the everlasting, unbottled vapors, were we granted a fleeting glimpse, hundreds of feet below on the bottom of the well, of the plummetless hole that spills upward its poisonous breath. If the frail-seeming ledge on which we hung had caved, not one of us could have reached bottom alive—the deadly fumes would have done for us far short of that.

A long, long, silent space we watched the phenomenon, thought robbed of definiteness by our abrupt and absolute removal from the blooming, springing, established world above the encircling palisade of dead and dying planetary matter. Jack's contribution, if inelegant, was fit, and without intentional levity:

"A hell of a hole," he pronounced.

Pélé, Goddess of Volcanoes, with her family, constituted a separate class of deities, believed to have emigrated from Samoa in ancient days, and taken up their abode in Moanalua, Oahu. Their next reputed move was to Kalaupapa, Molokai, thence to Haleakala, finally coming to rest on the Big Island. In Halemaumau they made their home, although stirring up the furies in Mauna Loa and Hualalai on occasion, as in 1801, when unconsidered largess of hogs and sacrifices were vainly thrown into the fiery flood to appease the *huhu* goddess. Only the sacrifice of a part of Kamehameha's sacred hair could stay her wrath, which cooled within a day or two.

Many, doubtless, have there been of great men and women in the Polynesian race; but the fairest complement to the greatest, Kamehameha, seems indisputably to have been that flower of spiritual bravery, Kapiolani, a high princess of Hawaii, who performed what is accounted one of the greatest acts of moral courage ever known—equal to and even surpassing that of Martin Luther. A woman of lawless temperament, her imperious mind became interested in the tenets of

Christianity, and swiftly she blossomed into a paragon of virtue and refinement, excelling all the sisterhood in her intelligent adoption of European habits of thought and living.

Brooding over the unshakable spell of Pélé upon her people, in defiance of their dangerous opposition, as well as that of her husband, Naihe, the national orator, she determined to court the wrath of the Fire Goddess in one sweeping denunciation and renunciation.

It was almost within our own time, in 1824, when she set out on foot from Kaawaloa on Kealakekua Bay, a weary hundred and fifty miles, to Hilo. Word of the pilgrimage was heralded abroad, so that when she came to Kilauea, one of the missionaries, Mr. Goodrich, was already there to greet her. But first the inspired princess was halted by the priestess of Pélé, who entreated her not to go near the crater, prophesying certain death should she violate the tabus. Kapiolani met all argument with the Scripture, silencing the priestess, who confessed that *ke akua*, the deity, had deserted her.

Kapiolani proceeded to Halemaumau, where in an improvised hut she spent the prayerful night; and in the morning, undeserted by her faithful train of some fourscore persons, descended over half a thousand feet to the "Black Ledge," where, in full view and heat of the grand and terrifying spectacle of superstitious veneration, unflinchingly she ate of the votive berries theretofore consecrate to the dread deity. Casting outraging stones into the burning lake, she fearlessly chanted:

> "Jehovah is my God!
> He kindled these fires!
> I fear thee not, Pélé!
> If I perish by the anger of Pélé,
> Then Pélé may you fear!
> But if I trust in Jehovah, who is my God,
> And he preserve me when violating the tabus of Pélé,
> Him alone must you fear and serve!"

Tears were in our eyes to vision how this truly glorious soul then knelt, surrounded by the bowed company of the faithful, in adoration of the Living God, while their mellow voices, solemn in the supreme exaltation, rose in praise. We cannot help wondering if Mr. Goodrich, fortunate enough to experience such epochal event, was able, over and above its moral and religious significance, to sense the tremendous romance of it.

Scarcely less illuminating was the conversion of that remarkable woman, Kaahumanu, favorite wife of Kamehameha, to whom I have already referred as one of the most vital feminine figures in Polynesian annals. Far superior in intellect to most of the chiefs, she had been created regent upon the demise of her husband, ruling with an iron will, haughty and overbearing.

At first disdainful of the missionaries, finally her interest was enlisted in educational matters, whereupon with characteristic abandon she threw herself into the learning of the written word as well as the spoken. An extremist by nature, born again if ever was human soul, from 1825 to her death in Manoa Valley, Honolulu, in June of 1832, she held herself dedicate to the task of personally spreading virtue and industry throughout the Islands. Her last voyage was to pay a visit to Kapiolani, after which she lived to receive the fourth reinforcement of American missionaries, who arrived in the *Averick* a month before her passing; and the crowning triumph of her dying hours was the first complete copy of the New Testament in the Hawaiian tongue. Alexander writes:

> " . . . Her place could not be filled, and the events of the next few years (of reaction, uncertainty, and disorder in internal affairs) showed the greatness of the loss which the nation had sustained. The 'days of Kaahumanu' were long remembered as days of progress and prosperity."

And yet, according to all research, the ancient Hawaiians were essentially a religious people according to their ideals. Almost every important undertaking was led by prayer to widely diverse gods, unfortunately not all beneficent. The "witch doctor," or *kahuna*, exerting a disastrously powerful influence in all phases of racial development, has not to this day entirely ceased to blight the imaginations, to the actual death, of certain classes. "Praying to death" is the most potent principle of kahunaism, and in the past played an important part in holding down the population of the never-too-prolific race. One prayer alone, related at length by Dr. J. S. Emerson, enumerates some eleven methods of causing death to any subject selected, and illustrates the unsleeping brain and artistry of the sorcerers, "assassins by prayer," who invented it. Still, kahunas were not an altogether enviable faction in the past, since on occasion they employed their own mental medicine against one another. A certain class of these "metaphysicians," as Jack dubs them, bore a reputation of being "more like evil spirits than human beings," so feared and hated that their practices constituted a boomerang, resulting in their being stoned to death.

All the foregoing, and more, we lazily discussed at length on the precarious shelf in Pélé's mansion, although often speech was interrupted by sulphur fumes that blinded and suffocated. And when we climbed into the pure air, Jack and I agreed that even in the quiescent mood of its least spectacular aspect, Kilauea is more than well worth a long voyage to behold.

At the Volcano House, Mr. Demosthenes led the way to his guest book in the long glass sun-room, and showed many celebrated autographs, reaching back into the years. Jack, upon request, added his own sprawling, legible signature that always seems so at variance with his small hand. Our joint contribution was as follows, with Jack leading off:

"'It is the pit of hell,' I said.

"'Yes,' said Cartwright. 'It is the pit of hell. Let us go down.'

"'And where Jack goes, there go I.' So I followed them down."

Next Day.

This blue and crystal morning, despite the pleasant bustle of packing for the return to Hilo, Mrs. Shipman was found seated sumptuously amidst cut flowers of her own tender care, weaving crisp leis for our shoulders and hats. This in itself was not surprising; but in view of the fact that she was to accompany our departure, it seemed the very acme and overflow of hospitality; and Jack, gazing upon this mother-of-many, his eyes brimming with appreciation, muttered under his breath: "Mate—isn't she wonderful?" Later, after a thoughtful pause in his writing, he broke out: "To me, Mother Shipman is the First Lady of Hawaii!"

To the garlands were added necklaces of strung berries, bright blue and hard as enamel, and strands of tiny round rosebuds, exquisite as pale corals from Naples. It was a custom in less strenuous years to present these plant-gems laid in jewel cases of fresh banana bark split lengthwise, the inside of which resembles nothing so well as mother-of-pearl. Can anything lovelier be imagined?

And so, wreathed in color and perfume, we dropped down the fragrant mountain, ourselves a moving part of the prevalent luxuriance of blossom and fern and vine. One mile is as another for unspoiled beauty, although turns in the magical pathway open up pictures that surpass beauty if this may be. Great trees, living or dead, their weird roots half above ground, form hanging gardens of strange flowers and tendrilly things imagined of other planets or the pale dead moon. Giant ferns, their artificial-looking pedestals set inches-deep in moss on fallen trunks, crowd the impenetrable, dank undergrowth. Climbing-palms net the forest high and low with fantastic festoons, and star the glistening wildwood with point-petaled waxen blossoms of rich burnt-orange luster, while the decorative ie-ie sets its rust-colored candelabra on twisted trunk and limb. If you never beheld else in all Hawaii Nei, the Volcano Road would impress a memory of one of the most beautiful journeys of a lifetime. Of the thirty miles, the twenty nearest to Hilo wind through this virgin forest garden, into the picturesque outskirting lanes of the old town.

When the carriage left the bridge that crosses Wailuku's roaring gorge into the Shipmans' driveway to their castle-white mansion overlooking Hilo, a pair of white-gowned daughters, brunette Clara, and Caroline tawny-blonde, ran to meet mother and father and younger ones as if from long absence, and lo, also Mary, now Mrs. English, who proved to be an old classmate of Jack's in the Oakland High School. Behind them, Uncle Alec, another hale example of Hawaii's beneficence to the old, stood apple-cheeked and smiling under his thatch of vital, frosty hair, and joined in a welcome that seemed to seal us forever their very own.

BALDINGS', WAINAKU, Sunday, September 15, 1907.

We did it! we did it! And, as so often happens, the giddy experience came through a remembered suggestion of Mr. Ford, who has long wished to coast the cane-flumes of the Big Island. Jack made a tentative bid to the Baldings for this rather startling entertainment, and the pair, "good fellows" to their finger tips, entered into the spirit of the idea, which, however, was not altogether new to them.

One of the flimsy aqueducts runs just beyond their rear fence, on the seaward slope, and any weekday we can follow with our eyes the loose green faggots slipping noiselessly toward the toothed maw of the sugar mill, the whistle of which marks the working hours of its employees.

To the right is a gulch, crossed, perhaps two hundred feet in air, by the flume's airy trestle; and over this, in swimming-suits, a merry party of us essayed the narrow footboard that accompanies the flume elbow high at one's side.

Each had his or her own method of preserving balance, mental and bodily, above the unsettling depths. Jack sustained his confidence by letting one hand slide lightly along the edge of the flume, with the result that his palm, still calloused from the *Snark*'s ropes, picked up an unnoticed harvest of finest splinters that gave us an hour's patient work to extract. My system was first deliberately to train my eyes on the receding downward lines to the tumbling gulch-stream, and at intervals, as I walked, to touch hand momentarily to the flume. Martin, debonair stranger to system of any sort under any circumstances, paced undaunted halfway across, and suddenly fell exceeding sick, grasping the waterway with both hands until the color flowed back into his ashen face.

The wooden ditch is just wide enough in which to sit with elbows close, and the water flows rapidly on the gentle incline. If one does not sit very straight, he will find himself progressing on one hip, and probably get to laughing beyond all hope of righting himself. With several persons seated say a hundred yards apart, the water is backed up by each so that its speed is much decreased, and there is little difficulty in regulating your movements and whatever speed is to be had—and mind the nails! Lying supine, feet-foremost, arms-under-head, the maximum is obtained; sit up, and it slackens.

The ride was great fun, and, safely on the ground once more at our starting point, Jack was so possessed with the sport that he telephoned to Hilo for "hacks" to convey us a mile or so up the road to a point where the flume crosses. A laughable crowd were we: the men, collarless, in overcoats on top of their dripping suits, the women also in wet garments under dry ulsters.

In a sweltering canefield, Mr. Balding directed the binding of small, flat bundles of the sweet-smelling sugar stems, and still with the fear of nails, however smoothed and flattened, strong upon us, remembering tragical cellar-doors of childhood, we embarked upon our sappy green rafts.

Just fancy lying on your back, the hour near sunset, in a tepid stream of clear mountain water, sliding on under the bluest of blue skies with golden-shadowed clouds, breathing the sun-drenched air; then lifting slowly, to glance, still moving and strangely detached, over the edge, to canefields far beneath and stretching from mountain-forest to sea rim; picking out rocky watercourses, toy bridges and houses, and Lilliputian people going about their business on the green face of earth; while not far distant a gray-and-gold shower-curtain, rainbow-tapestried, blows steadily to meet you in mid-air, tempering the vivid blues and greens of sea and sky and shore. In the void between ourselves and the shimmering green earth, ragged bundles of cane, attached to invisible wires, drawn as by a spell toward the humming sugar mill at sea-rim, looked for all the world like fleeing witches on broomsticks, with weird tattered garments straight behind. You glide in an atmosphere of fantasy, "so various, so beautiful, so new," in which every least lovely happening is the most right and natural, no matter how unguessed before.

Over-edge and on the ground again, at exactly the proper spot to obviate feeding one's shrinking toes into the sugar mill machinery, one can only think of a longer ride next time—which Jack is planning to the tune of a ten-mile-away start.

Belike our latest skipper is a better man at sea than ashore. Certain rumors lead us to this hazard. Early in his employment by Jack, I had taken him aside in Honolulu, and outlined what Jack had been through during the post-earthquake building and first sailing of the *Snark*. In voice quivering with emotion, and with moist eyes, he implored me to harbor no doubt that he would devote the coming years to making our voyage the success it deserved to be, et cetera. "Mrs. London," he said, "believe my word when I tell you, now, that if I don't take the *Snark* around the world, and back through the Golden Gate into San Francisco Bay, it will be because I am dead!"

Perhaps a professional sailor is always "a sailor ashore"; and doubtless the captain has by now read my easy-going husband well enough to know that he will not be left to settle the personal bills incurred in Hilo over and above his salary.

SHIPMANS', HILO, Monday, October 7, 1907.

To-morrow the dream-freighted *Snark*, carrying only three of her initial adventurers, Jack, Martin, and myself, sails from Hilo for the Marquesas Islands lying under the Line, toward which Jack's sea-roving spirit has yearned from boyhood, since first he devoured Melville's tale, "Typee," of months detained in the cannibal valley on Nuka-Hiva. And soon, by the favor of wind and current, we shall drop our modern patent hook in Melville's very anchorage at Taiohae Bay, which was also that of Robert Louis Stevenson's *Casco* in later years; and together we shall quest inland to Typee Vai.

Besides the captain, there is a new Dutch sailor, Herrmann de Visser, delft-blue of eye, and of a fair white-and-pinkness of skin that no lifetime of sea-exposure has tarnished. The berth of the sorely regretted Tochigi is occupied by a brown manling of eighteen, Yoshimatsu Na- kata, a moon-faced subject of the Mikado who speaks, and kens not, but one single word of English, same being the much overtaxed Yes; but his blithesome eagerness to cover all branches of the expected service prom- ises well. Martin has been graduated from galley into engine-room; and Wada, a Japanese chef of parts, bored with routine of schooner schedule between San Francisco and Hilo, is in charge of our "Shipmate" range and perquisites in the tiny, under-deck galley.

Jack had confidently assumed, after four months' re-pairing in Honolulu, that the new break in the seventy-horsepower engine could easily be mended, and that in a week or ten days at most we might resume the long-delayed voyage. But alas, as fast as one weakness was dealt with another appeared, until even that long-suffering patience which Jack displays in the larger issues, was worn to a thread, and at times I could see that he was restless and unhappy. Nevertheless, he worked doggedly at the novel, missing no forenoon at his table behind a screen on the lanai of the Shipmans' high house, where we came, follow- ing the visit with our friends at Wainaku. But too often I could sense the strain he was under, and ached to see drawn lines around his mouth and a blue wanness, like shadows on snow, beneath his eyes.

Among other exasperating discoveries, the cause of a hitherto un- accountable pounding of the engine was found to lie in an awryness of the bronze propeller blades, probably sustained at the time the yacht was allowed to fall through the inadequate ways in the shipyard at San Francisco. This corrected, something else would go wrong, until we became soul-sick of sailing-dates and hope deferred.

One day, packed and ready for an early departure, Jack, who had answered the telephone ring, called that the captain wanted to talk to me. As I passed him, Jack whimsically remarked: "I hope it isn't some- thing so bad he doesn't want to break it to *me!*"

It was precisely that, and the captain's opening words made me swallow hard and brace for the worst: "Mrs. London ... I couldn't tell him. ... I couldn't do it .... You can do anything. But after all he has had to bear lately, I just simply couldn't break it to him."

Some day I may learn that in *Snark* affairs nothing is too dread- fully absurd nor absurdly dreadful to occur.

Jack had such difficulty in getting the ill tidings out of me, and I myself was so cast down, that the information savored strongly of anticlimax when finally I told him that the five-horsepower engine had fractured its bedplate, and the repairs would hold the *Snark* in port at least a week longer. This engine and the big one are of different makes and were built in different parts of the United States; and yet each had been set in a flawed bedplate! Jack was forced to laugh. "I see these things happen, but I don't believe them!" he repeated an old remark. How much of despair there was in his mirth I had no way of knowing; but when he went into town to inspect the latest wreckage, he was called upon to cheer his own men, for the captain met him with tears, and Martin was discovered lying face-down on his bed. We named no more sailing-dates for a while—until to-day, when *almost* we believe we shall get away tomorrow at two o'clock; and in our cool bathroom lie the farewell leis, of roses, and violets, maile and ginger, that the Shipman girls, entirely undiscouraged by the fact of more than one withered supply, have already woven.

In face of *Snark* annoyance, our more than kind friends have seemed to redouble their efforts to beguile us from the not unreasonable fear of outstaying our welcome. Always the carriage is at our disposal, and beautiful saddlers, one of which, Hilo, coal-black, possessed of all the docile fire of the young horse, is our especial delight; and for love of him we have written the ranch foreman at home to give this name to the newest colt, which is also black.

One day the girls have taken us horseback to see where the latest lava-flow encroached to within five miles of the town, threatening to engulf it. This having been in 1881, the inhabitants must have thought Mother Shipton's notorious prophecy was coming to pass.

Another fine afternoon, to Rainbow Falls we rode, toward which no photograph, nor even painting, can do justice, because the approach is impossible to the use of lens or brush. One rides peacefully along a branch trail from the road, when unexpectedly, into a scene that has hinted no chasm or stream, there bursts a cataract of the Wailuku, eighty feet of it, into a green shaft lined with nodding ferns, where the fall, on a rainless day, sprays its deep pool with rainbows.

There came a day of "Hilo rain," when Mrs. Shipman tucked us into the curtained rig and haled us about town to observe an example of what the burdened sky can do in this section. Since the Hiloites must endure the violent threshing of crystal plummets of their overburdened sky, they make of it an asset. The annual rainfall is 150 inches against

Honolulu's 35 on the lee side of Oahu. And we must see Rainbow Fall, now an incredibly swollen, sounding young Niagara born of the hour. Chaney wrote: "It rains more easily in Hilo than anywhere else in the known world . . . . We no longer demurred about the story of the Flood . . . . Let no man be kept from Hilo by the stories he may hear about its rainfall. Doubtless they are all true; but the natural inference of people accustomed to rain in other places is far from true. There is something exceptional in this rain of Hilo. It is never cold, hardly damp even. They do say that clothes will dry in it. It is liquid sunshine, coming down in drops instead of atmospheric waves . . . . Laugh if you will, and beg to be excused, and you will miss the sweetest spot on earth if you do not go there." And that is Hilo.

Aboard the *Snark*, Monday, October 7, 1907.

Half-past one, and early aboard. With the help of moon-faced, smiling Nakata, all luggage has been stored shipshape in our wee state-rooms, and we await a few belated deliveries from the uptown shops, and the friends who are to see us off.

Frankly, I am nervous. All forenoon, doing final packing, I have startled at every ring of the telephone, apprehensive of some new message of the Inconceivable and Monstrous quivering on the wire. And Jack—has done his thousand words as usual on the novel!

He now stands about the shining, holystoned deck, unconsciously lighting cigarettes without number, and as unconsciously dropping them overboard half-smoked or dead full-length. He is not talking much, but nothing of the spick-and-span condition of his boat escapes his pleased blue sailor eye. And he hums a little air. Over and above the bad luck that has stalked her since the laying of her keel, the *Snark* indubitably remains, as Jack again assures, "the strongest boat of her size ever built"; and we both love her every pine plank, and rib of oak, and stitch of finest canvas.

Later: We got over the goodbys somehow—even dear Uncle Alec came to see us off. I hope nothing better than to have a kiss of welcome from him years hence when we come again to beautiful Hilo, which means "New Moon," fading yonder against the vast green mountain in a silver rain, as I had his kiss of parting this day.

"And there isn't one of them ever expects to lay eyes on us again," Jack said low to me as the captain pulled the bell to the engine-room and Martin started the bronze propeller, and the little white yacht began to move out from the wharf on her outrageous voyage. They tried hard to look cheerful, dear friends all, and Mrs. Balding's "Do you *really* think you'll ever come back alive?" would have been funny but for the unshed tears in her violet eyes. And little convinced was she, or any soul of them, by Jack's vivid disquisition on this "safest voyage in the world."

And so, waving our hands and calling last good-bys, we made our way out through no floating isles of lilies, down from the Waiakea River's marshes, for Hilo Bay lies clear and blue, in a fair afternoon that gives promise of a starry night. The captain of the Bark *Annie Johnson*, in port, a favorite poker antagonist of Jack's the past week, accompanied us a distance in the Iron works engineer's launch, and the big American-Hawaiian freighter, *Arizonan*, unloading in the stream, with a great sonorous throat saluted the little *Snark*, who answered with three distinct if small toots of her steam-whistle.

A westering sun floods with golden light the city clearing from its silver shower, and we know that some at least of her thoughts are with us happy estrays on the "white-speck boat" adventuring the pathless ocean.

And one beside me in a hushed voice repeats:

"'The Lord knows what we may find, dear lass,
And the deuce knows what we may do—
But we're back once more on the old trail, our own trail, the out trail,
We're down, hull down on the long Trail—the trail that is always new!'"

Thus, on our Golden Adventure, we set out to sea once more, answering its clear call; and it is Goodby, Hawaii—Hawaii of love and unquestioning friendship without parallel. Her sons and daughters, they have been kind beyond measure.

Great love to you, Hawaii—"until we meet again," as you sing in your sweetest song of parting grief and joyful welcome:

"Aloha oe."

JACK LONDON, KAMAAINA

The other day a man stood, uncovered, beside the red bowlder that marks by his own wish the ashes of Jack London, upon the little Hill of Graves on his beloved Ranch in the Valley of the Moon. Set in indestructible cement, about those ashes for he desired to rest in the ashes rather than any dust of him are wrapped two cherished leis of ilima that he had brought withered from Hawaii.

The man, there among the trees of the whispering ridge, told me how, only a week earlier, he had been talking with a simple ukulele-player in a Hawaiian orchestra at one of the San Francisco theaters. The Hawaiian boy had spoken haltingly, with emotion:

"Better than anyone, he *knew* us Hawaiians . . . Jack London, the Story Maker . . . . The news came to Honolulu and people, they seemed to have lost a great friend auwe! They could not understand . . . . They could not believe. I tell you this: Better than any one, he knew us Hawaiians."

Months before, a friend wrote from Honolulu: "These many weeks, when two or three who knew him meet upon the street, they do not speak. They cannot speak. They only clasp hands and weep."

And another: "Jack's death has done a wonderful thing. It has brought together so many of his friends who had not known one another before. It has brought together even those of his friends who did not previously care to know one another."

What sweeter requiem could be his?

Could he only know could the thrill of this knowledge only have been added to his "crowded hour of glorious life"!

It was not an easy nor a quick matter for Jack London to earn his kamaainaship. Nor did he in any way beg the favor. Time only has been the proof whether his two masterly stories, "The Sheriff of Kona" and "Koolau the Leper," have made one tourist stay his foot from the shores of the Hawaiian Islands.

And yet, these stories, sheer works of art that had nothing to do with his visit to Molokai, in no way counteracting, to his judgment, the admitted benefit of his article on the Settlement, were the cause of bitter feelings and words from what of provincialism there was in Hawaii and was ever island territory that was not provincial?" Provincial they are," reads a little penciled note of his: "which is equally true, nay, more than true, of New York City."

And untrue things were spoken and printed of Jack. Erect, on his "two hind legs" as was his wont, he defended himself. In the pages of Lorrin A. Thurston's *Pacific Commercial Advertiser*, following some ill-considered remarks of the editor, Jack and Kakina had it out, hammer and tongs, without mincing of the English, as good friends may and remain good friends. Even now, it is with reminiscent smile of appreciation for the heated pair of them that I turn over the pages of Jack's huge clipping scrapbook of 1910, for a moment forgetting the grave on the Little Hill, and once n ore live in memory of the brilliant discussion and Jack's own hurt and indignation that he should have been accused of abusing hospitality. There is no space here for the published letters; and besides, it is the long run of events that counts.

Kamaaina, desire of his heart, he became, until, in the end, the Hawaiians offered him the most honored name in their gift, which is my pride forever. In Hawaiian historical events, Kamehameha I was the only hero ever designated

"Ka Olali o Hawaii nui Kuaulii ka moa mahi i ku i ka moku,"

which is to say,

"The excellent genius who excelled at the point of the spear all the warriors of the Hawaiian Islands, and became the consolidator of the group."

And to Jack London, this is their gift:

"Ka Olali o kapeni maka kila."
"By the point of his pen his genius conquered all prejudice and gave out to the world at large true facts concerning the Hawaiian people and other nations of the South Seas."

The First Return

And we came back, as we had always known we should.

The *Snark*'s voyage ended untimely in 1909—because we paid too little heed to Dr. E. S. Goodhue's warnings against "speeding up" in the tropics. Jack's articles, collected under the title of "The Cruise of the *Snark*," and my own book, "The Log of the *Snark*" tell the story of the wonderful traverse as far as it attained. To this day, friend and stranger alike occasionally write from the South Seas that the little *Snark*, now schooner-rigged, has put in at this bay or that in the New Hebrides, under the flag of our French Allies—*Snark* Number One of a fleet of *Snark*s trading and recruiting in the cannibal isles.

We came back: and on the wharf at Honolulu that morning of the *Matsonia's* arrival, March 2, 1915, in the crowd we thrilled to meet the eyes of Gretchen and Albert Waterhouse, Harriet and Lorrin Thurston, dear Miss Frances Johnson, faithful and full of years, and the Goodhues all, with many another who had kept us a-tiptoe for days aboard ship with their welcoming wireless greetings and invitations.

An amusing incident did much to mellow the pleasure-pang of our returning. Nearest the stringer-piece of the pier stood a beautiful brown-tanned girl in an adorable bonnet of roses, her dark eyes searching the high steamer rail.

"Gee! what a pretty girl!" exclaimed a voyage acquaintance at Jack's elbow. "Wouldn't you take her for at least half-white?" Jack, following the directing gesture, enthusiastically agreed that she must be "all of hapa-haole," and added:

"Furthermore, I'll show you something; I'll throw her a kiss, see? and I'll bet you 'even money' that she'll respond. Is it a go?—you just watch."

And the conspicuous wafted caress arresting her eye, the young woman answered with blown kisses and outstretched brown arms.

"Gee!" was the awed whisper. "Are they all like that?"

It was Beth, my cousin from California—Beth Wiley, who is as much or as little Spanish as I, but shows it more. By several months she had preceded us, and had become well-browned by unstinted sunning on the beach at Waikiki.

The malihini's confusion was almost pathetic when Jack introduced "Mrs. London's cousin—I taught her to swim when she was a gangly kid!" and he continued mischievously, "I'll leave it to you, Beth, to convince him that *part* of that color of yours has been acquired since last I saw you!"

Tremulous with memory of those hack-drives in the silver and lilac dawns of eight years gone, we entered one in the crush of automobiles outside the wharf's great sheds, and proceeded to the Alexander Young Hotel, of coatless remembrance, for one night. Kilauea being in eruption, we were to go aboard the *Matsonia* next day for the round trip to Hilo.

On this short voyage, for the first time from sea vantage, we saw the Big Island's matchless green cliffs, stepped in dashing surf and fringed with waterfalls, with Mauna Kea's fair green knees and lap of cane extending into the broad belt of clouds—and, glory of glories, Mauna Kea's wondrous morning face white and still against the intense blue sky.

(1) Halemaumau, Kilauea, 1907. (2) Jack in Kilauea. (3) Bedecked
with Leis. (4) Halemaumau, 1917.

At Hilo, dear old Hilo, we were met by Mr. R. W. Filler, manager of Mr. Thurston's concrete dream of a Hilo Railroad, over which, in an automobile on car wheels, we made the thirty-four miles to Paauilo in the Hamakua District, and pronounced it one of the most scenically beautiful rail journeys we had ever had the good fortune to travel. It was hard to realize the accomplishment of these trestles, one horseshoe of which, we understood, is the most acute existing. And thus, high in a motorcar, upon steel tracks, we looked fascinated into the depths of the same gulches, unbridged and perilous in Isabella Bird's time, and laboriously journeyed by ourselves nearly a decade before. Sections of the railroad, instead of skirting the bluff coast line, run through passes that have been sliced deep through the bluffs themselves, the narrow cuts already blossoming like greenhouses.

Reaching the terminal, Paauilo, a pretty spot on the seaward edge of a great coffee plantation, we lunched capitally in a rustic hotel, before starting on the return. Partway back, we left the train, at a station where kind Mr. Filler had been especially urged by Kakina to have an automobile waiting to take us mauka to the Akaka Fall, seldom visited and rather difficult of access. A muddy tramp in a shower brought us to the fall—a streaming ribbon five hundred feet long, trailing into an exquisitely lovely cleft, earth and rocks completely hidden by maidenhair and other small ferns.

Strange it seemed to speed over the old road into Hilo in a "horseless carriage," deeply reminiscent as we were of the four-mule progress of other days. And good it was to meet up once more with the Baldings and their half-grown family, Mrs. Balding dimpling at Jack's reminder of her pessimism concerning the *Snark*; and with Jack's First Lady of Hawaii, "Mother" Shipman, her curly hair perhaps more silvery, but her face beaming as ever. And there was Uncle Alec, smiling only more mellowly; and I received my welcoming salute.

"Is Hilo still alive?" was one of Jack's first inquiries.

Whereupon the venerable coal-black horse was led out, still beautiful, but lacking the pawing eagerness of old. "His namesake is my favorite horse on the Ranch to-day," Jack told them, tenderly smoothing the nozzling velvet muzzle.

The following morning, in an unyieldingly new hired machine, up mountain we fared, noting a considerable lessening of the forestage along the route, due to the encroachment of sugar cane. And in some of the cleared areas we recognized the familiar 'ava plant of the South

Seas. Still remained untouched stretches, as of a dream within a dream for beauty, and again I could vision the evanescent minarets and airy spans of the Palace of Truth I had once liked to fancy growing before my eyes in the delicate tracery of tropic foliage. Nothing seen in all the *Snark*'s coming and going among the isles under the Line had surpassed this enchanted wood.

Saving the Volcano for evening, we spent the day horseback, visiting Kilauea's environs of sister craters, some still breathing and others dead and cold, shrouded in verdure. Kilaueaiki, one of the nearest to the Volcano House and the new Crater Hotel, is an 800-foot deep sink, with a circumference of half a mile. The neighborhood is pitted with these void caldrons, and one could spend wonderful weeks in the jungle trails. The Thurstons have made a thorough study of the region, and pronounce it one of the most interesting in the Islands. Into a number of the more important craters we peered, and our native guide finally led the way up Puuhuluhulu, around whose mellifluous name we had been rolling our tongues from Honolulu, where Kakina's last adjuration was not to miss a sight of this particular blowhole.

Leaving the animals with the sandwich-munching guide, we carried our own lunch to the summit, where, lying prone, we ate with faces over the edge of the bewitching inverted green cone. For an hour, like foolish children, we played with our fantasy, planning the most curious of all contemplated Hawaii dwellings, this time in the uttermost depths of Puuhuluhulu's riotous natural fernery, with a possible glass roof over the entire crater!

Already, as we returned, low-pressing clouds above Kilauea were alight with the red-rose glow of Halemaumau. And no remembered volcano of Tana or Savaii made me any less excited at prospect of at last beholding Pélé's Gargantuan boiling well.

Not by the old trans-basin trail did we pilgrimage to the House of Everlasting Fire, but upon an automobile road graded through stage-scenery of ohia and tree ferns that were like fairyland in the brilliant headlights. One encircles nearly half of the great sink until, on the southeastern section, the road winds westerly down into and across the floor to Halemaumau.

It was the weirdest drive I have ever known; and weirder still it became when, within a few minutes' walking distance of the pit, the machine, making for a walled parking circle, ran into a great waft of steam like a tepid pink fog. Out of this, or into it, the eyes of an oncoming car took form, burning larger and brighter through the downy smother, and safely passing our own.

A well-defined pathway is worn in the gritty lava to the southeast edge. Soon we were settled there waiting for the warm mists to incline the other way and disclose the disturbance of liquid earth that we could hear hissing, softly, heavily, hundreds of feet beneath, like the sliding fall of avalanches muffled by distance and intervening masses of hills.

And then, suddenly, the mist drafted in a slanting flight toward the western crags, sucked clear of the inland sea of incredible molten solids. Open-mouthed we gazed hundreds of feet into the earth and saw nothing like the colored representations of Halemaumau, but a tortured, crawling surface of grayish black, like a mantle thrown over slow-wrestling Titans in a fitful, dying struggle. Then a crack would show—not red, but an intensely luminous orange flame-color— a glimpse of earth's hot blood. As our eyes became accustomed to the heaving skin of the monstrous tide, they could follow the rising, slow-flowing, lapsing waves that broke sluggishly against an iron-bound shore. And never a wave of the fiery liquid but left some of itself on the black strand, its ruthless, heavy-flung comb resistlessly imposing coat upon coat of this gore of rock that cooled, at least in comparison to its source, in its upbuilding process. Once in a while a bubble would rise out in the central mass, and burst into a fountain of intolerably brilliant orange fluid, its scorching drops fading on the heavy black surge.

There is no use trying to tell of this wonder of the world. From the seduction of its merest smoke display to this deep-sunk eruption of 1915, it is all one in its confounding marvel.

On this night, when the first vivid crack broke the oily dark surface, Jack, with a gasp of delight, seized my hand, lighted a match above it, and peered closely at a big black opal, precious loot of Australia's Lightning Ridge, that I had named "Kilauea" before ever we saw Pélé's colors. Tipping the stone from slanting plane to plane, its blue-gray dull face cracked into flaming lines for all the world like the phenomenon before us in the bowels of Mauna Loa—a truer replica of Halemaumau than any painting.

Upon our return, Mr. Demosthenes had the old guest book lying open in the same long glass room, and again we read the page written years before, regretting that Bruce Cartwright, Jr., was not there with us. His extraordinarily charming wife, Claire Williams, a connection of the Castle family, we had come to know on this voyage from San

Francisco, returning from Paris with her equally charming sister, Miss Edith. The Cubist-Futurist party that Mrs. Cartwright, Jr., gave at their Nuuanu home a few months later, on which her fancy had been nearly three years working, will never be forgotten in Honolulu, and beyond Honolulu by those who were fortunate enough to be bidden.

"Be sure, now, Lakana," had been another final behest of Kakina's, "to call up Sam Johnson in Pahoa, when you get to Hilo. I'm writing him to expect to take you from the Volcano down to Puna. He's a delightful fellow. Never saw such a man for *punch*. Don't miss seeing him—and he's an immense admirer of your stuff."

And so, this next morning, there arrived at the Volcano House, in an apparently reckless manner of speeding, this black-eyed Russian, a Samson for strength of muscle and of will, breathing vitality and abounding health—once sailor, ex-soldier of the Regular Army of the Republic of Hawaii, retired Colonel of her National Guard, athlete, builder of good roads, born commander and organizer of men, forester, and for the nonce in charge of the Castles' Pahoa Lumber Company's mill in Puna. Incidentally, he had been savior, single-handed except for the assistance of one Hawaiian youth, of the entire crew of the barkentine *Klikitat*, wrecked on the rocks above Hilo two years before, while from the top of the almost perpendicular bluff, Hilo's population looked on. This Russian-born American, whose natal name was too much for the officials when he first came ashore and applied for citizenship and enlistment at Honolulu, was forthwith given the unmusical if sturdy name of his vessel; and, having made good his adoptive sobriquet, loyally he has stuck to it.

The Colonel's exuberant coasting was exhilarating if rather amazing; but soon I came to realize that he was blessed with a correlation of eye and brain and hand that qualified him for judicious chancing. They do relate how, on this same road, he tilted his machine at a vicious bull that had for long terrorized the countryside, neatly scooping and incidentally slaying it upon his radiator.

Nine miles from Hilo, at the mill of the enormous Olaa Sugar Plantation, we branched off southwest on the picturesque Puna Road, which, once clear of certain beautiful miles of jungle, crosses an interesting if monotonous desert of aged lava. Mauna Kea and her sister mountain were good to us that day, for both going and returning we had fair view of their snowy springtime summits.

The mill at Pahoa demonstrated to us how the forests of lehua, koa, the scarcer kou, the ohia, and all the valuable timber of the rich woods is converted into merchantable lumber. And we came away with a handsome souvenir, a precious kou calabash, heavy and polished like brown marble, a product of the mill.

Pearl Johnson, the Colonel's wife, variously dubbed Pearl of Pahoa, and the Princess thereof, fragile-dainty as her husband is husky, might have stepped out of the pages of Tennyson's "Idylls of the King," so ineffably is she like one's ideas of the ladies beloved of the Knights of the Round Table.

After luncheon, they summoned three sweet part-Hawaiian sisters, the Mundon girls, cultured and modest-mannered, to sing. And there, my initial time in the District of Puna—scene of Richard Walton Tully's "Bird of Paradise,"—quite unexpectedly I learned something of what these isles of the *Snark*'s first landfall meant to me, over and above my knowledge of Jack's own undying regard for them. For, while the contralto and treble of their limpidezzo voices sang the beloved old "Sweet Lei Lehua," "Mauna Kea," the "Dargie Hula," and the dear heart-compelling "Aloha oe," suddenly I fell a-weeping, quite overwhelmed with all the unrealized pent emotion of what I had seen and felt the preceding days, and the gracious memories that flooded back from the older past.

Once more at Hilo Harbor, the *Matsonia*, out in the stream, her siren sounding the warning hour, was reached by launch from the little oriental waterside at the mouth of the Waiakea. Our eyes were more than a little wistful as in memory we sailed out with the *Snark*. But we did it! "With our own hands we did it," thus Jack; and the glamorous voyage was now an accomplished verity, from which we had come back very much alive and unjaded.

Back in Honolulu, Jack declined to be ousted by any officious steward from our stateroom until the final period was dotted to his morning's ten pages. Eventually he issued upon deck almost into the arms of Alexander Hume Ford, whom we were no end glad to see, buoyant and incessant as ever, brimful of deeds for the advantage of Hawaii as ever he had been of their visioning.

The first responsibility, not to be neglected for a single hour, was the hunting of a habitation that we might call our own for the time being. Beth had reported the total failure of her exhaustive search.

Honolulu was chock-a-block with tourists. "Beginning to realize what they've got," Jack observed with satisfaction, although a trifle put out that his prophesied appreciation of the Islands by the mainlanders, should interfere with his own getting of a roof-shelter.

With Mr. Ford was Mr. Harry L. Strange, a brilliant young Englishman who had in the past several years converted the Honolulu Gas Company into an efficient corporation capitalized in seven figures, and who put himself and his machine at our disposal in the agent-visiting expedition. We learned from one of the great Trust Companies that the Oliver C. Scott cottage on Beach Walk, a newly opened residence street not far from the Seaside Hotel, was to be let a couple of months hence, and we found it eminently suitable for our little household of four, for Beth was to be one of us, and Nakata, as usual, was our shadow. And then we devoted all our powers to persuade the somewhat flustered Mrs. Scott that she needed an earlier visit to the Pan-American Exposition than she had planned, and proceeded to move in before she and her excellent husband could change their minds, while Jack wirelessed to the Coast for Sano, our cook. Temporarily ensconced in the Hau Tree Hotel half a block away, Mrs. Scott, still wondering how they had consented to such an abrupt arrangement, was more than generous in lending every assistance in the way of advice as to best ways and means of housekeeping and marketing.

Not a day passed before, in swimming-suits, we walked down Kalia Road to the Seaside Hotel, and once more felt underfoot the sands of Waikiki. But such changes had been wrought by sea and mankind that we could hardly believe our eyes, and needed a guide to set us right.

The sands, shifting as they do at irregular periods of storm, had washed away from before the hotel, leaving an uninviting coral-hummock bottom not to be negotiated comfortably except at high tide, and generally shunned. A forbidding sea-wall buttressed up the lawn of the hotel,[1] while the only good beach was the restricted stretch between where the row of cottages once had begun, and the Moana Hotel.

And what had we here? In place of those little old weather-beaten houses and the brown tent, the Outrigger Canoe Club had established its bathhouses, separate club lanais for both women and men, and, nearest the water, a large, raised dancing-lanai, underneath which reposed a fleet of great canoes, their barbaric yellow prows ranged seaward. At

[1] At this writing, 1917, the sands are again level with the seawall, shoaling as far as the diving-stage, rendered useless for lack of deep water.

the rear, in a goodly line of tall lockers, stood the many surf-boards, fashioned longer and thicker than of yore, of the members of the Canoe Club.

A steel cable, whiskered with seaweed, anchored midway of the beach, extended several hundred yards into deeper water where a steel diving-stage had been erected, and upon it dozens of swimmers, from merest children to old men, were making their curving flights inside the breakers. Several patronesses of the Club give their time on certain days of the week, from the women's lanai inconspicuously chaperoning the Beach.

Actually, the only landmark recognizable was the date-palm still flourishing where had once been a corner of our tent-house, now become a sheltering growth with yard-long clusters of fruit, and we were told it was known as the "Jack London Palm." For it might be said that in its shadow Jack wove his first tales of Hawaii.

And all this progress meant Ford! Ford! Ford! Everywhere one turned evidence of his unrelaxing brain met the eye. But he, in turn, credits Jack with having done incalculably much toward bringing the splendid Club into existence, by his article on surf-board riding, "A Royal Sport." Largely on the strength of the interest it aroused, Mr. Ford had been enabled to keep his word to Jack that he would make surf-boarding one of the most popular pastimes in Hawaii. Upon his representations the Queen Emma estate, at a lease of a few dollars a year, to be contributed to the Queen's Hospital, which her Majesty had established, had set aside for the Club's use this acre of ground, which, with the enthusiastic revival of surf-boarding, was now become almost priceless.

Queen Emma was the wife of Kamehameha IV, mother of the beautiful "Prince of Hawaii," who died in childhood, herself granddaughter of John Young, and adopted daughter of an English physician, Dr. Rooke, who had married her aunt, Kamaikui. The Queen owned this part of the Beach, from which her own royal canoes were launched in the good old days, and where she also used the surf-board.

"Her estate holds this land," Ford had said in 1907, "and I'm going to secure it for a Canoe Club. I don't know how; but I'm just going to." And Jack, when writing "A Royal Sport," was not unmindful of the kokua (assistance) it might possibly prove in bringing about Ford's ambition for Waikiki. So keen had our friend been on the trail, that we had half wondered how soon we should be turned out of our Seaside quarters to make room for lumber and carpenters!

And Fred Church—is he here?—and his pretty wife. Where are they? Auwe!—the pair, long since separated, the wife gone somewhere East, and the man dead these several years. Jack, thoughtful over the passing of so good a fellow, sighed regretfully; and then, sighing again but with a difference, enounced:

"Mate Woman, we've got them all skinned to death, you and I!"

And Honolulu had of course altered, and grown. New streets, like this our Beach Walk, had been laid on filled marshlands at Waikiki, and bordered with sweet bungalows set in lovely unfenced gardens, while the lilied area of duck-ponds along Kalakaua Avenue had shrunken to the same populous end. Beyond the Moana, Heinie's, an open-air cafe chantant—and dansant—beguiled the up-to-date residents and tourists, and a roof-garden, with like facilities, was bruited for the Alexander Young. The Country Club, out Nuuanu, boasted what we heard many a mainlander term "the finest golf-links anywhere." Diamond Head's rosy cradle had become unapproachable as a heavily fortified military position. Residential districts of beautiful homes had extended well into the valleys, and Kaimuki, on the rolling midlands beyond Kapiolani Park, formed quite a little city by itself. Some of the vernal ridges of Honolulu's background had blossomed into alluring building-sites—such as Pacific Heights; and Tantalus had developed to a large extent its possibilities.

Automobile traffic had drawn the island closer together, and a drive around Oahu, by the route we had formerly traveled, was more often accomplished in one day. Once we spent a night on Kahuku Plantation, guests of Mr. and Mrs. Macmillan (we had known Mrs. Macmillan when she was a newspaper woman in California), and visited the huge Marconi Wireless Station near by. Our return to Honolulu was made by way of the railroad around the extreme western end of the island. This trip should not be missed, for it shows a most beautiful coast line, and splendid valleys of the mountain ranges, on the slopes of which one may see the ruins of old stone walls and habitations of long-dead generations. Automobile picnics from Diamond Head to Koko Head, and others over the Nuuanu Pali to points on the eastern shore, like Kailua and Waimanalo bays, together with a visit to Kaneohe Bay and its wondrous coral gardens, and swimming and sailing in pea-green water over jet-black volcanic sands, nearly completes the circuit one may make of this protean isle.

This summer of 1915, during a warm spell in town, bag and baggage we moved for a week to the little hotel at Kaneohe Bay. Each time we emerged over the Pali into the valley of the Mirrored Mountains, Jack would exclaim at the vast pineapple planting that had flowed over the carmine hillocks below. Instead of bemoaning this encroachment of man upon the natural beauty of the landscape, Jack hailed it with acclaim. To those who complained, he would cry:

"I love to see the good rich earth being made to work, to produce more and better food for man. There is always plenty of untouched wild that will not produce food. Every time I open up a new field to the sun on the ranch, there is a hullabaloo about the spoiling of natural beauty. Meantime, I am raising beautiful crops to build up beautiful draft-animals and cattle—improving, improving, trying to help the failures among farmers to succeed. *And*, don't you see? don't you see?—there's always plenty of wild up back. I haven't spoiled one of the exquisite knolls. And suppose I had—to me the change would be from one beauty to another; and the other, in turn, would go to make further beauty of animal life, and more abundance for man."

Indeed, from its small beginnings of but a few years before, the pineapple industry had risen to the second in importance in the Islands, giving place only to sugar.

Mr. Thurston, on a vacation at Kaneohe, one day took us horseback for one of the most interesting and least known jaunts on Oahu. From the hotel we held east a quarter-mile to the sandy mouth of the Kaneohe River, across a spit of mountain-washed debris, through abandoned fishing villages and little groves, and then skirted an arm of the bay, outside the ancient wall of a fish pond nearly half a mile in diameter, where the tide washed our horses' flanks.

Thence we reached a plain partially covered with sand and sand hills washed up out of the ocean, and rode across an old coral bed formerly undersea, which had been elevated several feet. Northwest to the point at the entrance to Kaneohe Bay, from a small fishing village, we climbed a low volcanic cone to see the ruins of an old heiau, where some seventy years ago a church was erected by the pioneer Catholics. The church is now in ruins, for the inhabitants, numbering several hundreds, have passed away. The pathetic remains of their little rocky homes are still to be seen scattered about the slopes of the green hills and upon surrounding levels, where plover run, with skylarks soaring overhead. And for the first time in our lives, in this lonely deserted spot, we heard the celestial caroling of these lovely flying organisms, English skylarks, which our old friend Governor Cleghorn, now dead, first imported from New Zealand. Ainahau, auwe and ever auwe, had been broken up into town lots, and was become the site of a boarding-house! Never, once, did Jack or I, in passing along Kalakaua Avenue, glance that way. Too sorrowful and indignant we were, that the home of Likelike and Kaiulani should not have been held inviolate.

On the seashore, inside a glorious surf, in view of Na moku manu, or Bird Island, where we could see myriad seabirds nesting and flying about in clouds, we lunched under grotesque lava rocks, carved by the seas of ages; and Jack and I studied the green and turquoise rollers that thundered close, driven by the full power of the trans-Pacific swell, figuring how we should comport ourselves in such waters if ever we should be spilled therein. Again in the saddle, we let the horses run wild over a continuous, broad sand-beach, for a mile and a half, to our right a line of glaring sand hills, called Heleloa. Mounting these later on, Kakina led us to the battle field of a century before, where the Mauis, landing, had fought with the Oahus. The winds had uncovered a scattering of bleached bones, whiter than the white sand, and Jack, always interested in skulls, was able to find one perfect jawbone, larger than his own, with several undecayed molars firm in their sockets.

Near the shore at one point we turned aside and dismounted to hunt for land-shells in the bank of a small gulch. For Lorrin A. Thurston had become a land-shell enthusiast, and by now possessed a fascinating collection of over 200 varieties, laid out like jewels in shallow, velvet-lined drawers.

Following the northerly shore of Mokapu Point, presently the trail mounted the outside of the little mountain till, entering at the open south side, we were in the green half-crater where cattle and horses grazed. Tying our animals, we lay heads-over the sea wall of the broken bowl, looking down and under, two hundred feet and more—"Kahekili's Leap"—where the ocean surged against the forbidding cliff, from which our scrutiny frightened nesting seabirds.

So far, we have met no one who has taken this little journey of a day, but it is easily accessible and more than worth while. Nothing can surpass the magnificent view one has of the blue Pacific, white-threshed by the glorious trade wind; and the prospect, landward to the Mirrored Mountains, is indescribably uplifting.

Returning from Kaneohe to Honolulu by motor a few days later, after heavy rains, we thrilled to the sight of those same mountains curtained with glorious rainbowed waterfalls; and once in the pass, the mighty draft of the trades revealed fresh cataracts behind torn cloud-masses, and looped and dissipated them before ever they could reach the bases of the green palisades. Another attraction of the Islands, fathered by Alexander Hume Ford, is the Trail and Mountain Club, which has developed a system of mountain pathways and rest houses that is a paradise for hikers. One of these rest houses stands on the rim of Haleakala, furnished with a large number of bunks and camping accommodations for the public.

Entertained one evening at dinner by Harry Strange and his mother, we became acquainted with Colonel and Mrs. C. P. Iaukea, part-Hawaiian, and aristocratic-looking to their finger tips. He had been Chamberlain to King Kalakaua, and accompanied Kalakaua's queen, Kapiolani (probably named after the illustrious defier of Pélé), to London at the time of Queen Victoria's Jubilee. At present Colonel Iaukea is one of the trustees of Liliuokalani's estate. He stated that the Queen had expressed a wish to meet Jack London, and Jack, pleased that the meeting should come about in this way, arranged to be present at a private audience the following Thursday, March 11, together with Mrs. Strange and Harry.

The Royal Hawaiian Band, conducted by the venerable Henri Berger, now in his seventy-first year, after forty years' leadership of the band, was in full attendance in the Queen's Gardens at Washington Place, which, in this city of notable gardens, is cited as the most beautiful. Berger, owing to age and failing health, has since been retired upon a pension.

The dignified white mansion is as beautiful in its own way as the gardens, and tastefully tropical, surrounded as it is by broad lanais, with large pillars supporting the roof in Southern colonial style. As William R. Castle, Jr., writes: "The whole has an air of retirement expressive of the attitude of the Queen herself."

And on the white-columned veranda, robed in black holoku, tender old hands folded in her silken lap, Her Majesty sat in a large armchair, at her back certain faithful ladies—Mrs. Dominis, wife of Aimoku Dominis, the Queen's ward, with her cherubic little son; Mrs. Irene Kahalelaukoa li Holloway; and Mrs. Iaukea, all of them solicitous of their loved Queen's every word and gesture. Their veneration is a touching and beautiful link to the close and vivid past.

Liliuokalani's fine face, as we saw it this day, was calm and lovable, as if a soothing hand had but lately passed over it.[1] She raised quiet, searching eyes to our faces, and upon Colonel Iaukea's introduction, smiled pleasedly and extended her hand, which it is the custom to kiss, and which we saluted right gladly. A few low-voiced questions and answers concerning work Jack had done on Hawaii; the listening to a number or two from the Band; and we were free to wander among the treasures of the house, than which are no finer specimens of royal insignia outside the Museum. At length, Hawaii's National Anthem, rising outside under the palms, brought us all to the lanai again, where the men stood uncovered.

Queen Liliuokalani's own book, "Hawaii's Story, by Hawaii's Queen," published in 1906, by John Murray, London, should be read not only for her viewpoint, but also because it is piquantly entertaining in its lighter humors, and her naïve descriptions of travel and characters in the United States and England are delicious.

Upon our arrival in Honolulu, we found that Nakata had employed his time in visiting his uncle and cousins in Lahaina, Maui, where he had contracted an alliance with the oldest of the cousins, Momoyo. And thus we faced losing the boy after eight years of mutually enjoyable association, for the wife was ambitious for him to become a dentist, and found a family of his own.

Returning from a luncheon given by that vital institution, the Honolulu Ad Club, Jack burst into the house:

"Guess whom I met to-day! Two men, both of whom you have known, one here and one in Samoa—and now risen to different positions and titles. I give you three chances. Bet you 'even money' you couldn't guess in a thousand years."

That was "easy money" for him, and I threw up my hands. Our fearless old friend, Lucius E. Pinkham, once president of the Board of Health, was now become Governor of the Territory of Hawaii, appointed in 1913 by President Wilson, for a term of four years; and the other we

---

[1] I note, in a late issue of the *Pacific Commercial Advertiser*, that for the first time since the Queen's abdication, the American Flag floats over Washington Place, indicating her sympathy with America's entry into the war against Prussianism.

As this book goes to press, I am profoundly touched by announcement of the death of the beloved Queen of the Hawaiians, Liliuokalani, on November eleventh.

had known in Tahiti and Pago-Pago, C. B. T. Moore, erstwhile Governor at the latter American port, and Captain of the *Annapolis*, now Rear Admiral, stationed at Pearl Harbor. Later we exchanged visits with Admiral and Mrs. Moore, and colorful were our reminiscences of days and nights under the Southern Cross.

It would require a book in itself to tell of the revolutionary alterations in Pearl Lochs, now possessed of all the circumstance of a thoroughgoing naval station. As for the old Elysian acre, we were informed it had changed hands and the bungalow had been replaced by a much more ambitious one. It would be difficult to express why we never went back. Perhaps it had been a perfect thing in itself, that experience, finished and laid aside in heart's lavender.

So much, briefly, for naval activity on Oahu. As for the Army, in addition to the older forts, and the new fortifications on Diamond Head, Schofield Barracks had sprung up, a city in itself, over against the Waianae Mountains on the table-land, and we could hardly believe our eyes, motoring from Haleiwa Hotel by way of Pearl Harbor, when they rested on the modern military post that spread over the green plain to the mountain slopes. Here we spent two or three days, guests of Major (now Colonel) Guignard. Oahu had become the greatest military station of the United States.

One Sunday we spent outside Honolulu Harbor on the famous racing yacht, *Hawaii*; and in our hearts and on our lips was the wish that again we were "down, hull down on the old trail," with a hail and farewell to every glamorous link of the *Snark*'s golden chain of ports, thence on and on through the years, from the Solomon Isles to the Orient, beyond to the seas and inland waterways of Europe. "You never did gather all that lapful of pearls I promised you," Jack mused regretfully.

Four days after this yachting party, Honolulu and the rest of the Union shuddered to the loss of the Submarine F-4. They went out merrily in the morning—F-1, F-2, F-3, F-4—and all emerged but the last. For weeks and months, during the work of raising, under supervision of the U. S. S. *Maryland*, Captain Kittelle, there was a subtle gloom over the gayest life of the capital. Outside the Harbor channel, where the submarine had eventually slipped off coral bottom into deep ocean, from steamer and sailer, canoe and fishing boat and yacht that passed in or out, leis were dropped upon the mournful waters.

Upon the Beach at Waikiki it was seldom we missed the long afternoon. Jack worked in a kimono as of yore, his face and figure little
changed, if more mature. After luncheon, in bathing suit, bearing towels and a white dangling bag of blue-figured Japanese crepe, knobby as
a stocking at Christmas time with books and magazines selected from
the boxes regularly shipped from the Ranch at home, and bountiful
cigarettes and matches, he would be seen walking along Kalia Road
with his light and merry gait to the Outrigger Club. And "I'm glad
we're here *now*" he would ruminate; "for some day Waikiki Beach is
going to be the scene of one long hotel. And wonderful as it will be, I
can't help clinging, for once, to an old idea."

Under the high lanai of the Outrigger, we lay in the cool sand
between canoes and read aloud, napped, talked, or visited with the
delightful inhabitants of the charmed strand, until ready to swim
in the later afternoon. One special diversion was to watch several
Hawaiian youths, the unsurpassed Duke Kahanamoku among them,
performing athletic stunts in water and out. And that sturdy little
American girl we had known before, Ruth Stacker, now a famous
swimmer herself, could be seen instructing her pupils in the wahine
surf. George Freeth, we heard, was teaching swimming and surf-
boarding in Southern California. Our own swims became longer from
day to day. Still inside the barrier reef, through the breakers we
would work, emerging with back-flung hair on their climbing backs
while they roared shoreward. Beyond the combing crests, in deeper
water above the coral that we could see gleaming underfoot in the
sunshafts, lazily we would tread the bubbling brine or lie floating
restfully, almost ethereally, on the heaving warm surface, conversing sometimes most solemnly in the isolated space between sky and
solid earth. And once Jack told me a thing that will abide like a dove
of peace until I die, as one of my sweetest touches with this sweetest
of men:

"I never told you this," he began, "but many years ago, before I
knew you existed, I lay one afternoon on a California beach—at Santa
Cruz—in one of my great disgusts . . . you know—when I have dared
look Truth in the face, and become blackly pessimistic about the world
and the men and women in it. It was a quiet day; and while I lay, with
my face on my arms, over and above the steady breathing of the ocean
and plashing of a small surf, there came to me, from very far off, almost
like skylarks in the blue, the voices of a man and a woman."

He righted, from where he had been floating on his back, and slowly trod water while he went on, dreamily:

"I couldn't for the life of me figure where the voices came from. I raised my head, but no one was in sight on the beach; and at last, the nearing conversation guided me seaward where I could just barely make out the heads of two persons very leisurely coming in, talking cozily out there in deep water, as unconcerned and comfortable as if sitting in chairs or on the sand.

"Something inside me suddenly yearned toward them—they were so blest, those two together. And I wondered, lying there sadly enough, if there was a woman in the world for me—the little woman who would be the right woman—with whom I could go out to sea, without boat or life-preserver, hours in the water holding long comradely talks on everything under the sun, with no more awareness of the means of locomotion than if walking.—I could have told you this eight years ago," he recalled, "the day we swam across the bay at Moorea. I thought of it at the time. But we were not alone. The stage was not set for you and me."

Touched and gratified, I reminded him of the afternoon that first I swam to the *Snark* in Pearl Lochs; and more than many times, swimming free in the breakers at Waikiki, hailing with shout and wave of hand the surfing canoes and boards flashing and zipping to every side, we referred to those days when the farthest we swam together was an eighth of a mile—Jack held back because I could do no more.

Deep thinker though he was, and worshipful of the brain-stuff of others, he ever found shining things of the spirit in courageous physical endeavor. I think, in a dozen close years with him, year in and year out, "in sickness and in health," till death did us part, that never have I seen him more elated, more uplifted with delight over feat of one dear to him, than upon one April day at Waikiki.

An out-and-out Kona gale had piled up a big, quick-following surf, threshing milk-white and ominous under a leaden, low-hanging sky. At the Outrigger beach no soul was visible; but a group of young sea-gods belonging to the Club sat with bare feet outstretched on the railing of the lanai above the canoes. Joining them, Jack inquired if they were "going out." Young Lorrin Thurston tossed back his sun-bleached mop of gold hair from his golden-brown eyes and looked at the others quizzically. "Nothing doing," one laughed. And another, "This is no day for surf-boards—and a canoe couldn't live in that water." "But we are going to swim out," Jack said. "You'd better not, Mr. London," the

(1) Kahilis at Funeral of Prince David Kawananakoa.   (2) Kamehameha the
Great.   (3) and (4) Sport of Kings.

boys frowned respectfully. "You couldn't take a woman into that surf."
"You watch me," Jack returned. "I could, and shall."

We went. Now, understand. It was not in order to be spectacular
that Jack took me out that day. This was not bravado. With the several
weeks' training he had given me in sizable breakers, he expected as a
matter of course to see me put that training to use. And I felt as one
with him. The thing was, first, to get beyond the diving-stage, for a
big freshet had brought down the little river a tangled mass of thorned
algaroba and other prickly vegetation, which, with a wild wrack of
seaweed, made the shallow water almost impassable.

Very slowly we forged out, and at length were in position where the
marching seas were forming and overtoppling. Rather stupendous they
loomed to small me, I will confess; but, remembering other and smaller
ones and obeying scrupulously Jack's quiet "Don't get straight up and
down—straighten out—keep flat, *keep flat!*" I managed not badly to
breast and pass through a dozen or more that followed fast and faster,
almost too fast for me to get breath between whiles.

But when I finally ventured "I think I have had enough," immediately Jack slanted our course channelward where the tide flows out
toward the reef egress. Once in this smoother water it was plain sailing,
so to speak, except that after half an hour we found we were not getting
anywhere—worse than that, drifting willy nilly out to sea. By now, the
young crews of the Outrigger had followed with their boards, fearing
we might come to grief, and upon Lorrin's advice we made back toward
the breakers and out of the current, and "came in strong" with our best
strokes to the Beach.

Again, one less stormy day, in deep water Jack was seized with a
cramp in his foot, from which often he suffered at night—a painful
and increasing symptom of break down in his ankles, accompanied as
it was by rheumatism in both wrists and ankles. Between us, he floating, I treading, we rubbed and kneaded the foot as best we could, until
a strange surf-boarder hove in sight, fighting seaward, whom I hailed
at Jack's suggestion through set teeth. We got Jack on the board, and
went more thoroughly at the ironing-out of the cramp with our palms,
and presently he was able to swim ashore.

There was nothing whatever remarkable in these two incidents.
Having learned to put implicit faith in Jack's judgment, which I had
never had reason to doubt, I merely followed his directions and knew
that he would give instant heed, in the first instance, when I claimed

weariness. But that a small, sensitive female of the species should follow him in water where experienced members of the Outrigger hesitated to go, and that she should not lose her head in his disablement, from his angle surpassed intellectual achievement, because it called for spiritual courage. "I'd rather see my woman be able to do what she did, than to have her write the greatest book ever published or unpublished," tersely summed up his philosophy of values.

Once more, near this the end of my story, as in its Foreword I pray indulgence for what seems the necessary sprinkling of the perpendicular pronoun, in order to present the values of the things that were, as Jack would say, his bribe for living. Courage, to him, was the greatest thing, after love and loyalty, in the world. The combination of these formed, for him, the only divinity he recognized.

The newest brood of surf-boarders had learned and put into practice angles never dreamed of a decade earlier. Now, instead of always coasting at right-angles to the wave, young Lorrin and the half-dozen who shared with him the reputation of being the most skilled would often be seen erect on boards that their feet and balance guided at astonishing slants. Surf-boarding had indeed come into its own. And the sport never seems to pall. Its devotees, as long as boards and surf are accessible, show up every afternoon of their lives on the Beach at Waikiki. When a youth must depart for eastern college-life, his keenest regret is for the loss of Waikiki and all it means of godlike conquest of the 'bull-mouthed breakers.' No athletic-field dream quite compensates. It remains the king of sports.

One night in early May, Mayor John C. Lane of Honolulu gave a great luau in Kapiolani Park, where some fifteen hundred of us sat under a vast tent-roof and listened to the flowery eloquence of Senators and Congressmen from Washington. And it was to the venerable but sprightly "Uncle Joe" Cannon we awarded the triumphal palm for the most sensible, logical speechifying of the event. This magnificent luau, presided over by the handsome Mayor, surpassed any in our experience the South Seas over. "Mayor Lane ought to be reelected indefinitely," Jack would say, "to do the honors of his office!"

The following day Jack and I both sailed from Honolulu for Hawaii, but on separate ships. The *Mauna Kea* was charted to take the Congressional party junketing about the Islands, and Jack was bidden to be one of the Entertainment Committee. Owing to the fact that the *Mauna Kea* was full to overflowing, even so that many of the Committee bunked on deck, we resident wives were blandly uninvited. But I, through a timely invitation from the Johnsons on the Big Island, was enabled to come in contact with the august picnic party.

And so, with "*Aloha nui oe*" one to the other, Jack saw me off for Hilo on the *Kilauea*, sister of the smart *Mauna Kea*, while twelve hours later he was headed for Maui. My roommate on the crowded steamer was an Englishwoman, Mrs. Russell, busily knitting socks for her brothers fighting in France. She told me how her husband, who had worked on the *Snark*'s machinery eight years before, when confronted with difficult or unsurmountable obstacles or problems, had ever since declared: "This is as hard as repairing Jack London's engines!"

On Maui, Jack became much interested in the experiment that had been made in small homesteading on government land; but he did not foresee success in the venture. "You can't turn the clock back," he said. But his reasons for his opinion in the matter are set forth in his own book, "My Hawaiian Aloha," which will be published in 1918. This series of articles, written in 1915, Mr. Thurston has declared, are of a value to Hawaii that cannot be estimated in gold and silver.

And so I next saw Jack at Napoopoo, on Kealakekua Bay, with the Blue Flush for background, and we agreed warmly that never anywhere had we seen anything like it, and nothing to surpass. Here the Congressional party disembarked to see the Cook Monument, and from Napoopoo were whirled south and around through the Kau District, over a new and wonderful lava highway, to the Volcano House. It was during this day's ride, at luncheon by the way, that the wires flashed to us the stunning news of the sinking of the *Lusitania*, and a stricken look was upon the faces of all for a time.

Following our greeting at Napoopoo, Jack had whispered to me:

"See that man over there, talking to Sam Johnson? He's the managing editor of the *Advertiser*—the very man, I feel confident, who started the old row I had with Kakina on the leper stories. And we've been roommates on the *Mauna Kea*" he broke into his irresistible chuckle, "—the joke is, I didn't know who he was, and we promptly became the best of friends. He is a dandy fellow. Now it's all made up—and I want you to forget the old hurt, Mate Woman, and be awfully nice to him; and you'll like him immensely. He's delightful."

I allowed myself, with Mr. Roderick O. Matheson, but one reference to the old affair. "You're going to be good to Jack henceforth—and love us?" He looked at Jack with Gaelic blue eyes brimful of affection: "I can be an awfully good friend, Mrs. London," he said, "and Jack London belongs to Hawaii, now."

The Johnson machine, in which I had come to Napoopoo, carried a full and very jolly cargo back to Pahoa on the Puna coast, for in addition to its driver, the exuberant Colonel, and us two, there were Senator and Mrs. Warren, Mr. Matheson, and "Bob" Breckons, one of Hawaii's most brilliant attorneys.

Again on the sulphurous brink of Halemaumau, Jack, who cared comparatively little for spectacles of this ilk, remarked to me after a long gazing silence at the increased flow and disturbance of the mountain's internal forces:

"I'm coming personally to understand your fondness for volcanoes—I myself am getting the volcano habit. I shall come here every time there is a chance; and in future, if this pot boils up and threatens to boil over, and we're in California, we'll take the first steamer down to see it!"

The fame of Mrs. Johnson's house party the next twenty-four hours, given to her allotment of members of the junketing party and their Entertainment Committee, is still talked in Hawaii. Among others from Washington, besides Senator and Mrs. Warren, who proved the best of "good fellows," there were Senator and Mrs. Shaffrath, and Mrs. Hamilton Lewis, wife of the Senator, who had remained East. What with certain city officials of Honolulu and Hilo, and their wives, the Pearl of Puna's slim ladyship presided over a circular table that accommodated a round two dozen of us, and a merry time was ours.

On the following Saturday, our two steamers arrived back in Honolulu within an hour of each other. Mr. Thurston, who was aboard mine, carried me up Nuuanu for breakfast on the well-remembered and lately visited lanai over the rocky stream; and Harriet, and the daughter Margaret, now grown into a stately and beautiful young woman, again led me down into the magnificent fernery they had connected to the lanai, roofed over a grotto hewn in great bowlders on which the house rests. While still at breakfast, we spied the *Mauna Kea* entering harbor from Kauai, and a taxicab delivered me on the dock exactly as my man, beaming at my precise calculation, descended the gangway.

Shall I ever see Kauai? I had planned to do so; for this 1915 visit to Hawaii I had expected to make alone, returning with my cousin, Beth. Meanwhile Jack, for an eastern weekly, was to sail on a battleship with President Wilson, attended by the Atlantic Fleet, through the Panama Canal to the Exposition at San Francisco.

But Jack repeatedly complained: "If you knew how *much* I'd rather go to Hawaii—but I need the money, my dear, if I'm to carry out my schemes on the ranch!"

The official cruise being abandoned on account of war developments, he contentedly declared:

"*Now* I can go to Hawaii with you for a few weeks. And I'll write a new dog book while I'm there. And we'll see Kauai, too."

The few weeks lengthened into five months, and "Jerry of the Islands" was begun and finished, to be followed by "Michael, Brother of Jerry."

And so it came to pass that Jack alone of our small family saw the Garden Island, and came back promising that next trip to the Islands we should stand together on the brink of Hanalei, Kauai's famous valley, which he said beggared description. He was especially fond of a new song, "Hanalei," and often asked the Hawaiians to sing it for him. For one reason or another, we never saw Hanalei together.

The president of the Board of Health, Dr. John S. B. Pratt, being absent from the Territory, Governor Pinkham, always full of aloha toward us, gave to Mr. D. S. Bowman, Acting, his earnest kokua (recommendation) that we be furnished with a permit to revisit the Leper Settlement. Long since we had heard from Jack McVeigh, who affectionately assured us of his personal welcome. He had lately asked Jack to give a lecture in Honolulu, the proceeds to be applied toward erecting a new motion-picture theater at Kalaupapa; but shortly the means came from some other source, and the lecture did not take place.

Jack always disliked repeating even the most desired experience in exactly the same manner; and this time, with gracious permission from Mr. Bowman, for the sake of variety we were to *descend* the Molokai Pali. To this end, we landed from the *Likelike* one midnight, bag and saddle, at Kaunanakai, where waited Henry Ma, a wizzled, clever little old Hawaiian, sent all the way from Kalaupapa with horses. Miss Myers, a sister of Kalama of hearty memory, going home from Honolulu, accompanied us up-mountain.

Thus, under a full moon, we retraced the road descended eight years earlier in the heat of midday. The moonlight bewitched the re-membered landscape, and silvered the receding ocean floor; and very tenuous and unreal it all seemed, as the eager horses forged lightly up, mile upon inclining mile, into chill air, for which I, for one, was unpre-pared. To Jack's insistence that I wear his coat I refused to listen, until, riding alongside, he pressed his warm hands to my cheek. "See—how warm I am—you know *me!*" His circulation was always of the best, and never have I known his hands to be cold. Even on frosty days, tobog-ganing or sleighing, or long, damp hours at the *Roamer's* winter wheel up the Sacramento or San Joaquin rivers, it was the same; "See—how warm my hands are!"

Ten very short miles to ourselves and the home-bound animals lay behind when we reached the Myers' house-gate. I shall always blame sweet Hawaiian backwardness that set a silence upon Kalama's red lips. No word she spoke except "Aloha," as smiling she led the flagged way to the guest-cottage. And how were we to know that this imperial-bodied, full-blossomed Juno was molded on the frame of that tall, slim, strapping cowgirl we had met nearly ten years ago? There was some-thing only vaguely familiar about her, and I dared to ask: "We knew you here before?" Oh, shades of night, protect and hide! "Why, yes," quietly, "I am Kalama—don't you remember?" Kalama! Kalama! Will you ever forgive? Why were you so gorgeously, amply different that we knew you not?

"Do you know where you are?" this, when, after three hours' sleep, Henry Ma had tapped upon the begonia-screened window, and we had breakfasted and mounted and were galloping over green pastures to Molokai's great falling-off place. Almost, as one hesitates to unlock a long-sealed box of letters and pictures, I drew back from the imminent verge. How I should like to have been the first who ever came suddenly upon this unexpected void of disaster and gazed upon the incredible lapse of the world below! We had yet to search for its equal.

A very different trail from the one we had never forgotten was that we now descended,—wider, and so depressed in the middle that the earth was raised at the outer edge. Man nor beast could fall off the pali-sade except he went out of his way to do so. But the action of water had on the steepest declivities exposed large bowlders that were exceeding disconcerting to horse and rider. Still hanging with hind-hoofs, while feeling below with fore-, a grunt from the cheerfully alert buckskin pony would advertise that its unprotected belly had come in contact or impact with an equally rounded if less yielding object. Several times our saddles slipped so far over-neck that the beasts almost overbalanced to a somersault.

"It would be far simpler to walk and lead them," Jack giggled. "But I rode up the trail without getting off, and I'm going down the damned thing the same way! What do you say?" And we did not dismount, save when necessary to set back our saddles.

Once at the doubly luxuriant kukui cluster at the feet of the pali, we saw a rider urging his flying steed in our direction—Jack McVeigh, could it be? But it was only a half of the big bluff man we had known. A severe illness had rendered him almost unrecognizable; but the hand-clasp and voice were the same, if more than ever cordial. One of the first remarks was: "I wish you were going to be here for the Fourth. We're going to whoop it up in grander style than ever. The Fourth you saw won't be a patch on what's going to happen this time."

Dr. Will Goodhue, a little heavier, and if anything more benign if that could be, with his beautiful Madonna, and in her arms their newest babe, waited at the arbored gate to welcome us of the wayward feet. Dr. Hollmann was now with the indefatigable Dr. George W. McCoy, at the Kalihi Receiving Station in Honolulu, where subsequently we renewed acquaintance.

The huge Belgian dairyman, good Van Lil, of old memory, now a patient, had married another, and the pair lived happily in a vine-hidden cottage near Kalawao, making the most of their remaining time on earth. Beyond a fleeting embarrassment in his vague blue eye, he met us on the Damien Road with the undimmed buoyancy of other years, and our eyes could see no blemish on his face. Probably we were more affected than he, for in the main the victim of leprosy is as optimistic as he of the White Plague.

And Emil Van Lil was not the only one whom we saw who had perforce changed his status toward society in the intervening eight years. The little mail-carrier who had led us up out of the Settlement, we found in the Bay View Home, cheerful as of yore, although far gone with the malefic blight. And, auwe!—some of the men and women we had known here before as extreme cases still lingered, sightless perhaps, but trying to smile with what was left of their contorted visages, in recognition of our voices. Others, whose closing throats had smothered them, breathed through silver tubes in their windpipes. Strange is this will to persist—tenacity of life!

To light the almost desperate gloom of pity that could not but overwhelm me, Jack, with the shadow on his bright face too often there since the Great War commenced, said:

"Dear child—awful it is; but awful as it is, think of how thousands of healthy, beautiful human beings are making one another look in the shambles of civilized Europe right now while we stand here looking at these."

Annie Kekoa, we were cheered to hear, had been discharged years before, all tests having failed to locate further evidence in her of the *bacillus lepra*, the depredations of which had ceased with her slightly twisted hand. She was now married and living in Hilo.

With pardonable pride the Superintendent showed us through the new "McVeigh Home," for white lepers; and next forenoon, while Jack finished writing a chapter of "Jerry," I visited the Nursery, also new, where, behind glass, mothers may see their babes once a week until the tiny things are removed to the Detention Home in Honolulu. Born as they are "clean" of the disease, they are taken from their mothers immediately after birth, since further contact is a peril most strictly to be avoided.

Probably not one remained of the Bishop Home girls who had wrung our souls with their plaintive singing; but for Mother Marianne, wraith-like in her frail transparency, with blessings in her blue-veined hands and old eyes that seemed to look through and beyond us, we endured, as in the past, a concert. And it was no easier for them and for us than it had been for us and those who had gone before. Again were the tender things more sorrowful for my unconcealable grief than for their own.

But facts are facts, and joyous ones must overbalance the sorrowful. By stern and sterner segregation, as was done in Europe, leprosy is being successfully stamped out of the Hawaiian Islands. Eight years before, on Molokai, there were nearly a thousand lepers, and the *Noeau* made four yearly trips to carry the apprehended victims of the Territory; now there are a trifle over six hundred, and but one human cargo in the twelve months disembarks at Kalaupapa. This diminution of roughly thirty per cent of patients led Jack to prognosticate that fifty years hence the good rich acres of the Molokai Peninsula will be clean farmland for the clean, and moreover an accessible and unparalleled scenic wonder for the travelers of the world.

"I am happier about this place than I ever hoped to be," he impart-
ed to me. "Oh, don't think for a moment that I minimize the dreadfulness of leprosy. But I am certain now of the passing of it, if the Islands
persist in this rigid segregation."

And Jack ever stood reverent before the beyond-price work of Dr.
Will Goodhue in freeing the inhabitants of the Settlement from their
thrall. Let me quote from his article, requested by the *Advertiser* upon
our return to Honolulu:

> "I insist that I must take my hat off in salute to two great, courageous,
> noble men: Jack McVeigh . . . and Dr. Will Goodhue . . . . My pride
> is to say that I have had the vast good fortune to know two such men.
> McVeigh, sitting tight on the purse-strings of the one hundred and fifty
> thousand dollars a year appropriated by the Territory, sitting up nights
> as well, begging money from his friends to do additional things for the
> Settlement over and beyond what the Territory finds itself able to-day to
> appropriate, is the one man in the Territory to-day who could not be re-
> placed by any other man in his job. Dr. Goodhue, the pioneer of leprosy
> surgery, is a hero who should receive every medal that every individual
> and every country has ever awarded for courage and life-saving. . . . I
> know of no other place, lazar house or settlement, in the world, where
> the surgical work is being performed that Dr. Goodhue performs dai-
> ly. . . . I have seen him take a patient, who, in any other settlement or
> lazar house in the world, would from the complications of the disease die
> horribly in a week, or two weeks or three . . . and give it life, not for
> weeks, not for months, but for years and years, to the rounded ripeness
> of three score and ten, and give to it thereby the sun, the ever chang-
> ing beauty of the Pali, the eternal wine of wind of the northeast trades,
> the body-comfort, the brain-quickness, the love of man and woman—in
> short, all the bribes and compensations of existence."

In a machine, by way of a new boulevard on the coast, we went to
Kalawao, and saw our good friend the faithful Brother Dutton, alert
as ever among his pupils; and passed on to the imposing Federal Leprosarium on the wind-swept shore in view of the lordly front of promontories with their feet in the deep indigo sea. This Leprosarium had
been built at a cost of $300,000, and was now abandoned and falling
into the swift decay of disuse in the tropics. Such a Leprosarium was
never known. Jack McVeigh almost wept as he fingered the full equipment of blankets molding in their original wrappings: the beds, the
washstands, the endless costly paraphernalia of a hospital, lying inutile
and deteriorating, which he was unable to put into needful circulation
in the Settlement. Even the fine dynamo, which a caretaker was paid

to keep from rusting—"Think how this could furnish my people with electricity!" he mourned. O red, red tape—what a curious institution dost thou create!

Jack London very shortly got himself into trouble by airing his views in the *Advertiser*, which stirred up a tidy tempest of protest in Washington, D. C.; but he was, after much hot correspondence in the press, the means of Jack McVeigh finally getting his selflessly covetous hands on the outfit of the ambitious edifice.[1]

Mr. Thurston had long planned a Japanese sampan trip from Honolulu to the non-leper valleys of windward Molokai, which lie between those stately promontories beyond Kalawao. And so, early on Sunday, "Decoration Day," according to prearrangement by wireless and telephoned to the Settlement, a smart blue sampan hove in sight around the pali headland, and lying off-shore sent in a coffin-shaped tender with an alarming freeboard that made it appear topheavy. Kakina possessed no permit and therefore did not so much as step on the Kalaupapa breakwater-landing.

Aboard the outlandish powerboat, we found Mr. W. L. Emory, an architect of Honolulu, and his son Kenneth, both engaging personalities, and, to our hearty delight, Mr. Jack Atkinson, who had not yet decided whether or not he would be seasick. We decided for him, if unwittingly. A rainbow-and-silver sickle of an aku, bonita, was presently seen tripping the wave-tops at the end of the Japanese sailors' trolling-line. This, promptly dispatched and prepared with Japanese soyu—to Jack and me more toothsome than any raw oysters—proved the last straw, not to mix metaphors, to Mr. Atkinson's camel of control.

Oh, the rich life we lived on our *via regia* of happiness! Here were we again, in a small boat, sixty feet over all—"Only five feet longer than the *Snark*, Mate-Woman!"—running before the big coastwise seas that heaved and broke in jeweled chaos almost over the fleeing stern. Again the "stinging spindrift" was in our faces, and I could have cried for joy at being on even so small a portion of "the trail that is always new."

Skirting the black lava-bound peninsula, with its combing surf, we were soon in calmer water off the mouth of the riotous valley where we

---

[1] Eight months after Jack London's passing, the *Pacific Commercial Advertiser* contained a column stating that the Federal Leprosarium would probably be torn down and the material used for building cottages in the Settlement, which, J. D. McVeigh is quoted as saying, "it would be a God-send to secure." In this column Jack London is mentioned as having been the first to suggest such action.

had ridden that long-ago day, its walls rising thousands of feet into the blue. It gave us an adventurous, alert feeling to skim the glassy swell under those overtowering somber cliffs, in the passes between shore and the three dark-green abrupt islets, fragments left from old convulsions of the riven island. The largest, Mokapu, over a hundred feet high, is crowned with mosses and shrubs, and a species of stunted palm tree found nowhere else in the world save, perhaps, on Necker, another islet of Hawaii.

The air rustled with wings, around and overhead, and Jack and I thrilled again to the call of the bosun bird, puae, and watched rapt its flight, high, high, and higher, above the pure white waterfalls that, spent in the wind, never reached the sunshot dark-sapphire brine.

Two miles or so beyond the last valley we had known, the sampan rounded into Pelekunu, unknown to the tourist, and visited by no one we had ever met. No vessel can approach the beach of its U-shaped bay, which shelves steeply out of deep water, bluer than the staring-blue sampan. "Why, the valley ran into the ocean," Kenneth observed.

No possible landing place could we detect, and followed the slant eyes of the Nipponese skipper and his men while the oriental launch chugged steadily into mid-bay, presently making in closer to the beetling cliff on our right. A ledge of volcanic rock, jutting into the ocean-deep water, was indicated as the landing; but slow surges swept rhythmically across it. "Can't help being glad we know how to swim," Jack remarked, every sailor-sense of him on the *qui vive*. Our problem lay in gauging our leap from the top-heavy marine coffin at the exact right moment. Only in quiet weather can any sort of connection be effected. If it be a trifle rougher than on this day, a basket on a derrick is lowered into the boat for passengers to climb into.

I decided to try both ways, and once safely on the ledge, indicated to several native youngsters who had run the half mile from the village at the head of the U, to send down the rattan car. Swinging up in the air, the cable manipulated by two mere children, I had a decided if precarious advantage over my companions who clambered a long vertical ladder.

Our slight luggage disappeared like magic villageward in the arms of the natives, and we followed at leisure the tropic trail. It is a story in itself, that night and the next day in the isolate valley of Pelekunu. The sea, and this only at rare intervals, is its sole egress, except for those who have clinging abilities second to none but wild goats. The few inhabitants, living in weather-grayed houses almost as picturesque as their hereditary lauhala huts, welcomed us with wide arms, and, like souls of grace we had known so sweetly in the South Seas, gave us their best. A Hawaiian pastor and a Belgian priest vie in kind-ness to their limited flocks, and all proffered us the freedom of the place.

Up wet and steaming paths we strove through hot-house plants that shook perfumed raindrops upon us, into the short, mounting vale; and I, while the men went landshell-hunting with and for the eager Kakina, idled in deep grass like that remembered of Iao and Tantalus. I tried hard to realize the earthly actuality of this sheer amphitheater of greenest green laughing with swishing water-courses and long falls, and the intense inshore peacock-green of the precipitously walled bay, turning to intenser peacock-blue outside, clear to the low white wool-packs on the intensest indigo horizon.

"We'll return here some day, when we needn't hurry; and then we'll go into Wailau, too," Jack, who had been especially happy himself on this little side-voyage, endeavored to compensate my regret in passing the next lovely rent in the shore—lovely as Pelekunu, with an almost impregnable partition between the two. What we saw from the resumed sampan trip, young Kenneth Emory, in Ford's *Mid-Pacific Magazine*, later on described too happily to omit:

"With each revolution of the propeller, scenes were laid open whose mag-nificence and beauty surpassed all that we thought impossible to surpass the day before. A plateau three thousand feet high and a mile long ended in one vast pali—cut down as if by a knife. Waterfalls, peaceful vales, lagoons hidden under dark caverns, tropical birds floating above, vines swaying in the wind, every form and color of beauty lay revealed upon the grand precipice above us."

How strange to ascend Haleakala in an automobile!—oh, not to the summit, but even to the Von Tempskys' and some miles above.

Kahului had fulfilled its promise and become a lively young town, and Mr. and Mrs. H. K. Duncan, kind friends who entertained us at their pretty beach home, took us to Wailuku, unchangeably quaint, and into fabulous Iao, that transcended all our recollection of it. And then the voices of the Vons over the telephone from Kaleinalu by the sea, and next from their smart machine at the Duncans' gate—the same debonair Von, and the two elder girls grown to beautiful woman-hood, all of us with tears in our joy of reuniting, for Amy the mother had died untimely. During our subsequent visit at the Ranch we missed her presence at every turn. Lorna, thirteen, brought up as a girl in Hawaii may gloriously be, to the free life of saddle and range, could rope cattle with the best; and the young son, Errol, was not far behind. At the races in Kahului, we saw Jubilee's colt, Wallaby, carry off honors for Gwen; and the Welshman and Bedouin, as well as Pontius Pilate, were reported still alive on the Ranch.

During the weeks spent there, I noticed with surprise and faint misgiving that Jack stayed rather close to the house. "Oh, you girls run along ... I think I won't ride to-day. There's so much to read—I can never catch up. Perhaps I'm lazy; I'd rather lie around and read. We'll do Haleakala next time we come." But he never looked into Haleakala again. Even then the Shadow was upon him.

THE SECOND RETURN

Voyaging back to California in time for Jack to attend the High Jinks of the Bohemian Club at their Grove, which is within a few miles of the Ranch, we spent a gay summer and fall, with a continuous house party making merry upon Sonoma mountain side. Jack's 7,000,000-gallon reservoir impounded behind his new dam, of summerwarm water encircled by redwood and madrono forest, made it possible to keep up our swimming condition. Too often, however, I could not but notice that he sat and watched the rest swim, or, in bathing-suit, paddled guests about in the canvas canoe or the larger skiff—items of *Snark* outfit that had never got aboard.

And long horseback rides seemed by him to have been relegated to the past. To be sure, his increasing devotion to agricultural problems on the "Ranch of Good Intentions" necessitated close supervision; but otherwise he appeared to prefer quiet riding, and the mild brown Prince stood saddled under the big oak more frequently than the growing colts or the skittish Hilo. Many a day he begged:

"Will you go out with the folks over the trail?—I think I'll take a sleep this afternoon, if you don't mind." Or, I rode alone; but always out of the house he stepped to meet my returning, with a pleased word about the particular colt I bestrode, and a beaming "If you knew how I love to hear you coming up the hill!"

All the while, the Great War weighed upon his spirit, sleeping or waking.

As the autumn wore, again he turned to Hawaii. "Why not spend our winters there?" he suggested. "We'll take the whole household down,"—and thereupon set the wires vibrating, to the end that when we arrived in Honolulu, December 23 of the same year, 1915, on the *Great Northern*, by way of Hilo and the volcano, we went right into a delightful house, 2201 Kalia Road, around the corner from the Scott cottage on Beach Walk. Amongst other acquaintances of the *Great Northern* voyage we especially valued one, Mr. James D. Dole, who is the young "pineapple king" of Hawaii—the most unassuming self-made millionaire imaginable. "Oh, Mr. Dole's just *folks*" I once heard a New England woman observe. "Nothing airish about *him!*"

At Hilo Bay, where the *Great Northern* first touched, certain glaring inefficiency on the part of the launch owner at Waiakea, in handling passengers to and from the steamer, caused Jack to go right up in the air, on the spot and later in the press, with a righteous wrath that stamped him true promoter of Hawaii's interests.

Our place at Waikiki, adjoining the grounds of the quiet Hau Tree Hotel of old, now the Halekulani, had once been the property of one of the Castles, and next of Judge Arthur Wilder, cousin of James and Gerrit Wilder, whose suicide at the Beach in the fall of 1916 shocked the Islands. It was now owned by a Chicago millionaire.

Mr. Ford and Harry Strange met us at the wharf, but before getting into the machine, we must shake hands and condole with our old friend Mr. Kawehaweha, of Keauhou memory, just returning to the Big Island from burying his sweet life-partner.

And then we were driven to Kalia Road, where, in the old house that was to be our new home, we discovered Harry's mother putting the last touches to the perfect sunny orderliness she had wrought out of the chaos of unoccupiedness of disarranged furnishing covered with spiders and dust and mold. In reply to our laughing protest that any one in this matter-of-fact world should do so infinitely much for any one else, she exclaimed, "Why, it's nothing at all, my dears; in England, just as a matter of course, we always open up returning neighbors' homes!"

This was welcome indeed; and day after next, she had us to a real English Christmas dinner, with holly all the way from "Home." Harry came to fetch us, in a violent, warm, delightful Kona storm that turned streets into rivers and vacant lots at Waikiki into lakes, where Hawaiian youth for days frolicked and caught many a meal of derelict fish.

Jack, so frequently and viciously misrepresented, found he had dived full tilt into a cool wave of hostility in Army and Navy circles, due to the recrudescence of a canard which for years he had vigorously denied, and which had occasioned endless annoyance at most inopportune moments. One such was when, at Galveston in 1914, he was ready to sail as war correspondent with General Funston for Vera Cruz. This canard, "The Good Soldier," purported to be an address by Jack London to the youth of America who might have a mind to enlist, exhorting such, in no uncertain terms, to avoid military service.

"If the Army and Navy men would only take the trouble to read their own official sheets," Jack would fume disgustedly. "But they don't know their own papers. How the *hell* am I going to tell them all, separately, that I didn't write a word of the thing! I deny, and deny, and deny, until I am tired, and what good does it do, when they don't see the denials?" For in the *Army and Navy Register*, as well as the *Journal*, and in the general press, he had repeatedly disclaimed authorship of or sympathy with the sentiments of the canard. Mr. Matheson saw to it that Kakina's *Advertiser* gave full publicity to Jack's real views, and, as in Vera Cruz, we made good friends in the Army and Navy. This "Good Soldier" canard, with Jack's letter of denial and his decided views upon preparedness, written to Lieutenant James D. Willson, U. S. N., has subsequently been circulated by the Navy Recruiting Stations, before and after the entry of the United States into the War.

Also I found a silly impression persisting among the charming Army women:

"Your husband does not like us," they voiced their belief. "He made derogatory remarks about Army women in 'The House of Pride.'"

Jack fairly sizzled, with despairing arms flaying the air: "Don't mind my violence—I always talk with my hands—it's my French, I guess.—But these people make me tired. If they'd only really read what they think they're reading. Because I have a bloodless, sexless, misanthropic, misogamistic mysogynist disapprove of décolleté and dancing, and all and every other social diversion and custom, I myself am saddled with these unnatural peculiarities. A merry hell of a lot of interesting characters there would be in fiction if they all talked alike and agreed with one another and their author!—What's a poor devil of a writer to do, anyway?" he repeated his wail of nine years earlier at Pearl Lochs when "The Iron Heel" had been rejected of men. "Of course I like Army women—just as I like other women!"

On New Year's Eve, we attended a reception in the Throne Room of the old Palace, where Queen Liliuokalani sat at Governor Pinkham's right hand. "And it's the first time in over twenty years that Her Majesty has received in this room," he whispered his satisfaction with what he had been able to bring about.

Followed a great military ball in the Armory, dinner and dance at the Country Club, and a wild night of fun at Heinie's. Nowhere in the world could there be such a New Year as in this subtropical paradise. Rain it did, and bountifully—a tepid torrent of liquid jewels in the many-colored lights of the city streets, which kept no Pierrot nor Pierrette indoors. The very gutters ran colored streams, what of the showers of confetti.

"Can you beat it?" Jack murmured when, at dawn, our machine threshed hub-deep in water down our long driveway under the vine-clambered coco-palms, to the ceaseless rhythmic impact of a big gray surf upon our sea wall.

Carnival Week was in February—a succession of pageantry opening with the Mardi Gras. No one with steamer-fare in pocket should forego Carnival Week in Honolulu. The unflagging Governor Pinkham and I vied in seeing who could last out the greater number of occasions that crowded each of the seven days from morn till midnight and later; and to this day we agree to disagree as to which of us was one event in the lead.

Polo, the best in the world, automobile races, equine races, took place at Kapiolani Park, with Diamond Head, green for the first time in many years and spilling with waterfalls, for background; and there were aquatic contests at the harborside, where Duke Kahanamoku added more emblems to his shield than he lost, and where Mayor Lane's slim kinswoman, Lucile Legros, won over the famous Frances Cowells from the Coast. And Jack and I could not refrain from working, with every nerve of desire, on behalf of our Hawaiians in their own waters!

The military reviews were especially imposing. Brigadier-General Samuel I. Johnson's remarkable National Guard, which he had made second to none in the Union, Jack vowed surpassed the showing of the regulars; while others declared that the cadets of the Kamehameha School founded by Mrs. Bernice Pauahi Bishop, for Hawaiians, put both regulars and militia in the shade. The splendid work that had been done with the Boy Scouts was evidenced by their orderly discharge of their Carnival duties of assistance in maintaining order. Punch Bowl, sprouting with unwonted verdure, was now become the cradle of Scout as well as militia encampments. James Wilder, who is always beaming, beamed harder than ever at praise of the Scouts, in whose training he had put much time and endeavor.

And pa'u riders turned out in full panoply, as did great floats of wondrous construction and significance; and there were historical pageants at Kapiolani Park that left little to be desired in illustration of old sports. Jack was especially impressed by the remarkable spear-throwing done by certain descendants of warriors, who had not allowed their valorous traditions to rust. And at Aala Park, in another part of the merry metropolis, an excellent "Midway Pleasance" furnished entertainment that was anything but historical, but thoroughly enjoyable.

In train came a succession of balls, civic as well as military, in the enormous Armory. Every moment was filled and packed down, and little did Honolulu sleep that week. Jack relinquished all work and accompanied me throughout the whole gay rout, sitting the long night sipping soft drinks and an occasional "small beer," while he talked with our many friends and shed his ever benignant, bright approval upon my delight in dancing. And I, in turn, took equal pleasure in his frequent card-parties, at home and elsewhere, although more than often I tried not to worry that he sat playing long hours he would better have spent swimming or otherwise keeping fit. "Oh, you run along with the others, Kid-Woman," he would smile, with a hand on my arm. "I'll come in after Jack Hawes and I win one more rubber."

Lavish entertaining we did this spring and summer in the old house at Waikiki—luncheons, dinners, dances, card-parties, teas under our own hau tree, with ever the swimming between whiles. Sometimes, after the day's round of social events, winding up with dancing, our guests and we trooped out of the spacious, half-open bungalow, through the great detached lanai roofed with a jungle-tangle of blossomy hau trees old in story, across the lawn bordered with low young Samoan coco-palms planted by Arthur Wilder and along the sea-wall right-of-way to a tiny beach two gardens away toward Diamond Head. Here we slipped into the sensuous lapping waters under a rust-gold moon, or the great electric-blue stars, and swam for a wonderful hour.

"The Southern Cross rides low, dear lass . . . and the old lost stars wheel back," Jack would paraphrase softly while we timed our strokes for the diving float in the channel. "What shall it be, Twin Brother? The house over there is for sale. Shall I buy you it, now, for the first of our string of island homes?—or a sweet three-topmast schooner after the War, to do it all over again, only better—though never more sweetly than in the dear little old tub—and sail on round the world as we love to plan?"

What other choice for me, who had heard and answered "the beat of the offshore wind"? The three-topmast schooner, by every wish, with all it implied of resumed adventure overseas. Our dreams had been rudely cut mid-most by ill health. But those we had realized, instead of seeming true, were still wrapped as in a blue and rose glamour of untried desires. "Which way I feel goes to prove," I wound up somewhat of the above to Jack, "that the becoming of them, as far as they went, was in excess of the anticipation." And he, to withhold me from the verge of sentimentality, made the shocking rejoinder: "You mean to say,—am I right?—that the young fuzz has not worn off your enthusiasms! Never did I see woman who wanted to go to so many places!"

Ah yes, Jack had learned full well to "loaf" in the tropics. With his comprehensive knowledge, mastery of his implements, and his alert sense of form and color, those inexorable thousand words a day consumed little energy; and there was scant exertion in his habit of life in the palm-furnished, breezy bungalow of wide spaces, and the deep gardens of hibiscus and lilies. Too little exertion. Too seldom was the blue-butterfly kimono changed for swimming-suit or riding togs; too often, from the water, I cast solicitous eyes back to the hammock where, out of the blue-figured robe, a too white arm waved to show that he was watching me put to use the strokes in which he had coached me. "Oh, yes—no—yes—no, I think I'll hang here and read," he would waver between two impulsions. Or, "No, thank you—I'll read instead—all this war stuff I want to catch up on. I'm glad you asked me, though," half-wistfully, "—you forgot, yesterday, and went in alone." Forgot, no! Never once did I forget.

I was avoiding all approach to the "nagging" we still never permitted in our family of two.

And ever the War pressed upon spirit and brain and heart, from the first shock to his belief that the time of great wars between great nations was past, all through his undying exasperation with the powers that were, which held his own country back from more formidable protest against Hun atrocity. To think he should have missed any thrill of the consummation of his hope to see the Stars and Stripes in France! Again and again, before, during, and after that last visit in Hawaii, have I heard him solemnly deliver himself:

"There's only one end to this conflict, in my judgment; it is *unthinkable* that the German Idea should predominate and survive to a 'place in the sun.' If I thought there was the least possibility of Germany winning in this struggle, I promise you I should go to die in the trenches with France and her Allies."

Never had I seen him more deeply stirred than when Harry Strange left the Honolulu Gas Company, his mother, and his children, to sail for England to join the colors, where, having earlier distinguished himself in the Boer War, he was soon in France. After being thrice wounded he received the Military Cross and mention in dispatches for conspicuous gallantry on the Arras Front. To certain harsh criticism in Honolulu that Harry should have left his dependents, Jack pleaded with blazing eyes:

"You do not seem to understand: He *had* to go. He walked the floor night after night trying to see the way out—the right way. There was no other way out, for him, than the one he took; he could not have done other than he did. .... As well criticize the flame that burns, as criticize this royal thing of the spirit within him that drew him from success, and love of children, and fat security, half across the world to fling himself into the maelstrom of battle—all for an Idea."

As for Emma Strange, his mother, more than once we heard her say that he or she would have had to go to help England.

That Jack London was not in Europe as war correspondent was due, over and above the pressing responsibilities that kept him forever writing, writing, to the fact that he saw nothing but baffling disappointment and failure for correspondents on any front. "Japan sounded the death-knell of the war correspondent. I should be balked of getting what I went after, and it would drive me madder than I was in Korea and Manchuria in 1904. You remember, I came home in the middle of things there, simply because of my disgust at being unable to earn my salary from the newspaper that sent me, in the way I thought it should be earned. Marking time in a military camp is not war corresponding."

All during these last months of his life, there was in Jack the widening gratification that he was advancing in his conquest of the heart and understanding of the people of Hawaii, Hawaii-born Anglo-Saxon and part Hawaiian, and the ever dear and dearer Hawaiians themselves.

(1) Jack and Charmian London, Waikiki.   (2) A Race around Oahu.
(3) Sailor Jack Aboard the *Hawaii*.   (4) Jack on Beach Walk.

And then, one day, we met Mary Low—Mary Eliza Kipikane Low—
a connection of the Parker family. At a midday luau in a seaside garden
at Kahala, on Diamond Head, we came together with Mary and, as if it
had been foreordained, were forthwith adopted by her capacious heart.
Like a devoted elder sister, she assumed a sort of responsibility for us
twain with her people. Only an eighth Hawaiian, no malihini would be
competent to detect her Polynesian affinity. But, to us, the royal arches
of the black eyebrows on her broad forehead, and the high aquiline nose
and imperious lift of the upper-lip of her small, fine mouth, expounded
the quintessence of Polynesian aristocracy as we had come to know it
here and under the Equator.

Already Jack was in the way of becoming ineffaceably associated
with the interests and affections of Hawaii—was there not more than a
hint of intention to enshrine him in the inner circle of that seclusively
exclusive lodge, Chiefs of Hawaii?—and he was bound in good time
to come into his own with them all; but Mary, bless her forever, hastened the day, else he might have faded back from the world ere he had
known the "Kamaaina" that had begun to form upon their lips.

At this poi-luncheon, as a noonday luau is now called, demand was
made of Jack for a speech. "My Aloha for Hawaii" was his topic, and he
gave a glowing brief resume of the history of that aloha nui in his life.
And then Prince Cupid, in a brilliant and logical address, delivered a
tribute to the incalculable gifts Jack had brought to the Islands with
his discerning brain that had interpreted to the world much of the true
inwardness of hitherto misunderstood aspects of the country and its life
and people.

And upon a later occasion, a luau at the home of the Prince and
Princess, Mayor Lane humorously declared, to hearty applause, that
he should like to nominate Jack London to succeed him in office. For
often Jack, rare genius of previsioning, and with the added advantage of perspective, had thought a step in advance of the dwellers
in the Islands, and had fearlessly expressed his earnest convictions.
A few Hawaiian-born Americans have realized this, one or two even
going the extraordinary length of consulting his opinions upon how
best to apply their millions to benefit their sea-girt land which they
love better than mere personal gain. In time, as in case of Jack's protest on the idleness of the Federal Leprosarium, his ideas and protests
had been substantiated; and none so ready as these people to proclaim
him right.

A PROGRESS AROUND THE BIG ISLAND

"Why can we three not go around Hawaii together? I will take you to some Hawaiian homes, and you will love them and they you," urged Mary Low, perhaps the third time we met.

"Why not?" Jack brightly took her up. "I'm ready as soon as I finish 'Michael, Brother of Jerry.' When shall it be? Set the date. Any time you say—eh? Mate?"

And so it came to pass that on the Big Island we spent six weeks going from house to house of the Hawaiians, some strangers to us, some old acquaintances, in a round of entertainment and hospitality that set us on tiptoe with the unstudied human beauty and wonder of it all.

"I question—*do* you really get what this means to you and me, in our present and future relation to Hawaii?" Jack would reiterate with that adorable eagerness that I share in his vision. "I have read more, listened to more, than have you, of the ways of the people in the past generations—of the royal progresses of their princes, their kings, and their queens. This way of ours, led by Mary Low, is of the nature of a royal progress, but with the difference that, not being born into the honor, it is up to us to be worthy of its being thrust upon us. Do you get me?—Oh, pardon my insistence," he would relax his high, sparkling tension, "but I do so want you, my sharer, to enjoy with me the knowledge of what all this means for you and me."

Ah, I did, I did. And I do. My own heart and intelligence, further quickened by his still more sensitive divination, lent to the otherwise vastly interesting experience an appreciation that will abide for all my days. The imperishable charm of what it meant and means has come back a thousandfold, pressed down and overflowing, his share and mine together, to me in my singleness.

"Mary Low is a wonder, I tell you! "Thus Jack, elate. "She is a mine of interest and information. Her mind a kingdom is. I haven't talked with a woman in Hawaii, of whatever nationality or blend of nationalities, whose brain can eclipse Sister Mary's for vision of the enormous dramatic connotations of the race as it has been and is being lived out right here on this soil which you and I love. Listen here," breaking off to read me his scribbled notes, "think of the story this will make—why, I want to write a dozen yarns all at once. I become desperate with my inability to do so, when, any hour of the day, Mary chats about say the Parker Ranch history, or, for that matter, almost any big ranch on this isle of ranches. She might, with her memory and adjustment of values and her imagination, have been a great writer of fiction."

And so, in such company, we disembarked one morning before daylight on the wharf at Kailua, Hawaii, where, far cry to the old time Goodhue surrey, in the darkness we made our way toward an electric-lighted 1916 motor that had cost its owner, Robert Hind, Mary's brother-in-law, some eight thousand dollars to land here from the East.

Effortlessly we surmounted the familiar road, to a point where our way turned to the left. In a gray car in a gray-and-silver dawn we passed the home of the Maguires (Mrs. Maguire is sister to Mary Low and Mrs. Hind), and with Mauna Kea's icy peak flushing in our eyes, pursued the drive toward Parker Ranch. Bending off to the right for a remembered sugar-loaf hill, Puuwaawaa, we came to the home of the Hinds, and there spent a fortnight with Robert Hind and his beautiful wife, Hannah, whose eyes and smile Jack more than once preserved, for what time may be, in written romances. Their sons and daughters were absent in eastern colleges. Here, in terraced gardens of lawns and every flower and plant that will grow at this 2700-foot elevation, we worked and played; and each morning, before breakfast, Jack and I made it a point to attend the toilette of a great peacock, whose absorption in the preening of his black-opal plumage was little disturbed by our admiring scrutiny and conversation. And there were horseback rides, and long trips in the machine. One of these picnics was to the great heiau of Honaunau, south of Kealakekua Bay.

To reach Honaunau, one is obliged to leave a vehicle of any kind and take to the saddle. Horses were furnished by Miss Ethel Paris, an energetic young woman who is capable of running a cattle ranch unaided if need arise, and who entertained us right royally. This is the most famous and imposing of Hawaii's ruins, covering nearly seven acres. The walls of the Temple of Refuge, still intact, protected thousands of fugitives in the olden days, and measure a dozen feet in height by eighteen in thickness. Those of the Tower of London retire into insignificance before this savage architectural achievement.

On this night we slept at the Tommy Whites', following a luau at their house. Here, to our joy, we found Mother Shipman, carrying on a little "progress" of her own; and her greeting was: "My own son and daughter!" Next day there was still another luau, mauka at the old Roy place, Waihou, where again we met the Walls. Mrs. Roy, mother of both Mrs. Shipman and Mrs. White, had passed away several years earlier. Her garden remained, more beautiful than ever in its fragrant riot of roses and blumeria and heliotrope, and the begonias had surpassed all promising.

Kiholo, seaside retreat of the Hinds, was enjoyed for a night and a day—miles down-slope over the lava; and again we drove to Parker Ranch, guests of Mary and Hannah's Aunt Kalili, Mrs. Martin Campbell. The great holding, nearly doubled in acreage, is now the fortune of one tiny part-Hawaiian lad, Richard Smart. For Thelma Parker had sacrificed herself for love in a tragic marriage, and died untimely, survived by but one of her children, who, the father shortly following his child-wife to the grave, is now sole heir to the estate. On the side of Mauna Kea, in the old family cemetery walled with sepulchral cypresses, rest the ashes of beautiful Thelma, taken there with all fitting pomp, mourned by every Hawaiian heart born on her lands. Standing beside her grave, we tried to vision that long funeral cortege winding up the green miles she had so often galloped wild in her childhood. Poor little maid—one is thankful that at least she had that wonderful maidenhood.

Near the cemetery is Mana, old deserted home of Parkers, rambling in a great courtyard. Mary wept amidst the ruined fountains, for here her own early years had been spent. An Hawaiian caretaker let us in, and through the koa rooms we wandered, touching almost reverently the treasures of generations—furniture, pianos, china, and moldy albums of photographs. One curio especially appealed to Jack, who uses a similar incident in "Michael, Brother of Jerry"—a whale-tooth, sailor-carven, with an inscription referring to the sinking of the Essex by a cow-whale. Coincidentally, a man, claiming to be a survivor of the Essex, died in Honolulu about this time of our visit to Mana.

It was a distinct pleasure to learn that Frank Woods, of Kohala, had lately bought the old place for his wife, Eva, who is a daughter of the famous Colonel Sam Parker, Minister of Foreign Affairs during the reign of Liliuokalani. The early home of the original Parker, built with his own hands, stands in a corner of the inclosure. One aches with the romance of it all, and would like to write an entire volume upon the history of the Ranch that started on this spot.

Mr. and Mrs. Carter we met again, and, among other events, recalled Jack's accident on the old gray horse. To our astonishment, we were told that the animal, still alive, ever afterward had to be given up as unsafe for the young folks. It will remain a mystery for all time.

"It's like an old Morgan mare my father had," Jack said. "One day, when she was about twenty, she kicked up her heels, and with tail and head straight up, vaulted the fences and ran away, clean mad."

At the historic old port, Kawaihae, where the Ranch does its shipping, we were entertained for luncheon by pretty Mrs. Todd, and shown Queen Emma's home, eloquent with decay, still dignified in the age-wreck of its palm gardens. It was off Kawaihae, in a gale, that Captain Cook's *Resolution* sprung her foremast, which caused him to put in at Kealakekua Bay for repairs, to his doom. Only the heat prevented us from making an effort to walk to the ruins of the important heiau of Puukohala, erected upon advice of the priests, to secure to Kamehameha the Kingdom of Hawaii.

Picking up our mail on the way through Waimea, Jack found his first author's copy of "The Little Lady of the Big House" and also of "The Acorn Planter."

"Well, here's 'The Acorn Planter,' Mate," he said. "It isn't lost, even if it was considered too primitive for the Bohemian Club's Grove Play.—Darn it—I wish they could have seen their way to the thing. I *like* its big motif, myself."

Upon our final leave-taking of Puuwaawaa, the Hinds' open-handed hospitality sent us in one of their cars to Hilo. On the way, Mrs. Tommy White ran out with an addition to our lunch—a marvelous cold red fish, the *ula-ula*, baked in ti-leaves, and a huge cake, compounded of fresh-grated, newly plucked coconut and other delicious things we could not guess. Of course we visited the Maguires, as well as the Goodhues down their lovely winding lane. And we must slip in for a moment to the wide unglassed window-ledge, to gaze once more from that vantage upon the divine Blue Flush.

And again we passed beyond the Blue Flush of Kona, and sped over the road traveled by the Congressional party the year before, through the village of Pahala, and on up Mauna Loa for an all-too-short stop-over with Mr. and Mrs. Julian Monserrat, on Kapapala Ranch in the Kau District, before pushing on to the Volcano.

Different again from other lava deserts of the island is this of Kau, made up of flow upon succeeding flow from Mauna Loa, in color black and bluish-gray. Vast fields of cane alternate with arid stretches, and west of Pahala is a sisal plantation and mill, the most extensive on the Island. Mauka of the road one sees a fertile swath of cane growing on a mud-flow of Mauna Loa at an elevation of 1200 feet. This mud-flow was originally a section of clay marshland which, in 1868, was jarred loose by an earthquake from the bluff at the head of a valley. In but a few moments it had swept down three miles in a wet landslide half a mile wide and thirty feet deep. Immediately afterward a tidal wave inundated the entire coast of Kau, while Kilauea, joining the general celebration, disgorged lava through underground fissures toward the southwest.

And now, full majestic lies Kau under the deep-blue sky, and as majestic moves the deep-blue, white-crested ocean that washes its lava-bound feet. From the Monserrats' roof we made a side-trip to the coast, where in the black sands we gathered the "breeding stones" which the old-time natives believed to reproduce themselves. Being full of holes, these large pebbles secrete smaller pebbles, which roll out at odd times, thus furnishing grist for the fancy of simple folk. Jack, immensely taken with the conceit, in no time had several brown urchins earning nickels collecting a supply which, he declared, he was going to turn loose on the Ranch at home. Another curiosity in the neighborhood is a fresh-water pool just inside the high beach where the Pacific swell breaks. One of the attractions of Kau is its good plover hunting.

A pretty story is told of a small fishing place, Manilo, near Honu-apo on the coast. A trick of the current eternally brought flotsam of various sorts from the direction of Puna into the little indentation at Manilo. Over and above the driftage of bodies of warriors who had been slain and thrown over the cliffs along the coast, the tiny inlet became famous as a sort of post office for the lovers of Puna, whose messages, in the form of hala or maile leis, inclosed in calabashes, could dependably be sent to their sweethearts in Kau.

Near Punaluu, the landing place for East Kau, are the remains of a couple of heiaus—Punaluunui and Kaneeleele, said to have been con-nected in their workings with the great Wahaula heiau, of Puna.

And thus we merely glanced through the District, making mental notes for a return.

The Monserrats', on Kapapala Ranch, is another of the homes that quaintly combine the lines and traditions of prim New England ar-chitecture with a lavish charm of subtropic treatment of interior and garden compound. In the latter, high-edged aloofly with cypress and eucalyptus from the winds of the surrounding amplitude of far-flung, treeless mountain areas, one feels bewilderingly lifted apart and set aside, amidst an abandon of flowers, from the rest of the kingly island.

Julian Monserrat, with keen appreciation of Hawaii's turbulent history, filled Jack with valuable material for fiction.

And from this Ranch, one may ride to the summit of Mauna Loa, which is overtopped by its sister peak only by the few hundred feet height of small cones in Mauna Kea's immense crater. But Mary Low's time was limited, and there was still so much ahead of us, that this venture, too, was set forward into the ever receding allure of future returnings.

Still another sumptuous luau, at which we came in contact with some of the Pahala neighbors, and we set out for Kilauea, where, in broad daylight, at last we beheld the bursting, beating wonder of her heart of lava quite as blood-red as all its painted or sculptured imagings. Thus it must have been when a churchman half a century ago wrote:

"Wine of the wrath of God, which is poured out without mixture into the cup of His indignation."

We amused our fancy with trying to believe that this unusual manifestation was the reward of certain offerings, of flowers and tid-bits saved from the Monserrat luau, which Mary and ourselves cast into the burning lake!

From Hilo, where our Shipman family once more enfolded us, even to Uncle Alec, the dear, we made another flying trip down the Puna Coast, leaving Pahoa behind on our second quest into idyllic Kalapana by the turquoise sea. Here the natives are still "natives" in simple mode of life and attitude toward the same, and here one finds, at the village of Kaimu, what is said to be the largest grove of coconut palms in the Islands. On the high-piled crescent of sand, overrun by a blossoming vine, under the angled pillars of the great grove lolled a scattered group of Hawaiians. From the noble silvered head of one of the benevolent old men Jack bought me a coral-red lei, one of a sort seldom seen these latter days in Hawaii—a solid cable full an inch in diameter, made by laboriously perforating, below the center, hard red berries or seeds, resembling the black-eyed Susan, but smaller, and sewing these close together around a cord.

The village of Kalapana, farther south, supports quite a large population, and is very lovely with its fine growth of coconut, puhala, and monkey-pod trees. Near by are to be seen the *niu moe,* or sleeping-coconuts—palms that are bent, when young, by visiting chiefs, and thereafter called by the names of the chiefs.

Kalapana landing has become so rough that it is used only for canoes, and not far off rises a bluff from out the sea. From a little inshore dell we clambered a gigantic litter of bowlders to the plateau of this bluff, and looking down from the top could glimpse shoals of large fish directly below in deep water. Jack, bargaining for raw fish at a native hut, missed this side-diversion, which included the exploring of a rocky tunnel beginning midway of the plateau, its mouth surrounded by broken old stone fences. Reached by this eerie passage is a large chamber, once used as a place of refuge. The tunnel, made winding so that spears might not be cast after the fleeing, works out from the main chamber to a place on the cliff, high above the sea. There is also, in this neighborhood, the remnant of the Niukukahi heiau. From Kalapana runs a native trail to the Volcano, but no road farther than the village itself.

That night we spent in Kapoho, to the north, the beautiful old home of Henry K. Lyman, whom we had known for some time, Road Supervisor of the Puna District, and part-Hawaiian, descended from the old missionary stock, and a most attractive and interesting personality. At the Chicago Convention of Delegates, he was affectionately known as Prince of Kapoho. And right princely does the tall, suave-mannered gentleman live in the lovely house of his childhood.

Not far away is a famous spring in the lava-rock, always at blood heat, which forms a bath sixty feet long by thirty wide, and twenty-five deep. Also near Kapoho is Green Lake, a deep pond in a volcanic cone, in which it is said the bodies of swimmers under water show brilliant in shades of blue and green. And in this environ, on a verdant bluff above the sea, is the ruin of the Wahaula heiau, the last where idolatry was extensively practiced. It is said to have been builded by Paao, a powerful priest, in the eleventh century. This temple, by the way, is the original of the restored model in the Bishop Museum at Honolulu.

Many lava trees are to be seen in the Puna District—trees once surrounded and preserved by upstanding lava—great vases sprouting from their tops with living growth. Certain emerald-green hills seen from the lanai showed as if sculptured by the hand of man; and it is not unlikely that they were fortifications in their day. This Puna coast is packed with beauty and historical interest. Sitting on the fragrant lanai at dusk, listening to a serenade by Henry Lyman's plantation boys after their day in the canefields, Jack assured me we should come back to explore Puna to heart's content.

In the morning our host drove his grateful guests to Hilo, in a steady downpour that almost made a motorboat of his car. At Hilo we boarded the train for Paauilo, the end of the railroad, and were confirmed in our belief that Kakina's brain had conceived one of the world's wonder railway routes.

From Paauilo Mr. Peter Naquin, young manager of two big sugar plantations, took us to Honokaa above the sea, whence we had ascended to Louissons' eight years before. Next day Mr. Naquin and his rosy wife carried us on to their other plantation home at Kukuihaele, an enormous house, sedately paneled the height of its gloomy walls, and set in a terraced park of lawns and umbrageous trees. But the gravest Scotch architecture of fun-decrying managers of eld could not dampen our spirits, and a contented time we had in the dark interior, playing cards by a large fireplace of an evening, and working by day, meanwhile delaying for the unobliging weather to clear, that we might see Waipio and Waimanu valleys near at hand. And Jack, who ever sought argument, in the young couple found an adequate grindstone upon which to sharpen his faculties, both being exceedingly up-to-date in methods of reasoning as well as information. "Mrs. Naquin," Jack praised, "is the most logical woman I have met for some time—quite extraordinarily logical, indeed."

From the deck of the *Kilauea* the previous spring, Mr. Thurston had pointed out these grand valleys, telling me that above all places of beauty and interest in Hawaii we must not miss them. If possible, he urged, rather than enter by trail, surf in from seaward in canoes. This latter we had hoped to do; but the natives reported too great a swell from the continued bad weather. Moreover, from the almost incessant rains, the trail up the pali out of Waipio into Waimanu was not considered any safer than the beaches. But one day, riding in a drizzle, Jack and I happened upon the broad, steep trail into Waipio, and followed it down into a sunnier level, meeting strings of ascending mules laden with garden produce. This was one of the prettiest little adventures we two ever had together, dropping down the declivity into the sequestered vale that opened wondrously as we progressed to the lovely banks of a wooded river that wound to the sea, widening to meet the salt surf. On its banks we could see and hear the ringing sweet voices of wahines at their washing and babies at play.

At the head of this great cleft in the coast nestles the half-deserted, half-ruined village of Waipio, with behind it a tremendous rock bastion veiled in waterfalls to its mist-hidden summit. We rode on across river-shallows to a pathway once sacred to the sorcerers, kahunas, the which no layman then dared to profane with his foot. Only the approaching twilight held us back from a beach trail that leads to a clump of tall coconuts, marking the site of a famous temple of refuge for this section of Hawaii, Puuhonua, built as long ago as the thirteenth century, with Lono for deity. About 1790 it was destroyed by a Kauai king. I shall never cease to deplore the weather that prevented us from seeing more of Waipio and climbing the trail, stark above our heads, into Waimanu.

This day, moving along the bases of the mighty precipices, we planned happily how we should some day come here, restore one of the abandoned cottages and its garden, and live for a while without thought of time. What a place for quietude and work. Even Jack seemed to welcome the idea of such seclusion and repose. Little as he ever inclined toward folding his pinions for long, Hawaii stayed them more than any other land. "You can't beat the Ranch in California—it's a sweet land," he would stanchly defend, "but I'd like to spend a great deal of my time down here."

An accession of the storm began tearing out the road to Honokaa, and even a section of the plantation railway which skirts the seaward bluffs. That repaired, we heeded the warning of Mr. Naquin, aware of our schedule, that we might not be able to leave for weeks if we did not avail ourselves of this route. And so, in a heavy downpour and wind that turned our futile umbrellas inside-out, we made the several miles in an open roadster on the track, the spanning of rain-washed gulches recalling our flume-coasting of 1907.

Eventually, after an equally drowning automobile passage over the roads of our journey of years earlier, we arrived once more at Waimea, on the Parker Ranch. Here, turning off into North Kohala, the machine emerged into better weather and dryer roads along the flanks of the Kohala Mountains, which are over 5000 feet in elevation.

Both Jack and I, carelessly enough, had somehow pictured the North Kohala District as in the main a wilderness of impassable gulches. And to be sure this feature is not lacking, for the district embraces some glorious country that is a continuation of the gulch and valley scenery of which Waipio and Waimanu form part.

So imagine our surprise to find ourselves at the Frank Woods' home, Kahua, on a magnificent green-terraced sweep from mountain top to sea rim, in the midst of a ranch or conglomeration of ranch-es covering many thousands of acres, whose volcanic rack had been rounded by the ages and clothed with pasture. Frank Woods, in laying out his grounds, had roughly been guided by the natural lines of the incline, and from his house, where the living-room extended full width overlooking the splendid panorama, it was hard to discern, except by the finer grass of his lawns, where garden and wild ended and began. Never have I seen Jack so pleased over any gardening as with the wide undulating spaces of Kahua. And in this house of valuable antiques we slept in a high koa bedstead, crested with the royal arms, that had belonged to Queen Emma.

Motoring across to the northwest coast, our surprise grew. A perfect road ran through an ordered landscape that was unescapably English in its general trimness as well as in the architecture of its buildings. Of course, there was everywhere a waving expanse of the fair green cane, and near the oceanside were ranged the sugar mills of Kohala. At the town of Kohala, where Kamehameha began his conquesting career, one happens suddenly upon the original Kamehameha statue, spear in hand, helmet and cape gilded to simulate yellow feathers. This fig-ure, by T. R. Gould of Boston, cast in Italy, was lost coming around Cape Horn. The exact duplicate, which stands before Honolulu's Court House, was ordered and set up previous to the salving of the original from the wreck, which was sold to the Hawaiian Government.

The rich plantations formerly depended upon rainfall for irriga-tion; but in 1905 and 1906 they became independent of this more or less sporadic source by constructing the Kohala Ditch on the order of those of Maui and Kauai. The indefatigable M. M. O'Shaughnessy was chief engineer of this nine miles of tunnel-building and fourteen of open wa-terway, that supplies five plantations. He was assisted by Jorgen Jor-gensen, whose own remarkable Waiahole Tunnel and ditch on Oahu, aggregating nearly 19,000 feet, we had seen; and P.W.P. Bluett, whom we visited following our stay with Mr. Woods.

Mr. Bluett took us a-horseback up the mountain to show us this Kohala Ditch, and also the second great engineering feat, of his own designing and supervision, the Kehena Ditch, consisting of fourteen miles of tunnel and ditch line, some of it through rank jungly swamp-land. This Ditch supplements the Kohala viaduct by conserving storm-waters which had heretofore been wasted. Along the Kehena we rode at an elevation of thousands of feet, through some of the most gorgeous country of the whole Territory of Hawaii, culminating in that of the valley Honokane Nui, into which we peered while Mr. Bluett described the perilous building of a trail we could see scratched on the almost perpendicular wooded side of the giant gulch, this being the line of communication for the O'Shaughnessy system.

Jack, with his unquestionable love of natural beauty, was ever impressed with man's lordly harnessing of the outlaw, Nature, leading her by the mouth to perform his work upon earth.

"Do you get the splendid romance of it?" he would say. "Look what these engineers have done—reaching out their hands and gathering and diverting the storm wastage of streams over the edge of this valley thousands of feet here in the clouds.

"Look what Bluett has accomplished, and he isn't shouting very loud about it, either. Do you remember Jorgensen, what a modest, unassuming fellow he was?—and Peter Bluett here—look at him: Anglo-Saxon, big, strong, efficient—you have to draw out such men to learn what they've done in making the world a better place to live in . . . . And yet," he would lapse sadly, "just such men are devoting their brains to producing destructive machinery for making anarchical chaos out of Europe, where there should be only constructive work . . . all because a crazy kaiser and his lot want a place in the sun, and the whole earth to boot."

The story of this Ranch alone, of which Mr. A. Mason is manager, and the old headquarters, Puuhue, of its original owner, James Woods, an Englishman who married a sister of Colonel Sam Parker, is inextricably woven with the dramatic lore of the Parker Ranch. Puuhue is a house of connected as well as detached houses, strung over a terraced green court high-hedged from the Trades and shaded by fine trees. Here lives Mr. Bluett, with Lucy his wife and his beautiful little daughter, Treva. In one section of the home, a large, cool room of stone, Jack, having finished his three spirited, pithy articles, under title of "My Hawaiian Aloha," and one short story, "The Hussy," commenced upon a strange South Sea fantasy, "The Message."

Again is the compulsion strong within me to expatiate upon the place of our blissful tarrying; but my book would needs start a yard-shelf of books—none too long to do the subject justice—were I to let pen stray among the unwritten stories that Mary's active memory, impelled by her untrained sense of artistry, spun for us on the way to and from charming social functions given by the hospitable dwellers of the English countryside, from Kahua and Puuhue to Kohala and beyond.

There was an afternoon in Miss White's entrancing British gardens on a Hawaiian hillside; tea with Mrs. H. H. Renton, whose husband we knew so long ago at Ewa Plantation; or with Mr. and Mrs. Sam Woods; and tea or luncheon at Mr. and Mrs. E. Madden's in Mahukona; with dinners and card parties at Mr. Bluett's, and a wonderful evening with the Bucholtzs at the Bryant place. And Mr. Paetow had us for tea in his quaint garden lanai past Kohala, on the beautiful Niulii Plantation, its little gulches choked with ferns and blossoming ginger. Afterward, he drove us to inspect a less modern ditch, tunnel and all, that still irrigates a large tract of taro—another ebullition of the constructive genius of Kamehameha.

There is a prehistoric chart laid upon the long incline of the Woods Ranch. It resembles the map of a vast scheme of town-lots, the rocks, overgrown with green, windrowed into age-leveled partitions. An explanation which has been offered is that this was not a continuously inhabited district, but the chance halting place of chiefs, who, ever migrating with their retainers, often settled down for months and even years, raising their produce as well as depending upon the commoners of the invaded land. These miles-broad checkerboards of windrowed stones are also to be seen in Kona and Waianea, both sections being, like this portion of Kohala, more or less dry in certain seasons, where sweet potatoes were of old the principal crops, growing abundantly in the wetter months.

This location was the point at which Kamehameha from time to time converged his great armies, for the invasion of Maui, Molokai, and Oahu. Several years, for example, were consumed in assembling his legion of 18,000 fighting men and a fleet of war canoes to transport them to the conquest of Oahu alone. It is likely that many of these troops practically supported themselves in and around this section, which would account for the large operations in rock-gathering that fenced and divided their myriad plots.

"And they, too, whispered to their loves that life was sweet—and passed," Jack would muse with great eyes upon their disappearance; "and we, too, shall pass, as they passed, from the land they loved."

Mr. Frank Woods lent me a chestnut horse that had been in training for his wife, absent in Honolulu with her declining father, Colonel Sam Parker. She had not yet seen her husband's surprise gift, and I was the first woman to ride the splendid creature, while the Hawaiian cowboys who had broken and trained him stood about waiting for whatever might happen. For be it known that Eva and Frank Woods are notable specimens of Polynesian "physical aristocracy," despite their slight Hawaiian blood, and this animal, his dam a cow-pony and his sire a thoroughbred race-horse belonging to Prince Cupid, had been chosen for size and power to carry his Amazonian mistress about the mountain ranch, and broken by heavy men. Little was he held down to the springy earth by my light weight, and we spent much time in mid-air, it seemed to me, for he touched ground as seldom as possible in his leaping uphill or down, over the high lush grasses, as if conquering a never ending succession of hurdles.

It was from the hospitable Maddens', at Mahukona, after a luau, that finally our truly royal progress around the royal island came to its end. Laden with their leis, and those brought or sent by others of our friends in Kohala, we embarked in whaleboats for the *Mauna Kea* anchored outside. And while the steamer edged along the southerly coast before squaring for Oahu, stopping off several familiar landings, over again we lived what Jack sweetly vowed were six of the happiest weeks he had ever spent in the Islands.

Back at Waikiki, the spreading bungalow seemed home indeed, with our own servants, always adoring of Jack, smiling welcome from the wide lanai.

"Almost do we feel ourselves *kamaaina*, Mate Woman," he would say, arm about my shoulders, while we welcomed or sped Honolulu guests, or watched, beyond the Tyrian dyes of the reef, smoke of steamers that brought to us visitors from the Coast. "Only, never forget—it is not for *us* to say."

One thing that earned Jack London his kamaainaship was his activity for the Pan-Pacific Club. Under the algarobas at Pearl Harbor, in 1907, one day he and Mr. Ford had discussed socialism—upon Ford's initiative. "Well," the latter concluded, "I can't 'see' your socialism. *My* idea is, to find out what people want, help them to it, then make them do what you wish them to do; and if it is right, they *will* do it—if you keep right after them! ... Now, I'm soon leaving for Australia and around the Pacific at my own expense, to see if there is a way to get the peoples to work together for one another and for the Pacific."

"That's socialism—look out!" Jack contentedly blew rings into the still air.

"I don't care if it is," retorted his friend. "That won't stop me. Walter Frear has just been appointed Governor of Hawaii, and I've interested him, and carry an official letter with me. Hawaii, with her mixture of Pacific races, yet with no race problems, should be the country to take the lead. I'm going to call a Pan-Pacific Convention here."

"Go to it, Ford, and I'll help all I can," Jack approved.

"All right, then," Ford snapped him up. "Address the University Club next week!"

"Sure I will, and glad to, though you know how I despise public speaking." And Jack kept his promise, while Mr. Ford was presently off on his mission to Australasia.

On the day of our return from California to Honolulu in 1915, while helping us find a house at Waikiki, Mr. Ford recounted the growing of his venture, which he declared needed only Jack's further cooperation to carry it through to success. "It's big, I tell you; it's big!" Weekly dinners were given by Ford in the lanai of the Outrigger Club, at which on occasion there were present a score of the leading Hawaiians, or Chinese, or Japanese, Koreans, Filipinos, or Portuguese, to exchange ideas with the leading white men who were behind the movement. The speeches and discussions were of vital interest, all bent toward bringing about a working in unison for the mutual benefit of Pacific nations.

Out of these affairs sprang up interesting friendships between ourselves and these foreigners and their families, resulting in social functions in our respective homes and at the foreign clubs, and also at the Japanese theaters. Would that all the international differences of the Union might be handled as harmoniously as they are in Hawaii. During our last sojourn in Honolulu, more than one Japanese father assured us: "My sons were born under your flag. I should expect them to fight under your flag if need arose."

One evening, at the Outrigger Club, Jack spoke the Pan-Pacific doctrine of friend Ford before the Congressional visitors and three hundred representatives of the various nationalities in Hawaii, all of whom responded enthusiastically through their orators.

The Pan-Pacific Club grows apace, with headquarters at the University Club in Honolulu, in the room where Jack first fulfilled his pledge to speak on the subject. In this room, on Balboa Day, 1917, Finn Haakon Frolich's splendid bust of Jack London, modeled on the Ranch in 1915, was unveiled; while at Waikiki, beneath the date-palm

(1) Queen Lydia Kamakaeha Liliuokalani.   (2) Governor John Owen Dominis,
the Queen's Consort.   (3) A Honolulu Garden—Residence of Queen Emma.

that marks the site of the brown tent-house, a Jack London Memorial drinking fountain, is to be erected.

In San Francisco, Alexander Hume Ford has under way the project for a great skyscraper to be called the Pan-Pacific Building, with headquarters therein for this club the name of which is now ringing around the Pacific Ocean. And while he, Mr. Ford, is the discoverer of this New Pacific, humbly he insists that without Jack London it would have been a longer, stronger pull to bring about the present situation.

I did not dream how ill a man Jack was. I often wonder if he himself possessed any inkling of the gravity of his condition. But slowly it began to dawn upon me that matters were radically wrong with him. Else why did that "cast-iron stomach," as he loved to boast it, decline to retain even the food he only played with? "You must remember," he would parry questioning, "that breakfast is my meal of the day. Why, this morning I had, in addition to my cups of Kona coffee, a half of a papaia, a large dish of mush and cream, and my glass of soft-boiled eggs." That sounded reassuring; but what for a long time I did not know was that this much-enjoyed breakfast seldom remained with him beyond the hour. At the home table, or dining out, to guests' or hostesses' query, "You are not eating! Don't you *ever* eat?" he invariably replied, "Oh, I'd always rather talk than eat, you know. I can eat any time."

And more frequently, on the rare days we lacked company, he slept the afternoon away, merely mentioning, without complaint, that he had lain awake most of the night reading. With delight he listened to Robert W. Shingle's proffer of his own polo ponies to ride about Kapiolani Park or anywhere we chose; but I alone availed myself of the genial Senator's gift.

Always was he ready for cards at Mrs. E. S. Cunha's, or one of her wonderful luaus; or dinner and cards at the Harvey Murrays; or with Charles Chillingworth, President of the Senate, and his adorable wife, Ann; or maybe it would be with Francesca Colonna Hawes, in Princess Kawananakoa's lovely old home on Pensacola Street, or a game with Mr. Hawes at the University Club. Princess Kawananakoa we had never seen since 1907, but had come to know her sisters, Mrs. Shingle, Mrs. Walter Macfarlane, and Mrs. George Beckley. Then, too, there were dinners exchanged with our army and navy friends, and Governor Pinkham and Dr. and Mrs. C. B. Cooper, with whom he lived; or

Claire and Bruce Cartwright gave a dance in their open ballroom up Nuuanu; and we made exchange dinner and theater parties with the C. B. Highs, the Frank Thompsons, the William Williamsons. Not least amongst our good friends was Charles Dana Wright, of the *Star-Bulletin*, who held his family silver ever ready to accommodate our increasing table, in the rented house of limited furnishings.

And there were days and nights when we met Prince Cupid and our First Princess, at Sam Parker's, where the old Colonel's devoted girls, Eva Woods and Helen Widemann, entertained informally, and we saw the gallant spend-thrift host of other days failing, failing. ... It was the year before, one of the last days he ever left the house, that in our Beach Walk cottage we had Colonel Parker for luncheon, together with his life-long friend, that good Bohemian and gentleman, Frank Unger, since dead. The two wore about their Panama hats orange leis of ilima, now so rarely seen in these days of careless paper imitations, which they presented to Jack and me. And it is these cherished garlands of wilted flower-gold that now wreathe their friend's ashes in the Valley of the Moon.

And there were times when we twain were included in affairs that were solely Hawaiian except for the few who had married into the families—as at Charles W. Booth's beautiful house, Halewa, one night in Pauoa Valley, where a hundred sat down to a great banquet, with a dance to follow in the vine-screened lanai, from which one could see up the valley the hundreds of acres that were as a back-garden of the estate. Mrs. Booth, herself part Hawaiian, and daughter of a Maui chief, let us roam about the absorbing apartments, each a veritable museum of treasure trove inherited from her aunt, Malie Kahai, a celebrated beauty—feather leis, tapas, calabashes, finest of mats, and, prize of all, a feather cape that had belonged to her princely father. Some of the furniture had come from the palace of the king and from Queen Emma's residence. Here we met Stella Keomailani, Mrs. Kea, "Stella" to her intimates, last living descendant of the high chiefs of the Poohoolewaikala line—a sort of royal Hawaiian clan descended from kings. Blue-blooded pure Hawaiian, she is a remarkable type—tall, slender, with brown hair and hazel eyes and a skin as of ivory washed with pale gold. One would call her almost fair. On her father's side she is cousin to Queen Emma, and one of the heirs mentioned in the Queen's will.

But there—to mention all who blessed us with their friendship would be almost to quote our Honolulu telephone directory, which hangs now at my elbow, with its markings desolately reminiscent of the roof under which Jack London dwelt those seven months on Kalia Road.

Anxious for the criticism of Honolulans upon certain stories he was writing at this period, "On the Makaloa Mat," "The Water Baby," "When Alice Told Her Soul," "The Bones of Kahekili," Jack often had me telephoning for a party to come for luncheon or drop around for tea under the hau, for the reading, with a swim to follow. Other new stories he wrote and read aloud—"The Kanaka Surf," "The Message," "The Princess," and "Like Argus of the Ancient Times." With the exception of "The Kanaka Surf," which was a haole tale placed in Honolulu, none of these latter are Hawaiian fiction. The next novel he contemplated settling down to was to bear the title of "Cherry"—a Japanese heroine with an Islands setting and a potent radical motif. And this work, "Cherry," was the broken thing he left behind when he died on November 22.

One morning Jack was obliged to have me call in Doctors Herbert and Walters, for he had been seized with the agonies of kidney stone. Shortly before, he had been very ill all night, as if from ptomaine poisoning. And within a week of his death, home on the Ranch, there was a repetition of both these symptoms of a condition that he would not regard seriously. "Don't worry," he would brush aside attempts to diagnose or to call in medical advice. "It will pass—look at me: I am in good weight, and shall live many happy years, my dear." But there was that in his face which brought me white nights, and caused his friends to ask, "What ails Jack? He looks well enough, but there's something about him ... his eyes ..."

And so the gay wheel turned in Honolulu, as the golden days and star-blue nights came and went. And yet, for all Jack courted more or less excitement—I quote from my pocket diary, and the date is June 14, 1916: "Mate said tonight that this has been the happiest day he ever spent in the Islands. And what did he do? Write, read me what he had composed; and we lunched and dined conjugally alone together, with a little swim in between whiles; and in the evening he read to me from George Sterling's latest book of poems, 'The Caged Eagle,' just received from George, and broke down in the reading before the deathless beauty of the poem called 'In Autumn.'

Before we sailed for home, which was on July 26, that Jack might attend the Bohemian Jinks, we put our heads together with Mary's for the planning of a luau, just before our departure, under our own roof and hau tree for our own Hawaiian friends, with a night of dancing and music and cards to follow. The only haoles to be bidden were their close connections. Forty they sat at the great board that was entirely covered with deep layers first of ti-leaves and then ferns, strewn with flowers and fruit of every description, native and imported. It was a feast served by women whose business it was to see that every detail was in the most approved Hawaiian fashion.

To Mary Low must be given the praise for the success of this occasion, for under her superintendence it was produced. And upon her unerring knowledge and tact the place-cards, bearing embossed the royal coat-of-arms of Hawaii, were laid. The ends of the enormous table were seated in this wise: Jack center, with Princess Cupid to his right, and Mrs. Stella Kea left. Myself at opposite end, with Prince Cupid on my right, and Mayor Lane at my other side, while his wife, Alice, sat at the Prince's right—she of the beautiful hands that are her husband's pride, exquisitely modeled by a mother's early manipulation, lomilomi, after the charming Hawaiian practice.

Our friends will not, I am sure, be offended if I mention a laughable incident that all took in jovial good part. Next the Princess, "Bob" Shingle, best of toastmasters, had concluded his opening brilliant speech, and sat down amidst hearty applause. But his sitting was not of a permanence that was to be expected, being in fact an entire disappearance to those at my end of the long table, and alarm widened the blue eyes of Muriel, his wife. Alack, the floor of the aged lanai had not upborne such weight of Polynesian aristocracy these many years, and the hind-legs of even this medium-sized haole's chair went incontinently through the rotten planking.

Hardly had the bubble of merriment subsided when, to my speechless horror, Prince Cupid vanished from my side in a clean back-somersault. He was on his nimble feet almost before he struck the sand nearly a foot below the lanai-level—not for nothing had he learned football tactics in his university days. His good-natured mirth put all at ease, and the alert nervousness of Senator Chillingworth and others of his stature and avoirdupois called forth much funning. However, there were fortunately no more accidents, and the speech-making in appreciation of Jack and his services to Hawaii was gratifying in the extreme.

I can see Jack now, as he rose, all in white save for his black soft tie, hesitating half-diffidently with the fingers of one hand absently caressing the flowers on the ti-leaves, before raising his eyes, black-blue and misted with feeling. At first his voice, low and clear, shook slightly, but gathered, with his beautiful, Greek face, a solemnity that increased as he spoke his heart to these people among whom he loved to dwell.

Secondarily to the pure aloha motive of this luau, we had assembled our friends for the christening of the Jack London Hula, chanted stanza by stanza, each repeated by the celebrated Ernest Kaai and his perfect Hawaiian singers with their instruments. Mary was the mother of this mélé, for in her fertile brain was conceived the idea of immortalizing, for Hawaii, Jack London himself and more specifically his progress around the Big Isle of Mounts, as was done for the chiefs of old by their bards and minstrels.

The Hawaiian woman best fitted, in Mary's judgment, to recite the saga, was Rosalie (Lokalia) Blaisdell, who had helped in the versifying; and all Lokalia asked in return for the long evening's effort, which with lofty sweetness she assured us was her honor and pleasure, was a copy each of Jack's "Cruise" and my "Log" of the Snark.

Thus, during the eating of the hundred and one Hawaiian delicacies that a bevy of pretty girls prepared and served from the kitchen, never was the gayety so robust that it did not silence instantly when Lokalia's voice rose intoning above the gentle wash of reef waters against the sea wall thirty feet away, followed by the succession of Kaai's lovely music to the mélé. Each long stanza, carrying an incident of the progress around Hawaii and those who welcomed Jack, closed with two lines:

"Hainaia mai ana ka puana,
No Keaka Lakana neia inoa."

"This song is then echoed,
'Tis in honor of Jack London."

Listened critically all those qualified to judge, and now and again a low "Good," or "Perfect," or "Couldn't be better, Mary," or "All honor to Mary Kipikane!" would be forthcoming from Prince or Mayor or Senator. And there was in the mélé a lilting Spanish dance song for Lakana Wahine—Kaikilani Poloku, which is myself; for kind hearts gave me the name of a beloved queen of the long gone years, whose meaning is passing sweet to me, for Jack loved it too.

And now, through tears I write of the end, when, laden to the eyes with no false leis by the hands of Hawaii, Jack looked down from the high steamer deck into the up-turned faces of the people of his Aloha Land, standing ankle-deep in flowers and serpentine. The great *Matsonia* cast off hawsers, and, moving ahead majestical-slow, parted the veil of serpentine and flowers woven from her every rail to the quay.

"Of all lands of joy and beauty under the sun ..." Jack began, the words trailing into eloquent silence. He had approached Hawaii with gifts of candor and affection in hands, and eyes, and lips. And Hawaii, impermeable to meanness or harboring of grudge over franknesses that had but voiced his grave interest in her, has been the greater giver, in that she granted him the joy and satisfaction of realizing that they had not known each other in vain.

Not alone because it was Jack London's Loveland do I adore Hawaii and her people. To me, native and haole alike, have they expressed their heart of sorrow in ways numerous and touching. To them, this book, "Our Hawaii." To them, greeting and farewell:

"Love without end."
"Aloha pau ole."

JACK LONDON RANCH,
    IN THE VALLEY OF THE MOON,
        September 1, 1917.

Jack London State Historic Park

Located in Glen Ellen, California in the "Valley of the Moon", the park includes the large ranch and buildings owned by Jack London that he purchased over a number of years in the early 1900's. It includes the museum, several buildings, and a number of ruins of old structures including the burnt-out Wolf House.

Museum

The Museum was built by Charmian London after London's death in 1916. The House of Happy Walls was designed to be a museum as well as Charmian's home. She lived in the house from 1935 until 1945 (when she was not traveling abroad or staying with relatives). Today the museum in-cludes displays in many rooms, with a complete set of first-edition books by Jack London, Charm-ian's 1901 Steinway pia-no, and many unique crafts and mementos  Jack and Charmian collected in their travels.

This house is similar to the Wolf House in some ways—the Spanish-style roof tiles and walls of field stone, for example—but it is much smaller and more formal. Much of the furniture in the house was designed by the Londons and custom-built for use in Wolf House, though never used there due to the fire that destroyed Jack and Charmian's dream home. Several times a year small concerts are held upstairs in the historic building.

Grave Site

During the last few years of his life, Jack London's health declined rapidly from the effects of failing kidneys. On November 22, 1916, at only forty years old, Jack London died after a brief coma. His death certificate states that the cause was "Uraemia following renal colic".

On November 26, 1916, in a silent ceremony, Charmian London placed her husband's ashes on the chosen knoll under a large rock from the Wolf House. After she passed away in 1955, Charmian's ashes were laid under the same rock, next to Jack.

Wolf House

Started in 1911 and designed by architect Albert Farr, Jack's dream home was four levels comprising 15,000 square feet, 26 rooms and 9 fireplaces. It was constructed with beautiful locally-cut redwood logs, stone walls, and even contained a reflection pool.

Jack London wrote so many books about wolves and dogs that his friend George Sterling gave him the nickname 'The Wolf'. So when Jack started to build his dream house in 1911, it was only fitting that people would call it the 'Wolf House'.

Jack and Charmian never got to live in their home because one hot summer night in August 1913, spontaneous combustion

started a fire in the house. Nobody was living near the house so the fire was quite advanced before anyone became aware of it. The Londons were sleeping in the Cottage about a half mile away and were awakened by a farm worker who saw the red glow in the sky. They got on their horses and rode to their beloved dream house. By the time they got there, the house was completely engulfed in flames and beyond saving. Although Jack vowed to rebuild the house, he did not live long enough to rebuild. Today, we have a beautiful ruin.

Cottage

The Cottage was London's principal home on the Beauty Ranch. This wood-framed cottage was purchased by London in 1911 along with the Kohler and Frohling winery build-

ings. It was enlarged after 1911 until it included some 3,000 square feet of living space. Here he wrote many of his later stories and novels.

In 2006, restoration of the cottage was completed and the re-furnished cottage and Stone Dining Room were opened to visitors. These two buildings capture Jack and Charmian's bohemian lifestyle and close working relationship.

Beauty Ranch

The Beauty Ranch is the legacy of Jack's passion for the land. The Cottage, the Winery Ruin, the Silos, Barns and

Pig Palace are remnants of Jack and Charmian's life on the ranch. Combined with scenic beauty and miles of hiking and riding trails, the park attracts fans of the writer and nature lovers year round.

In 1905 London bought the first of several ranches on Sonoma Mountain in Glen Ellen, California. Using proceeds from his prolific writing career, London acquired adjoining parcels over several years and expanded his ranch, also known as the Ranch of Good Intentions.

By 1913 London owned 1400 acres on the slopes of the mountain and by 1916 employed nearly fifty workers building, farming, and tending prize livestock. Self-taught and inventive, London sought to improve farming methods using common sense, research, and concepts gleaned from travel.

The "Pig Palace"

Visitors to the ranch today will see examples of his ingenuity and foreshadowing of organic and biodynamic methods popular today. He planted 65,000 eucalyptus trees hoping to use them for lumber but they eventually proved unsuitable.

Lake

Jack London designed a stone dam on the slope of Sonoma Mountain, creating a lake at the headwaters of Kohler Creek. His plan, to capture water for his farming needs and to remediate erosion from the logged out hillsides above, worked well. He also saw the resulting lake as a cool respite for swimming and boating with Charmian and friends during the hot summers. The four-acre lake was completed in 1914 and became the topic of the first water rights trial in California. When London won the dispute, he invited all the neighbors for a barbecue beside the lake. The floating walkway, along with piped in fresh

spring water for showering, was state of the art in 1915. Charmian and other riders used the lake to swim their horses. During the Depression, Beauty Ranch was converted to a Guest Ranch that offered fishing, swimming, boating and picnics at the lake.

In 2010, London's lake was designated "one of the ten most threatened cultural landscapes in America". An assessment is underway to repair the dam, refresh the lake, and revitalize the adjacent wetland. These improvements will substantially reduce sediment downstream and provide fresh open water and wetland habitat for amphibians, reptiles, birds, and mammals on the mountain. Park visitors can still view the graceful stone dam and log bathhouse.

I would rather be ashes than dust. I would rather that my spark should burn out in a brilliant blaze than it should be stifled by dry-rot. I would rather be a superb meteor, every atom of me in magnificent glow, than a sleepy and permanent planet. The proper function of man is to live, not to exist. I shall not waste my days in trying to prolong them. I shall use my time.

—Jack London, 1916

Map of the Park

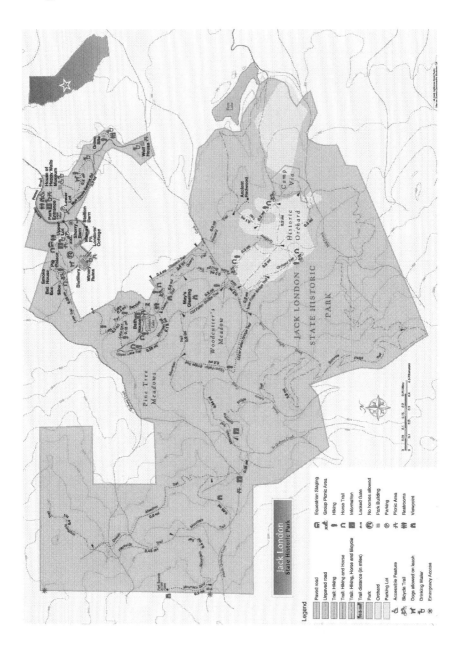

Made in the USA
Columbia, SC
06 January 2020